# ACCLAIM FO...

"I have always loved a good love story. When I read *Remember the Lilies* and the romance of two young people in the Philippines during WWII, I knew this was a book to awaken my senses . . . Tolsma has the uncanny ability to relate events in Santo Tomas as they were and to couple these facts with a good, romantic war story."

—*Sascha Weinzheimer Jansen, interned in Santo Tomas Prison Camp, Sr. Vice Commander, Bay Area Civilian Ex-POWs (BACEPOW), featured in The War: A Ken Burns Film*

"Tolsma isn't afraid to detail the horrors of war as she depicts how tragedies can be obstacles to one's Christian beliefs. She also illustrates how Gisela and Mitch, though questioning if God has abandoned them, unite in their hope for the future and shared faith."

—*RT Book Reviews, 4-star review of Daisies Are Forever*

"Excellent storytelling, accurate historical reporting and gritty, preserving characters make this WWII-era novel a must read. In this moving, historically accurate portrayal of WWII Germany, the characters learn that, even with destruction all around them, some things last forever."

—*CBA Retailers + Resources (on Daisies Are Forever)*

"[*Daisies are Forever*] is a compelling and fast-paced tale about the atrocities and tremendous losses endured by those marked forever by World War II. The theme of faith despite all odds will resonate with readers. Recommended for fans of Rosamunde and Robin Pilcher, Kate Morton, and historical romances."

—*Library Journal*

"In an adventurous tale that reads like a movie script, Liz Tolsma weaves faith in seamlessly, moving the reader with her characters' convictions to create a captivating debut novel."

—*BookPage (for Snow on the Tulips)*

"This book was a fascinating look at WWII from the Netherlands perspective, one I hadn't heard before. It captured my interest and wouldn't give it back until the last page!"

—*CBA Retailers + Resources (for Snow on the Tulips)*

"Tolsma crafts strong characters and easy-to-visualize scenes. The inherent danger of Nazi occupation is apparent. Relevant biblical connections remind the reader that God is always in control, no matter how dire the situation may seem. Tolsma's story is a way to remember the past and those who gave their lives for freedom."

—*RT Book Reviews (for Snow on the Tulips)*

"Based on the author's family history, this moving tale not only offers insight into the moral and physical struggles of those under the duress of war but also vividly captures the time and place. A good choice for readers who enjoyed Mary Doria Russell's *A Thread of Grace.*"

—*Library Journal (for Snow on the Tulips)*

All the best!

# *Remember the Lilies*

# ALSO BY LIZ TOLSMA

*Snow on the Tulips*

*Daisies Are Forever*

# Remember the Lilies

LIZ TOLSMA

THOMAS NELSON
*Since 1798*

NASHVILLE MEXICO CITY RIO DE JANEIRO

Published in Nashville, Tennessee, by Thomas Nelson. Thomas Nelson is a registered trademark of HarperCollins Christian Publishing, Inc.

Thomas Nelson titles may be purchased in bulk for educational, business, fund-raising, or sales promotional use. For information, please e-mail SpecialMarkets@ThomasNelson.com.

Publisher's Note: This novel is a work of fiction. Names, characters, places, and incidents are either products of the author's imagination or used fictitiously. All characters are fictional, and any similarity to people living or dead is purely coincidental.

Scripture quotations are taken from the King James Version of the Bible.

**Library of Congress Cataloging-in-Publication Data**

Tolsma, Liz, 1966–
Remember the lilies / Liz Tolsma.
pages ; cm
Summary: "Irene and Rand come from very different walks of life. Will they find common ground in their fight to survive? Irene has grown up in the jungle as a missionary with her Aunt Anita, but now she and countless others are imprisoned by Japanese soldiers at the Santo Tomas Internment Camp in the Philippines. Irene and her aunt are safe there, and she keeps busy with her duty of delivering censored messages to the camp's prisoners, but like everyone else, she prays for the war to end and for her freedom. Rand is a wealthy, womanizing American, whose attempted escape from the internment camp has put himself and others in danger. When Rand and Irene's Aunt Anita meet one another in the hospital, Irene learns more of his story and her heart is determined to save his family. But the danger outside the walls of the hospital worsens every day, and life in this exotic place is anything but luxurious. Can Irene find Rand's family before they disappear forever? And can a humble missionary woman and an arrogant man find common ground in the face of their biggest fears?"-- Provided by publisher.
ISBN 978-1-4016-8914-8 (softcover)
1. World War, 1939-1945--Philippines--Fiction. 2. World War, 1939-1945--Concentration camps--Philippines--Fiction. 3. World War, 1939-1945--Prisoners and prisons, American--Fiction. 4. Philippines--Fiction. I. Title.
PS3620.O329R46 2015
813'.6--dc23
2014032852

*Printed in the United States of America*

15 16 17 18 19 RRD 6 5 4 3 2 1

*To my son, Brian. This story was born from your suggestion that one of my books needed to take place in the Pacific theater. I am so proud of the young man you are and proud that you have chosen to serve our country in the Marines as thousands of brave men have in generations past. May the Lord richly bless your life.*

*"For evildoers shall be cut off: but those that wait upon the* Lord, *they shall inherit the earth. For yet a little while, and the wicked shall not be: yea, thou shalt diligently consider his place, and it shall not be. But the meek shall inherit the earth; and shall delight themselves in the abundance of peace."*

Psalm 37:9–11

*"I will be as the dew unto Israel: he shall grow as the lily, and cast forth his roots as Lebanon."*

Hosea 14:5

*"The flowers appear on the earth; the time of the singing of birds is come, and the voice of the turtle is heard in our land."*

Song of Solomon 2:12

*"I shall return."*

General Douglas MacArthur, shortly after he escaped from Corregidor, Philippines, and arrived in Australia, 1942

*"Faith is not simply a patience that passively suffers until the storm is past. Rather, it is a spirit that bears things—with resignations, yes, but above all, with blazing, serene hope."*

Philippine president Corazon Aquino

# GLOSSARY OF FOREIGN WORDS

## Tagalog (Filipino language)

*Amah*—nanny
*Bakya*—traditional Filipino wooden-soled, open-toed clog
*Baryo*—neighborhood or subdivision
*Byaya*—grace
*Camote*—sweet potato
*Carromatas*—traditional horse-drawn buggy
*Dabakan*—Filipino drums
*Kuliglig*—cicada
*Lugao*—a tasteless mixture of rice and ground corn
*Mestizo*—a person of half-Filipino, half-Caucasian descent
*Sawali*—coarse twilled matting made of flattened bamboo strips, most commonly used for walls
*Talinum*—Philippine spinach

## Japanese

*Socho*—Japanese Sergeant Major

# Prologue

## Manila, Philippines

*December 8, 1941*

The cool breeze off Manila Bay swept around Rand Sterling as he maneuvered his red Mercedes Sports Roadster convertible down Dewey Boulevard, past large Italianate homes and Spanish-style mansions much like his own. They were all on his right. On his left, coconut trees waved their fronds in the wind, and they were accented by the blue of the bay. Salt scented the air, and he took a deep breath, unable to keep a wide smile from spreading across his face. The beautiful woman in the seat beside him, Peggy Brambly, laughed as a gust tugged at the brightly colored scarf on her head.

"Can you go any faster?"

Faster, yes, faster. Rand pressed down a bit on the accelerator, the needle on the speedometer inching up. "Better?"

She sat back against the black leather seat, her cream-colored face lifted to the sun. "I've looked forward to this picnic all week. Then you had to break our date . . ."

"Nightclubs don't run themselves, you know. Something came up at the Azure."

"Or someone."

"Comes with being the boss." He grinned at her.

"No matter." She waved a manicured hand. "We're going now."

That's the only reason he took Peggy places from time to time. She understood that he wasn't a one-woman man. Not since Catherine. Peggy made no demands on him, and he appreciated that.

He steered around a slow-moving *carromatas* and through the heavy traffic of Studebakers, Packards, and Nashes clogging the roads even at this early hour. Turning onto the side streets, they passed Filipina women in striped skirts and white blouses with full sleeves selling mangoes, *camotes*, or sweet potatoes, and other produce along with such Filipino treats as cassava cake and a steamed rice cake known as *puto*.

"I was afraid you'd cancel again after I heard about Pearl Harbor. Nasty business, that. At least it's far away from us."

A bit of Rand's own lightness evaporated with Peggy's words. The Japanese had launched a surprise attack on Hawaii just hours ago. Yes, for now it was far away. But for how long? What was in store for them? MacArthur had promised to protect them. Rand had to trust in that.

"Oh, bother, Rand. Wipe that scowl from your face. Things won't be that bad. You'll see. We have the American forces to defend us." She touched his knee, the warmth of her hand traveling through the fabric of his chino pants and up his leg. "Where are you taking us? This isn't the way to the Taal volcano."

"All in good time. I have to stop at the Monarch first."

"Why do you have to own two clubs? All work and no play makes Jack a very dull boy." She stuck out her painted lip in a most becoming pout.

Now he laughed as he passed the Jai Alai Club with its glittering, turret-style, all-glass front. No one had ever insinuated that he was dull. Just the opposite. "If I wasn't a bit dull, you would have no place to play."

"I could go to the Metropolitan Club. Peter Williams has quite the place."

"You wouldn't." He gripped the wheel as he continued down the bustling street, sidewalks filled with Filipinos, Americans, and Brits hurrying to their jobs at the banks, the import/export companies, and businesses of all sorts that lined the road. The stone and brick buildings towered over them.

He glanced at Peggy brushing a strand of dark hair from her face. "You have me there. I haven't been to that place since that awful deal with Bernice. Poor thing. Sent away to live with her aunt in Chicago, and we all know why. He's a cad, and I'll never darken his doorstep again. No one will. The scandal will ruin him, mark my words."

Rand didn't doubt it. In their business, they were to flirt and dance with their patronesses but to stop the relationship at that. Everything kept light and aboveboard. No woman wanted to associate with a man who used her like yesterday's *Manila Times.* A fine line, to be sure. A shiver raced through him. "Let's not talk about Peter. He cooked his own goose. Today it's you and me. No Japanese, no business . . ."

"You mean after you stop at the Monarch."

"Right." He slid his sports car into a spot in front of his club and jumped out. He tingled all over as he always did when he arrived here. His father, a mining executive who had come to Manila to live and work soon after the Great War, had given him the Monarch, telling him to make something of himself.

And so he did.

He and Peggy strode into the cool of the building with its high, curved ceilings, lavish chandeliers dripping with crystals, and polished wood floors. In twelve hours, the place would be packed, the liquor flowing freely, the cash filling his coffers.

He liked being noticed. Rubbing elbows with all of Manila's elite. So Rand opened the Azure, equally as popular, maybe even more. He had arrived. Perhaps it was time to expand the sphere of his influence.

At the opposite end of the room, a curvy young Filipina, Bethel Ocampo, stood in front of a microphone, belting out "All of Me" while his club manager, Henry Lansdale, looked on with shining eyes.

"You're here early, Henry."

His associate turned and ran his hand through his curly brown hair. "I can see what got you out of bed at this hour, Rand." Henry had the gall to wink. Peggy's fair face flamed scarlet.

Rand crossed the immense dance floor, tables with white cloths and miniature lamps lining each wall. "Just needed to check something in the books."

When he reached Henry, his friend clapped him on the shoulder and walked with him. "I've never met anyone more concerned with the books. Since that trouble with Walter What's-his-name, you're positively obsessed."

"It's not that I don't trust you, Henry."

"It's just that you don't trust me."

"Exactly. I knew you'd understand."

"Always."

Rand opened the heavy, carved mahogany door into his office, dominated by a large desk and a tufted leather chair. Peggy positioned herself on the matching couch under the bank of windows overlooking the Pasig River. This morning it shimmered in the sun. She crossed her ankles, her black-and-white striped shirt and black skirt hugging her body. She batted dark eyelashes at him. Tearing his gaze away, he opened the red-covered ledger and ran his finger down the column of numbers.

The corners of his mouth hooked up. The Azure had passed the Monarch in revenue. And a hefty profit it was. He saw visions of clubs in Singapore and Hong Kong and Saigon. Rand would be known all over the Orient. He warmed even though the air conditioner cooled the room. Bruce Tarpin and John Mitchell would drool over the chance to invest in such a successful venture.

"Ready yet?"

"Finished." He shut the book. While he could spend all day examining the numbers, plotting how to grow the business, he needed to show Peggy a good time. As the popular daughter of a Pan Am executive, she had friends not only in Manila but throughout the Far East. He needed to stay in her good graces.

She stood and patted her hair, rolled in the front, curls in the back. "I'm famished. Let's get this show on the road."

She hooked her arm through his, and they strolled into the main room. He waved at his two employees. "See you later, Henry. Bethel, you sound swell. Billie Holiday suits your voice. I'll be back before your performance tonight. We're expecting a full house."

"Don't do anything I wouldn't do." Henry grinned a wicked grin.

Rand wanted to slug him.

Instead, he led Peggy to the car, and soon they were winding their way through the city once more. Sleek art deco buildings stood side by side with centuries-old Spanish-style stone churches and homes.

Knowing the Azure continued to rake in the money, he relaxed against the back of the seat, driving with his right hand on the wheel, his left hanging out of the car. From time to time he stole a glance at Peggy. Not a flaw marred her perfect complexion set off by her dark hair. Just the kind of woman he liked.

"Rand!" Peggy tightened her grip on the door handle.

He stepped on the brake hard to avoid hitting a woman crossing the street from between two parked cars. Vehicles behind him honked. He leaned over the driver's side door. A fabulous platinum blonde stood stock-still, her glassy blue eyes wide in her round face. "Are you hurt?"

She shook her head.

"I didn't see you. I'm sorry."

She smiled. "I should have been more careful. I apologize." Then she looked both ways and finished crossing the street. He and Peggy continued on their way, but he couldn't erase the image of that woman's fresh, innocent face from his mind. So opposite from the polished Peggy's. He didn't think he'd ever forget it.

They had reached the heart of the city when Rand heard the strangest sound behind them. A low, droning humming. At first he thought it might be his car giving him trouble, but no. The sound grew louder. He looked around but saw nothing.

Peggy's forehead creased. "What is that noise?"

They drove by a newspaper hawker staring at the sky, a copy of the morning paper in his hand, the headline shouting the news about Pearl Harbor.

Cold dread shot through Rand.

No, not here. Not this place.

Not his beloved Manila.

# Chapter One

## Santo Tomas Internment Camp, Manila

*October 15, 1943*

For almost two years, Rand Sterling had stared at the heavy iron bars that trapped him in this prison. The clanging of the iron gates behind him all that time ago continued to ring in his ears. Just the thought of it dampened his hands.

He glanced at the small piece of paper he clutched in his hands. He didn't need to read the words he had received a few weeks ago. He had memorized them.

*Papa is dying. Please come.*

He had asked the release committee for a pass to see Armando. But they refused to go to the Japanese commandant with his request because Armando was only his houseboy.

Only.

The man was more like a father than his own father. Armando had taught him everything. And Rand still had much to learn. He had lost so much to this war, including the Monarch and the Azure. He couldn't bear to lose Armando too.

He'd begun formulating a plan to escape as soon as he had received the note from Armando's son, Ramon. To be sure, it was risky. Very Clark Gable–esque. But worth it.

Only a few men had attempted this feat before him, and that was in the first days of their internment. They failed. Their Japanese captors had executed a swift and deadly punishment. Since then, no one had taken the chance at freedom.

All of his plans had fallen into place. And now that darkness had descended, it was almost time to implement them. He had been sending messages back and forth with Ramon via the packet line—secret, coded letters that would pass through the Japanese censors with ease.

The one he received from Ramon today puzzled him. It didn't make sense. Something had to be missing.

*Tonight was terrible. The time was set. The bright lights blinded me.*

What wasn't he understanding?

He turned and wound his way through the large Shantytown the prisoners had constructed on the university grounds, down packed-dirt streets such as Camote Drive and Tiki-tiki Lane. He wiped the sweat from his brow, sure it didn't come because of the typical hot, humid Manila evening. A few quiet voices floated on the night air, mingling with the music from the variety show set up on the main square. The crowd brought their woven *sawali* mats and sat on the damp ground, laughed, sang, and forgot their status as civilian POWs for a while.

His heart pounded as he entered his little nipa hut. The *sawali* mats that made up the walls provided protection from the hot mid-day sun and a quieter place to sleep than the main dormitory. Here he had a small kitchen in one corner, a living area with a table, a bed complete with mosquito netting, and a porch. He had snagged a prime location in the area known as Glamourville—near the wall along Governor Forbes Street. Perfect for his escape.

He swallowed a few times, willing his small chicken dinner to stay down. What if the Japanese guards changed their patrolling routine tonight? What if he had trouble climbing the high concrete wall? What if . . . ?

"Are you ready?"

Rand just about shot out of his skin at the sound of the voice behind him. "Jeepers, Henry, you scared the bejeebers out of me."

Rand's former club manager stood in the hut's doorway leaning against the bamboo pole, a lopsided grin spread across his boyish face. "What if I had been a guard?"

"If you had been a guard, I'd have jumped a yard and hit my head hard." Rand tipped his head and grinned.

Henry stood straight. "Not really a time for fun and games. You know how serious this is, right? You've heard of Fort Santiago."

The grinding of his stomach gave him the answer. "I know, I know. Trying to keep my mind off of it. If I'm caught, torture at the fort is the best-case scenario. But I won't be. The plan is perfect."

Henry rubbed his stubbly chin. "Anything can go wrong."

"Only if you nark on me. And so far you've kept my indiscretions from the society page."

"Your secrets are safe with me. You have a whole bunch of them, you know? Though, if they throw me into Santiago with you, I can't promise I won't crack under the pressure."

"Good man." Rand slapped him on the back. "I knew I could count on you. Just hold on to your end of the rope. Ramon will have the other. Once I'm up and over, just let it go and get out of there. Fast."

"That part I can handle."

Rand didn't doubt it. Between the softball and football teams the organizing committee had put together and his work in the community garden, Henry managed to stay in shape. So had Rand. "Don't let me down."

Henry guffawed. "Not on your life."

That's what Rand counted on.

⁂

"Miss Irene, please stay with me."

Irene Reynolds leaned over Sheila King's bed, held the child's hot hand, and smoothed a strand of black hair from her feverish face. "I won't go anywhere. I promise." She understood what it was like to be motherless.

Sheila closed her eyes, and a sad smile crossed her lips. Irene sat on the cool tile floor. After working this afternoon at the censor's office, then volunteering at the infirmary all evening, she wanted nothing more than to return to the Main Building, curl up on her cot, and sleep for a very long time.

Irene's young charge moaned in her sleep, the intense pain of malaria disturbing even her slumber.

If only they didn't have to be in this dreadful, God-forsaken place.

Sheila moaned again and turned in bed. She opened her sea-green eyes. "Miss Irene, I don't—"

The girl didn't finish her sentence before she got sick. Then her tears flowed. "I'm sorry. So sorry."

Irene hushed her. "You couldn't help it. Just hang on. Let me get the orderly and we'll clean you up."

She made her way through the hall. Sheila should have a mother to tend to her. It was the ones like her who drove Irene to spend so much time here. Sheila's American father had been captured on Bataan, her Filipina mother dead of cancer.

Children she wanted to help.

She didn't have to go far before she found an orderly, his tall, lean frame hunched over as he washed the floor in one of the doctors' offices. "Andrew, I could use your help with Sheila."

He looked up, his green eyes bright even in the pale light. He ran his hand through his shock of bright-red hair. "She's sick again?"

"I'm afraid so." Irene's wooden-soled *bakyas* clapped against the hard floor as she made her way down the hall to Sheila. The orderly followed, hard on her heels as she set a quick pace.

"You need to slow down, Irene."

She answered him over her shoulder. "Can't you keep up?"

"Not that. You are working too hard. You spend so much time here with the children. You're tired yourself."

"That's one way to flatter a woman."

A blush crept up his skinny neck. "I meant, well, you need to sleep a little. I'm worried you'll end up sick. Then who'll sit with you?"

"You're very sweet." She entered the ward and made her way to Sheila's bedside. "Let's get her comfortable again."

They worked in silence as they changed the sheets. Irene sent Andrew off with an armload of dirty linens, then slipped a clean nightgown over Sheila's head. Within seconds of lying down, the child fell into a more restful sleep.

The room silenced as one by one the patients slumbered. Mothers rose and stretched, yawning a few times before heading outside for a breath of fresh air or to tend to their other children. How awful to have your little one so very, very sick. And so unnecessarily. Not enough mosquito netting. Not enough toilets. Not enough soap and hot water.

Irene had promised Sheila she would stay with her until she fell asleep, but she couldn't tear herself away from the child tonight. She did want to leave before the nine o'clock curfew so she could return to the Main Building, where the women were crammed into university classrooms never intended to be dormitories. Anita would be waiting for her in room 40 to have devotions and prayer before lights out.

A heavy mantle of fatigue descended on Irene, and she caught her head bobbing more than once. To try to stay awake, she ran over in her head the censored notes she retyped this morning before the Japanese would allow them to be passed to their recipients.

One from today stood out in her mind. At first glance, it appeared to be innocuous.

*Tonight was terrible. The time was set. The bright lights blinded me. Perhaps another night will be better. Be thankful you are where you are.*

*Perhaps another night will be better. Be thankful you are where you are.* The words the Japanese censors had stricken sounded like a warning, a caution to stay put. And how could he stay put unless he intended to leave?

Could he be thinking about escaping? Surely he knew the fate that awaited him if he was caught. They all knew what happened to those three who tried to escape in the first months of their captivity.

Beaten.

Shot.

Buried alive.

She stood so suddenly, her knee knocked against Sheila's bed, almost tipping it over. Irene steadied the cot, kissed the girl's forehead, and raced down the hall. The orderly flagged her down, but she waved him away. She clattered down the stairs, out of the building, and through Jungletown.

By the time she rounded the Main Building and came to Glamourville, sweat poured down her face and her back. The air clung to her bare arms and legs like a heavy winter coat.

Sharp pains stabbed her side, but she ignored them as she wound her way through the maze of streets, hoping she'd find Mr. Sterling's shanty. She knew his nipa hut backed to the wall.

Not having occasion to come to this part of the compound often, she got turned around in the dark. She ran up and down the streets.

The note had said tonight. It was tonight.

And if she didn't find him in time?

She didn't allow that thought to continue.

# Chapter Two

The world around Irene buzzed, and her heart bounced against her chest. A light mist began to fall, mingling with the sweat running down her face. She forced her legs to stop running, her hands on her knees, her neck bent to keep from passing out. She didn't know where Mr. Sterling's hut was, only that it was in Glamourville.

Perhaps he had figured out from the remainder of the sender's note the message he'd been trying to convey. But if he hadn't and Irene's detective work was correct, he could be in a great amount of trouble.

No one survived an escape attempt.

No one even tried.

She finger-raked strands of damp hair from her eyes. In the daytime, each shanty had its own personality. At dark, they blurred together, one indistinguishable from the other. She straightened to resume the search, not knowing how she would find him. Her legs protested, but she urged them forward. She had to make sure Mr. Sterling had the complete message.

She knocked on the bamboo and *sawali* mat door of one of the huts. A surly middle-aged man answered. "What do you want?"

"Do you know where Mr. Sterling's hut is?"

"Why would I know something like that?" He squinted and scrunched his forehead.

She bit back her caustic reply. "It's important that I find him."

"What does that have to do with me?"

"Please, if you know, tell me." She clenched her fists.

"I've never heard of the man." With that, he slammed the door as hard as possible. It lacked the *oomph* of shutting a wood door, but she understood the meaning behind it. And here she stood, wasting time. She rapped on a few more huts. Some of the residents were either out for the evening or had returned to their dormitories for the night. Others answered with the same reply. No one appeared to know the mysterious Mr. Sterling.

A Japanese patrolman strode in her direction, his trousers ballooning around him, his tall black boots silent on the dirt street. To avoid having to bow, she turned her back on him and moved to the door of the next shanty. He passed without a word, and she released a breath she hadn't realized she'd been holding.

On her fourth attempt, she found someone who knew where Mr. Sterling lived. Now she just had to get there in time to stop him from making a huge, life-threatening mistake.

She moved faster and faster, stumbling at last on the hut. The lily blooms in front drooped. No lights shone through the mats. When she peeked in the opening on the side, the one commanded by the Japanese to be kept so privacy between men and women was impossible, she spotted no movement.

But from the corner of her eye, she caught a flurry of activity.

She had found Mr. Sterling.

He had not figured out the rest of the message.

---

Rand and Henry squatted behind Rand's nipa hut. Off in the distance, the crowd at Dave Harvey's variety show laughed. A cat mewed not far from them. The sun had set. The sky was dark.

Every one of Rand's muscles was poised for action, tense and alert. His lungs allowed him only to draw shallow breaths. His heart thumped in his ears, and he was afraid the noise would drown out the possible approach of Japanese footsteps.

He peered around the bamboo corner of the shanty in time to watch the guard move down the street. His back would be to Rand for several minutes. His chance to escape. His chance at freedom.

With a nod, he motioned for Henry to follow him. Ramon should be in place on the other side of the wall on Governor Forbes Street, ready to take him to Armando. Never in his life had Armando failed him. When Rand's parents had been too busy with their social life to stay by his side when he had the measles, Armando was there. When he tore his best trousers after Mother told him to stay clean, Armando covered for him.

He vowed not to fail the man. He would take care of him until MacArthur returned and freed them all.

Rand rolled the rope between his hands. If they didn't sweat too much and if the mist didn't make his ascent too slippery, he should be able to scale the wall with little trouble. He'd been doing push-ups and pull-ups every day since he had received the note, while Armando clung to life.

He stared up at the monstrous concrete-block structure in

front of him. All that stood between him and the outside world. He had to succeed.

If any soldiers appeared in the area outside the wall, Ramon was to whistle like a bird. Armando loved to imitate their calls—bush larks, Pacific swallows, paddyfield pipits. Rand remembered lessons from Armando on how to identify different birds. The same lessons Armando taught his own son. Who knew how handy they would be?

The wall jutted into the sky. With a little concentration and a whole lot of luck, he could do this. Couldn't he?

He squared his shoulders. Yes, seeing Armando one more time was worth the effort. Worth the risk.

Henry slapped him on the back. Rand's breath caught in his throat. Henry slapped him again.

Rand grasped the thick hemp rope and flung it over the wall, hoping he'd gotten enough on the other side for Ramon to take hold. Hoping that Henry would be able to hang on so he could scamper over.

Henry grasped the rope and gave it a tug, then shook his head. Rand shrugged. What was the problem? His buddy pulled the rope. Slack. Hadn't Ramon been able to grab it?

Rand listened for the birdsong. Nothing. Absolute silence, save for the distant laughter of the crowd at Dave Harvey's variety show.

The guard would return within a few minutes. Rand would have to move fast if he expected to be over and out of here by the guard's return. Another tug of the rope. More slack. Still no sign of Ramon.

Rand pivoted, sure he heard footsteps. A woman appeared at the side of the hut, leaning in the opening, calling for him in a low voice laden with fear. He recognized the Jean Harlow white-blond hair and the curve of the hips.

The one he'd nearly run over two years ago.

What a knockout. But why was she here?

He didn't want to acknowledge her presence, but she drew attention to his activity. Even in the darkness, he felt Henry's scowl. Rand motioned for his friend to stay still. Perhaps when she realized he wasn't in the hut, she would leave.

Of course she didn't. She walked around the outside of his humble abode. When she discovered what he and Henry were up to, would she turn them in?

He couldn't chance it. So far tonight, nothing had gone according to plan. As soon as she rounded the corner, he sprang on her from behind, crushing her in the crook of his left arm, clamping his right hand over her mouth. A single scream and they would all be dead.

She wriggled and fought, landing a few good kicks on his shin with the hard wooden sole of her *bakya*. He bit the inside of his cheek to keep from crying out in pain but held her fast. He leaned in to whisper in her ear. "If you promise not to make a sound, I'll uncover your mouth. Do you understand?"

She trembled under his hold but nodded.

He withdrew his hand only a little bit, ready to clamp down on her if she didn't keep her part of the bargain, maintaining a tight grip on her. "What do you want?"

"To deliver a message."

"Why should I trust you?"

"I'm from the censor's office. I typed a note from your houseboy, leaving out the censored parts."

"And you didn't have the delivery boy share them with me? All the others do."

"I didn't think they were important. Now they make sense."

He came in closer so his lips brushed her neck. She shivered. "What did the note say?"

"'Perhaps another night will be better. Be thankful you are where you are.'"

He growled, then released her so suddenly she fell against him. He pushed her away. Ramon hadn't planned on being on the other side of the wall tonight. "Now's a fine time for you to deliver that message."

"You're escaping, aren't you?"

"Get out of here." He turned and tugged the rope over the wall. The knot on the end, however, got caught on the corner of the wall. No matter how hard he pulled, he couldn't release it. He would need it for the next attempt. He couldn't leave it there. The Japanese would discover it come morning.

Cheers rose from the group watching the show on the main square. The male attendees would soon return to their nipa huts for the evening while the women would retire to the classrooms in the Main Building or Annex. Too much unwanted attention.

Henry joined him in trying to free the rope. No success.

Then the woman was at their side. "Let me help you. Maybe with three of us, we can get it free."

But the wall was too high for them to maneuver the knot.

Voices drifted their way. Not cheery English voices returning from the evening's entertainment. Not the Dutch or Polish voices of some of their fellow internees.

The very distinct, nasal voices of the Japanese.

Rand dared to peek around the shanty to the dirt road. A pair of guards clad in drab olive uniforms sauntered down the muddy road, their machine guns clasped in their hands.

They swept the area with their flashlights, the beams dancing over pretty patches of flowers and mingling with the light from a few of the huts.

Each step brought them closer to Rand and Henry. And the woman. Rand's dinner threatened to evacuate ship. They had to make a beeline out of here.

Just as he turned to go, the searchlight found its mark.

Right in his eyes.

# Chapter Three

Irene sat on the floor of the dark nipa hut, damp and out of breath after her sprint away from the Japanese guards, hugging her knees to her chest. Through the opening, she heard the choppy words of the soldiers as they fell on Mr. Sterling and his friend.

Though the air was heavy and warm, she shivered and couldn't stop. She clasped her hands tighter and pulled her legs in closer. What was happening to the two men?

Whatever it was, it was her fault. She should have realized right away what the note was about and told Mr. Sterling earlier. Why hadn't she thought it important? *Stupid, stupid.*

And now her actions—rather, inactions—would cost two men their lives. She swiped at a stray tear. The Japanese would not spare them. They hadn't spared the three who escaped early on in their confinement, despite the protests of Mr. Earl Carroll, the head of the internee government, who had pleaded for their lives.

The Japanese commandant refused to budge.

Cupping her hands over her ears, she tried to block out the

noise. Still, the sounds of the captors' blows falling on the men reached her. At least one of them cried out in pain, cursing God, cursing the heavens, cursing the Japanese.

*Father, forgive me.* Clamping her teeth together, she waited for the blast of a gunshot.

The crowds began to return from the night's entertainment. "What's going on there?" one internee asked.

She crawled to the door and opened it a crack. The mass swarmed around Mr. Sterling's hut. A buzz ran through the audience.

"What's happening?"

"I can't see."

"What did they do?"

"They're crazy for trying to escape."

The guards raised their weapons and shouted. The people fell back but didn't leave. With the onlookers packed shoulder to shoulder, she couldn't see the men's fate.

Keeping her trembling arms tucked against her body, she pushed open the flimsy door the rest of the way with her shoulder and stepped down to the dirt lane. Part of her wanted to help in some way or another. She owed it to Mr. Sterling.

Yet she knew any attempt to save them would be in vain. And at the cost of her own life.

She wriggled through the crowd. The Japanese asserted their authority. "Get back. Get back. Go home. Nothing to see." Again they raised their weapons.

Duly convinced that the guards meant business, the people dispersed. Irene couldn't turn away. She stayed after the majority of the spectators left.

And she got a good view of the men. Both faces were raw and bloody. Mr. Sterling's right eye was swollen and his nose crooked.

His friend bore similar injuries and staggered when the Japanese lifted him to his feet. Two guards half carried, half dragged Mr. Sterling away.

As they passed her, she shrunk against the corner of the hut next door, praying the shadows would hide her.

She dug her fingernails into the bamboo.

Mr. Sterling passed. He turned his head and stared in her direction.

Right at her.

Into her eyes.

His expression was unreadable.

*Fort Santiago.* The words alone sent a shiver down Rand's spine. Never mind the sight of Henry beaten to a pulp, slumped over beside him on the hard wood bench in the back of the truck. The vehicle sped away from Santo Tomas.

He knew where he was going.

He knew what fate awaited him there.

The Japanese weren't going to end his misery in one swift blow. They would siphon the life from him little by little.

The tires screeched as the truck rounded a corner a little too fast. Rand slid across the bench and banged into the side, his ribs paining him. Henry also moved down the bench.

Why had he even tried to escape? Now he would never see Armando again. And how foolish to clue Henry in on his scheme and ask for his help. He had a wife and a son he had shipped to Australia before the war.

Rand's temple throbbed and each breath was excruciating. A

bullet to the head would be too merciful. That punishment was too easy. Before he would find relief from his agony, the Japanese would pile on more and more. Until he broke.

Then they would execute him.

Those who had witnessed the killing of the first three escapees told of the moans still coming from the men even as their captors piled dirt on their graves.

Rand broke out in a cold sweat. Anything but that. Any torture but that.

With each bump over the pothole-riddled street, blackness tugged at the corners of his brain. Perhaps it would be best to give in to it. Just let go. Inexplicably, the picture of a lovely round face framed by white-blond hair flashed in front of his eyes.

He must be hallucinating.

With another sharp turn, Henry screamed in pain. Rand stumbled toward him, biting his lip. The taste of blood had never left his mouth. Would this ride never be over? Yet Rand didn't want the ten-minute trip to end.

Because death awaited him.

Henry gave Rand a long glance. His eyes glazed over. He moved his mouth but no sound came out.

Rand held his friend's hand. "Hang in there. If they take us to the jungle, there might be a way of escape. We can hide in the hills."

With a groan, Henry shook his head. "All you ever think about?"

"Escape? Yes. I like my freedom too much. My parents were forever chastising me because I would go off on my own and do my own thing. Poor Armando had a devil of a time keeping up with me."

Armando. Ramon. What if the Japanese caught him too? The cost of this crazy scheme continued to rise.

"I'm sorry. Should have never gotten you involved."

"Edna and Charlie."

Henry's wife and son. "You fight to get back to them. Don't let them down."

The truck lurched to a halt. Within moments, Japanese guards opened the doors and pulled out Rand and Henry by their hair. Rand squared his shoulders and held his breath, refusing to give the soldiers satisfaction in the pain they inflicted.

He released the air in his lungs once his feet hit the ancient stones of the old Spanish fort. Thick-walled Santiago had overlooked the Pasig River for four hundred years.

A gun in his back and a stream of what he assumed to be Japanese curses spoiled the view of Manila, the Pearl of the Orient, at night. The soldiers led both men down below, into the deep recesses of the fort, now an enemy stronghold.

A place of torture for those who refused to cooperate with the occupiers.

A dread word among all of the Santo Tomas internees.

A hole almost no one survived to tell about.

The stench of mold and mildew, death and dying, excrement and vomit almost overwhelmed Rand. He breathed through his mouth, able, though, to taste the odors. He swallowed hard.

The guard took Rand to a small room. As he entered the door, he looked back at Henry. Another guard led him farther and farther into the bowels of the dungeon.

Would he ever see his friend again?

The soldier slammed him into a cold metal chair in front of a battered desk. A single lightbulb illuminated the space. Other than that, the room was bare. The only noise came from the pounding of Rand's heart against his rib cage.

No sooner had the door behind him clanged shut when the door in front of him clattered open. A small but powerful-looking man entered the interrogation room. He wore the Japanese secret police Kempeitai uniform—drab olive, a hat with a red band and shiny black bill, a red-and-yellow collar badge. No white armband with red Japanese lettering. He was an officer. He strode about for a bit, around and around the cell, his gaze never leaving Rand.

Abruptly, he slammed his hand on the desk. "Why were you trying to escape?"

The man's English was impeccable. "You speak very well. Studied in the States, I presume?"

"Harvard. Class of '36. Summa cum laude. Who helped you in the attempt, poor as it was?"

The man would get nothing from him. "If my parents had their way, I also would have graduated from Harvard in '36. USC, class of '37. Summa cum nothing." It stung just a bit to know this Oriental man was more intelligent than him.

Eyes narrowed, scowling, the inquisitor leaned in, his heart-shaped face within inches of Rand's. Trying to catch him off balance. "I need names. All of them. Whoever was involved in this. Whoever knew about this."

One thing Rand Sterling never did—make the same mistake twice. He kept his mouth shut. Mostly to prevent his dinner from a return engagement. Though he wouldn't be the first to lose his supper in this place.

"Names." The officer withdrew a sheet of paper and a pen from the desk and pushed them in Rand's direction.

He crossed his arms and clenched his fists. It would be easy, so easy, to write names. But to betray those who loved him best . . . And for what? His execution orders had already been signed.

The soldier slapped him open palmed across the face. Red, blue, and green lights flashed in front of him. Rand now understood the meaning of seeing stars. Then the little vision he had in his right eye was extinguished.

"Why so reluctant, my friend? Don't you want to save your skin?"

"Nothing I do will save my skin."

"So impertinent." The interrogator's voice grew hard once more. "Write. Or I'll go back for that pretty little blonde the guards reported running away from the scene."

Rand shifted on the chair, his surely broken ribs making any movement unbearable. Could he sacrifice her to save Armando? He didn't know the woman. "No one helped. It was me and me alone."

"How did you get the rope?"

"It was left by the man who built my hut. I had no way of returning it."

The soldier's face grew red. "You. Are. Lying."

Rand didn't cower. "I. Am. Not."

Again, the soldier slammed his hand into the desk. A wonder that he hadn't broken a bone. "You must write." From inside the desk, he produced a hammer. "I will give you ten minutes to write. If you do not, I will come and break a finger. Ten more minutes, another finger. You may not have gone to Harvard, but you can see the pattern here."

Loud and clear.

The prison door rattled shut, the noise echoing down the long, desolate hallway.

Rand tussled his hair. Who to give up? Whose life would be lost along with his? He wrung his hands, one of the few places on his body that didn't hurt. At least for now.

If he were a praying man, he'd ask God for discernment. He remembered Armando teaching him about wise King Solomon. He needed just a bit of that wisdom.

His thoughts paced back and forth. The woman? Armando? Ramon? *Which one? God, which one?*

The heavens remained silent. He wasn't surprised. God didn't have time to bother with a heretic such as himself.

He stared at the pen on the pitted gray metal desk. If only it would pick itself up and make the choice for him.

Armando had never failed him. Ever. He was always the one to comfort him, the one to cheer him on, the one to help him.

Rand didn't blame Ramon either. Tonight wasn't his fault. He'd tried to warn him.

Rand didn't even know the woman's name. How could he write it if he didn't know it? She played no part in the escape except for bringing the message to him a bit too late. Honestly, it was a miracle she had figured out the meaning. Perhaps the Japanese had too. They might have been lying in wait for him.

Maybe he had never stood a chance.

With cold, clammy fingers, he picked up the pen and began to write.

# Chapter Four

Irene stood against the side of the nipa hut for a few more minutes, until she knew the guards and Mr. Sterling and his friend were gone. Covering her mouth with her hand, she made a mad dash for the safety and security of the Main Building. Funny that it would be a haven for her now when most of the time it was a prison.

Her muddy *bakyas* slid on the polished floor, and she held on to the banister so as not to trip as she flew up the stairs. She scampered into room 40, cots shoulder to shoulder covering almost every available inch of floor space. She stepped over and around and picked her way among the sleeping and half asleep to where Anita sat on her bed, her hands clasped in her lap, her back ramrod straight, her unseeing eyes staring straight ahead.

As Irene passed, a smile lit Anita's pale face. "I didn't know if you'd be back tonight."

Irene slipped off her wooden-soled shoes and sat on her cot. "Sheila is sleeping. She seems a bit better."

"Then what has you all flustered?"

"Who says I'm flustered?"

Irene's aunt shook her head, her honey-colored curls framing her face. "You may be nineteen, but you can't fool me even though I can't see."

Irene flopped back on her cot. "I made a mistake that is going to cost two people their lives."

"Sheila? I thought you said she was better."

"Not her. Two men I don't know."

Anita furrowed her brow. "You're going to have to explain."

"I didn't deliver a message I should have. I mean, I delivered it, but not all of it, thinking it wasn't important."

"But it was."

Irene nodded and choked back a few tears.

"Should you have known?"

"I should have guessed." She rolled over and buried her head in her pillow, hoping to block out the sounds of the soldiers' fists and boots connecting with Mr. Sterling's body. All to no avail.

Anita rose and sat on the edge of Irene's cot, smoothing back her hair. The mother-like touch that Irene had never known from the woman who had given birth to her. "We should pray for them."

Prayer was always Anita's answer to any sort of trouble. "Not even prayer will save them. I wouldn't be surprised if they are already dead."

"What can it hurt?"

Irene questioned more whether it would help. Still, she closed her eyes and allowed Anita's soothing words to wash over her. She prayed for the men, for Sheila, and for their Japanese overlords.

Spending the last nine years among missionaries, she knew God commanded them to pray for their enemies. Anita taught the women of the village this over and over. Anita, a gracious teacher, leader, example to the women. All despite being sightless.

But this—this was so hard. Her enemy was not wounded, lying on the side of the road needing assistance. Her enemy was brutal, keeping women and children imprisoned, torturing men without a second thought.

Anita pulled the light blanket over Irene's shoulder. She grasped the edge of it, hot tears washing down her cheeks.

Would this nightmare ever end?

~

Rand's fingers trembled, and he bit his swollen lip as he put the pen to the page.

*Franklin Roosevelt*
*Douglas MacArthur*
*Dwight Eisenhower*
*George Washington*
*Thomas Jefferson*

He set the pen on the desk and wiped the sweat from his forehead. For better or worse, it was done.

Goose bumps broke out all over him as the heavy metal door opened and the officer returned. Rand was sure the man could see his chest pulsing. He crossed his trembling arms in front of him.

The interrogator picked up the page and stared at it. Rand held his breath. The man's eyes widened and his face grew red. He wadded the paper into a ball and threw it across the room. He grabbed the hammer, his knuckles white, pulled Rand's right hand from against his body, and smashed his thumb.

Pain seared his hand.

He pulled it back, cradling it against his body.

Screams ripped from his throat.

The soldier held the hammer over Rand. "I will not tolerate your little games." He walked to the door Rand had come through and knocked. A soldier, armed with a machine gun, entered.

"Take this man to a cell. I am finished with him for tonight."

The guard pulled Rand to his feet, stuck the barrel of the gun in his back, and led him out of the room. They continued through the dark, dank hallway and down a flight of stairs. Every step, every little motion, every little jar brought excruciating pain.

His guard opened a heavy, solid steel door and shoved Rand inside. With a clink, the door shut behind him, the key grating in the lock.

Through a haze of pain, Rand noticed the cell was tiny, a few feet by a few feet. The walls and floor were stone. Two inches of water flooded the room. There were no furnishings—no bed, no sink, no toilet. The eye-watering odor in the place led him to believe that all of the cells were like this. Above him, maybe thirty or forty feet straight up, was an opening covered with an iron grate.

He sat in the water in a corner, still holding his wrist, shivering from the cold and wet and shock—the only things keeping him from passing out. Tears of pain mingled with the light rain that fell.

Two years ago this time, he had been waltzing with one of Manila's fine, eligible bachelorettes, puffing on cigars with his friends Bruce and John, eating the finest foods his cook prepared. He never had to lift a hand to care for the garden. He never had to wash or mend his own clothes. He never had to do any menial task. He was at the pinnacle of success.

If only he could turn back the clock, go back to that life, not take anything for granted. Or anyone. Like Armando.

He saw nothing through his right eye. With his left eye, he gazed at his injured hand, the thumb mangled.

If the Japanese kept breaking his bones, he would be good for nothing.

⁂

All through the night, a steady, heavy rain fell. The Pasig River, already swollen from the usual seasonal tropical storms, overflowed its banks. Water poured into Rand's cell. He sat in it, now up to his knees. He shivered, unable to stop the tremors. A few times during the night he nodded off. True, deep sleep remained elusive.

He drifted asleep, reality mixing with his subconscious.

> Armando ran toward him, his hands outstretched, his smile bright. Then arms grabbed him. Rand could only see the arms, not the body of the man who caught Armando. He screamed, pleading with Rand to save him. But Rand's swollen hands were tied together, each finger bent in a different direction.
>
> "I can't reach you. Armando, come here. Please don't take him."
>
> But the door slammed and he disappeared.

Rand woke with a jerk of his head. Armando's face, the terror in his eyes, haunted Rand.

At long last, gray light filtered into the cell. The dim morning revealed blood and moss and mold on the stone walls. The water around him was filthy.

His tongue stuck to the roof of his mouth. When would they bring food and water? Did they feed their prisoners?

Even though he was surrounded by water, he knew one sip of it would bring on dysentery or typhoid or a host of other diseases. His body ached and his hand throbbed. Around him, men groaned and screamed. Obscenities filled the air.

Rand stood and stretched. He stifled a cry when his ribs protested the movement. He wanted to get out of here whatever way possible. Escape wasn't an option. Release was his only chance, however slim. Perhaps he could persuade the Western-educated jailer to let him go. Appeal to his connection with Americans.

If all else failed, death would be a way out. But the Japanese didn't go for a quick, easy, painless demise for their prisoners. No, they would make sure he would have to endure endless torture before death would claim him.

But if it claimed him, it would be a release.

He didn't want to live like this.

Reduced to nothing.

A guard came and handed him a bowl of thin gruel. Nothing to drink. Perhaps he would die of thirst in a matter of days. End the torture early. He downed the soup.

The rain continued, heavier than ever. Above him, the wind howled. He thought about the mud at Santo Tomas and the flimsy little huts. He imagined himself lounging on his leather sofa at his home on Dewey Boulevard, a brandy in one hand, bright red, green, and blue Persian rugs accenting the cool marble floors. Armando would shutter the windows against the storm. Rand never worried about the weather. His house was well built, and he was safe and secure there.

The water level in his cell rose at an alarming rate. Even now as he stood, it came to his waist. Despite the stifling heat and humidity, the water was cool.

Drowning might be another path to freedom. Much faster than torture.

The guard came to his cell after a while and led him to the same interrogation room he'd been in last night, sat him in the chair with a rough push, then slammed the door shut behind him.

The same soldier who had broken his thumb entered the room, his uniform clean and pressed, a brown belt around his waist, high black boots polished. "I trust your accommodations are satisfactory."

Rand didn't move, didn't say a word.

"Ah, you are giving me the silent treatment now. Very well. It is perhaps for the best. You can get right to work on the list of names I requested last night." He leaned in, his face mere inches from Rand's, his breath hot. "You think you are very clever, Mr. Sterling. Let me give you some advice. Do not play games with me. I am in charge here. If you follow my directives, things will go well for you. If you insist on frustrating me, there will be consequences. How is your hand feeling this morning?"

A torrent of words dammed up behind Rand's lips. He clamped them shut, refusing to let the man have his satisfaction.

The inquisitor withdrew another sheet of paper from the desk drawer and pushed it and a pen in Rand's direction. "I realize you may not be able to write very well, but give it a try. I will return shortly to check on your progress. I suggest that you comply with my demand."

With a clang of the door, Rand was again alone in the room. At least this one wasn't flooded. His cold, wrinkled toes were grateful.

He refused to even entertain the thought of divulging the

names of those who helped him. They already had Henry. Had they broken his fingers? Or had he spilled Ramon's name and mentioned the woman?

He hoped his friend would have the strength to resist.

Perhaps this was an exercise in futility. Perhaps they already possessed the information they needed.

He stood and paced the room. It was about three feet longer and wider than his cell. With his left hand, he rubbed his aching forehead.

The man warned him not to be such a smart aleck today. Too bad. He figured he'd use movie star names. Carole Lombard. Cary Grant. Greta Garbo. Tomorrow, perhaps he would move on to cartoon characters.

He owed Armando that.

As the door opened once more, he stared at his hand.

Which finger would his captor break today?

# Chapter Five

Irene woke from her fitful sleep as light began to filter through the large windows. A few other women sat on their cots, combing the tangles from their hair. She wanted to be at the head of the line to use the restroom, so she threw aside the blanket and rose.

As she started to tiptoe to her destination down the hall, Anita called for her.

Irene stopped. "What do you need? Are you ready to get up?" Irene would have to help her through the maze of cots. They were shifted almost daily, as one woman had a tiff with her friend and moved to another part of the room or as a resident came or went. Anita couldn't manage to navigate it alone.

"No. I don't feel well."

Irene kneeled beside her aunt, feeling her forehead with the back of her hand. Hot. "What's wrong?"

"My stomach hurts. Very much. My head too."

"Let me help you up. Once you're dressed, I'll take you to Santa Catalina to see the doctor."

"But roll call will begin soon."

"Don't worry about that. Bertha will count you and me and all will be fine. She's a good room monitor that way."

"And your breakfast?"

"Stop worrying about me. I'll get something at the hospital or buy some fruit from the vendor once we have you settled."

Anita leaned on Irene and shuffled her way to the washroom. When the other women heard that Anita wasn't well, they stepped aside and let her use the facilities first.

The walk to the hospital wasn't far, but as they made their way there, the rain began to fall faster and the wind blew with such ferocity they were almost knocked off of their feet.

"I should have tended to you myself in the room. You shouldn't be out in the storm." But Irene worried about her aunt. She hadn't protested actually going to see the doctor—only about missing roll call and breakfast.

Anita slogged forward, putting more and more of her weight on Irene with each step. She didn't know how long she'd be able to support her aunt. A few more steps and Anita's knees gave way. It was all Irene could do to hold Anita out of the mud.

Two young men passed by on their way to the kitchen.

"Help us. Please help me. I need to get her to Santa Catalina."

They walked over. One was tall and thin with wavy hair. The other was shorter and squatter. "You're headed to the hospital?"

Irene nodded. "Can you help me carry her? She's too weak to walk."

The wavy-haired one grabbed Anita under her armpits while the other held up her legs. They made quick progress to their destination.

A nurse in her brown collared Army uniform scurried over, a creased cap on her head. "Irene, are you here to see Sheila? She's been asking for you all morning."

She nodded in Anita's direction. "That visit will have to wait until later, Marge. My aunt is ill. She's running a fever and has stomach pains."

Marge frowned. "That's too bad. Boys, why don't you bring her to this seat, and I'll take it from there."

Irene thanked the young men and went to Anita's side. "What can I get you?"

Before she had a chance to answer, Marge returned with a thermometer and a stethoscope. She took Anita's pulse and marked her vitals in a chart. "Your fever is quite high. We'd better have Dr. Hadley take a look at you."

Anita's face grew paler, her cheeks brighter red. "Can I lie down, please?"

Marge nodded. "Sure, sweetheart. Can you stand or shall I get an orderly?"

"I'll manage if you and Irene help me."

It took a few minutes, but Anita shuffled to the bed and lay down with a grateful sigh. She flashed a small smile in Irene's direction. "Quit worrying."

Anita knew her too well. "I'm not."

"Sure. And I'm the Queen of England."

Irene fussed with the blanket. "Is that better, Your Royal Highness?"

"Yes. My next command is for you to sit down."

Irene obeyed. She sat and waited, and waited and sat. About the time breakfast would be ending, more patients entered to see either the doctor or a nurse. Irene crossed and uncrossed her legs. Still no Dr. Hadley. She didn't even see Marge or any of the other nurses.

Coughs and sneezes and even a moan or two drowned out the ticking of the round wall clock. "Let me get you a drink."

Anita nodded as her eyes drifted shut.

Happy for an excuse to get out of the hard, straight-backed chair, Irene went in search of a glass of water. And Dr. Hadley. On her way to the faucet, she stopped by Sheila's room. "How are you doing this morning, sunshine?"

Sheila's round face shone. "I'm better. Nurse Hughes told me I might even get to leave the hospital soon, when I'm stronger."

"That's wonderful." Irene squeezed Sheila's shoulder.

"But I'll miss you."

"We'll see each other around. Listen, I'll be back later, but right now I'm here with my sick aunt, and I have to get her a glass of water and find the doctor."

Sheila nodded. "I promise not to go anywhere."

"You do that, sweetie."

Irene got a cup of water from the hospital kitchen. Still no sign of the doctor. No one she asked seemed to know where he was.

She put her head down, mumbling to herself about his absence when people needed him when she ran into a solid chest.

Sneaking a peek up, heat rose in her neck when she met Dr. Hadley's dark eyes. "Miss Reynolds. So nice to bump into you. I hear you've been on a manhunt for me."

She nodded. "My aunt is here." She led him to Anita.

He listened to her heart, looked down her throat, read the nurse's notes, asked her for her health history, nodded, and cleared his voice. "Typhoid fever, I'm afraid."

Irene's hands became clammy.

"Poor living conditions, especially now in the rainy season." He patted Anita's hand. "We'll keep you here, take good care of you, and have you back on your feet in no time."

Tingles traveled up and down Irene's arm. She appreciated

the doctor's encouraging words, but she knew drugs were in short supply. Another complication was that she and Anita didn't have much money to purchase medicines. And typhoid fever could be—and often was—very serious.

She lifted Anita's head to give her a drink of water. "There. What else can I do for you?"

"Go to work."

Irene took a step back. "Don't you want me to stay with you?"

"Right now I want to sleep."

Anita's hint wasn't subtle. She didn't want to be fussed over. "I'll be back when I'm finished. I promised Sheila I'd see her later."

"Come after lunch. When you've had something to eat."

"Yes, ma'am." She ducked out of the room.

As she hurried to the administration offices, she couldn't help but fret about Anita's illness. Since scarlet fever robbed her of her sight about fifteen years ago, her health had been fragile.

Fighting off disease in this cesspool was no easy feat.

Unending, unendurable days passed for Rand as he rotted away in the cell. The filthy water receded a little before another typhoon hit and the river overflowed its banks again. The mosquitoes swarmed his face, and he no longer had the strength to swat them away. Malaria became a very real possibility.

The only blessing was that his Japanese interrogator didn't send for him again. He had broken the pointer finger on his right hand when he'd seen the list of movie star names and his middle finger when Rand had turned in a page full of baseball players' names. By now he expected his entire hand to be broken.

Why did Mr. Harvard-summa-cum-laude leave him alone?

Rand stared up at the sun streaming through the grate at the top of the cell. The heat from it never quite permeated the thick stone walls. He'd love to feel the sun on his face once more, speed along Dewey Boulevard. He missed it.

In those days, he was somebody.

Right now he simply wanted to be nobody.

Each day, as his death approached, he welcomed it more and more. The beauty of its release brought him to tears.

He was glad his parents had been in the States on business when the war broke out. He didn't want them to see him like this. His mother forever chided him if his clothes were stained, or if he had a hair out of place, or if he had dirt under his fingernails. They would turn their heads in disgust at their son.

The unappetizing gruel was delivered again. No point in eating it. Rand's nauseous stomach wouldn't allow him to suck nutrition from it even if he wanted to. He sat in the wet corner waiting to die.

Then a key scratched in the lock. A bolt of fear shot through him. With a groan, the door opened. The guard lifted him to his feet and dragged him out.

Perhaps this would be the end. They realized they would get nothing out of him. Time to do away with him.

In that moment, a spark flamed to life in his soul. He wasn't ready to die. Not yet. He wanted to be out of this dungeon, but he didn't want to die. He was only twenty-nine. There was so much of life still in front of him. So much living left to do.

He wanted to hike the Taal volcano. He wanted to swim in the Philippine Sea, feel the sand between his toes. He wanted to dance until the sun rose.

The soldier led him down the hall, the ever-present machine

gun in Rand's back. Several times he had to reach out and steady himself as he rode a wave of dizziness.

Was Henry in any of these cells? Was he still alive?

His stomach rolled over.

They passed the room where he'd been interrogated before. Perhaps he would have a new inquisitor. Perhaps they were leading him to his execution.

He trembled. Wasn't this what he wanted?

Not anymore.

His foot caught on an uneven stone in the floor. He tripped and fell, pain racing up his arm when he broke his fall with his right hand. The soldier lifted him to his feet and continued prodding him toward his certain fate.

The dungeon was eerily silent. No moans of pain or screams of anguish. Were they clearing out the place? Getting rid of all of the residents to make room for more?

He couldn't stand it. He turned to the guard behind him. "Where are we going? Where are you taking me?"

The soldier answered with a jab of his gun in Rand's back.

They came to a large door. Rand wrinkled his forehead, tried to remember. This was Fort Santiago's entrance. He was sure of it.

The guard hollered at the soldier stationed at the door, and the portal swung open.

Bright light stung Rand's eyes. He gulped fresh air. Wherever they were taking him, he was grateful for these few moments outdoors.

A truck sat idling outside of the prison, its back doors flung open. With the prodding of the gun, Rand climbed into the truck, protecting his hand. The driver locked him in and revved the engine. Were they on their way to the cemetery, where he would dig his own grave?

It took Rand's single-seeing eye a few moments to adjust to the darkness again. He hoped to meet Henry here, but no other passengers occupied the space.

He fell against the side of the truck as they rounded a corner, sucking in his breath at the pain in his chest and hand. They zigzagged through the streets. Because the truck had no windows, he had no idea where they were.

With a squeal of the brakes, the truck stopped. He heard the cab door slam shut and Japanese voices.

They had arrived.

He trembled.

His end was near.

# Chapter Six

Irene knelt beside Anita's bed in the hospital, sponging her hot face with cool water. Five days had gone by since Anita had come down with typhoid fever. Each day her aunt became more and more ill.

Every minute she wasn't working at the censor's office, she was at her aunt's side. Irene couldn't force food into her mouth. And sleep? She would sleep on the floor, but Dr. Hadley refused, forcing her to leave before curfew.

Irene prayed her way through the night, asking the Lord to heal her aunt. He was great enough to do it. Capable of doing it.

But He didn't.

Had He turned a deaf ear to her?

She thought of the great number of sick and suffering.

Had He turned a deaf ear to them all?

Her knees ached from her position on the polished tile floor. She stood and returned the damp washcloth to the basin of water beside Anita's bed. Anita had slept the entire two hours Irene had been here today. She wound a curl of hair around her finger. There had to be something else they could do for Anita. Some medicine, some way to make her better. She released the curl and it sprang back into position. Irene missed her aunt's smile, her warm heart.

Again she went on the hunt for Dr. Hadley. This time she found him consulting with Dr. Young. She stood with her arms crossed, waiting for them to finish their conversation. She had to restrain herself from tapping her foot.

She pounced on Dr. Hadley the minute Dr. Young walked away, grabbing his forearm. "My aunt, Anita Markham, is so much worse this morning. She isn't waking up, and her fever is as high as ever. What can we do for her? There has to be other medicine. Maybe your diagnosis is wrong."

As soon as the words flew out of her mouth, she wished she could gather them back. Dr. Hadley's face grew red. "Do you have any medical training, young lady?"

Irene stared at her *bakyas*, the leather straps cracked. "Only caring for sick or injured missionaries and villagers."

"Then I would thank you to leave my job to me." He walked in the opposite direction of Anita's room.

Irene's shoulders slumped even as fire burned her middle. She meandered her way back to Anita's bedside. Instead of doing her aunt good, she may have done her harm. If the doctor didn't come soon and examine Anita, Irene was afraid of what her aunt's condition would be when he did arrive. To her, time had become critical.

Anita continued to sleep while Irene kept her vigil. About an hour after her run-in with Dr. Hadley, Dr. Young came to them. The man matched his name—young, tall, thin, with a shock of sandy-colored hair. "I hear you would like a second opinion on your aunt's condition."

Irene fanned her hot face. "I didn't mean to insult him."

"You're concerned about her. I understand. But you also have to understand that we are understaffed here. We do our best to give whatever care we can, but we have just a few doctors for the more than three thousand camp inmates. We're dealing with a lot of disease here. We need your patience."

"I apologize."

"Why don't you get a cup of coffee while I examine her? Be back here in, say, ten minutes, and I'll share my thoughts with you then."

Irene didn't want to leave. Anita had taken such good care of her when she had no one else. She owed Anita the same.

On the other hand, she didn't want to risk offending Dr. Young, so she made her way to the kitchen in search of a cup of whatever was passing for coffee today.

A commotion caught her attention. Staff and visitors streamed toward the front door and congregated there. Behind their hands, they whispered words Irene couldn't make out.

"Can you believe it?"

Her friend Mercedes Knapp's voice at her elbow startled Irene. "Believe what? What's going on?"

"Have you not heard? The most exciting news in camp since we arrived." She tucked a strand of dark hair behind her ear. "Those men who tried to escape and were captured about a week ago, remember them?"

"Yes, yes." If only she could forget. She wiped her damp hands on her light-brown skirt.

"Well, one of them is back. Alive."

"Alive?" She must have water in her ear.

"That is what I said. I do not know anything else, but I am going to look when they bring him in. Maybe then we will learn more." Mercedes muscled her way through the crowd. "Excuse me. Excuse me."

Irene followed in her wake. Could it be true? At least one of the men had survived? Which one?

The man approached the hospital, laid out on a stretcher borne by two orderlies. He wore no shirt and held his right hand to his sunken chest, his head turned away. His pants were caked with dirt as was every exposed area of skin. Even though she stood several feet away, she smelled a horrible odor.

She squinted as he passed by, hoping his clothes or hair would give away his identity. They didn't. She slunk behind her friend.

The men passed into the infirmary, and the crowd dispersed. Irene clutched Mercedes's arm. "Which one of them is he?"

She shrugged. "I don't know. But I will find out."

Irene tugged on her. "No. Don't. I mean, don't bother him. He's badly injured and doesn't need to be pestered by gawkers and onlookers."

Mercedes squinted her already narrow, dark eyes. "You're behaving very strangly. What are you not telling me?"

"Nothing. Nothing at all. Let's leave him in peace. By dinner word will be all over camp, and we'll know for sure then."

"If that is what you want. Paulo will be done with school, so I have to get back to the shanty. I will tell you his name if I find out." After a quick hug, Mercedes slipped away.

Anxious to get back to speak to the doctor, Irene hurried to the kitchen for her coffee substitute. The women cooking were abuzz. A thin teenage girl brought her the cup. "Did you see him?"

Irene blew away the steam. "See who?"

"The man they brought in. The one who tried to escape."

"Yes, I saw him."

The conversations around them came to a screeching halt. "What did he look like?"

"Skinny, dirty, and smelly."

"I heard they brought him from Fort Santiago."

A tremor passed through Irene. She took a sip. "But no one survives that place."

A plump, matronly woman joined them. "They don't. That's what makes this so unbelievable. They shot those other three at the beginning, but not him. Makes one wonder what he did to get himself out of such a pickle. Whichever one it is, he's plenty rich, from what I hear, so it could be that he bribed his way out."

"I suppose that's a possibility." To her, it didn't matter how he earned his release, just that he was alive. Perhaps the other one was too. "Thanks for the coffee."

As she made her way down the hall, back to Anita's bed, Irene could think of nothing but the shell of a human carried into this building. He may have survived, but at what cost—physically, emotionally, financially?

Dr. Young hung his stethoscope around his neck when she returned. He turned to face her and scrubbed his stubble-studded chin. "I'm hearing signs of pneumonia in her lungs. We don't have the means to treat her here. I'm going to recommend that she be sent to an outside hospital."

The room spun around Irene. "It's that serious?"

"It's that serious. Let me get to work on getting her a pass."

"She'll be there alone. I have to go with her."

Dr. Young sighed. "I'll see what I can do. It's difficult enough getting a pass for a spouse, much less a niece."

*Please, God, grant both of us passes.*

She needed Anita, and Anita needed her.

Rand floated on a bed of air as the orderlies carried his stretcher to the waiting ambulance. The morphine cooled his veins and gave him complete relief from his pain. What blessed relief. He wished they would give him more.

Somehow, in a few short days, Dr. Young had managed this pass to the outside hospital for him. He hadn't been able to believe it when the good doc brought him the news. The war must be going well for the Japanese. Leniency toward the internees was always a sign of Japanese victories. After Corregidor fell, their captors had eased up on them a good bit. For a while, anyway.

The closing of the doors extinguished most of the light, only a sliver eking through the gap. And Rand saw less of it than a normal person, the sight never having returned to his right eye. The driver slammed the cab door. The gears ground, and the vehicle lurched forward. Rand clutched the edges of the stretcher.

Or tried.

He caught a glimpse of his mangled fingers. Useless. Hopeless. He'd never hold a pen or a cigar or a glass of brandy in his right hand again. He'd never slip it into the soft hand of the newest debutante.

Curse that Kempeitai.

He fisted his left hand and banged it on the stretcher's metal frame.

Before they had traveled one hundred feet, the brakes squealed and they came to an abrupt halt. His litter slid.

"You have another patient for me?"

Rand didn't hear the answer to the driver's question, but a moment later, bright sunshine streamed in and another stretcher was loaded into place. The woman was thin and frail, her skin almost translucent.

"I see I have a companion on this trip."

She turned her head in the direction of his voice. "I'm Anita Markham."

"Rand Sterling."

"You sound funny."

He felt funny. "Morphine."

"Are you injured?"

"Just smashed to a pulp. Don't the bruises give it away?"

"I'm blind."

He hated himself for having to make her explain. Yet he understood her darkness. "I'm sorry." Whether for himself or for her, he couldn't tell.

"You had no way to know."

She turned away. He enjoyed the light, airy sensation that filled him. The trip may well jar his bones. He wouldn't care. But even the medication couldn't help him forget about Armando. Was he still alive? Rand had to get to him. Had to find a way.

The heavy iron gate of Santo Tomas clanged behind them.

It startled him out of his daze. "Freedom. This is what I wanted in the first place."

"Freedom, you say?" Her voice was thin and raspy, her breathing labored. "Did you try to escape?"

"You heard of my exploits?"

"My niece told me. You survived."

"I don't know how. I didn't cooperate."

"God's ways are not our ways."

That's why he was better off making his own way.

"I'm surprised the Japanese gave you a pass."

"You would think that after they tried to kill me, they wouldn't want me to heal. But they all have their price."

The ambulance hit a bump and bounced the occupants. "Jiminy Cricket, can't that driver be a little more careful?"

Mrs. Markham clung to the edge of her litter, her knuckles white. "Please watch your language. The monsoon rains make it difficult to keep the roads in good repair. I'm sure he's trying his best."

"Are you always so cheerful?"

"Are you always so grumpy?"

The ambulance careened around a corner. "Do you still think the driver is being careful?"

"He should slow down a bit. Unless you are in urgent need of care?"

"I spent five days in that hole they call Fort Santiago. If I survived that, I will survive this trip." He could survive anything.

Another sharp corner flung Rand against the side of the vehicle. Mrs. Markham began to pray. "Dear Father, please cause this driver to see the discomfort he is bringing us. May he slow down. Ease Mr. Sterling's pain. Bring us safely to our destination."

"You like to pray, don't you?" He tried his best to keep the mocking tone out of his voice.

"Wouldn't you agree that we need it?"

"What good does it do?"

The gears shifted again, and the ambulance tilted as it rounded a corner. The brakes squealed. Rand hung on to the stretcher with his left hand, hoping he wouldn't fall out. Hoping his companion would stay put.

The vehicle continued to tilt. Mrs. Markham cried out.

Next thing he knew, the ambulance was on its side. He slid and, because of his broken fingers, couldn't hold on. He fell to what was now the floor with a thump.

Mrs. Markham yelped as she crashed beside him.

Rand lay stunned on what had been the side of the ambulance. The eye-watering odor of gasoline filled the air.

# Chapter Seven

Mercedes Knapp sat in her tiny shanty kitchen. A small opening gave her a spectacular view of the back of another hut. The sounds of her son, Paulo, playing in the dirt street with the other children drifted in muffled, muted.

He didn't know, didn't understand today's significance.

She placed a candle on the small table. One year. One year since Charles had his heart attack. One year since he died at the age of forty-three. She struck a match and lit the wick.

Things like that happened to old men, not to her husband. Not to such a strong, vital man.

He left her alone with a seven-year-old son to raise. Being Filipina, she could leave Santo Tomas, but she remained with Paulo, an American citizen, a half Filipino *Mestizo*. As she had stayed with Charles. By choice.

She muddled through life. She loved her boy, worked in the censor's office, and tried her best to conserve the stores of food

Charles had stockpiled for them before . . . A physical ache tugged at her chest.

The future taunted her. Where she would live? How she would provide for her son? How she would face tomorrow alone?

"Charles, what am I to do? How am I supposed to survive?"

No answer.

The air around her remained silent save for the voices of the children, the flickering of the flame, and the song of the *kuliglig*—cicada.

A thump against her *sawali* wall broke the silence. She jumped and held her hand over her racing heart. The shanty shook, and she feared it might fall right over, like the middle pig's house in the book she read to Paulo.

Footsteps moved around the hut to the back. She stepped away from the opening, hoping whoever prowled outside wouldn't see her. Might it be a guard looking for a little fun? Or a thief coming to take what few possessions she had?

She glimpsed the back of a head with light, curly hair. A man's head. A tall man's head. Had she seen him somewhere before? Mercedes drew in a breath, letting it out little by little so he wouldn't hear her.

An unusual odor drifted in. A salty smell like that of the Philippine Sea. But you didn't expect that here. Not in the city, so far from the bay.

Men's deep voices came from the front of the hut. "Have you seen him?"

"I saw him go down this way."

"Where is he?"

Ah, the picture grew clearer. These people were looking for the man hiding behind her shanty. But why? What had he done?

She took another step backward, her knees knocking together. He might be dangerous.

"We can't let him get away with it."

Curiosity drove her to peek out of the window. Charles had scolded her often because of her insatiable need to know. The man stood against the wall, panting. He clutched his hands to his chest. The salty, fishy odor stung her eyes.

Now she remembered. He stayed down the street, alone with five children. Mark was his name. His boys played with Paulo.

"Start looking between the huts. Maybe we can flush him out."

Mercedes wiped her hands on her skirt and held her breath.

Mark swiveled his head.

Someone ran down the space between her shanty and her neighbor's.

The wanted man made a move, but his pursuer caught him and tackled him to the ground. "Hey, Luke, I got him."

More footsteps and another man arrived.

"Get that fish from him."

That explained the ocean smells emanating from him.

The three wrestled and fists flew. They shouted and cursed.

"Stop. You there, stop." A Japanese guard appeared on the scene. Mercedes backed away from the opening.

"No fighting. You stop, or I will take you all away and lock you in the prison."

She thought of those five children without a father. Of her own fatherless son. Who would help them? Who would take care of them? She had to prevent that guard from hauling them off to custody.

Without thinking, she stepped through the door and to the scene of the commotion, standing between the now-breathless men and the soldier. "Leave this man alone. All of you." She raked her gaze over the Westerners and the soldier.

The guard stared at her, his dark eyes large. He took one step forward.

"These men have families who depend on them." She crossed her arms in front of her, hoping his English was good enough for him to understand.

The soldier's mouth formed a large O.

Mercedes glanced over her shoulder at the internees behind her. "Get out of here. And stop stealing fish." She glared at Mark before returning her attention to the guard in front of her, hearing the men run away.

The soldier took another step forward. Her stomach fell. What had she done? She had a child too. Without her, Paulo had no one. *Dear God, protect me.*

"Why did you help them?"

"One man took food that did not belong to him to feed his children. His friends didn't like that." She was a bit surprised at his mastery of the English language. He had less of an accent than she did.

"They cannot make noise like that at night. And no fighting." The guard scowled, but in the depths of his eyes, she read understanding.

"They won't. I promise. You know what it is like to try to feed your family."

For a moment, his features hardened, his jaw clenched, the muscles in his face tight. Like he fought himself. Then they relaxed. "They should not dishonor their families."

"They are trying to give their children food."

Paulo picked this moment to run to her, clinging to her leg. She ran her fingers through his riot of curly, dark hair.

"That is your son?"

She nodded.

Something akin to a smile lit his face before disappearing behind the hard soldier mask. "I will not arrest them. Not this time."

"Thank you, Mr. . . ."

"Tanaka. Hiroshi Tanaka." He stuck out his right hand to shake hers. He was missing the tip of a finger.

"I will talk to them. Make sure they do not disturb the peace again."

He bowed to her before turning away.

Mercedes stood in place for a few minutes, Paulo still at her side. She bit her lip. All in all, a strange encounter. First Mark and the men, and then the soldier who had been almost friendly.

He should have taken all four of them into custody. The Japanese maintained strict control over the prisoners. But the guard didn't. In fact, he smiled when he saw Paulo. None of his other countrymen had done such a thing.

What was his story?

She heard Charles's whisper in her ear as clearly as if he stood beside her. *One of these days your curiosity will get you in trouble.*

---

Gasoline fumes choked Rand. Warmth trickled down his arm. He must have cut himself when the ambulance flipped over. Funny, but he didn't feel pain—not from his arm or hand or any other part of his body. Mrs. Markham's screams abated, but she continued to moan. With weak, trembling arms, he pushed himself up and crawled in her direction.

The floor was uneven. His left palm landed on a sharp piece of glass. He felt pressure but nothing else. At last he reached her. He sat down and squeezed her shoulder. "Are you okay?"

She drew a few ragged breaths. "I'm fine." Her cough made him believe differently. She was a very sick woman who needed help fast. How would they ever get out of here?

Within moments, voices speaking the Tagalog language—a mix of Filipino, Spanish, and English—surrounded them. He heard them tugging at the door. He patted her hand to reassure himself as much as her. "They will have us out of here soon. We can't be that far from the hospital."

There was more shouting. He understood the words, "Can't get it opened."

Jammed. The door must be jammed. The smell of petrol intensified. Any moment they might be blown from here to kingdom come.

"Dear Lord, get us out of here. Protect us and deliver us."

He tuned out Mrs. Markham's prayer. God wasn't going to reach down and pull them from the ambulance. They needed help from the men on the outside. The smell of fuel and the rubbing of metal against metal as they attempted to open the door made his heart flip. Any little spark . . .

"Why aren't they coming?" Mrs. Markham's voice sounded weak and tired. She coughed and coughed.

"We'll be out of here as soon as they get the door opened. And that will be anytime now. Hang in there."

"I'm cold." His companion moaned.

Shock, most likely, combined with her raging fever. With every last bit of strength he possessed, he moved away from her, careful of the broken glass from IV bottles littering the interior. He collapsed on the floor. If he could get to the doors, he could help push against them. He scooted forward.

The crowd shouted all around. The noise made his head pound like *dabakan*—Filipino drums. Now his hand, his arm, his body ached despite the dose of morphine. He began to shiver as well. Would they never be rescued?

Then a different banging began. Loud. Insistent. Purposeful. "Hello? How are y'all in there?" A deep, definitely American voice.

Mrs. Markham remained silent. Rand mustered his strength. "There are two of us. Please, we need help. I can push from the inside."

"Hang on. We're working to get to y'all. The door is stuck, so we might have to find another way. But y'all stay with me. We're right near the hospital, so when we get y'all out, y'all will get taken care of."

Why was this healthy-sounding American not in Santo Tomas? He couldn't be a hospital patient, could he? No, his voice was strong. Trying to think about the possibilities increased the pain behind Rand's eye.

"There's gas in here." The odor had not diminished.

No answer.

"Did you hear me?" He was so weary, speaking was an effort. If only the American could hear him. A wave of chills racked his body.

Still nothing. His heart kicked against his ribs.

A few minutes passed before the now-triumphant voice returned. "Okay. We think we have a way out. I found us a saw."

"Gas!" Rand shouted with all he had. Metal against metal would be deadly. They couldn't saw. "Stop!"

"What's wrong there?"

"Fumes. Gasoline. The vehicle is filled with them. You'll blow us up."

The saw clattered to the ground. "Back to the drawing board, then. But don't y'all fret." The man's voice became muffled, as if he'd turned his head away.

More time passed. The Tagalog chatter faded. The world grew hazy. Sleep pulled Rand down.

A banging on the side of the ambulance roused him to consciousness. He pounded on the side, now floor, of the vehicle. "Get us out of here. Get us out of here."

"We'll have y'all out in no time, mister. I think we can open the door without making sparks."

The corners of Mrs. Markham's mouth curled upward. Her cheeks burned red. A coughing fit overtook her. Rand crawled back to her and helped her sit, pounding her on her back. If only he had water for her. Heat radiated from her body.

She needed treatment. Now.

More noise from outside, scraping, clattering. The odor of gasoline hadn't receded. Couldn't they be careful?

Then light flooded the compartment. The clean scent of fresh air filled his nostrils. A man crawled toward Rand, and strong arms came around him.

"How're y'all doing there, sir?" That sweet tea-flavored drawl again.

"Take her first." He pointed to Mrs. Markham. "She's very ill."

The man with the strawberry-blond hair went to the woman's side and lifted her tiny body with ease. She coughed once more, deep, wracking, wrenching coughs. Would she ever catch her breath?

Perhaps she would die just this close to the hospital.

She turned her head in his direction as she passed. "Wait."

The man carrying her paused.

"Are you here, Mr. Sterling?"

He nodded, then remembered she couldn't see. "Yes."

"My niece. Forgive her. Promise me."

Why on earth would he need to forgive a woman he never met? But he couldn't deny Mrs. Markham her dying wish. "I promise."

"Don't forget."

# Chapter Eight

Irene paced in front of Dr. Young, her hands swinging, her *bakyas* clacking on the polished hospital floors. "I don't see why they won't issue me a pass to be with my aunt. She needs me. They've let others go to take care of sick relatives. Why not me?"

"That's where the problem comes in. You're only a niece."

Irene stopped so suddenly her momentum carried her into Dr. Young's chest. He grabbed her by the upper arms to steady her. Heat rose in her face, and she took a quick two steps backward. "Only a niece? I'm not *only* a niece. I'm the closest thing she has to a daughter."

Dr. Young held up his hands. "I understand. I've pleaded your case with the committee. Right now it's out of our control."

"So that's it? She's to be left there, helpless, afraid, with no one to look after her?"

"The staff at Hospicio de Santiago in Makati is excellent. She should have no reason to be afraid because there are plenty of people there to take care of her. In no time she'll be stronger and will be able to return. You can be with her for her convalescence here."

Irene balled her fists. The answer didn't suit her. "Who makes up these rules?"

"The release committee decides which cases to bring before the Japanese officials. It's not an easy process. Be thankful we were able to get your aunt out."

Irene rubbed her forehead. "I know. I am. But don't you see? I want to be with her. In the opposite situation, she wouldn't leave me alone."

Dr. Young patted her shoulder. "Trust me, I do understand. These are trying times. Nothing is easy. Nothing is the way it should be."

"No need to tell me that." The hospital pass slipped through her fingers, her heart sinking with it. "I'll have to wait here until she's well enough to return."

He nodded. "I'll keep working on that pass. And if there is any change in her condition, I'll let you know as soon as I have word."

As it appeared that would be the only consolation she would get today, she turned away and headed down the hall. Her chest burned, though. Only wild animals should be caged like this. What harm was it to the Japanese if she left the campus? She was no spy.

Well, perhaps in a way she was. She looked at her watch with its small, square face and black-braided cotton band and gasped when she read the time. Eleven o'clock. She needed to hurry to the censor's office. By the time she got there, she would be late.

After a couple of dry days, the seasonal rains had started again. She sloshed through yet more mud puddles as she crossed the yard. Her bare legs were stained with dirt, and she'd have to wash her dress the first chance she got.

She slid into the swiveling chair at her metal desk at five minutes past the hour. Around her, women at similar desks clacked away at their typewriters. Mercedes tore her attention from her work and gave Irene a smile, which she returned.

Already a stack of notes had piled up, awaiting her attention. She sifted through them, none very interesting. They sent words of love from Filipino spouses on the outside. A few times she had to black out complaints about Japanese treatment of the island natives. There were business updates from outside partners. With great reluctance, she marked out reports of declining sales and Japanese restrictions. She made note of those, to pass on the word of the true state of affairs to the owners of those businesses.

The letters from children to their fathers brought a bit of sunshine into her dismal day. The childish scribble, the poor spelling, the darling little pictures.

She imagined the day she opened Byaya Children's Center, the yard filled with little ones playing, shouting, singing. She could see their happy faces, joyful to have a place to call home.

"Good morning. Or should I say afternoon?"

Irene looked up to see Mercedes standing beside her. "I've been trying to get a pass to go with Anita to the hospital."

Mercedes shook her head, her short, dark curls springing with the motion. "No luck?"

Irene scrunched her mouth. "No. I don't have a chance because I'm only a niece. Imagine that, only a niece."

"The committee studies the facts. They don't understand the relationship you two have."

"Don't they have hearts?"

"Is it not most important that Anita got out to get the help she needs? And Mr. Sterling?"

Mercedes had this way of zeroing in on the heart of the matter.

No beating around the bush. It's one of the things Irene loved about her. "You're right, as usual. At least Anita has a chance of recovery there. Here . . ." She refused to think of the possibility. "Mr. Sterling?" The rich one. The handsome one.

"Yes, the man who tried to escape and who survived Fort Santiago. He went in the ambulance with Anita. I told you I would find out."

"You're incorrigible, Mercedes."

"Maybe so. Wait, though. I have to tell you about the most unusual encounter I had the other day."

Some of Mercedes's curiosity must be rubbing off on Irene. "What?"

"I don't know how to even say it." Mercedes pulled a chair beside Irene and sat. "My neighbor stole a fish, and a Japanese guard came to break up the fight that ensued. He intrigues me."

"The neighbor?"

"No, the soldier."

"Don't think about it. You'll only find trouble."

"You sound like Charles."

"He was a wise man. I miss those days when Anita and I would come visit you in Manila. You both were great supporters of our mission."

Mercedes swallowed hard, then brightened. "You know, at first the soldier was so hard, but then he saw Paulo and he softened. Like a heart of flesh beat inside of him. He even told me his name."

Irene leaned forward and whispered, "You would do best to forget the incident. And the soldier. He is the enemy, locking us in here and not giving us enough to eat. Keep that in mind."

"And we are his enemy. I'm not a monster. I don't believe he is either."

"It's a dangerous game. Think of Paulo."

"I do. I will. It's always about him." Mercedes rose and returned to her desk. "Thanks for listening."

*Lord, keep her from getting involved in a situation she'll regret.*

Irene returned her attention to her work, picking up one of the last notes she had to sift through today. It was addressed to Mr. Rand Sterling. Her hands shook, and the dampness from her fingers marked the page.

She unfolded the note. Small, round letters covered a single line. Her brain interpreted the words her eyes scanned. Unlike the first cryptic note, this one left little to the imagination.

*You got lucky. Next time Fort Santiago will look like a picnic.*

She squinted at the print, trying to recall if the handwriting was the same as the one in the first letter. Unfortunately, so many notes came through this office every day she no longer remembered.

Had Mr. Sterling been betrayed?

She swiveled in her chair. The office was almost empty, many of those who worked here having left to get lunch. Only buxom Roxanne remained, her head bent over her typewriter, the keys clacking and the bell ringing. She didn't look up even to slide over the carriage.

Irene wiped her hands on her dark-blue cotton dress. Her fingers trembled and blood whooshed in her ears as she picked up the note.

The office door opened. A Japanese guard clad in olive drab, feet shod in shiny black boots, strode in. Irene held her breath, along with the note in her hand. The soldier moved to the chief censor's desk and began sorting through papers, his back turned to her. Closing her mind to all of the torment that would be unleashed on her if anyone discovered what she was doing, she slid the message into her pocket. It felt like it burned her thigh.

He turned around just as she removed her hand from her pocket. "Good afternoon." He exited the room. Irene let out her breath and took in another deep one.

She swallowed hard, straightened her papers on her desk, stood, and walked out of the room as if she didn't have a care in the world. She even waved to Roxanne on her way out.

Although she wanted nothing more than to race across the university grounds to the relative security of her little nipa hut, she steadied herself and strolled along. She stopped and used a few precious pesos to purchase a mango and a roll of toilet paper, much like she would do on any given day. She had to lock her knees while she stood there. She had to remind herself every now and again to breathe before she fainted.

She smiled at the boys playing baseball in the school yard and at a toddler jumping in a puddle, his mother a step too far behind him. Irene's laughter at his antics sounded forced, even to her own ears.

She turned down Shantytown's main street, then down a few other roads until she came to the little hut where she and Anita spent their free time during the day. The primitive dwelling bore signs of neglect. Weeds grew up between her flowers, and a mouse had chewed a hole through one of the *sawali* mats that made up the walls. She would need to get that replaced.

She climbed the two steps into the relative darkness of the shelter. A few moments passed before her eyes grew accustomed to the dim interior. She hadn't been here since Anita took sick. Without her aunt's laughter and her stories, the place was hollow and empty. Irene's throat burned. How was Anita doing? Was she improving? Or . . .

She must banish that thought. Her mother and father had both left her. Just up and walked out on her. She took a deep breath and steadied herself. Anita was all she had left. She couldn't leave too.

Irene moved to the small sink and counter at the far end of the single room to check on their meager food supplies. The rice sack was full of grain and a few bugs and weevils too. Some internees had decorated their shanties with a few luxuries—rugs, clocks, small tables from home. Irene and Anita had been in Manila for the Christmas holiday, spending time with Mercedes and Charles, when the Americans gave up the city and the Japanese entered, rounding up all Westerners. They had no access to their few belongings, no one on the outside to help them. The Knapps had little enough themselves.

Their hut boasted a scarred, wobbly table that Mercedes had given them, a bed made of lashed-together bamboo poles that provided a place to lay during siesta time, and an old wooden rocking chair from Mercedes's mother, with a bright rag rug–style cushion on the seat.

Irene lowered herself to the chair, running her hands over the well-worn armrests. The woman had rocked thirteen babies to sleep here.

But rest was the furthest thing from Irene's mind. She sat for a while, hoping the note would vanish, that her discovery was nothing more than a bad dream. She picked up her pace, the chair rocking to and fro at a rate that wouldn't lull any child to slumber. Then she stood so suddenly that the chair continued to move without her.

She peered out the uncovered window meant to keep men and women from using the privacy of the hut to be intimate with each other. In the heat of the day, the area remained quiet. Most had fled inside for their usual siesta.

She returned to the chair, picking at the blue fabric-covered buttons on the bodice of her dress. She tugged at the end of the matching belt. Taking a deep breath, she reached into her pocket. Her fingertips brushed the edge of the page. She withdrew it, shaking so much that the paper fluttered to the floor.

Outside she heard footsteps and the sounds of Japanese voices. The guards often conducted random searches at random times, hoping to discover couples together or uncover a hidden radio.

She stared at the paper on the floor. If they found that she had taken it from the censor's office and intended on delivering it, she would learn firsthand what Fort Santiago was like.

The voices grew louder. She bent down. Their tone was insistent, demanding, stopping in front of her shanty. Her fingers closed around the note. As they flung open the door, she stuffed the letter into her brassiere.

# Chapter Nine

Rand struggled to open his eyes. He pried them to slits. The sights weren't familiar. He lay in a bed, a real iron bed with a mattress and clean sheets. The pale-blue paint on the footboard was peeling, but it was a bed, though a far sight from Dewey Boulevard. Beside him was a small table with a pitcher of water on it and a glass. He tried to roll over to reach it, but even the smallest movement brought excruciating pain.

Where was he?

He forced himself to remember. He recalled the sensation of falling. Screams. The odor of gasoline.

In the midst of it, he heard a soft voice, calm and peaceful, praying. In the recesses of his mind he heard another voice, deeper, masculine, speaking words so similar.

For some reason, he longed to hear those words again.

A quiet whisper of shoes came down the hallway, and Rand turned his head. A Filipina nun, dressed in a white habit, her eyes and skin dark, stopped in the doorway and smiled. "Good morning, Mr. Sterling."

"Where am I?"

She entered the room, almost floating as she moved. "You're at Hospicio de Santiago. I'm Sister Francis."

He remembered. The ambulance driver took the turn too sharply.

She poured him a glass of water and held it to his lips for him to sip. It was cool and soothed his parched throat.

"What about Mrs. Markham? How is she?" It was she who prayed.

"Holding her own. It's a small miracle neither of you was seriously injured." Sister Francis put a thermometer under his tongue, wound a blood pressure cuff around his arm, and pumped it up. Satisfied with both readings, she felt his pulse and recorded the information in his chart.

"Will I live, Sister Francis, or is my demise imminent?"

She tapped her long finger on the chart, her lips hinting of a smile. "You can't flirt with me, Mr. Sterling. I'm a nun. And I suppose anyone who survives Fort Santiago can survive just about anything. The doctor will be in to see you shortly." With that, she floated out of the room.

He sank back in his pillows and sighed. In an attempt to cheer himself, he tried to remember all of the glittering parties he had attended. The women in their sequined gowns, feathers in their hair, gloves up to their elbows.

Voices came from the hall, soft female words with a French accent, laced with urgency. "*Socho* Endo, you must stay in bed. Wandering the halls is no good for you."

A reply came in Japanese.

"Tell *Socho* Endo that the jungle fever means he must stay still in bed."

Another voice in Japanese. More words Rand couldn't understand.

"Thank you. Remind him that he is not to get up at all. Help me get him back to his room."

And the door next to Rand's clicked shut.

A Japanese guard convalesced in the room next to his? Fire burned in Rand's chest. With his good hand, he gripped the edge of the blanket with all of his might.

It would take everything he had not to sneak into the man's room at night and suffocate him.

∽

Irene bowed to the two Japanese soldiers—something Anita would disapprove of—then came to attention, rooted to the ground in the middle of her shanty. She stood taller than either of those who conducted the search. They slit open the rice sack, the precious grain spilling on the floor. They overturned the table and ripped open the mattress. They tore the picture of her and Anita from its frame on the little shelf and smashed the glass. Her heart smashed along with it.

She had no idea what they were looking for, and she didn't dare ask them. Was this a random search, or had they come for something specific? Why had they picked her? The paper stuffed down her dress crinkled with every breath she took.

They yelled at her, but she didn't understand them. She remained silent, her hands clasped in front of her to prevent them from shaking. With a last grunt, they spun on their heels and marched out the door.

Five or more minutes must have passed before Irene was able to relax and take a deep breath. If they had come for something, they left without it, hopefully satisfied that she was innocent of whatever had caused them to force their way in.

She dropped to her knees and began to salvage whatever rice she could. It wasn't an easy task. With sweaty fingers, she sewed the rip the best she could, then returned every grain of rice she could pick from the ground. It might be a bit dirty, but it was food.

Was this what life had come to? Scraping rice off the ground so she didn't go hungry? Shaking in fear while men with machine guns searched her house? Protecting a man she didn't even know?

She waited another full hour until she brought herself to withdraw the crumpled letter and sit on the chair with it.

*You got lucky. Next time Fort Santiago will look like a picnic.*

There was no doubt about this note. No cryptic message or hidden meaning. Someone had it out for Rand.

And this time she wouldn't hesitate. She had delayed too long already. She must get the information to Mr. Sterling. But he was at the hospital, out of her reach.

Unless she got a pass.

She once again slid the letter into her dress. No use taking a chance that it would fall out of her pocket. She even wondered if she should commit it to memory and burn it so there would be no chance of being found with it.

But Mr. Sterling might need to see the handwriting, see if he recognized it so he could determine who was working against him. No, she had to keep it and deliver it to him personally.

And he needed to read it as soon as possible. With her mind made up, she raced out of the hut and back in the direction of the hospital. She flew up the steps and down the hallway until she reached Dr. Young's office.

Of course, he wasn't there.

One of the nurses followed her. "May I help you, ma'am?"

"I'm looking for Dr. Young. Is he here?"

She shook her head. "I'm sorry. He's gone for the rest of the day. Dr. Hadley is filling in for him. Do you need something?"

"Nothing Dr. Hadley can help me with."

"You're Irene, aren't you?"

"Yes, I am." With her chestnut hair gathered into a knot at the base of her neck, this nurse looked familiar to Irene. She couldn't remember her name, though.

"If you need Dr. Young before tomorrow, his hut is in Glamourville. It's the one beside the big palm tree. You can't miss it."

"Thank you. Thank you so much." Speaking to him at his shanty might prove to be better. She would be able to talk freely with him about the situation and why she so desperately needed that pass.

She dashed through the door and down the steps, almost knocking over a vendor with a cage of chickens on the back of his bicycle. She sidestepped a mother with a baby in a carriage and an old man hobbling along on his cane.

She had to force herself not to run the entire way and draw attention to herself. Running wouldn't get her out of here any sooner. The process to get a pass may take days or even longer. She didn't expect quick action.

Irene did know the shanty the nurse had described, remembering it from her search of Glamourville for Mr. Sterling. The huts here were larger and better built than her own was to withstand the monsoon rains. People of means lived in this place, people who had the money to hire a crew to build the best shelter possible. Like Mr. Sterling. Nothing like her poor hut with holes in the mats.

A large palm tree shaded this part of the town, and birds of paradise bloomed in the yard. She stood in front of the home, her heart pounding, and only in part from the exercise. She licked her lips and climbed the three steps to the front door.

Her father always said, "No time like the present." He had other opportunities in mind, activities he should never have been involved in, but she'd never get that pass standing on the step. She knocked three times on the bamboo poles that made up the door.

"Come on in," the doctor's cheery voice called from the back. Didn't he even want to know who it was?

Still, she did as he requested and entered the hut, bamboo floors covered with a rug, a mahogany table in the center of it all. He wasn't in here. She passed through the shanty before finding him lounging in a rattan chair on the screened-in porch.

The living was definitely much better here than in her part of "town."

He rose when she entered. "Ah, Miss Reynolds. What brings you by? Not bad news about Mrs. Markham, I hope."

"No, nothing like that." She put her hand to her chest, the paper sticking to her damp skin. "Well, maybe a little."

"Would you like a bit of scotch?"

"What? Oh no. I don't drink." Anita had pounded into her head the dangers of the stuff.

"What can I help you with?"

"I need a pass to go to the hospital."

"I'm doing all I can, Miss Reynolds, just like I said. It will take some time, supposing you get a pass at all."

"Circumstances have changed. It's very important that I get to that hospital as soon as I can."

"How so?"

She knew he'd ask her that question, but she wasn't sure how to answer. How much should she reveal? His young face appeared trustworthy enough, but you never knew what lurked behind baby-blue eyes. "I have an urgent message I must deliver to Mr. Sterling."

"What kind of message?"

"I'd rather not say. It's, well, private and sensitive. But of topmost priority."

"Not a little love note?"

Heat rose in her face at the hint of teasing in his voice. "No, not at all. It's a matter of life and death."

Dr. Young clasped his hands behind his neck and leaned back, staring at the thatched roof. "This grows more serious each minute."

"Please, Doctor, I'm not exaggerating this situation in order to get out. I work at the censor's office. When Mr. Sterling attempted to escape, I'm the one who arrived too late with the note telling him to abort the mission. This time I don't want to fail to get word to him."

"Is he planning another escape?"

She sucked in her breath.

The doctor waved his hand. "Never mind. I'm sorry. I was having a little bit of fun with you. I can see from your eyes that it is indeed a serious matter. Again, I can't promise results, but I will do what I can. I'll press the matter a bit with the board."

She released her breath. "That's all I ask. Thank you." She sighed and left the doctor's hut. What was she going to do? How could she get a pass? Fake an illness?

She dragged her feet through the mud as she made her way back to her own hut, not caring how her *bakyas* gathered dirt. A couple of nine- or ten-year-old boys ran past her, shouting as they played cowboys and Indians.

She used to love playing that game with the other children at the mission compound. She always volunteered to be the mother back at camp, cooking over the fire and tending to the babies.

When she got older, she continued to work with the babies and the little children who lived near their mission. They loved her and needed her. And she needed them.

As she approached Shantytown, she watched a little girl run to meet a man Irene presumed to be her father. The man picked up the child and swung her around before planting a kiss on her cheek. Hand in hand, they entered a nearby hut.

Irene's stomach hurt, and she hugged herself. Oh, to have known a father's love in that way. To have had a father who cared that much for her.

She kept her gaze averted as she walked, knowing the way through the university grounds well enough she didn't even have to look where she was going. Being here for almost two years did that for you.

And then a pair of black mud-spattered boots appeared in front of her eyes. Before she could stop herself, she ran smack into a Japanese soldier.

# Chapter Ten

The crickets' night song blended with the humming in Irene's head when she whacked into the Japanese guard. She lost her balance. His two muscular arms came around her and steadied her. "You must be more careful."

Her heart raced twenty miles a minute. Her mouth went dry. Would he be angry with her? Though Anita wouldn't like it, she gave a slight bow. "My apologies. I am very sorry. I will be more careful."

"I am afraid you are injured."

"No, I am fine. Thank you." This was the first soldier who ever expressed any concern over her well-being. She thought of Mercedes and her experience. Could this be the same guard?

"Let me walk you to your destination."

The paper stuffed in her undergarments scratched her skin. Even if he was the one who had been kind to Mercedes, she didn't want him around. "No, no, really, that's not necessary. I will be more careful in the future." She bowed again. *Lord, please make him go away. Let him leave me alone.*

"I will come with you."

Any more protesting and he might grow suspicious. "Thank you. My hut is down the street a little way."

Much to her surprise, he strolled beside her. Not in front of her to lead her to wherever he wanted to take her. Not behind her to prod her along with his gun.

"You are surprised by my English."

"Yes, come to think of it, I am." She'd been so startled before, she hadn't realized he'd been conversing with her in perfect English.

"University of Washington." He tipped his cap, and she noticed he was missing a fingertip on his right hand.

She nodded, not quite sure what to say. The Lord wasn't heeding her request to snatch him up in a puff of smoke.

"You were thinking very hard."

"Yes, I was. Again, I apologize."

"No need. What was on your mind?"

She couldn't tell him. He may speak the language very well, but he remained the enemy. She had reminded Mercedes of that fact. What could she tell him? "I was thinking about my aunt."

"Is she in the United States?"

As her mind formulated her response, she realized she might be able to use this encounter to her advantage. Perhaps like Mercedes. "No, at Hospicio de Santiago. She is very ill with typhoid and pneumonia. I've asked for a pass to take care of her, but so far, because she is only my aunt and not a close relative, I haven't had any success. But she has been like a mother to me. She is all I have, and I am all she has."

The soldier nodded. "Do you not believe she is getting adequate care?"

"No, that's not it. She is lonely without me, and she'll have a better chance at recovery if someone is with her, someone she knows and loves. I can encourage her to get well."

"I see. If it is a pass you want, it is a pass you shall have."

She stopped for a moment to process what he said. "You'll give me one?"

"Yes. Be ready to leave in the morning. I shall have it delivered to your room later tonight."

"Thank you." She gave him her information, and he left to take care of the matter.

She stood for a while in the middle of the street. Had he really consented to give her a pass? He must be playing a trick on her. A cruel joke. Getting her hopes up only to dash them to bits like a piece of clay pottery.

He would make sure she never got that pass.

Anita would die alone.

Rand sat in the bed, feather pillows stacked behind him, a bowl of warm chicken broth in a china bowl on a tray in front of him. He spooned the soup to his mouth with his left hand, spilling much of it along the way.

He would never get used to being left-handed. The doctor had performed surgery on his fingers, but they would never work properly again. He should have just amputated them.

Rand wiped his chin and blankets with a napkin and pushed away the rest of his meal. The sisters did a fine job with the food, but he had no appetite.

Sister Francis entered a few minutes later. "Don't you like our lunch, Mr. Sterling?"

"Don't give me your soup, but a chicken from the coop, with potatoes and gravy, and I don't mean maybe."

"And I say no, and I don't mean maybe. Once you begin eating what we put in front of you, perhaps then we can begin to take orders. Is that a fair deal?"

"My *amah* wasn't as strict with me as you are."

"It is likely your nanny was dazzled by your charm. I am not." She cleared away the dishes and left the room, then returned a few minutes later with a wheelchair.

"What on earth is that for? Am I being released already?" For what it was worth, this hospital was a palace compared to Santo Tomas. He had no desire to leave.

"Don't think I haven't given thought to turning you out myself. No, actually, the doctor feels it is time you got out of this bed and moved around a bit."

What if he didn't cooperate? Would he be allowed to stay here longer? "I'm not sure I'm ready. It still hurts to move even the least little bit."

"I'll help you into the chair. Fresh air will build your appetite, if nothing else. You will never grow strong if you don't eat." Sister Francis threw back the cotton sheet covering the lower part of his body. "Let's get you sitting."

The pain wasn't as bad as it had been in the beginning, and he managed to get his legs over the side of the bed. A tall, lean man entered the room.

"Ah, Wilson, just in time. I'll need help getting Mr. Sterling into the chair."

"Glad to oblige, ma'am."

A Dixie drawl if he'd ever heard one. The voice Rand remembered from the ambulance. Wilson grabbed Rand by the armpits and plunked him in the chair none too gently.

"Hey, watch out. I have multiple broken bones."

The Southerner dared to grin like a cattle herder who had swallowed a cow. "Then I reckon you won't mind another one or two." He grabbed the handles of the wheelchair and, with Rand curling his toes over the edge of the footrest, took off around the corner and down the hall like he was racing cars at a dirt track. Rand managed to get a peek into Mrs. Markham's room as he whizzed by. She was asleep.

They broke into the bright sunlight. Rand's eyes watered. He lowered his head.

"Now ain't that better? Just look at what a fine day it is."

Rand studied the man. He appeared healthy enough—thin, to be sure, but the right amount of color in his cheeks. No apparent illness, no apparent injuries. "How did you happen to end up here? Why aren't you at the camp like the rest of us?"

The man's Texas-size smile faded, and he took a step back. "It's a long story, and I have to help the sister with another patient. I'll be back for you in a while."

Very strange. Rand had heard of men escaping the city and hiding in the jungle. Was that where he'd come from? But why was he here? None of it made sense.

As his eyes grew used to the brightness, Rand surveyed his surroundings. He sat on a stone patio in the midst of a lush garden. Mango trees and palms gave shade while a riot of orchids, hanging lobster claw, orange peacock flowers, and scarlet bougainvillea colored the scene. A brilliant mangrove blue flycatcher sang in the trees, and a gecko played in the garden.

Japanese planes zoomed overhead, taking off from and landing at Nielson Airport, breaking the idyllic peace and quiet.

The November sun warmed him and made him drowsy. His eyelids drooped, and he imagined himself lounging beside his family's swimming pool, a pretty girl on either side of him. Any moment Armando would appear with a tray of cakes and glasses of iced tea.

"Mr. Sterling, I'm happy to have run into you."

The lilting, feminine voice snapped him back to the present day, though the woman before him was beautiful enough to have appeared in his fantasy. Her eyes were the color of the water in his dream, her nose pert and upturned, her mouth small and round. "Have I died and gone to heaven?"

"Pardon me?"

His vision cleared and he recognized her. "You're the woman who brought me the message. What are you doing here?"

"I managed to wrangle a pass to visit my aunt. In fact, I've just arrived"—she lifted a small blue suitcase—"and haven't even seen her yet."

"Your aunt?"

"Anita Markham."

"The woman from the ambulance?" The woman who made him promise to forgive her niece. It was beginning to make sense. Did she think he blamed her for not bringing the message in time? Did he blame her?

"Yes, I heard you came with her."

"And you are?"

"Irene Reynolds. I know you're Rand Sterling."

"My reputation precedes me, I see. Yes, I did share an ambulance with your aunt. I passed her room just a few minutes ago, and she was sleeping. Have a seat, and I'll try to keep you entertained until she finishes her nap. I've been told I'm good at that." He tipped his head in the direction of the wicker chair to his right. "Please forgive me for not standing."

She flicked her wrist. "I've spent a good deal of my life in the jungle. There's no need for such formality around me." She plopped in the chair and set her bag on the ground. "You have more color and aren't grimacing as much as when I saw you at the camp hospital."

He held up his heavily bandaged right hand. "Is that a compliment?"

She didn't even flush. He must be losing his touch.

"Take it any way you like. What did the doctor have to say?"

"No tickling the ivories for a while. Carnegie Hall will miss me." He tamped down the steam that rose in his chest. He might be able to forgive this gorgeous creature in time. He would never forgive the soldier who left him disabled.

"Carnegie Hall? Are you that good?" She grimaced. "Were you that good?"

"I was teasing, Miss Reynolds. I can't play a note. Enough about me. Now you've intrigued me, saying you spent most of your life in the jungle. Like Tarzan and Jane?"

She shuffled her *bakya*-clad feet back and forth and bit her lip, as red as the bougainvillea.

What had he done?

Tears shimmered in the corners of her soft blue eyes. "My parents both left when I was young, so my aunt graciously took me in." Her cheeks pinked. "I had nowhere else to go, being only thirteen years old. She just happened to be a missionary in the Philippine jungle. She taught the women about child care and nutrition and the Lord. I went with her and spent my time with the children. It was like having little brothers and sisters."

Her story was so different from his. Abandoned by her parents. Then again, his own parents had left him to the care of his *amah* and Armando. "Imagine a creature as beautiful as you emerging from the wilds."

"I did hear of you before our internment."

He raised his eyebrows. "Is that so?"

"Yes. The son of a mining executive and a longtime Manila resident. You have quite the reputation. Anita and I were visiting friends of ours in Manila, and she pointed out your little red convertible as it sped past. And then the day the war started, you attempted to run over me with the very same car." She uncrossed and crossed her ankles.

He did remember. How could he forget the curve of her long neck, her ivory skin, the legs that went on forever. "After the war, I'll take you for a ride in that car. I like having pretty women in the passenger seat."

"Mercedes was right when she talked about you."

"She only had good things to say, of course."

"Just that you were quite the rogue and I would do well to stay far away from you."

A bubble of laughter built in his chest and a chuckle escaped. "Ah, good advice, but not good for my clubs."

She leaned back and stared at the blue sky. "You fancy yourself a ladies' man. Do you like that moniker?"

"I opened two very successful nightclubs and have plans for a string of establishments all over the city and throughout the country. Maybe even into Thailand and Hong Kong and the rest of the Far East. As part of my job, I have to make my clients welcome. Make them feel special, like they are the most important women in the world."

"So flirting is work for you?"

He rubbed his left hand over the wheelchair armrest. "It depends on how you mean that. And what would be wrong with it?"

She came to her feet and grabbed the suitcase handle. "You have a suave and debonair exterior, Mr. Sterling. Dashing. Daring. That's who you want the world to see. But who are you, really?"

She spun around, her red-and-white print skirt swishing around her legs.

"Not swayed by my good looks or obvious charm?"

She pivoted to face him once more, then drew a crumpled piece of paper out of her pocket. "This came for you the other day."

She handed it to him and disappeared into the building.

He unfolded the paper, the ink smeared as if it had gotten wet.

Even so, he was able to make out the words.

The paper fluttered to the ground.

# Chapter Eleven

Rand picked up the paper from the patio before the breeze could blow it away and stared at it in his hand with his one good eye.

*You got lucky. Next time Fort Santiago will look like a picnic.*

His heart froze, and he shivered despite the tropical heat. Who was threatening him?

He concentrated on the paper until the words blurred. Then he set it on his lap, his bandaged hand covering it. The world narrowed, and all he saw was the trunk of the palm tree in front of him.

Was it even a threat? Could someone be playing a joke on him?

He discarded that ridiculous idea as soon as it came to mind. The tone was not teasing.

How in the world could he have enemies when he was locked in an internment camp? And here he sat at this hospital, unable to move much. He was no threat to anyone.

He scratched his head and then rubbed his eyes. The heat must be getting to him.

When he glanced at the note again, his heart rate accelerated.

Someone was after him. Wanted him back at the fort. Back to the unbearable torture. This time they would string him up by his thumbs, his shoulders popping out of their sockets, until he died of thirst.

And this time he feared not being able to withstand the pressure. He would give up Henry and Ramon for sure.

A shadow fell across his lap as Irene came to stand behind him. "Have you made sense of it?"

He shook his head, careful not to jar too much and get a headache started. "Who would threaten me this way? I have no enemies other than the Japanese."

"Perhaps that is who sent the note."

He leaned forward in his wheelchair. "That could be. My inquisitor spoke perfect English. The louse was educated at Harvard."

"What could he do to you here?"

"He could take me to Fort Santiago whenever the whim struck him." A cold vise tightened around Rand's stomach.

"Or perhaps a member of your household sent it?"

A pain began behind his eye and escalated until he thought it would pop from its socket. He clenched his teeth. "No one from my household would do this to me. No one. Armando, our houseboy, has been with my family since I was a baby. He protected me. Was more a father to me than my own. He is the reason I tried to escape. I was going to see him because he's very ill. His son was helping me. Never again suggest a member of my household. Never."

She took a step back, holding her hands in front of her. "I didn't mean to upset you. I was just throwing out an idea. If you are so convinced of your servants' loyalty, then discard that thought. Maybe I should have said a business partner instead."

"My father is my business partner. He financed me and has let me run my business the way I see fit. There is a former employee who hates me. Who promised to ruin me after I discovered his embezzling ways. I'll never forgive what he did, but I haven't seen him in years."

"You're sure he doesn't have someone feeding him information? Or he could be in camp with us."

"I would have bumped into him after two years."

"True enough. Do you recognize the handwriting?"

Rand studied the paper, squinting. The scrolled letters triggered no spark of familiarity. "No."

She plunked into the chair beside him. "I'm sorry. I hoped you would know who sent you this."

Rand crumpled it. "At some point, whoever sent this will have to play their hand. Give away who they are and what they want."

Wilson Jennings, the Southerner who rescued Rand and Anita from the ambulance, strolled across the grounds, his hand in his pockets as he whistled "Dixie."

Despite the seriousness of the news Miss Reynolds brought, Rand couldn't help but laugh.

The woman beside him held her sides and giggled. "He's whistling 'Dixie.'" Tears streamed down her fair face.

"Oh, don't. Laughing makes my ribs hurt." But try as he might, he couldn't stop. It was the best and longest laugh he'd had since the occupation.

A door slammed shut behind them, and he turned to find Sister Francis flying in their direction. He doubted her feet touched the ground. Red suffused her face. "Come quickly, everyone. Mother Superior is in her office with three Japanese soldiers, holding them off for as long as possible. We can't let them find you, Mr. Jennings."

The tall, thin man turned a shade of white Rand hadn't seen since the ski slopes.

Rand shot Sister Francis a questioning look.

She glanced around and leaned in. "Mr. Jennings is an American soldier."

Rand lay as still as he could in his bed, his sheet pulled to his chin. Despite the tropical heat and humidity, he shivered.

Mr. Jennings was an American soldier who had eluded the Japanese troops on the Bataan Peninsula, who worked with the guerrillas until a sore on his leg wouldn't heal, causing a high fever. This was Sister Francis's hasty explanation.

Rand struggled to breathe. If the Japanese discovered Mr. Jennings, Rand's experiences at Fort Santiago would pale in comparison to what the poor Southerner would face. His captors would show him no mercy.

And a Japanese officer lay in the room next to Rand's.

The sister told them that from time to time Japanese release officers came for an inspection, making sure that all who were here were truly ill enough to warrant their passes.

Rand could have opened five clubs in the time it took for Mother Superior and the soldiers to make it to the hall where Rand and Mr. Jennings had their rooms.

"Who is this? Why is he here? We have no record of him." The soldier's choppy English sent a shiver down Rand's spine. They stood in front of Mr. Jennings's room from the sound of it.

"Look at him, sir." This was Mother Superior's calm, unhurried voice. "He is German. That is why you have no record of him.

He is an attaché here and caught jungle fever. It is very contagious for those who are not used to the tropical conditions. If he is to recover, he must not be disturbed."

"German?"

"To the core. If you would follow me, please, it is imperative that we let him rest. You would not want to have to explain to the Germans why one of their most trusted men died in this hospital."

"I will see him for myself." Rand heard the door click open.

"I must insist that he be left in peace. Any disturbance could be fatal."

"Then what is this woman doing in here?"

Rand assumed he meant Sister Francis. Mother Superior remained unflappable. "She is tending to his physical and spiritual needs in the quietest of manners."

A moment of silence. Then, "This man is no German."

Rand heard a sharp intake of breath. "Are you accusing me of lying, sir?"

"I have little use for you or your God or your morality. Yes, you are lying." A pause. "This book is in English." A thump as the book hit the wall.

"You cannot take him." Rand imagined Mother Superior throwing herself between the soldier and Mr. Jennings. His shivers increased.

Sounds of a struggle came from next door—shuffling of feet, breaking of glass, thudding of fist meeting stomach.

Mr. Jennings cried out. Rand heard the guard drag him from the room and down the hallway. Heat spread throughout Rand's midsection, and he clenched his jaw and one good fist. From the deep recesses of his mind, he heard the voices of his Japanese captors, shivered with the intense hot and cold and dampness, felt the crack of the hammer on his fingers. Rand stuffed his fist into his mouth to keep from screaming.

Mr. Jennings was a good man. He didn't deserve this treatment.

The fire in Rand's stomach grew hotter.

---

Irene pushed back a stray strand of hair and leaned over Anita, patting her hand. Anita slept, not even stirring when Irene straightened the pillows behind her. "When is all of this madness going to end?"

She sat on high-back chair, the sun slanting through the windows, and sighed. Too many questions didn't have answers. "Rand is being threatened now. What more is going to happen?"

Unable to sit still, she rose and paced the room, peering out the window overlooking the garden. What a beautiful, restful place. A wonderful spot for meditation and prayer. The sisters must have planted it for that very reason.

But today her spirit was restless. Even the view didn't calm her soul. *Lord, be with Mr. Jennings. Protect him. Watch over him.* She turned away and adjusted the already-smooth blanket over Anita's feet.

Voices rose in the hallway, then faded, then rose again. The Japanese inspectors neared.

She dipped the washcloth in the basin of water on the table beside Anita's bed, wrung it out, and placed it on her warm forehead. After several more minutes the footsteps and voices paused outside of Anita's room, and Irene turned to find Mother Superior and the three Japanese inspectors entering. She stayed put, hoping she wouldn't be required to bow.

The shortest and stockiest of the men spoke. "Why are you here if this woman is nothing but your aunt?"

"She is the mother I never had. She raised me when my parents couldn't." Or wouldn't.

Mother Superior nodded her white veil-clad head.

"Who gave you this pass?"

"A Japanese soldier. I don't know his name. He helped me apply for it, that's all."

"She is to return to camp a week from today to reapply for the pass." He made a note in the booklet he carried.

Heat rose in her chest. He couldn't do that. Her pass was for a month. "But, sir—"

Mother Superior cut her off with a wave of her hand. "I hope that Mrs. Markham will be well enough by that time not to be in need of such intensive care. But her condition is grave."

The soldier scribbled more notes, and Irene prayed they weren't black marks against her for her outburst. She couldn't let her behavior affect her aunt. She bowed her head. "I apologize, sir."

"We will see you at Santo Tomas one week from today. At that time we will reevaluate your need here."

When they walked out, Irene slumped in her seat. She removed the cloth from Anita's head and cooled it in the basin before reapplying it.

Reapplying. Just like she would have to do with the pass. And without the favor of the guard, she doubted it would be granted. She would be forced to leave Anita alone.

Her aunt had never deserted her. How could she do it to her?

Trying to look for the blessing in all of this—something Anita had taught her from the first day she'd come to live with her—Irene supposed it was a good thing they said nothing about her aunt's pass. At least Anita would be able to stay here for a good long while and regain her strength. She wouldn't have to endure the crowded conditions for some time.

The ache at the thought of having to leave didn't lessen.

⁂

Irene stood in Mother Superior's office late that afternoon with trembling legs. The small room contained a mahogany desk with a neat pile of papers on one corner, a bookshelf crammed with reading material, two chairs for guests, and the chair Mother Superior occupied.

The older woman sat as she often did when her leg ailment troubled her. She folded her hands in front of her, a gold cross hanging from her neck.

Irene stood beside the chair, not quite sure why she'd been called into the office. She'd never been so nervous in her entire life. What had she done to earn a reprimand? Unless Mother Superior was about to tell her to go back to Santo Tomas now and not wait the week.

"Sit down, child, and stop shaking."

Irene sat but couldn't control the tremors. "I am sorry to have caused you problems with my presence. A kind guard took pity on me and secured my pass. I will understand if you want me to leave now."

"I didn't call you in here to scold you."

"You didn't?" Then what could she want? Irene gripped the chair's wooden armrest.

"This came for you today." Mother Superior slid an envelope across the mirrorlike surface of her desk.

Irene took the envelope and lifted the unsealed flap. The handwriting on the sheet was familiar, that of the guard who had secured her pass to come here.

This slip of paper granted her privileges outside of the confines of Santiago Hospital. Her heart surged. "I'm free to do as I please?"

"Not as you please, no. You are allowed to go home and gather what you may need from there. I warn you: your home has probably been looted and not much left of any value."

And just that fast, she deflated. "My home is in the jungle. Anita and I were staying with a Filipina friend when we were ordered to report."

Mother Superior tented her fingers. "I recommend you do not use that pass. For Westerners, it is dangerous outside of these walls. The Japanese roam the streets, and they aren't always kind. A woman alone would be too much of a target."

"But I have a pass."

"That won't matter to them. I urge you to stay here."

Irene stood and clutched the paper to her chest. "Thank you for this. I appreciate it."

"You would do well to heed my advice."

Irene smiled at the woman and left the room. Once in the hall, she dared to stare at the pass once more.

She didn't even need to consider her decision.

It was already made.

# Chapter Twelve

"Wowie-kazowie, aren't you the cat's meow? You're as pretty as any of the girls at the Monarch."

Irene broke out of her reverie and discovered Rand wheeling his way down the hall toward her, a twinkle in his honey-colored eyes. He had slicked back the light-brown hair that framed his narrow face with a square jaw. With a few pounds added since his release from Fort Santiago, he appeared more robust. She smoothed her brown poplin skirt and jacket with dark-brown satin edging and smiled. "Thank you. Is that your nightclub?"

He rolled to a stop inches from her scuffed brown oxfords. "Yes. And you do look beautiful. A vision."

"You've seen too many nuns lately."

"No. You make Jean Harlow pale in comparison. You do know who she is, don't you?"

"My father's favorite actress. He said she looked like my mother. You see, I'm not quite as naive as you think I am."

"I never said you were. In any of my clubs, you would be a

knockout. You even broke out the lipstick today." He flashed her a rakish smile that only accentuated the cleft in his chin. "What's the occasion? Did I miss Thanksgiving?"

"No, you're safe for a few days yet. I'm going out."

"Not out to the garden dressed like that."

"No. Out. To the world beyond our confinement." She pointed to her red armband, proof that she had permission to move about the outside world.

"To do what?" A crease appeared across his forehead.

"To do what you can't. Check on your houseboy. Armando—that's the name you said." She held up a rucksack. "I even have a few different medicines Mother Superior gave me for whatever might ail him."

Thunder broke over his face. "No. I forbid it."

She took a step back. "You can't forbid me. You have no hold over me. I'm neither your wife nor your daughter."

"You're acting like an impetuous child. What are you? Nineteen? Do you know how dangerous it is out there? You don't even know your way around, Jungle Girl."

"For more than seven years I've been going deep into the jungle with my aunt each time we hear of an illness. We bring medicines, help, and the gospel. Don't worry about me. If I can handle scorpions and centipedes, I can handle Manila."

Rand shook his head, a lock of his wavy hair falling into his eyes. He needed a cut and a shave. "If you go to Armando, you could put him in danger."

"Maybe he already is." She didn't voice her thought again that someone in his household might be behind the note. Someone like Armando's son who didn't show up as planned for the escape attempt and sent a more-than-cryptic-enough message.

"Why are you taking such an interest in this? As I said before, we're practically strangers." Red suffused his cheeks.

She shrugged. "It's what Anita and I do. We help people who can't help themselves." Something about him drew her like a magnet. She wanted to assist him and to protect him.

"I'll be the one to help Armando."

"You'll never get a pass outside, so you can't do this for yourself. Let me do it. It's true—we don't know each other very well." She grabbed the handles of his wheelchair and steered him toward the patio. "The rain has stopped for the time being. Let's sit outside and get acquainted."

He turned back and glared at her. "You're kidnapping me."

"It's for your own good. If you want me to be efficient and safe, this is the only way."

"How much time do you have?"

"I don't know. I'm supposed to be able to go home and get whatever I need from there."

His eyes narrowed. "Then you don't have free reign. You'll be in a heap of trouble if you're found somewhere other than your home."

"And that's the beauty. I don't have a home."

They arrived in the garden, and she parked his wheelchair, engaging the brake in case he decided to wheel away from her. She pulled a wrought iron chair to face him, wiped off the fallen leaves, and sat.

He crossed his arms. "Not the beauty. The problem. You shouldn't go out at all."

More than once, Anita had labeled her stubborn. She deserved the title. "What can you do to stop me? My mind is made up, so the better way to go about this is to cooperate with me. Ensure my safety in that way."

He rubbed his temples. "You are infuriating."

"Not a pushover like your little debutante friends?"

Rand grinned. "No, life is much more interesting with you around, Irene. Irene, Irene, you make me want to scream."

She tapped her foot, her toes pinched inside the oxfords, hoping to tamp down the giggle rising in her chest. "Good. The train runs both ways. Now to get down to business."

"You're all about business, aren't you? Don't you like to have fun? Do you even know how?"

"Of course I do." Of all the things to insinuate.

"But missionaries like you don't smoke or drink or gamble."

"There is much more to life than that, Mr. Sterling. You can have a swell time without participating in those vices."

"You will have to show me, then, as soon as we are back at Santo Tomas."

She hemmed and hawed, thinking that the owner of two of the most successful nightclubs in Manila wouldn't want to have anything to do with her form of entertainment. "We'll see. Work before pleasure."

He shifted positions in the chair and grimaced. "Fire away. If this private investigator job doesn't work out, you could always be a reporter."

"Where can I find Armando and Ramon?"

"I don't know. They lived in servants' quarters on our property, but not anymore."

Irene got up and wandered around the edge of the patio, drinking in the scent of the tropical flowers. "My father taught me the names of many of the different plants here." She ached for those times so distant, when he did care for her. "It was so long ago,

I've forgotten most of them. He loved the variety and the showy colors. And the fact that there was color all year long. Nothing like January in windswept Nebraska." She touched the delicate edge of a petal. "I bet your home has beautiful landscaping."

"There is a swimming pool surrounded by a large lawn. It's perfect for entertaining. We take dips in the water or lounge on chairs or play a game of badminton or croquet in the yard. The gardener keeps it in tip-top shape, and my cook is the best in the city. I miss those times."

"On Dewey Boulevard, I bet. I get the sense that you enjoy the best of everything."

"Of course. A gated entrance, walled garden, Spanish-style villa. Very Colonial looking. A great view of Manila Bay. But don't go there. Don't do this. I believe the Japanese have confiscated the house, and Armando and Ramon have had to move. I don't know how to get to their new place."

How could he forbid her now? She had the information she needed to start her search.

"Mama, Mama, that nice Japanese man is here." Paulo came skipping into the small shanty where Mercedes was opening a tin of Spam to go with his rice for lunch.

Mercedes turned as Mr. Tanaka strode into the hut, regal in his olive uniform and shiny black boots. He set his rifle in the corner. A tremor ran through her body. "I'd rather not have that thing"—she nodded in the direction of the gun—"in the house where a little boy could get at it."

"Ah, of course. I have no children, but I know my sister would not want my niece to play with it either. I apologize." He picked up the weapon and held on to it.

Mercedes supposed that he couldn't put it outside where an internee might pick it up and begin shooting soldiers. "I'm happy to see you."

"I brought a gift for you and your son." He reached into his breast pocket and drew out a chocolate bar. He laughed. "Your eyes got very wide when you saw this."

Her mouth watered. "Chocolate is my very favorite."

Paulo sidled up to Mr. Tanaka. "And mine too."

The guard broke the bar in half. "Here you are. Go share it with your friends. You will make many that way."

The boy began to skip away before Mercedes stopped him. "Paulo, where are your manners?"

"Thank you." Paulo was out of the shanty in a flash.

"Please, sit down, Mr. Tanaka. Can I get you a drink of water?" Mercedes needed one. Her mouth had gone dry.

"No, but thank you for your kindness."

They sat at the kitchen table across from each other, he in the chair Charles had always occupied. Her heart clenched a bit at seeing another man there. It didn't feel right, but she bit back the emotion.

She wiped imaginary crumbs from the table. "Why did you join the military?"

"To fight for the honor of my country."

Any soldier from any country would say that. "Is it something you always wanted to do?"

"Why all of the questions?"

"Each of us has a story. Where you came from and how you got to the place you are now. I'm wondering what your story is."

"I was married and working as an engineer on a road-building crew when the war broke out. I joined the military to protect and serve my country. That is all."

"What happened to your wife? Did she die?" Mercedes choked on the lump in her throat. Did he understand what it was like to lose a spouse?

"No. It is—was—a loveless marriage." He scraped back the chair and rose. "That is enough. I must return to my duties."

Mercedes was confused. Was he still married? Divorced?

He held her hand and helped her to her feet, then drew her close. "I like coming to see you. Next time I want to hear your story. You said we all have one." He kissed her cheek and then her neck.

She shivered and stepped back. "Please. You are Japanese, and I am Filipina. I lost my husband only a year ago."

He bowed. "My apologies. It is . . ." Then he turned and left the hut without another word.

Mercedes stood on the front step hugging herself. Her emotions were churning like the sea during a storm. What had just happened?

Paulo returned home, half of the chocolate bar still clutched in his little hand. "No one wanted any Japanese candy."

Mercedes hugged herself all the tighter.

❧

Not too long after lunch, Irene stood on the outside of the gates of Hospicio de Santiago. Freedom. After all of these months, it was strange, like putting on a pair of *bakyas* after wearing boots that pinched your toes.

She hustled down the street, not wanting to waste a moment of her liberty. Even though her resources were stretched thin and she needed to save every last peso for the foreseeable future in Santo Tomas, she hired a *carromatas* to take her to Dewey Boulevard.

Outside the walls of confinement, life went on. Shops lined the streets. Bundles of electric lines hung over the road. People bought, sold, and traded.

And the children. They were dressed in rags, running up and down the streets. She watched as one of them swiped an orange from a vendor. Manila had changed during the occupation.

Her heart bled for the little ones. “Stop, driver.”

The man reined in his horse and she hopped out. “Wait here.”

She dug deep into her pocketbook and pulled out a few coins. Not much, really. Not much at all. They had come into camp with precious little, and that had dwindled to almost nothing.

But she couldn’t let these children live like this. One little girl, her dark eyes wide in her thin face, came to her. Irene stroked her long, dark hair, matted as it was. “Here, this is for you. Buy some bread for your family.”

The child’s eyes glistened with unshed tears. “But I don’t have a family.”

Why did she have to be holed up in Santo Tomas? She should be out here, helping the helpless. “Then buy yourself some bread. And when the war is over, try to find me. My name is Irene Reynolds.” For now she could do no more. But when the fighting ended, she would. She would take care of the motherless and fatherless, like her aunt had taken care of her.

Saying nothing to the driver of her depleted finances, she returned to the *carromatas*, and he continued toward their destination.

She stopped at the nearby market to find out if anyone knew the Sterling residence. It took a bit of doing, but at last a woman said she had been a maid there for a short time and gave Irene the directions. Rand said Armando and Ramon didn't live at his home anymore, but it was a place to start.

And then, in contrast to the poverty, came Dewey Boulevard, a wide street lined with palms, following the curve of Manila Bay. She'd heard about the grand palaces that hugged this street, but she had to remind herself to keep her mouth closed when she saw them in person.

These homes were spectacular. Rand was more than rich. He was fabulously wealthy. Each home got better than the last. Large Italianate villas. Spanish-style residences. Greek revivals. As a child, she had poured over Anita's coffee-table book on architecture—the one non-necessity she owned—fascinated that people lived in places like those in the pictures.

Anita taught the village women that the Lord was preparing a mansion in heaven for them far superior to any castle on earth. At this moment, Irene couldn't imagine anything bigger or grander than these homes.

Rand's residence stood back from the street, hidden by a thick wall. Overgrown hot-pink bougainvillea spilled down the stucco wall. A wrought iron gate barred the entrance. When she had a house of her own, she would never have a gate. She would welcome all.

She stepped from the *carromatas* and asked the driver to wait for her. Once she had smoothed her skirt with trembling hands, she made her way to the fence. As she was about to press the bell, she noticed the latch wasn't shut all the way. Looking around and behind her, she slipped inside and hurried down the long driveway. The graceful arches of the Spanish-style home welcomed her, and she climbed the steps to the dark wood front door where she rang the bell.

The Westminster chimes played, then fell silent. She heard no scurrying inside or the footfalls of anyone coming to answer. No Armando or Ramon. She must have stood there for five minutes or more, grateful for the portico and its red-tiled roof that shielded her from the hot sun.

After waiting what she considered to be an appropriate amount of time, she turned the knob and was only a little surprised when the door opened. The bright-white marble entrance with soaring ceilings and double staircase took her breath away. She tiptoed down the hallway to the left and peeked in one door.

Books littered the floor and papers were strewn all over the place. The only furniture remaining was the built-in bookshelf. Rand's study, she assumed. The dark mahogany wainscoting gave it a distinctive masculine flair. But where had his desk and chairs gone? Even the pictures were missing, dark splotches on the stucco wall where they should have hung.

She strolled farther down the hall to a bright room that stood empty and forlorn. Not even a rug covered the marble floors.

Going on, she came into a spacious kitchen with windows overlooking the yard. The cabinet doors hung open, the shelves bare. She peeked outside. Leaves clogged the pool and weeds had overtaken the garden.

What had happened here?

"Armando? Ramon? Hello?" Only the echo of her voice answered her.

Her heart pounded in her ears and perspiration broke out on her upper lip.

Beside the pool, she spied a smaller house. That must be where Armando and Ramon stayed. The Japanese weren't using the place. Perhaps the houseboy and his son had returned.

A door banged shut.

With a *whoosh*, she let out the breath she didn't know she'd been holding. Armando must have arrived.

The clack of her shoes rang out as she headed toward the front of the house. "Armando?"

Silence.

"Armando? Ramon?"

She inched forward two steps. She couldn't breathe. Armando would have answered her. How could she get out of here?

Footsteps sounded behind her. She ran.

But not far.

Not far enough. Or fast enough.

With powerful, muscular arms, a man grabbed her from behind and dragged her toward the stairs.

## Chapter Thirteen

Rand wheeled himself up and down the busy hospital hall, past other patients and the nuns, until his arm burned. Outside, thunder rumbled in the distance. No sign of Irene anywhere.

The foolish, headstrong woman had gone off in search of adventure on her own. Really, he preferred the meek, moldable women who frequented his clubs.

No, if he was honest with himself, he liked women like Irene. And like Catherine, so long in his past. Real women. Women who put away pretention. Women who had minds of their own.

Though a woman with a mind of her own was the most frustrating thing in the world.

At last, Sister Francis arrived in the ward and made her way down the hall. He hurried to meet her halfway. "Have you seen Irene Reynolds?"

Sister Francis nodded, her double chin jiggling. "I met her in Anita Markham's room an hour or more ago. She told me she had a pass to go out for a short time and asked if I would keep an eye on her aunt. I could tell she hated to leave, but she said she had an important errand. I do worry about her in the city by herself. You can never be too careful these days. But she was determined to go."

"And you haven't seen her since? She hasn't returned?"

"No, not as far as I know. When she gets back, shall I tell her you're looking for her?"

"That won't be necessary. Thank you." He wouldn't need her to announce Irene's arrival because he planned to station himself at the gate and wait there until she marched onto the hospital grounds.

Crazy, stubborn woman.

She would never find Armando. She didn't know where to look. He couldn't direct her to the *baryo* where his most trusted servant now lived because he had never been there himself.

His stomach knotted. Those from Santo Tomas who had managed passes brought back word of the danger on the outside. The Japanese were not kind taskmasters. Homes had been looted, women taken advantage of, innocent Filipinos killed.

That was the world into which naive, all-too-trusting Irene Reynolds stepped.

He wheeled around in circles in the front of the building. When he tired of that, he pushed himself to his feet and, holding the handles of his wheelchair, paced along the wall.

He hadn't done enough to stop her. He should have warned her in more specific terms what could happen to her. Whoever was threatening him might not be so receptive to Irene snooping around. He suspected Dewey Boulevard teemed with Japanese living in the finest homes in the city. Why, oh why, had he ever let his emotions take over when he spoke about his house, giving away its location?

She was young. She didn't know the ways of the world. She

didn't understand hate and cruelty. She saw good wherever she looked.

Hadn't she learned anything during the almost two years of captivity? If nothing else, she should have learned from his experience at Fort Santiago.

He slammed his left hand against the back of the wheelchair.

At times like this, he wished he were a praying man.

---

Irene bit back a scream as her attacker tightened his grip around her shoulders. She focused all of her attention on delivering the hardest kick she could to his shin with her heel.

Unaffected, he yanked her hair and dragged her toward the stairs.

She couldn't let him reach the top.

Once up there, she would be at his mercy. He may be small, but he was strong. Powerful. Determined.

Bile rose in her throat and she swallowed it.

As much as possible, she squirmed and struggled. She freed herself enough from his stranglehold to bite his arm. She clamped down hard.

Her attacker let out a cry and kicked her feet from under her. Only his grasp around her kept her from falling to the ground. He held her tight against his side, the tip of his finger missing on his right hand. She scrambled to her feet, slipping on the smooth marble tile.

Only a few more steps and they would be at the stairs. *God, no. Give me strength, Lord. Give me Samson's strength.*

Thunder rolled in the distance.

She knew the fate that awaited her if she didn't escape. The soldier would steal everything important from her. A gift that could never be regiven. He would ruin her forever.

She tasted metal and blood. Her heart pounded in her ears and in her chest, an uneven rhythm no proud *dabakan* drummer would use.

She kicked again. This time she aimed her oxford higher.

Her assailant squealed like a pig, dropping his hold on her. Knowing she only had a moment, she sprinted away.

His boots thumped behind her.

Blood pounded behind her eyes. She focused on the front door. If she could make it there, she would be safe.

Safe.

Safe.

Her shoes pounded out the rhythm.

She slid. Her arms and legs flailed as she struggled to maintain her balance.

She screamed at the top of her lungs, "No, God, help me. Help me. Help me."

She stayed erect. Like a football player, she lunged for the doorknob. The brass was cool and smooth in her hand.

Her fingers and palms dripped with sweat. She couldn't turn it.

The soldier shouted at her. He was right behind her. She tensed, waiting for his hands to grab her.

*Let it open.*

And it did. The knob turned in her hand. She leaned her weight against the heavy door and it flung wide. Sunshine assaulted her eyes. She took a deep breath.

*Run, run, run.*

Her lungs burned, the fire in her legs matching them in intensity. Sweat dripped into her eyes and stung. The gate blurred.

Had the soldier been armed? Was he going to shoot her in the back?

"Driver. Driver." Perhaps the man in the *carromatas* would hear her. Help her.

The gate swung in the breeze on its iron hinge. Her pursuer continued to shout at her. By his voice, she knew he ran mere feet behind her.

She would not stop. Never. Ever.

It took a small eternity, but she reached the gate. Dashed through it.

Through her tears, she spied the *carromatas* waiting at the curb. She took a flying leap and landed on the tufted leather seat. "Go. Go. As fast as you can. Don't stop until you get to Santiago Hospital."

The soldier appeared in her peripheral vision.

"Get moving. He's after me." She hoped the driver understood. She wished she spoke more Tagalog.

He whipped the horse, and the *carromatas* took off with a jolt. Irene dared to look back. Her attacker stood at the curb, yelling and gesturing in her direction.

She gulped air, her heart galloping faster than the horse. Sweat covered her, and her arms and legs went weak as adrenaline coursed through her body.

As the driver rushed up and down Manila's streets, she lay panting on the seat. She combed her fingers through her hair, all of her pins having mutinied.

No matter how long she lived, she would never be able to erase the soldier's sneering image from her brain. She would forever remember the feel of his hands on her bare arms, the aroma of saki surrounding him, the tickle of his breath on her neck.

Rand and Mother Superior had been right.

How would she ever face them?

⁂

Rand watched from Santiago's gate as a *carromatas* careened around the corner on two wheels. Were all Manila horsemen crazy?

The driver reined his frothing horse to a halt in front of the hospital. Rand's heart zinged. Irene? Was this her returning?

Not caring how much trouble he could be in if caught outside of Santiago's confines, he went to the *carromatas* as a disheveled Irene stepped from the carriage. Her hair fell around her flushed, perspiring face.

He took her small, trembling hand, but she flinched and drew it back.

"What happened to you?"

"I didn't find them."

They walked inside the hospital walls side by side, him pushing his wheelchair, her stumbling on unsteady legs. "I told you they weren't there."

"You were right. Mother Superior was right."

"About what?" His stomach lurched at the thought of what they might have been right about.

"I don't want to talk about it."

"Did he hurt you? The soldier at my house?"

She stopped short, and he turned to face her. "How did you know?"

"Why else would that *carromatas* driver whip his horse into such a frenzy? What did he do to you?"

"Nothing."

He touched her upper arm, and she winced. A lump formed in his throat. "He hurt you. That dirty beast hurt you." His words seeped through clenched teeth.

"It will heal."

"Did he . . . ?"

She shook her head with great vigor.

"You can tell me. Please, tell me."

"I have to sit down."

She didn't object this time when he led her by the elbow to the garden. With as much gentleness as he could muster, he lowered her into the ornate iron chair. She crossed her long legs. He leaned on his wheelchair for support. "Tell me everything."

"You don't want to hear."

He cursed their occupiers. "I promise I won't think less of you. And I won't tell anyone if you don't want me to." The heat in his belly turned to ice.

"A soldier came while I was at your house." She bit her lip until it bled.

He stroked her hand, hoping to calm her, reassure her that she could trust him. "And then what?"

"I was looking for them. I was so sure I would find them or some trace of them at your home. Even if they weren't there, I might find a clue to their whereabouts. I didn't. I'm sorry. More than anything, I wanted to help you. To give you news about Armando's health."

"And that's what makes you a special lady. Crazy and headstrong, but special."

One corner of her mouth flicked up.

"What else happened?" He urged her on, but he wasn't sure he wanted to hear what she had to say.

"He tried to drag me up the stairs. I fought him, bit him, kicked him. God helped me, and I was able to get away."

Now Rand sunk to the chair beside Irene. "You're going to be fine?"

She nodded. "I'm sorry."

His heart flipped. "You have nothing to be sorry about." He leaned toward her.

"If I had only listened to you . . . This is all my fault."

"None of it is. He had no right to frighten you. Or to put his hands on you. Those Japanese are . . . are . . ."

Her soft blue eyes filled with tears.

Anger seared his heart. If he ever got his hands on that man . . .

# Chapter Fourteen

His dark eyes narrowed, a man with a round face approached Irene. A growl issued from his throat and talons sprang from the tips of his fingers. He prowled in a circle around her, stalking her like a lion. She tensed, ready for him to pounce. When would he get it over with?

Another man appeared, lighter haired, sneering, also with claws for fingernails. He marched in a circle, too, in the opposite direction of the other man. He sang a strange, haunting song, leering at her.

She turned in one direction, then the other. No matter where she looked, one or the other was there. They closed in on her, tightening the noose, ready for the kill.

An obstruction in her throat cut off her breath. Her pulse pounded in her wrists.

She tried to run but slipped.

She couldn't get to her feet.

And then four beast-like hands reached for her.

Irene woke with a start. Her heart raced as fast as the *carromatas* did yesterday. Rain pounded at the window overlooking the hospital garden. The rivulets streamed to the sill. When she was little, she loved to watch the droplets race each other down the pane. She always tried to guess which one would win. More often than not, she was wrong.

Like yesterday.

What had possessed her to go out at all? An unrequested pass could only mean trouble. And it did. As the *carromatas* drove away, she got a glimpse of the man's face.

A pockmarked face she had seen before.

A man missing part of a finger.

The man who had issued her pass.

He hadn't been kind. He'd been conniving. Duplicitous.

Why had she ever trusted him?

*Mercedes.* Irene sat up in bed so fast she got dizzy. She had to warn her friend. Tell her not to depend on the two-faced soldier.

Mercedes's soldier may or may not be the same man as the one who attacked her. Regardless, he was no friend. None of them were.

If she ever saw him at Santo Tomas, she didn't know if she would run away in fear or run toward him and give him a few more well-placed kicks.

She shifted positions, her bruised body a constant reminder of her folly.

Rand had been gentle, understanding, not judgmental. She hadn't expected the tenderness and compassion from a high-and-mighty society man. He had been genuinely concerned for her welfare.

He, who had warned her not to go, who could have given her the I-told-you-so speech, wanted to make sure she hadn't suffered more than physical injuries. Hadn't chastised her for her decision. Had been touched that she wanted to help him.

She stared at the ceiling, watching a black spider make its way from one side of the room to the other. When he anchored his tether and swung free, Irene gasped.

In an instant like that, life could change.

Sister Francis floated into the room. "How are you this morning, dear?"

"I'm fine."

"Good. You're not a patient here, technically, but I wanted to check on you, to see how you were making out."

"Other than stiffness, I'm well."

Sister Francis nodded toward the window. "Another typhoon. Don't you love the Philippines in November? Do you want me to bring you a little breakfast?"

"No, thank you. I can go to the kitchen for a tray later. How is my aunt?"

"She is doing better. Her fever broke yesterday afternoon. She's been asking for you."

Irene clung to the bedsheet. "Did you tell her that I went out? That I was attacked?"

Sister Francis nodded. "She asked us direct questions as to your whereabouts and why you didn't come to visit her last night."

And, of course, they wouldn't lie. Irene swung her legs over the side of the bed, pulling the white cotton nightgown over her knees. Sister Francis left, and Irene dressed in her plain brown cotton dress with red buttons on the bodice and red piping on the pockets.

Rand met her in the hall and his golden eyes widened. "You're up."

"And you're standing. I'm off to see Anita."

"Yes, I'm getting stronger each day. Let me walk you there."

"I'm steadier on my feet than you are."

"It's the gentlemanly thing to do, after all you've been through."

"You don't need to stick to such conventions for my sake." The very last thing she wanted was for him to feel obligated to be near her.

"We can lean on each other."

Irene offered him her elbow as they made their way to the end of the hallway. "It's the least I can do." He stood at least six inches taller than her own five feet six.

He cleared his throat. "Did you sleep well last night?"

"No. I kept seeing his face. And his hand. I remember that hand, missing some of a finger. He's the one who was kind to me, who gave me the pass."

Beside her, Rand stopped short and squeezed her elbow. His forehead creased. "The same one? You're sure?"

"Positive. He . . . he planned it all." She swallowed hard.

A muscle jumped in Rand's cheek. "That . . . that . . ."

"I'll never speak to another of the guards again. Ever. I promise."

"It's not your fault. Not at all." He took a deep breath. "You were set up. He planned the trap from the beginning."

Just thinking about yesterday's incident caused a shiver to run up and down Irene's spine, so she pushed it from her mind.

They came to the end of the hall. Rand had walked the entire way, not really leaning on her. "You'll be able to go back to Santo Tomas soon." The thought of not bumping into him in the hall brought a tinge of sadness.

"Unfortunately, yes. It's much nicer here, being pampered by the nuns."

And he would know about pampering.

He shrugged. "But it doesn't feel like real life. It's more of a holiday or a movie or a dream that has to end."

"I have to make the trek to the internment camp later this week to reapply for my pass." Dread grabbed her midsection and refused to let go. In every Japanese face, she would see that man. Maybe, because she would be requesting an extension, she would even run into him.

She shook away his image and focused on the man beside her. "Thank you, Rand. I appreciate your walking me here, unnecessary though it was."

He bowed just a little. "My pleasure. Really. Anytime." With a wink, he returned the way they came.

Irene tapped at her aunt's door. "Anita?" She wound a curl around her finger before letting it bounce back.

Her aunt sat up in bed, her breakfast tray on her lap. Her thin, wrinkled face brightened when she heard Irene. "Come in, my dear, come in. It is good to see you."

Irene shuffled to the chair beside her aunt, sure she would receive a tongue-lashing. "I'm glad you're awake. You've been ill for a long time. I was worried about you."

"The Lord spared me. How are you, darling?"

"You heard what happened?"

"Yes. My heart breaks for you. But God is gracious. You escaped with no permanent harm done. Praise Him for that. His angels were watching over you."

"I can't argue with you." Only angels could have protected her and given her the strength to fight that monster. "I'm sorry for what I did."

"My dear, don't be sorry. Perhaps you shouldn't have ventured out on your own, but that didn't give that man license to do what he did."

"I was foolish. Rand tried to talk me out of it, and Mother Superior, too, but I insisted. I even tricked him into giving me information on where he lived."

Anita laid her fork beside her plate on the tray. "That's what I don't understand. Why were you so insistent on going there? What business did you have to take care of?"

"I was trying to help him. His longtime houseboy is very ill. That's why Rand tried to escape. He's desperate to help the man." She just realized she'd dropped the rucksack with the medication somewhere along the way. Her stomach dipped, and she sobered at the thought that the enemy would have the drugs and not those who needed it most.

She pursed her lips, not wanting to say more. Anita would scold her for sure if she knew about the note.

"You're young and impetuous. You need to learn restraint. But as I said before, that doesn't make this your fault. Don't ever, ever think that. Lean on the Lord and on me, and let us help you heal."

"Will life ever be normal again? Will we be free?"

"Life will be good, though maybe not as we knew it. Bring me my Bible." She handed Irene her tray.

Irene found the large, heavy tome on the table beside Anita's bed. Her aunt ran her fingers over the Braille markings on the page, flipping through until she found the verses she wanted.

"'But fear not thou, O my servant Jacob, and be not dismayed, O Israel: for, behold, I will save thee from afar off, and thy seed from the land of their captivity; and Jacob shall return, and be in rest and at ease, and none shall make him afraid.' Jeremiah 46:27. That is God's promise to us."

"Life isn't as simple as the Bible makes it out to be." No matter how much time passed, she would never forget a single detail of what happened yesterday. Nor would she ever forgive the man for what he did.

"Yes, it is. Trust in Him. Put your hope in Him. You may suffer, but joy is on the horizon. God is taking care of you." Anita turned more pages, running her fingers over the Braille print. "'Consider the lilies how they grow: they toil not, they spin not; and yet I say unto you, that Solomon in all his glory was not arrayed like one of these. If then God so clothe the grass, which is to day in the field, and to morrow is cast into the oven; how much more will he clothe you, O ye of little faith? And seek not ye what ye shall eat, or what ye shall drink, neither be ye of doubtful mind. For all these things do the nations of the world seek after: and your Father knoweth that ye have need of these things. But rather seek ye the kingdom of God; and all these things shall be added unto you.'"

Irene wandered to the window and watched the raindrops splash in the puddles below. "It's too dark now for me to see."

"Come, sit beside me." Anita patted a spot on the mattress next to her, and Irene did her bidding. "Don't give up hope. Forgive. Forget. Trust. God is taking care of you, just like He takes care of the lilies."

The words slipped past Anita's lips with ease, as they had hundreds of times before as she taught the village women. But to live them out was so much more difficult. Impossible, really.

Anita's hands trembled as she closed her Bible's cover.

Irene kissed her forehead. "I've tired you out too much, so I'm going to leave and let you get some rest. We can finish our conversation another time."

She knew in her head all of what Anita had told her was right. But her heart refused to believe.

Behind Irene, the car that had brought her and Rand from Hospicio de Santiago idled. She stared at the heavy iron spear-headed gates at the entrance of Santo Tomas. Had she been coming here as a university student, she might have thought them grand or majestic. Now, as an internee, she found them imposing and intimidating. She hated them.

Rand harrumphed beside her. "We're back where we started from. Isn't this swell?"

"You sound a little bit too much like me."

"See, you're rubbing off on me." He laughed and held her hand. "I think the guard wants us to go in."

She nodded, and he gave her fingers a squeeze. Together they entered the now-familiar yard, rows of nipa huts greeting them.

A soccer ball rolled in their direction from a group of kids. Mercedes's son, Paulo, chased it. "Mr. Sterling, you're back. We heard you were sick." The boy with pale skin and dark eyes looked up at Rand.

Sheila King was hot on his heels. She ran and wrapped her arms around Irene's leg. "I missed you. And Mr. Sterling too."

Rand handed the ball back to Paulo. "I see you've been practicing your dribbling. Keep it up. I need to get a bit stronger, like Miss Sheila has here. Then watch out. Tell the goalie to be prepared."

"I am the goalie."

"Ah, then you'd best get back to your teammates and get practicing. I show no mercy."

Paulo grinned and picked up the ball. "We know that."

Irene kissed the top of Sheila's head, then glanced down at the child. "You play with these boys? And with Mr. Sterling?"

Sheila nodded, her dark curls bobbing against her slender neck. "And I'm good, aren't I, Mr. Sterling?"

"Well, not as good as me, but you're a swell player."

Irene chuckled. "And he's cocky too."

"Precisely." Rand grinned.

"I'm glad you're out of the hospital and feeling so much better. Enjoy your game." Irene gave Sheila one last hug before turning her loose.

The children ran off and resumed playing. A bit of normalcy in this crazy, mixed-up world.

Irene shook her head. "When I was out in the city, I saw children on the street. Poor. Hungry. Stealing. They were orphans, I'm sure of it, reduced to desperate measures to survive. They broke my heart. I gave one girl all of the money I had brought along for the *carromatas* driver. And the longer the war goes on, the worse the problem will get. These kids may be prisoners, but at least they have someone to watch over them. Even Sheila."

"You like kids."

"I spent all of my time at the mission with the village children. Those days taught me to love God's little ones, especially the most vulnerable."

They walked on for a short way. Rand nodded at a Filipino man driven in a jeep into the compound by a Japanese soldier.

"Who is that?"

"It's a classified secret."

She gasped. He had the nerve to laugh. "What is so funny?"

"I'll tell you. If you can't trust a missionary, who can you trust?" He leaned over to whisper in her ear, his breath tickling her neck, giving her goose bumps. "That man smuggles in briefcases full of pesos for the internee committee to buy extra rice on the black market."

"I didn't know."

"I imagine there is much that goes on behind the scenes that most people don't know."

"Why did you tell me?"

"Because I think I can trust you not to give up our secrets if you end up in Fort Santiago."

Irene gasped again. "You do like to have fun with me, don't you?"

There was that gleam in his eyes.

After a fashion, life had continued as it had before they left. The little stands selling staples, food, and basic necessities dotted the campus. Irene looked with longing at the bologna, fruit, and vegetables, going as far as to stop at the stand and handle a potato.

Rand came beside her. "I'm going to purchase some of that chicken and a bit of bath soap."

Irene drew in a breath and let it out slowly. The chicken was selling for the exorbitant price of six pesos a kilo and potatoes for four and a half pesos a kilo. She and Anita had no money for such things. They depended almost entirely on what they got in the food line. Already, before leaving for the hospital, the quality and quantity of the meals had dwindled. She envied Rand to be able to buy whatever he wanted. He must have brought a good deal of cash into the camp with him. And he must be hiding it from the Japanese.

"We don't need anything right now."

"Let me treat you. What do you want? Anything at all."

She didn't want to be beholden to him. "Nothing. We have all we need."

"Irene, Irene, haven't you seen, there's not a pickle nor a bean."

She stopped and stared at him, his light-brown beard scraggly. "Why do you make up those silly little poems? Conditions are a bit too serious to be fooling around."

"And that's why I do it." His golden eyes danced. "My parents were always serious. At first, I started rhyming to make them smile. When I got to be a teenager, I did it to annoy my father. The habit sort of stuck. Besides, being sullen doesn't help matters."

"You won't know until you've tried it."

Irene breathed a sigh of relief as Rand walked away from the stand. "I'll come with you to the release committee office and make my purchases later."

Though she protested, he insisted. They entered the building and climbed the stairs. A doctor from Hospicio de Santiago met them there. The stabbing pains in Irene's stomach felt more like bumblebees than butterflies. She didn't want to stay here, especially after seeing the conditions. She wanted to be with Anita. Needed her aunt when the nightmares came.

Irene swung her legs back and forth as they sat on straight-backed chairs and waited in the stuffy hallway.

"Irene Reynolds?" One rather flabby-looking gentleman indicated she should step inside.

"Good luck." Rand hooked both corners of his mouth upward, but she couldn't.

She wove her fingers together to steady them before entering, her *bakyas* clicking on the floor. The committee questioned her as to why she needed to return. "To care for my aunt."

One gentleman cracked his knuckles. "And what is your aunt's condition now?"

What could she say? Anita had taught her to always tell the truth. "She is improving, sir."

He shook his bald head. "The commandant has been stingy when it comes to handing out passes. We cannot go to him and argue your case. I'm sorry, you won't be getting a renewal."

Her heart nose-dived. "But, sir, I'm all the family my aunt has."

"From your description of her condition and the doctor's, she should be returning soon as well. We have to deny the pass."

And with that, he shooed her toward the door.

She would be interned at Santo Tomas until the end of the war.

If it ever came.

A lump grew in the back of her throat.

Rand rose and stared at her as she exited the room, asking the question with his eyes. She could only shake her head.

From the corner of her eye, she caught sight of a soldier moving their way, chin held high, strides long.

She clenched her fist until her fingers went numb. She'd never forget that face. "That's him."

# Chapter Fifteen

Rand turned from the Japanese soldier striding down the hall, his boots heavy on the tile floor of the cool Administration Building, to face Irene. "Who? Who is he?"

"Shh. The guard. That's him." Irene's hands were clammy.

"What guard?"

"Don't let him hear. Please don't let him hear you." The world buzzed around her. For the first time in her life, she thought she might faint.

Then Rand stood ramrod straight. "From my house?"

She nodded.

He leaned forward, but she pulled him back before he could interfere. "What are you doing?"

The soldier drew closer, a hard glint in his eyes.

She'd be expected to bow out of respect to their captors. She wouldn't. Would. Not.

Never.

He was now a few steps from them. He drew his lips into a firm line, nostrils flared.

Irene could see nothing but him. She heard nothing but her heart slamming in her chest.

He approached and raised one corner of his mouth, an evil snarl.

She turned her head.

His boots stopped. She didn't bow. She didn't feel Rand bow beside her.

*Thwack.* His hand connected with her cheek. The sting brought tears to her eyes. She crumpled to the ground.

He kicked her in the side.

Pain exploded in her midsection. She hugged her arms around herself, her breath coming in ragged gulps.

Rand lunged. She grabbed him by the ankles. He fell to the tile floor with a smack and a cry of pain. He tried to crawl after the soldier.

The soldier turned. "I'd love to take you back to Fort Santiago." The dare was unmistakable in his voice. Then he marched away.

Rand struggled to free himself from her grasp.

"Don't, please don't." The rock in her throat made it difficult to force the words through. "You don't want to go back there." *God, no.*

"I'm going to wrap my one good hand around his neck."

She turned cold all over. "You can't. Promise me you won't. They'll send you back to that horrible place. And the message writer wasn't kidding when he meant last time would look like a picnic."

The sound of the guard's boots faded. "He hurt you. That beast hurt you." Color heightened in Rand's neck.

"Not much." She was sure she sported a red mark on her cheek, and she must have a bruise on her side.

He touched her face, his fingers as light as feathers. "Don't lie. It's not becoming for a missionary girl."

She swallowed hard. "Don't ever leave me alone in a room with that man."

Dread occupied the space in her stomach that breakfast hadn't filled. What would Rand do if he ever encountered the man in camp? And before the war ended, how many times would she run into him?

*November 14, 1943*

Rain slashed at the windows and pounded the roof of the Education Building while lightning lit up the sky with the brilliance of noon-time. Thunder rumbled almost without ceasing.

Except for the four years he attended college in the States, Rand had lived in Manila all of his life. Never did he remember a typhoon of this magnitude. Rain fell in sheets so heavy it was impossible to see across the yard.

Men were packed into the building, internees ordered to retreat to their dorms during the storm. They were stuffed into classrooms built to accommodate thirty students. Each room now held one hundred or more, all sleeping on cots or desks. He lounged on the mattress on his cot, then stared at the strange curly-haired man in the bed to his left. The bed where Henry had slept when they first arrived.

Where was he now? Still in Fort Santiago? Dead? If he'd been there this long, there was no way he would have survived.

He should never have gotten Henry involved in his harebrained scheme. The cost had been too high.

The pain in his chest deepened.

He flopped back on the bed and stared at the white sheet hung like a hammock above him. A place where he could store a few possessions. Some of the men snored, cashing in on their midafternoon siesta. Some huddled in groups playing cards, and some wandered in circles around the outer edge of the stuffy classroom.

The wind howled, and Rand wondered how his hut was faring. Everything had survived his absence, but this gale was enough to rip off the roof and send a torrent of rainwater into the shanty, even though he'd ordered it built on stilts.

A short, thin man with a bald spot in the middle of his head and a thick, dark mustache wound his way to Rand's small claim in this mass of males. He looked rather familiar, but Rand couldn't place him. He sat on the empty bed to Rand's right, a spot vacated by a man sent to the camp hospital a few days ago with enteritis.

"How are you, Mr. Sterling?"

Rand sat up. "I'm sorry, but I'm afraid you have the advantage on me."

"I apologize." The man made a move to shake Rand's hand. "Frank Covey."

"Ah yes, Mr. Covey." Rand still didn't recall the man with a scar across his cheek and a crooked nose, even as he shook his hand. "How have you been?"

"Stuck in this hole, the same as you. Though I heard about your escape attempt. I'm unsure if it was brave or foolish. You paid a high price."

Rand couldn't put his finger on it, but the man's demeanor—something about the way he looked at Rand, gripped his hand a bit too hard—set him on edge. Frankly, Mr. Covey gave him the heebie-jeebies.

"I visited your club, the Monarch, in the summer of '41. You know, when things were still good here. I was very impressed."

At least Rand now knew the connection between himself and Mr. Covey. The man had been a patron of his club. Rand often circulated among his guests, making them as welcome as he could. It's what he loved best about the job. "I'm glad you were satisfied with your visit."

"Very much so. Do you plan to reopen after the war?"

"Reopen and expand. The Monarch and the Azure are just the beginning."

"Those are some pretty lofty goals."

"This place gives you plenty of time to dream." And for him, with his father's backing as well as Bruce's and John's, the sky was the limit.

Mr. Covey leaned forward, elbows on his knees. "Have you been dreaming about a gorgeous platinum blonde?"

Rand got up and strolled to the other side of his cot, with the mattress between him and Mr. Covey. How did this man know so much about him? And the fact that he mentioned Irene . . . Rand shoved his good hand in his pocket. "There are quite a few of those here."

Mr. Covey also rose. "I think you know who I mean. Have a good day, Mr. Sterling. I hope we run into each other soon."

The thought made Rand's palms sweat.

❧

"Three days of this, Anita, three days. How much longer is this rain going to last? We'll all kill each other if it doesn't let up soon."

A squabble over which woman was the better cook broke out at the end of the row of cots in Irene and Anita's room in the Main Building. A strange thing to be arguing about since they didn't have much food to go around. The women were short-tempered and suffering from being packed into such close quarters. The odor of sweaty, unwashed bodies was becoming unbearable.

"Sit down, Irene. Your pacing is giving me a headache."

Anita had returned from the hospital a day before the typhoon hit. Irene hated that she had to spend time in such crowded, filthy conditions. The power had gone off, and the drinking water was contaminated. She would suffer a relapse, Irene was sure.

Not wanting to cause her aunt any further distress, Irene sat on her cot, the deep bruise on her side still causing her some discomfort. "I can't stop thinking about our hut and how it's faring. I'm sure it will be destroyed by the end of this, and all that money we put into having it built will have been wasted. Did you know Mr. Sterling offered to buy us some food?"

"When was this?"

"When he and I first returned to Santo Tomas. I refused him, not wanting to take advantage of him. I don't want to be dependent or beholden to anyone. Now I wish I hadn't. Our rice must be mush."

Anita rubbed her pale, wrinkled forehead. "I haven't known you to be in such a foul mood since you were a child. What has gotten into you?"

"I want to get out of here. Just be free. No more soldiers. No more captivity and fear."

Anita smiled and picked up her Braille Bible, her fingers gliding over the page as she read. Irene pulled her legs under her and tried to shut out the racket that reverberated in the room. She never thought she would long for peace and quiet the way she did.

She studied her aunt. The woman, who had so little herself, had taken her in and cared for her as tenderly as a mother. For years, Irene had wondered about the mother who gave birth to her. Her father didn't say much about her. Just that they were better off since she'd run away. He had closed his heart. Irene always wanted to know more. What would have caused her to leave her newborn daughter and husband? Perhaps she hadn't wanted to. Maybe she had died and no one wanted to tell her.

"Anita, tell me what you know about my mother."

Her aunt turned her head in Irene's direction, her mouth set in a firm line. "What do you want to know?"

"Did she die?"

"Yes. About six years after she left."

Irene gasped, and a surprising rush of sadness washed over her. A small part of her had hoped that her mother still lived. That one day they might meet again. Might have a relationship. "Why didn't you or my father tell me?"

Anita held up her hands. "What was the point? She had never been a part of your life. You were so young and wouldn't understand, and then as you got older, there was no reason."

"The reason might have been that I wanted to know."

"You never asked."

"I'm asking now. I need to know. What did she die from?"

"Irene, really, why are you pushing the subject?" Anita slammed the Bible shut and rubbed her hand over the book's cover.

Irene had never seen her aunt so agitated. "I want to know."

"You don't. Her life—and her death—were tragic. But a tragedy of her own making. Leave it at that."

Irene twisted the sheet that covered her bed. Her stomach twisted in similar fashion. Why was Anita so closemouthed about this? "I wish you would tell me."

"Do you really want to know? Because once I tell you, there is no going back."

A jolt of fear ran through Irene. Did she want this information?

Would it change her life? Yet she would always wonder and would never be satisfied until she had the answer. The truth. "Yes."

Anita took a deep breath and opened and closed her mouth several times before speaking. "She was murdered by the man she was living with. A man who was not her husband."

Irene opened her mouth, but no words came out.

"You're surprised."

Irene nodded, unable to speak. From a few cots down, two women argued about whose can of Spam they would open today.

"You would have been better off not knowing."

"She left my father and me for another man?"

"Yes. Your father was broken up about it. He loved her without reserve."

"But he never let on to me."

"He was protecting his heart. And yours."

An image flashed through Irene's mind then, her father bitter and sullen. Nothing ever gave him pleasure—not a trip to the lake, not building a snowman in the yard, not laughing with her. "That's why he was sad all the time."

They sat in silence for a while, as quiet as it could be in a room packed with women. A few of them began singing "Chattanooga Choo Choo," then danced into the hall. Tessa, a Brit who usually slept near them, brushed her long, flaming-red hair over and over again.

Irene wrapped the corner of the sheet around her finger until it cut off her circulation. She longed to ask another question but was afraid of the answer. All Anita would tell her was that her father had to go. As a child, Irene had accepted that. Now she wanted more. At last, she opened her mouth and forced the words to march out. "Why did my father leave?"

"You remember coming to Manila. I suggested it, thinking the change in scenery would lift him from his melancholy. He got a job at a nightclub, starting as a bartender and working his way to a management position. Then, when the club changed hands, he began embezzling money from the new owner. The man caught him. Before the owner could file charges, your father fled to the jungle. I haven't seen or heard from him since."

"He left me, just like my mother."

Anita shook her head. "Not just like her. He cared about you. He didn't want to leave but didn't have a choice."

"No, he had a choice. He chose to leave me when he embezzled." Which brought up another question. Did Rand know the man her father had stolen from? "What was the club owner's name?"

"Your father never told me."

Irene's heart beat fast, and a loud buzzing filled her ears. Rand had told her of a man who embezzled from him. A man he would never forgive. "What was the name of the club?"

Anita bit her lip. "Goodness, it's been so many years. The, uh, the, um . . ."

Irene crossed her legs underneath her and leaned forward while Anita scrunched her forehead. "I can't remember. I thought it had something to do with a bird or an animal, but I can't recall."

A bird. Could she mean a butterfly? Irene whispered her next question. "Was it the Monarch?"

Anita nodded.

Irene's mouth went dry.

# Chapter Sixteen

*November 17*

Irene awoke, her heart racing, though she couldn't remember the dream. That was probably best. The early-morning light cast strange-shaped shadows on the classroom wall. She watched them, seeing the Japanese soldier running after her, grabbing her around the neck.

She turned away, trembling, shivering all over. She tried to put the images out of her mind, but she couldn't rid herself of the feel of the man's rough hands on her skin.

She flinched when Anita rolled over and rubbed her arm.

"What's the matter, Irene?"

"Just that . . . nothing. Nothing at all." She smiled even though her aunt couldn't see.

"Another nightmare?"

"The shadows on the wall frightened me. I see his face everywhere I look."

"'Whatsoever things are pure, whatsoever things are lovely . . . think on these things.'"

Irene knew the verse, but keeping her mind from those disturbing thoughts was impossible. "The storm seems to have subsided. Let me take you to the restroom, and then I'm going to check on the hut."

With all of the extra people in from their shanties, the line was longer than usual for the few toilets. Men hauled buckets of water.

A middle-aged man with a long, pointy nose and close-set eyes whistled, then raised his voice. "We have no water pressure, ladies. Please flush by dumping buckets of water into the bowl. And we need volunteers for mopping duty, especially on the first floor where the water is coming in."

Irene shifted her weight from one foot to the other as the line inched forward. Maybe after she returned, she would mop and try to keep her mind from wandering to places it didn't belong. Like the fact that Rand would hate her the instant he found out she was the daughter of the man who stole from him.

Her world tilted, and she leaned against the wall for support. The kitchen was closed during the storm and cooking impossible, so she and Anita were limited to a sleeve of crackers they had at the Main Building. She rode out the wave of dizziness.

She had grown fond of Rand. He had a strange sense of humor and an out-of-place optimism, but he made her laugh. Underneath that suave, upper-crust exterior, she had seen a glimpse of a man with a tender heart. She would hate to lose his friendship. And what that friendship might have become.

"You're very quiet this morning." Anita stood ramrod straight, her posture always perfect. Her mother had insisted her daughter be as elegant as possible, despite their reduced financial circumstances.

"I'm thinking."

"About what?"

She didn't want to tell her aunt what was bothering her. Didn't want to rip off that scab and expose herself in that way—and her growing feelings for Rand. She doubted Anita would approve. "The storm has me concerned. What about our hut? Mercedes and Charles were kind enough to help us build it, but we have no way to repair it. Besides, if I get one can of chili, maybe we can find someone with a stove on the patio to heat it for us." On each of the Main Building's two patios, enclosed on four sides, the Japanese allowed the internees to keep stoves and do a little cooking.

The gray-haired woman behind them, who stood on sticklike legs, shook her head. "Be careful out there, my dear. You never know what you'll encounter."

Anita smiled, a bit triumphant. "See, Irene, you need to listen to common sense. We know the dangers that are out there."

She kissed her aunt on the cheek. "What can possibly happen to me?"

A gust of wind tugged at Rand's hat as he sloshed through the receding water. He'd had all he could take in the Education Building, men piled on top of men. The reek of dirty bodies and dampness choked him.

There were still areas of the campus that were flooded. The stench the retreating water left was enough to make his eyes sting. Here and there, people milled about, but most had yet to return to their huts.

He recognized one young boy sloshing through the water, clinging to his mother's hand. "Hey, Paulo. Mercedes."

Paulo lifted his face. “Mr. Sterling, it sure rained.”

“Only ducks like that kind of weather.”

Paulo cracked a broad grin. “Mama and me were checking on the shanty. The water came up awful fast.”

“I bet you were a good help to your mother.”

The boy nodded. “When can we play soccer again?”

“Not until the field dries out.”

“Never, then.”

“It will. Then get ready to be pummeled.”

“No sir, it’s us who’s going to whoop you.”

Mercedes tugged on her son’s hand. “That is not a polite way to speak to an elder.”

Rand laughed. “He’s fine. We have fun together.”

“I’m going to get Mr. Tanaka to play on our side.”

The Japanese soldier? Irene had told him a bit about her neighbor’s interest in the guard. “You had better get somewhere dry now.”

Paulo and his mother continued on their way through the muck.

His heart ached for the children here. They didn’t understand. And for the children who didn’t have fathers or mothers. The nobodies. Those who were orphans, like Sheila King, watched over by the other women. What would happen to them after the war? Where would they go? He would be back in his mansion on Dewey Boulevard, but where would they live?

He shook off his melancholy and quickened his pace, eager to see what had become of his shanty. He had paid a handsome price for the workman to construct it, and he hoped his money had bought him the highest quality. Before the storm, he and many others had pounded metal stakes into the ground and tied their shanties down.

Some had ridden the typhoon well. Others had lost roofs and bore other signs of damage.

He worried more about the food he had stored in the shanty. With this much water, there were no guarantees that everything would survive. He had taken much of his stores to the Education Building with him, but he had been forced to leave some of it behind.

The sight that greeted him at his front door didn't make him happy. Though the roof had remained intact, water had poured over the top step and gushed inside. The rug was soaked and muddy. Perhaps he'd be able to dry it out and save it.

When he looked up, he stopped short. Mr. Covey stood in the middle of the little room, a kilo bag of rice hoisted on his shoulder.

Rand clenched his fists. "What are you doing here? Where are you going with that?"

The man's flaccid face reddened. "Mr. Sterling. I didn't expect you out in the storm."

"Of course you didn't. I would like answers to my questions. Now."

"Don't get upset. I thought I'd do you a favor since I was checking on my own place. I was merely moving the sack to a higher shelf to keep it out of the water."

Rand believed that like he believed his father was Emperor Hirohito. "And now for the real reason you have broken into my place."

Mr. Covey set the rice on the table and held up his hands. "Believe me or not, I'm telling the truth." He stared Rand in the face.

But Mr. Covey's brilliant-blue eyes were shifty, and the white scar crisscrossing his cheek stood out in contrast to his red face. His crooked nose lent an even more sinister air to him. Rand felt certain the man wasn't telling the truth. "I'm here now to check on my hut. It would be best if you leave. Immediately. And from now on, don't do me any favors."

The man nodded and beat a hasty exit.

Rand surveyed the room. Everything appeared to be in place, just as he had left it. As far as he could tell, Mr. Covey hadn't pilfered anything.

A knot hardened in Rand's stomach. The man was as slippery and as slimy as the mud that covered everything. Why, though, did the man have such an interest in him?

He secured his little home as much as possible and began the long walk through the mud back to the Education Building.

Home.

No, this place wasn't home. His mansion on Dewey Boulevard was. A grand staircase. Sparkling chandeliers. Heavy draperies.

He chafed, wanting to go back to those times with all of his heart.

Look at what had become of him. The war had robbed him of everything. Despite his connections and his work in accounting, handling the money needed to purchase rice and other supplies for the camp, he was another nameless face in this throng of thousands.

Then he thought of Anita and Irene. They were much worse off than he, yet they never complained. They didn't speak much about their reduced circumstances and never grumbled. How could they manage to keep such a stiff upper lip in such conditions?

In his mind, he heard Anita's prayers. Calming. Soothing.

He sighed. No use standing in the rain like this, thinking such philosophical thoughts. When they got out of here, he would resume the life he had before. He just wouldn't take so much for granted.

What a cliché.

But what a truth.

He found himself in Shantytown, a bit out of his way, but his legs had brought him here while his mind wandered. The huts here showed signs of more damage. More roofs gone. More walls with holes.

He lowered his head and forged onward, anxious to get back to the dry, if not stuffy, building.

A scream pierced through the howling of the wind.

The sound froze him.

~

Clenching her toes against the wooden soles of her *bakyas*, Irene turned toward the table in her shanty. She had to heft this bag of rice, their last precious bag, onto it. As it was, it had been sitting in water for who knew how many days and was probably spoiled.

A flash of bright green under the table caught her eye. She froze as icy fear settled in her stomach. The creature coiled, shooting out its black forked tongue.

Irene took a step backward, tripped, and fell onto the muddy floor. She attempted to scramble to her feet, but in the slippery muck, she couldn't get traction.

The pit viper slithered in her direction. She covered her mouth to stifle the scream building behind her lips, afraid to startle it. It fixed its glassy orange eyes on her. She imagined the pain she would feel at its bite, the numbness spreading through her body, the paralysis choking the breath from her.

She withdrew her trembling hand from over her mouth to draw in a little air, and the shriek she had held in burst out. "Help. Help! There's a snake in here!"

Not that she expected a rescue effort. Most of her neighbors had yet to return to their huts. "Help me!" The words tore from her throat.

The pit viper raised its head.

# Chapter Seventeen

Rand shivered as he stood in the drizzle in the middle of Shantytown. Another scream pierced the heavy air.

He started in the yell's direction, the slippery mud making sprinting difficult. More than likely it was an injured stray cat. Perhaps one facing a venomous snake. But the plaintive cry beckoned him. It could be a child. He picked up his pace.

The sound stopped.

He ran now, mud splashing his legs. At an intersection, he paused. Which way had the cry come from? He wished it would start again. Should he go left or right?

Should he bother searching? The cat could have met its end by now. He turned to the left, not certain of the direction. An insistence in his gut spurred him on.

The oppressive, humid air covered him. His threadbare cotton shirt clung to his chest. Sweat trickled down the side of his face.

Then he caught a quiet but insistent voice, its tones hushed.

"Our Father which art in heaven, hallowed be thy name." A sweet female voice, laced with pain, one with a familiar timbre.

He hurried toward the small shanty and flung open the door. Irene sat on the mud-covered bamboo floor, her long legs tucked tightly to her. He stepped forward. A wisp of her blond hair fell across her perfect but tearstained, dirt-encrusted cheek. Though she spoke to her Maker, her eyes were trained on a spot in the corner, not far from her.

Rand followed her line of vision. The perspiration on his skin turned to ice.

A bright-green pit viper wriggled toward her, ready to strike.

"Don't move."

Irene startled at Rand's voice, breaking off her prayer. She turned toward him, her blue eyes large in her round face. "Help me."

If he only knew how. "Just stay put."

A stick. That's what he needed. There were plenty of them littering the ground. He backed out with slow, deliberate motions, then turned and found an acacia tree branch snapped in half. Perfect.

He grabbed it and headed back for the hut, no plan springing to mind. When he was a boy, a snake had slithered into his family's compound and Armando poked it with a stick. He wished he remembered what else Armando did.

The snake inched ever closer to Irene. He didn't have time to waste. Stepping between the viper and its intended victim, he poked the snake. It hissed in anger and focused its attention on Rand with its creepy eyes.

"Run, Irene, run."

"I can't. The mud is too slippery. I have no traction."

"Are you hurt?" He didn't take his eyes from the creature.

"No."

"Then you have to get up." Another poke of the stick produced another venomous hiss.

"I've tried."

"I can't help you."

"You have to." Tears colored her words. "Or else I'm going to die."

"Their bite is rarely fatal."

"I don't care. With conditions here, it may well be. Please."

Rand moved forward, pushing the snake farther into the corner of the hut. It voiced its displeasure with the move. He gave it one more good poke and, in a single movement, dropped the stick, turned toward Irene, scooped her in his arms, and carried her from the hut.

Once outside, he dropped her without warning, and she stumbled to her feet. He reached to steady her.

Blond lashes framed her eyes, droplets of water clinging to them, her skin smooth and fair. Her nose was straight and upturned, her lips red. Even without makeup and with a smudge of dirt across her forehead, she was magnificent.

He leaned in to kiss her.

She stepped away with such abruptness that he stumbled. "What are you doing?"

"I'm sorry. I'm so thankful that you aren't hurt . . ." He crossed his heart. "It won't happen again."

"I'll hold you to that promise. Thank you, though, for rescuing me. I don't know what I would have done if you hadn't come along."

"Irene, Irene, and a snake so green. I've never seen a snake so mean."

"You're teasing me again." Her lower lip trembled.

He caressed her cheek. "I'm not, trust me. I wanted to make you laugh."

"There's nothing funny about a snake."

"True. They don't do cabaret."

She creased her forehead but didn't laugh at his joke.

"I gather you don't like them."

"No. Anita was bit once. I thought she was going to die." She shivered.

He clasped their damp hands together. "You're wet through. I'll walk you back to the Main Building."

"I still need to put our rice up higher. At least half of it is wet already."

He stepped into the hut. The snake had slunk to the other side of the room, away from the rice and the table. Rand hoped it would stay there. He kept his one good eye focused on it and avoided the worst of the mud.

Not turning his back on the viper, he hefted the almost-full bag of rice onto the table. It was twice as heavy as it should be. In no time it would be ruined. The wobbly table legs threatened to give way under the weight of it. Rand watched it for a moment before deciding he was satisfied it wouldn't collapse.

He wiped his hands on his pants as he emerged. "All done."

"Thank you. I just . . ." She stared at her stained blue dress and her muddy legs. Gorgeous muddy legs.

He forced his attention back to her face. "You're welcome. Now let's get you home."

She glanced around. For what? Then she flashed him the tiniest of smiles, a little dimple in her cheek he'd never noticed before. "That would be nice."

They started in the direction of the women's dorm.

"What are you doing out here on this lovely day?"

He appreciated her attempt at levity. "Because it was so ducky, I thought I'd take a stroll to my hut and find out if it's still standing."

"And is it?"

"Yes, for the most part. The floor is flooded, but it is still standing, and the roof held."

"That's good."

"The question is, what are you doing out?"

"That bag of rice. Rand, it's all we have. We didn't take it to the Main Building with us. I couldn't manage it with Anita. So I had to come and save it. I had to."

"Your life is more important than rice." He'd never met such a stubborn woman, one who never learned her lesson.

"Our rice is our life." Her lips pursed.

Jeepers creepers, he didn't think before he spoke. "Of course. I'm sorry."

"I'm fine." A rather fake smile lit her face, but he decided to drop the matter before he upset her further. Perhaps next time she would weigh her decision before embarking on a dangerous mission.

Like he should talk.

He sloshed beside her for a while. "The strangest thing happened to me when I was at my shanty."

She glanced at him. "What?"

"There was this man there. A Mr. Covey. He introduced himself to me when the typhoon first hit, although he acted as if he knew me quite well."

"Why would he be at your shanty? Is his nearby?"

"I have no idea. But he wasn't at the shanty, he was in it."

"In it. As in breaking in it?"

"He claims that he wanted to do me a favor and check on my

supplies for me while he was out. But he has these shifty eyes, much the same as your snake, but blue."

She sucked in her breath. "That was not my snake. But how odd that he would be in there. What do you make of it?"

He led her around a deep puddle. "I can't figure it out. Maybe he's nothing but a strange man, but my heart tells me it's more."

Irene sat at her desk in the censor's office and stared at the pile of notes stacked high. Everyone wanted to send a message after the typhoon, letting their interned friends and relatives know about damage and safety—or lack of it.

Though she tried, her mind refused to stay focused on the task in front of her. She had a difficult time memorizing the censored parts of the notes today. Instead, Rand and his almost-kiss dominated her thoughts. Was he developing feelings for her? And what were her feelings for him? She wound a curl around her finger.

They were from two different worlds—his glittery high society, hers plain and simple. And when he found out her secret, he would want nothing to do with her. Better to rebuff his advances and let him go now, while the going was easy.

"Irene, haven't you heard a word I've said?"

She snapped back to reality to find Mercedes leaning against her desk clad in a pretty red dress with beige polka dots. "Oh, Mercedes, I'm sorry. I didn't see you there."

"Didn't see me? What were you thinking about so hard?"

Heat rose in her face. "Nothing at all."

"I came to welcome you back from Santiago Hospital. And I heard your aunt is back too."

"Yes, she is and doing much better, thank you. Have you seen the Japanese guard again?" Just asking the question caused Irene's mouth to go dry.

"Yesterday. He walked Paulo and me to our shanty. He even gave Paulo a piece of peppermint candy before he left."

Irene cleared her throat. "Don't see him anymore. Don't talk to him. Don't get close to him."

"Why not?"

"Sit down and pull up close. I don't want the other girls to hear." Mercedes did as she bid. "The guard who arranged for my pass also produced a pass for me to be out in Manila. Foolish as I was, I went to Mr. Sterling's house to check on his houseboy. Anyway, the soldier followed me there and . . . well, he attacked me."

Mercedes's eyes grew large. "Attacked you?"

"Shh."

"Are you all right?"

"I got away. I don't know how, but I managed to escape. But you have to understand that these Japanese aren't nice. They pretend to be kind so they can trick us and take advantage of us. You have to be careful. Break off all contact with this guard." She grasped her friend's hands and squeezed.

Mercedes pulled them away. "But Mr. Tanaka would never do that. Never. He is too good. And he already knows where my hut is."

"You can't be too careful. The man who attacked me and who is kind to you might even be the same man. I am begging you. I don't want what happened to me to happen to you."

Mercedes patted Irene's hand. "It won't. I promise to be careful. But don't make generalizations. I'm sure this isn't the same man."

*February 1944*

"What did you say?" Rand stared at Irene, sure he must have heard wrong. He had met her and Anita on the grounds in front of the Main Building as they waited for an orchestra concert to begin. Families and couples filled the lawn.

"I am out of a job." Her face was pale, and she knotted her fingers together. "The new commandant has ordered the package line to be closed immediately. All vendors are to leave the grounds of Santo Tomas. That means no more messages will be coming in from the outside. No more notes to censor."

Rand walked in a circle and tried to control his breathing. "They can't do that to us. They can't cut us off like that." They couldn't cut him off from Armando. He rubbed the back of his neck.

"Our stipend will be increased to fifty-five cents per day."

"What good is that going to do us?" He flailed his arms. "Between inflation and no food from the outside, the money is worthless." He had never thought those words would pass from his lips.

The string quartet began to play. Only a few measures into their piece, the heavy iron gates clanged open and two trucks sped into the compound, sending the group gathered on the lawn scattering. Rand pulled Irene and Anita out of the way.

Irene held her hand to her heart. "What's going on?"

The same question raced through his mind. He shrugged. "With this new commandant, who knows. The war is going badly for the Japanese. He's more determined than ever to make us suffer."

He couldn't help but glance at Irene as he spoke. She and Anita, along with countless others, had lost much of their food stockpile in the typhoon. Now they had little money and no opportunity to replace their precious supply.

And yet they didn't complain. They had every right to. Some might expect them to. He thought they would. But they didn't.

How was it that they managed not to?

Several drab-dressed, dark-haired soldiers jumped from the backs of each truck and began tossing bags onto the ground.

"Rice!" someone in the crowd shouted.

Rand surged forward at the word, as did the rest of the throng, all determined to get their hands on as much of the precious commodity as possible. He could help himself, Irene, Anita, and countless others.

"Look out!"

Irene's shout didn't stop him. He drove forward, propelled by the force of the mob. He would run over his own grandmother to get some food for Irene and her aunt.

"Get back." A soldier shoved Rand in the chest, and he stumbled against Irene. Together they tumbled to the ground.

A bayonet affixed to the soldier's rifle glinted with the last of the sun's rays. "All stay away or we fire."

The group took several backward steps, Rand and Irene crab walking out of the guards' reach.

The orchestral music continued to float on the evening breeze.

Rand stood, then offered Irene a hand up. Hers was rough in his. He had never done hard work like she had.

The entire crowd stood still, breath held.

"Are they going to increase our ration?" Rand didn't miss the note of hope in Irene's voice.

"They must be. Why else would they bring in so much?"

"God has provided." Mrs. Markham's face shone as if heaven itself smiled on her. Perhaps it did.

He wrapped his arm around Irene's thin shoulders and watched as the Japanese unloaded the remaining bags of rice.

The soldiers then gathered around the stacks of burlap sacks, raised their arms, bayoneted guns in hand, and slashed open the bags. Rice flooded out, spilling onto the ground, mixing with dirt, trampled on by booted feet.

A collective cry rose. "No!"

Irene gasped. "They can't do that. They can't. What will we live on?" Tears tinged her words. "Anita, they're slashing open the bags of rice and spoiling it all."

Laughter rose from the throats of their captors.

Irene trembled in Rand's arms, and he clung to her all the tighter. "Those mosquitoes. Cruel, heartless. They intend to starve us."

# Chapter Eighteen

With no more work at the censor's office because of the closing of the package line, which included cutting off notes from the outside world, life turned dull and routine. Irene worked in the mornings in the kitchen, peeling vegetables such as *camotes* and cleaning the leafy *talinum*. She was allowed to take the peels home and use them to supplement the meager diet they got at the chow line.

Bile rose in her throat at the thought of all of that rice, spilled on the ground, useless, while men and women and children went hungry.

But this particular morning was difficult to get out of bed. The sun was already hot, and Irene hadn't slept well. She woke up grumpy and out of sorts.

"I wish we didn't have to stand for this twice-a-day roll call." She led Anita through the maze of cots and desks to the restroom line. "It's crazy. Another rule instituted just to cause more suffering. Let's hope the room monitor gets our count correct today. Twenty minutes is long enough. An hour and a half is too much."

Much of her consternation came from the fact that she was very worried about Anita. She wasn't eating enough and was showing signs of beriberi, especially swollen legs. Walking had become difficult for her.

"At least it's not snowing or raining today."

Irene sighed. "Don't you ever get discouraged or angry? You have a right to be. You are allowed to complain. Now that the Japanese have stopped the nightly music, it's the chief form of entertainment around here."

Anita flashed a half smile. "Of course I do. But then I remember all of the good things the Lord has done for me. I count my blessings every day. Some days, yes, it's difficult to come up with many, but I always do. Always."

"What would be on your list for today?"

"The sun is shining. The Lord gave us life today. We have a shanty where we can spend our afternoons resting."

Irene held up her hands. "Okay, I see now. You're right. I should count my blessings."

"And what would they be?"

She rubbed the back of her neck. "I have a job in the kitchen where I can get food. I have a roof over my head at night."

Anita laughed, and Irene was glad to hear the sound. "That's the spirit. God has been good to us. He hasn't neglected us. He clothes us and provides for us just as He does the lilies of the field."

But with their treatment at the hands of their new taskmasters, Irene wondered.

They finished their morning preparations and, after standing in queue for breakfast, lined up in the hall of the Main Building. Irene held Anita's elbow to support her. Anita's face paled and her legs trembled. Irene wished she had brought a chair with them.

As the soldiers came to inspect the internees, they were expected now to bow. Anita had forbidden Irene from doing so, saying they would bow to no man. She wished her aunt would relent. She usually sneaked a small dip of her head, hoping to satisfy the guard and to appease her aunt.

Today, as the armed soldier strode past, all of those around them gave the deep from-the-waist bow the Japanese demanded. Irene and Anita stood tall. The short but muscular man spotted them and made his way toward the two women. Irene's own legs began to tremble. She recognized the face.

"Bow." He gripped his gun, his knuckles white.

Anita shook her head. "We bow only to God."

A murmur rose around them. "Bow," a woman hissed. "Don't be stupid."

"Anita." Irene laced her words with pleading, remembering the pain he inflicted the last time she refused to bow.

But Irene's aunt remained stubborn. And she sent Irene a poisonous glare demanding that she not give in.

"It's him," she whispered.

"Bow."

Surely the Lord would forgive them if they bent at the waist just this once.

"I bow only to God."

"I have no use for your God."

Irene felt as much as heard the whack of the soldier's hand across her aunt's face. She gripped Anita's elbow and clenched her other hand. "She is ill." Her breath came at a rapid pace.

The soldier's hand connected with her own cheek. It stung and brought tears of pain to her eyes. Fear shot through her like an electric jolt.

Her stomach churned.

She stepped backward. What if he hit her again? What if he attacked her again?

"If she is ill, take her to the hospital. Next time I will not be so kind." With that, the soldier turned on his heel and stalked away.

Still shaking from head to toe, Irene turned to her aunt. "Are you hurt?" A gash marred Anita's bony cheek.

"I know you wanted to bow, but it is the right thing to do."

"There is one thing I agree with him on. I'm taking you to Santa Catalina as soon as we are dismissed."

❧

Rand pushed his way through the crowd of internees after they were let go from morning roll call. He heard the news that the guard slapped both Anita and Irene. Heat rose in his belly. From the time Rand was very young, Armando taught him never to hit a woman. Never. They were meant to be cherished.

He came upon them as they left the Main Building, not going in the direction of their shanty, but in the direction of the hospital.

The beast had hurt them. Rand clenched his fists.

He strode behind them and caught them in quick fashion. He touched Irene's shoulder, and she stopped and faced him. "What did they do to you?"

"It was him."

A tremor colored her voice. She didn't have to explain any further. After the attack at his home, the incident at the office building, and now this . . . He stroked her tanned, bare arm. "I'm worried about you."

She bit her small lip. "I'm much more concerned about Anita."

Her aunt shook her head, her honey-colored curls bobbing. "With a little rest, I'll be fine. She fusses over me too much." Blood oozed from a cut on her cheek.

"Irene's right." He lifted Anita off of her feet and headed toward the hospital. She weighed little more than a child. Irene had cause to be concerned. The brutes were starving even the women and children.

They entered the hospital, and the Army nurse got a wheelchair for Anita and swooped her off to visit the doctor. Irene sat in a straight-backed chair, and Rand settled in beside her. "How are you?"

"I wish she would have bowed. I don't want him to hurt her. I'm one thing, she's another."

Deep creases marred her face. He wished he could wipe them away.

"I don't want him to hurt either one of you."

Her blue eyes widened. "Don't get involved, Rand. I begged you before, and I'm begging you again. Don't make this situation worse for me."

He touched her smooth cheek, and she calmed. The last thing he wanted to do was to agitate her. "I promise."

He would do his best to keep that promise.

Would his best be enough?

"This will continue to be a problem twice a day for the duration. I have to figure out a way that she doesn't have to bow."

"Or be present at all." Rand swiveled in his chair so he faced her. "She is awfully thin and frail, Irene. Malnourished. Ill. Perhaps you can persuade the doctor to keep her here for a while. Patients aren't required to stand for roll call. At the very least, it will buy you time to either persuade your aunt to bow or figure out another way to keep her safe."

A smile broke across Irene's face, brighter than the Filipino sun.

She leaned over and kissed him on his cheek. A thrill ran through him at the touch of her lips on his skin.

"Has anyone told you that you're a genius?"

"A few people here and there, but I don't like to brag."

She gave him a playful swat on the arm. "No, I meant your plan is swell. I've been concerned about how thin Anita has become. I suspect she's not eating much to save food for me. But I refuse to allow her to sacrifice her life for mine."

"I'll make sure that both of you come through this thing. Before the gate closed, I purchased all kinds of eggs and limes and pork. I hired a woman to preserve the eggs in the limes and to cook down the pork and seal it with the fat. I'm only one man, and I don't need that much."

He sensed her distancing herself from him. "You were going to sell it. A businessman like you can't sit around the camp and not devise ways to earn a few pesos."

"Money means less to me today than it did in January of '42." Did he really just say that? But he did. And meant it. There was more to life than money. There was survival. "Please, let me take care of you." He clasped his hands as he spoke the words. They sounded like those of a man in love.

Could he be?

Dr. Young stepped into the waiting room. "Irene?"

She stood.

"I must talk to you about your aunt." He wrung his bony hands together. "She is suffering from beriberi and malnutrition. I'm very worried about her condition."

God wouldn't be so cruel as to take Irene's only family member.

He couldn't be.

He wouldn't be.

# Chapter Nineteen

"Mama, Mama, guess what I learned in school today?"

Mercedes held on to Paulo's hand as they made their way to their shanty after dinner. "What is that?"

"Two times two is four. I'm smart, Mama." He stood taller, and an adorable grin spread across his round face.

Mercedes smiled and tousled his curly brown hair. "You are for sure. What would I do without you?"

"You would have to eat all of our food by yourself."

Her son was like his father—practical. Charles had left them with a good store of provisions. Mercedes was thankful they weren't ruined during the typhoon. "That is true. You have to help me eat it all."

"But you could give some to Miss Anita. She's sick and needs some food."

Mercedes couldn't deny that. And, according to Irene, Anita's condition hadn't improved despite her hospitalization. "Yes, but you need to eat to become a big, strong boy."

Paulo stopped and flexed his arm. "See my muscle, Mama. I'm already the strongest."

"And so you are." She laughed as they arrived at their shanty, grateful they were now allowed to sleep here as the men had been able to do for a long while.

Her laughter dried up when she pushed open the flimsy door. A man sat on one of their two chairs. He scrambled to his feet when she entered. "Ah, Mercedes, I have been waiting for you."

She pushed her hand to her chest in an effort to stop the pounding of her heart. "Mr. Tanaka, you startled me. I did not expect to find you here." She remembered Irene's warning about the soldier who attacked her. Was he the same one? Should she trust him?

He bowed. "I am sorry to have frightened you. Please accept my apology. I have a little time off, and I didn't want to be seen lurking in front of your hut. It might make people wonder."

She laid their meal tickets on the table. "Yes, I suppose it would. Paulo, run along and see if William would like to play with you."

"Okay, Mama. I'm sure he will. He's my best friend." The door slapped shut behind him.

"Was there something you wanted?"

The Japanese soldier rocked back and forth on his feet. "Just to see you. I have been thinking about you and wondering how you have been faring." He stepped forward and held her hands in his.

Irene's warning again rang in her head, but his grip was firm. "We are well, thank you. As well as anyone here. We are hungry, and there is much disease."

"I am sorry about that. The next time I come, I will bring you a bag of rice. And vitamins and meat for your son." He took a step forward. "You look lovely tonight."

A strange, fluttery sensation filled her stomach. One she had once before, with Charles.

Or was it fear? She stepped back. He might be dangerous. Such a look of tenderness crossed his face. "One of your soldiers attacked a friend of mine a couple of months ago." She wished those words had not just popped from her mouth.

He paled. From the horror of the thought or from the revelation of his secret? "That is terrible. Who was this man?"

"The same one who was friendly to her and helped her get the pass to Hospicio de Santiago."

"Does she know his name?"

"No." She paused. Did she dare confront him? He promised to bring food and vitamins for Paulo. For her, she didn't care. But for him? She had to provide for her son whatever way she could. And Mr. Tanaka was that way.

But could she trust him?

He stepped toward her once more. She moved in his direction. When he was within arm's length, he drew her close and kissed her cheek.

Mercedes heard a gasp.

Irene stood in the doorway, red-faced. "How could you?"

Rand took the long way home from the chow line, through Shantytown, nowhere near Glamourville, in the hope he might see Irene. It had been a few days, and he missed her smile. Strange. He never missed any of his lady friends once the evening ended.

The only woman he had ever missed was his college sweetheart,

Catherine. And once he returned from the States to Manila, that feeling faded.

All of the other women he knew wanted to be near him only because of his social status. Neither Catherine nor Irene knew or cared how many clubs he owned or who his father was. And the thought warmed him more than he ever believed possible.

He started down the street Irene's hut was on. Paulo stood at the side of the road, a football in his hand.

Rand joined him. "What's the problem?" He noticed a group of boys playing a little bit away.

"My friends won't play with me."

Rand shrugged. "Why not? I like to play with you."

"Because sometimes Mr. Tanaka comes to visit us."

"The Japanese soldier?"

Paulo nodded.

Mercedes was hurting her son by speaking to the enemy. Didn't she realize the harm she was doing? The trouble she was bringing on not only herself but also her child?

"I'll play with you." Rand sprinted down the lane, waving his hand. "I'm open. I'm open."

Paulo threw the ball in his direction. Rand caught it, cradled it against his body, and ran at top speed toward the boy, allowing him to catch him.

"Okay, my turn to be the quarterback now. Go long."

Paulo raced a good distance away, and Rand tossed him the ball. The boy ran in his direction. Rand pretended he couldn't catch him.

"Touchdown." Paulo jumped up and down.

"Good job. You're a great player. It's their loss."

A woman shrieked. "That's him. That's him."

It couldn't be. The second time he heard Irene scream when he was in Shantytown?

The hysterics came from the hut next to hers. Mercedes's shelter. He tossed Paulo the football and raced toward the shanty. Upon flinging open the door, he recognized the curve of Irene's neck and hips and her mustard-yellow dress. He ran to her. "What's going on?"

He was in time to witness the back of a soldier disappear through the porch and into the gathering darkness.

"Get him. That's the man who attacked me." Fear filled Irene's high-pitched voice.

*No. No.* Rage bubbled in Rand's veins. "Wait until I get a hold of him." He sprinted for the door, but Mercedes blocked his path.

"Don't. It is not him."

Irene came alongside him. "You don't know. I do. It's him. He haunts me. Get out of his way. Our way."

Rand held her back. "Stay out of it."

"I'm in it."

"Let me by, Mercedes." Rand didn't want to lay a hand on her, but if she forced him . . . "He's getting away."

She stepped to the side. "He has gotten away. You would end up back in Fort Santiago if you went after him on the streets. I did you a favor."

Irene wept beside him, tears streaking her beautiful face. "Why did you let him go? Why would you do that to me?"

Mercedes collapsed onto a chair. "Because it is not him."

"Do you care more about me or some Japanese soldier?"

"He is only doing what his country demands of him. He has no choice."

Rand shook his head. "How can you defend him? If he's innocent, we'll find out soon enough. If not, we'll bring him to justice."

"It is better you not find him. Your justice will cost you your life. And maybe Irene's too."

Irene sniffled. "You kissed him. After I warned you."

Rand clung to Irene, more to keep himself upright. "You kissed him? You're playing a dangerous game. Think about your son, if nothing else. Already the other kids don't want to play with him."

Her black eyes blazed as she came to her feet. "I am. I did not invite him to kiss me. And it was only on the cheek. But if he can help me and my son survive this place, all the better. Friends matter little when you're starving."

"Yes, I can see how little friends mean to you." Irene spewed venom. "That soldier will hurt you like he tried to hurt me. You will be sorry you trusted him. And sorry you believed him over me. Sorry to lose a wonderful, years-long friendship."

Rand rubbed Irene's shoulder, holding her back as she leaned toward Mercedes. "Whether he is the man who attacked Irene or not, you are asking for trouble. If you continue to see him, it will not end well. Think about that if you are so concerned with helping him."

"Please listen to us." Irene turned and left the shanty.

Rand followed. "Wait up."

Irene, already past her own hut, spun around. "I can't believe she would do that to me."

"You're jumping to conclusions. You don't know that he's the same man."

"But I do. Every time I close my eyes I see his face. I will never forget it. And his missing finger. That man was missing part of a finger."

"Mercedes is a grown woman."

"I thought she was my friend. I warned her, and she still did this to me. I'll never be able to forgive her." Irene stalked by in his direction. He tried to catch her as she passed him, but she pushed herself free. "Leave me be. I need to be alone."

With that, she disappeared into her hut.

❧

"I don't know what I'm going to do, Bruce." Rand marched in step beside his friend and business colleague as they patrolled the wall separating Santo Tomas from the rest of the world. Darkness had fallen on the camp, and with it, small relief from the heat of the day.

"You're doing it by watching for theft. Curse those who steal from those who have so little."

"Not about that. Every time I see that soldier and imagine him with his hands on Irene, and now Mercedes, I want to strangle him."

Rand imagined Bruce rubbing the back of his neck with a weathered hand as he thought about the problem. "Be careful, Sterling."

"Trust me, I will be. But it's so unfair that a man like him gets to go free after attacking a woman."

"Nothing about war is fair."

"I thought all was fair in war."

"And love. Speaking of which, I've never seen you so hung up on one dame before. What do you see in her? She's a missionary girl. Sweet, but not your usual cup of tea."

Bruce didn't understand. "She's pretty swell."

"But a missionary? She'll convert you."

"No worries there." The best people he knew were Christians. Was it the worst thing?

"It's too bad Peggy went to the Los Baños camp. She would give you a dose of reality."

"Peggy doesn't hold a candle to Irene."

"Yes, she's beautiful in an innocent way, maybe, but you need a woman who fits into your lifestyle. Who understands the circles you move in. Flirt with Irene if you want to, but don't keep Peggy and the other prominent ladies hanging too long."

"Nobody said I'm ready to settle down yet."

"Sure. But if I invest in you, I don't want you to end up like Peter Williams."

"No problem there. I wouldn't do anything to risk my clubs."

Bruce clapped him on the back. "I knew you wouldn't."

A light mist began to fall. "Hopefully this rain will keep trouble down tonight." Rand had never caught an intruder, and he wasn't keen to start now.

The camp was far from quiet as Rand and Bruce patrolled, even though curfew had passed. From one hut came the sound first of Benny Goodman and then Kate Smith on a phonograph. Two men argued in another shanty over who had gotten the larger portion of a can of beans, a common problem these days. Rand thanked his lucky stars he could afford a private hut. Cats screeched in another location, likely in a food fight similar to the two men.

Bruce stopped at one point to rub his legs. "All this walking is killing my calves."

"Haven't you been taking your vitamin tablets?"

"The measly few that came in the one Red Cross box we've received so far? Have you seen what they're feeding us? And no more vegetable stand."

Rand's own legs ached from time to time. "Never thought I'd wish for some vegetables. Armando would laugh to know. Hey, why don't you go back to your shanty? Everything is quiet."

"Are you sure?"

"I wouldn't have said so otherwise."

"Thanks, I think I will. I'll return the favor."

"I'll make sure you do."

In the stillness of the wee morning hours, an owl hooted. A rustle came from farther down, and Rand's pulse rate climbed a few notches. He went to investigate. With the clouds hiding the moon, it was difficult to see. He switched on his flashlight and waved it back and forth, searching for the source of the sound.

Into the light popped a short, thin Filipino man.

Rand approached the man. The tilt of his head and the shape of his face were familiar. Then a glint of metal caught Rand's eye.

The intruder carried a knife. "Stay back."

Rand stopped about fifteen feet in front of the man. "Who are you?"

"You don't need to know." The man backed away.

"I do know you." The voice was familiar.

"No, you don't."

"Ramon, it's me. Rand Sterling."

The teenager lowered the knife. "Rand?"

"What are you doing here? How did you get in?"

Ramon snarled. "I prefer to keep that secret. What matters is that you have done nothing to help my father."

"I'm sorry. If I could do anything, you know I would."

Ramon took three steps in Rand's direction. In a flash, he tackled Rand, his arm around Rand's throat, the knife sharp and cold against his windpipe. "Take me to your hut. I'll make sure you help him."

"I got caught that night and sent to Fort Santiago. By the time I was able to contact you, sure that my note wouldn't be intercepted and put you in danger, they had closed the packet line."

Rand had to walk bent backward because he was taller than Ramon, but he didn't dare straighten, afraid of what the blade would do to his neck. "Listen, just tell me what you need and I'll give it to you. I promise not to turn you in to the Japanese. For your father's sake and because I know firsthand what Fort Santiago is like."

"I don't trust you anymore. This is how it will work. If you help me, you won't get hurt. But if you try to turn me in, you'll wish you were back in Fort Santiago."

*Fort Santiago will look like a picnic.*

It couldn't be.

It just couldn't be.

# Chapter Twenty

Rand's shanty lay not far from the spot where he found Ramon. About halfway there, Ramon moved the knife from Rand's throat to his kidneys. At least he could walk upright. If this had been any other miscreant, he would have taken the opportunity to escape from his grasp and turn the tables.

But he did want to help Ramon. Armando deserved that much.

They entered Rand's hut, and he turned up the lamp. "Please put that knife away. There is no need for threats. I'm willing to help you, but only if you get rid of that weapon. Your father came to my family as a teenager, much the same age as you are now. He has been loyal to the Sterlings for many years. He killed a snake for me, fixed all my toys for me, acted as a buffer between my father and me when I was a kid. I owe him."

"That's right, you do." Ramon's words hissed between his teeth. "He gave so much to you. All you did was take and take. You took time from him, time that should have been mine. Love that should have been mine. He deserved better from you. From your family. And I'm going to make sure he gets it. That we both do."

"Why resort to this?"

Ramon's eyes darkened, his voice singsong. "Poor Rand. You have it so bad here." He sneered. "You are not the only one in the world suffering, you know. My father is sick. There is no medicine, no food. We cannot afford anything for him. And what do you do? Sit in here and let the Red Cross feed you."

Rand bit his tongue to keep back the caustic words he wanted to hurl at the young man, to tell him the way it really was. "Where were you the night I tried to escape?"

"The place was crawling with Japanese the night before. If you wanted to get over, fine, but I wasn't going to get sent to Fort Santiago. Then where would my father be? I value his life."

"And now? Why come now?"

"You never showed up, so I had to. Just like you to let us down."

Rand thought he understood. The boy was young, frightened, and now, desperate. He moved to the kitchen area, Ramon not lowering his weapon. "What do you need?"

"Flour. Sugar. Meat."

Rand procured those items from his stores.

Ramon glared. "More."

"And what do you have to carry it with?"

Without putting the knife away, Ramon pulled out a canvas bag.

"How are you going to get it home? The Japanese aren't going to let you waltz through the front gate."

Ramon scrunched his thick brows together. "Do not worry about that. Just keep putting in there what I tell you to. More."

Rand obeyed the order.

"Now clothes and shoes."

"I don't have much."

Ramon chortled. "You have more than I do. They were in the Red Cross box."

"How do you know about that?"

"Word gets out and around." He waved his knife.

Ramon was not making this easy. Rand rummaged through the trunk in his sleeping area and came up with a pair of shorts and two shirts. He added the precious pair of shoes he'd received in the Red Cross package, even knowing that his size twelves would never fit any Filipino. At least he was finally able to help Armando.

Ramon lifted the sack, testing its heaviness, smiling at its weight.

Rand's heart broke that Armando's son had been reduced to stealing. "How is your father?"

"Hungry and sick, like the rest of us. You left, and he has no job, no money. Not that there is anything to buy."

"Those Japanese. Doing this to innocent civilians." Rand took a breath to steady himself. "Don't let your father know you've been here. It would not make him happy to know his son is stealing. And don't you dare come back. You are risking your life. It's not worth it."

"You owe us."

Rand was well aware of that fact.

Ramon slipped away into the darkness of the night as mysteriously as he had arrived.

∞

A few days later, as Rand made his way back to his hut from the chow line, he spotted Mr. Covey headed in his direction down Tiki-tiki Lane. And Mr. Covey spotted him. It was too late to turn around without being rude.

"Ah, Mr. Sterling, what a nice surprise running into you here." Covey stopped so they could shake hands, then fell in beside Rand.

"Did you have business you needed to take care of?"

The mustached man shook his head in an eerily familiar way. "I was out for a stroll, so it's no problem for me to go this direction. I was hoping to run into you, in fact. Let's walk together for a while."

In this moment, Rand wished his mother had not raised him to be such a gentleman. He would have made up an excuse and slipped from Covey's slimy grasp. "What can I do for you?"

The street was quiet, many having retired to their shanties for siesta. Covey rubbed his crooked nose. "I need to talk with you."

Rand didn't want to play games with this little, slimy man.

Covey directed them to Father's Garden, a peaceful spot behind the hospital. At this time of day, they had the place to themselves. "You are a man of mystery, Mr. Sterling."

"I didn't realize that." Covey was a mystery Rand was desperate to solve.

"You have a public persona. Gallant ladies' man. Gracious host. Shrewd Manila businessman. On top of the world. We all have the image we want to present to the public, don't we? It's who we want to be. We erase the negative and highlight the positive."

"I suppose that's true." Rand shivered despite the tropical midday heat.

"Do you have much that you want to hide?"

"No. I have conducted my life with integrity." Rand crossed and uncrossed his arms.

"But you don't deny that you enjoy the company of lovely young ladies."

"What is your point?"

Covey rocked back and forth on his feet. "You have been seen around the city squiring more than one debutante on your arm."

"Is it a crime that I haven't chosen one woman to be with?"

"You enjoyed the company of several coeds when you were at school in the States, didn't you?"

Rand sat in one of the wrought iron chairs in the garden and gripped the armrest with his left hand. What did this man know? "Mr. Covey, please tell me what you are getting at."

"Does the name Catherine McLeod mean anything to you?"

A vision of a beautiful brown-haired, brown-eyed woman sprang to his mind. She loved to laugh and had an amazing singing voice. In many ways, Irene reminded him of her. "What does Catherine have to do with anything? I haven't seen her in more than six years. We lost contact soon after I returned to the Philippines."

"Curious." Covey walked a circle around Rand, then stopped short in front of him. "Did you know that she has a six-year-old daughter?"

"Am I on trial?" Rand leaned forward, hearing his heartbeat in his ears.

"Yes. And you are guilty. You are this girl's father."

Rand ground his teeth. He and Catherine had made a mistake, but only once. This girl couldn't be his daughter. Catherine must have married right after he left. It would explain why she answered none of his letters. "You have no evidence."

Covey reached into his pocket and withdrew a photograph. Rand held it, scrunching his eyes to examine it. Hadn't he seen this picture before? Then he realized. Except for the ringlets around the cherubic face, the child looked like him.

His heart froze in a chunk of ice. All of the fight drained from his body.

"I can see by your face that you agree with my assessment."

"I will agree to nothing until I hear it from Catherine. And that won't happen until after the war."

"Funny thing about that." Covey reached into his pocket once more and handed Rand the paper he pulled from it.

With clammy fingers, Rand unfolded the sheet. The handwriting swam in front of his eyes. He didn't recognize it.

Dear Rand,

We made a mistake almost seven years ago. But to me, it was no mistake because it produced our daughter, Melanie. She is a beautiful child and the love of my life. I don't know how Mr. Covey located me, but he wanted me to write this letter for you. When I found out I was in the family way, I moved to Virginia to live with my aunt and uncle as their widowed niece. We are happy and have made a life for ourselves. Please understand, I'm not asking for anything. I have a job as a nurse that I love. My aunt watches Melanie when she's not in school. We have a good life that I don't wish to be disturbed. Mr. Covey wanted me to let you know. He said you deserved it, and I suppose he's right.

All the best to you,<br>
Catherine

Rand took a deep breath, trying to steady his nerves. A daughter. He had a beautiful daughter. His insides churned. He didn't know a thing about her. Was she like he was at that age?

And now that he knew the truth, he was stuck in this hole in the middle of the Pacific gone crazy.

Catherine didn't ask for money or support. She said she didn't want anything. But judging by the grin stretching across Mr. Covey's face, he did.

Rand balled the page in his fist. "You are a lying, conniving snake in the grass."

"You can't call me a liar when you have the evidence of the truth in your hand. It arrived in the Red Cross package a few weeks ago."

"Get out of my sight. Don't you ever come near me again, or I won't be held responsible for my actions."

"Now, now, Mr. Sterling, don't be hasty. You don't want this information to be made public, do you? It might damage your reputation with the well-heeled women of this city. You want to rebuild your clubs after the war. Well, the ladies won't be as willing to flirt with you knowing what might happen to them."

He recalled his conversation more than two years ago with Peggy. And recently with Bruce. They agreed that Peter Williams's dalliance would cost him his business. If the news got out about Catherine and Melanie, he'd never be able to get either of his clubs off the ground again. Bruce and John and even Father would withdraw their financial support. And Peggy would make sure none of her many friends would ever visit the club.

Then he would be nothing. A fate worse than Fort Santiago.

It wasn't Ramon who sent that second message. It was Mr. Covey.

"You wouldn't." He begged the heavens to let this man be bluffing.

"I would. But you can keep your little secret. It will cost you."

Rand felt like a boxer backed into a corner. "How much?"

"Not much, Mr. Sterling, not much. Nothing outright monetary. Just a stake in your business."

"A stake in my business? No. Out of the question. You will

never lay a hand on either the Monarch or the Azure. Do you hear me? Never."

"I don't like the word *never*. I have the power to ruin you right in my hands."

Rand had found it. A way to duck out of the corner. He held up Catherine's crumpled letter. "No, it's in my hands."

"Do you think I would be as careless as to not make a copy? The original is safely in my possession."

"My business lays in shambles, Mr. Covey. The clubs have been shuttered for more than two years."

"I have faith in you. If anyone can cause the phoenix to rise from the ashes, it's you."

What price would Covey demand if he never reopened the clubs? But that wasn't an option. Without the clubs, he was empty.

"I can't give you an answer right now. I need to think about this."

"There isn't much to ponder. If you value your business and your reputation, you will give me controlling interest in the Monarch and the Azure."

Rand sprang to his feet, his face inches away from Covey's. "Controlling interest? It's gone from business partner to controlling interest already?"

"If I were you, I'd make my decision by the morning or the price will rise again. To heights you might not like." Covey grinned a crooked grin.

Rand doubled over.

∞

Long into the night, Rand lay under the mosquito netting on his bed in the hut. A daughter. That made him a father. One thing he wasn't sure he wanted to be. The single life had been good to him. True, he was nearing thirty, but he liked having a different lady at his table each evening. He enjoyed being able to flirt with whichever girl he chose.

Catherine had been his one and only serious relationship. In a way, he supposed he loved her. She was sweet and innocent and the only girl he knew who wasn't all about furs and cars and diamonds. She was about people and her horse and laughing with her friends.

Real. Like Irene. It was one of the things that first attracted him to her.

Did Catherine hate him? Resent him for what he did to her?

And what about the girl? Did she know anything about him? What had Catherine told her about her father?

There was that word again. *Father.*

A role he felt completely inadequate to fulfill. He had missed her first smile, her first steps, her first words. Things that couldn't be replaced.

What was he going to do?

He flipped over on his mattress.

His businesses were on the line. Everything he had worked for these past seven years, all he had ever dreamed of. When he was young, his parents showed him pictures of themselves at these clubs, having a great time. He wanted to be in the middle of the action. Important, like them. Even at ten years old, he knew he wanted to own and run clubs like those.

All at stake now. Because of one small mistake, everything he ever wanted was at risk.

About three o'clock in the morning, he gave up on sleeping. He rose and sat on the porch, staring at the stars and the moon hanging in the sky.

He needed to decide in the next five or six hours what was most important in his life—his Philippine dream or his daughter in Virginia. Or Irene.

What would Irene think?

No, she could never find out.

He buried his head in his hands. A missionary would never forgive him for his indiscretion. She would shun him, and he would never see her again. The thought made him sick, then made him sit back in his chair.

His feelings for Irene were similar to those he'd had for Catherine. Maybe even stronger because when he didn't hear from her after his return to the Philippines, he didn't mourn the loss of that relationship for too long.

How long would he mourn Irene? A day? A week? A month?

The difference was that he and Catherine were an ocean apart. He and Irene lived on the same university campus. He wouldn't be able to get away from her. She would haunt him.

And every time she passed his way or he caught her eye at roll call, his knees would go weak.

What should he do? Was there a right or wrong answer in this mess?

He had never been a praying man. Armando had tried to take him to mass a few times, but Mother and Father had forbidden it. Right now, though, he wished he could offer up a few words on his own behalf.

It couldn't make matters worse, that's for sure.

He knelt beside his chair as Armando had always knelt when he prayed. "God, please help me. I don't know what to do. I need to figure out a way to save my business. Show me the right thing. Amen."

He sat back on his haunches and waited for an idea to strike. For something, anything, to happen.

Nothing did. The heavens remained silent. No lightning bolt lit the sky. No meteor fell to earth. No choir angels sang.

Rand rose from his knees and paced the small porch, mussing his hair and rubbing his eyes.

If God wasn't going to answer him, he had to come up with the solution to the dilemma himself. Before, solving crises had never been a problem. If the clubs encountered any difficulties with suppliers or staff or customers, he knew how to handle them. A calm demeanor, a firm tone of voice, a confident carriage. Most often it got him what he wanted.

Then again, he'd never been at quite such a disadvantage. In the past, he never would have lost the upper hand. That was key.

Covey had him over a barrel, for sure.

Thoroughly exhausted and thoroughly defeated, Rand made his way back to bed. If he wanted to keep control of his clubs, if he wanted to woo Irene, he knew what he had to do.

# Chapter Twenty-One

Mercedes shifted her weight from one foot to the other as she stood in the hot kitchen, her paring knife grasped in her hands. The pile of *camotes* waiting to be peeled beckoned to her as her stomach rumbled and growled. Every part of her wanted to slip one in her apron pocket and take it to Paulo. Every part but her conscience. Was it wrong to steal food if you were starving to death?

Even with Mr. Tanaka's help and Charles's forethought, they were hungry. She worried most about Paulo. A growing boy like him needed proper nutrition to become a healthy man. She remembered her father, struggling with a large family to feed and no funds with which to do so. He had wasted away before their eyes.

She wanted so much better for her son. Would fight for that for him.

She ran the knife over the orange-colored peel, careful to leave as much flesh as possible. The internees needed every calorie, every bit of food they could manage.

Irene worked beside her, her lips drawn into a thin line, puffy dark bags under her eyes. She tipped her head to the left and then to the right and gripped her paring knife so her knuckles were white.

The pile of peeled *camotes* grew until they were both down to their last few. "I didn't mean to hurt you."

Irene dropped the knife and bent to retrieve it. "I warned you."

"He's been kind to me and Paulo. He helps us. Helps my son."

"That doesn't make a difference. He was kind to me too. To get what he wanted."

Mercedes sighed and let her hands fall still. "If he wanted to hurt me, he's had plenty of opportunities. I don't believe it's the same man." But she thought of his advances, the way he kissed her.

What would be the price for his kindness?

"I will never forget him. He is missing a fingertip on his right hand."

Mercedes leaned against the sink, then straightened. "Many men are missing fingertips. That doesn't make Mr. Tanaka unique." She wasn't sure she believed her own words.

"Why won't you listen to me?" Irene stabbed her knife into the heart of the *camote* in her hand, her fair face reddening.

"Look at me. I am a woman alone here. I have my son to think of, to feed and care for. With Charles gone, I need all of the help I can get. Befriending a Japanese guard ensures our survival. At the least, aids in it greatly." She began working once more.

"Don't be so sure. Rand is right. The game you play is more dangerous than Russian roulette." Irene wagged a long finger at her.

"If I play it right, I win." Mercedes tucked a stray strand of hair behind her ear. She had to win.

"He will hurt you, sooner or later. Spare yourself that trouble. Rely on God."

"The heavens are silent now." God felt very far away, like He had brought them to this camp and forgotten about them.

"Do you know what Anita would say to that? 'The Lord will open the heavens.'"

"I can't wait around for Him to do so. In the meantime, my son and I will die. Don't condemn me."

"He's a monster. There are other ways to survive. Many other ways."

"I do not have a wealthy patron like you." Mercedes's voice rose. Another peeled *camote* hit the pile.

Irene sucked in her breath. The barb hit its mark. "Money doesn't make a difference anymore."

"Exactly my point."

"If you were my friend, you would understand what he did to me and stay far away from him. I can't be around you if he's lurking behind your hut. And next to mine. How will I ever sleep?"

"I'm sorry, Irene. I truly am." And she was. She hated to lose Irene's friendship. She, Irene, Anita, and Charles had spent many pleasant evenings talking and laughing. Most of the other women in the camp shunned her because of her relationship with the Japanese soldier. She had thought Irene, a Christian, to be different.

But could there be a chance Irene was right? How far should she trust Mr. Tanaka?

Irene rubbed the back of her neck after Mercedes stormed from the kitchen. From now on, she would have to sleep in the relative safety of the Main Building. How could she even go to the shanty alone? Her attacker might show up anytime.

How could Mercedes do this to her? Did she crave the attention so much she would risk her reputation and perhaps her life? Or did she sympathize with the Japanese?

By rote, she whittled away the remainder of the *camote* peels and slipped off her gingham-print ruffled apron. On her way out the door, she filled the pot from home with vegetable peels to supplement her meager diet.

The sun shone with a brilliance that belied the grim reality of Santo Tomas. She didn't need to tend to her garden plot right away, so she took a detour to Father's Garden. After her conversation with 0ees were turning over as much land as they could to grow food for themselves, but Father's Garden remained untouched.

For now.

By the time Irene walked the short distance past the washing troughs, she was tired. The lack of food along with the physical labor took its toll. Even the young, like herself, didn't have the stamina they did before the new food restrictions.

She turned the corner of the Annex and saw two men huddled together at the far end of the garden. One's wavy, light-brown hair struck a familiar chord. He stood a full head taller than the other man. He was thinner these days, but so were they all.

Rand.

What was he doing here? And who was that man?

They were so deep in conversation they didn't notice her. She didn't hear their words, but she detected agitation in Rand's voice. The shorter man turned away. Rand scurried to cut him off. He shook his finger in the man's face. The man returned the gesture. Rand nodded and bowed his head, his hands limp at his side.

The man left.

Irene gave Rand a moment before making her way to him. "Rand."

He lifted his head, sadness brimming in his eyes. "Have you been here long?"

"I only just arrived. I'm taking the long route home from the kitchen." She held up her pail. "Who was that man?"

"Mr. Frank Covey."

"The man who broke into your shanty?"

"That's the one."

"You were agitated. What was he saying to you?"

Rand scrubbed his long, thin face. She loved the cleft in his chin. "It's complicated, Irene. A delicate situation that I don't want to explain."

"I'm not smart enough to understand, you mean."

"You are much smarter than any of my usual circle of women."

"Is that a compliment?"

"If you want it to be. But this story has more twists and turns than a mountain road."

Why was he so evasive? "Who is this Frank Covey?"

A crease marred his forehead. "I believe he's the man who has been threatening me."

Irene grabbed his upper arm to steady herself. "Why?"

"Why do I believe it?"

Irene nodded, unable to force any more words through her tight throat.

"Just some of the things he's said to me. He's a slippery fish, that's for sure."

A thought raced across her mind, and she relaxed a bit. "But that note came from the outside."

Rand bit the inside of his cheek. "True. But that doesn't mean he couldn't have had a friend on the outside write and deliver it."

"What reason would he have to do that to you?"

Rand twisted his hands and directed his gaze downward. "I don't know."

She thought he did. "Maybe you're jumping to conclusions."

He shrugged. No, he did know why Mr. Covey threatened him. He knew but refused to share with her.

Much more was going on than he was saying. They both had secrets.

Goose bumps broke out on her arms.

# Chapter Twenty-Two

*April 1944*

Irene stood in the chow line, waiting for the meager meal of rice and beans, tapping her tin plate against her thigh. The intense late-afternoon sun beat down on her, and rivulets of sweat tracked down her face.

She dreamed of a cool stream, the water trickling in from the mountains, the brooks converging into a river that then plunged in a deafening spray to a placid lake. She imagined herself in her green-and-black swimming suit, the chilly water washing over her hot body, cooling, soothing, relaxing.

Tessa Wainwright, a friend from the Main Building whom she'd been working next to in the kitchen lately, nudged her. "Where were you off to, love?"

"To this beautiful waterfall near where Anita and I ministered. If you come back here after the war, I'll take you there. It's the most beautiful place God ever created."

"What I want right now is shepherd's pie." Tessa tucked a stray strand of red hair behind her ear. "The ground lamb in a dark, rich gravy, the corn golden and sweet, the mashed potatoes creamy and browned and crisp on the top. Just imagine digging your fork into that, the crust crunching, the potatoes melting on your tongue."

Irene laughed. "Stop it. You're making my mouth water."

"When I eat my dinner, that's what I'm going to imagine. I can taste it already. Now if only this line would move along. What about you? What's for dinner tonight?"

"Christmas ham, salty and sweet at the same time, and green beans browned in butter and sautéed with almonds." Irene had to swallow the saliva gathering on her tongue. "And cherry Jell-O with a dollop of real whipped cream on the top."

"Good afternoon. Miss Reynolds, I believe?"

Irene spun around to find that a short, thin man with a dark mustache and a scar across his cheek had appeared at her side. She hadn't seen him before. Or had she?

"Hey, mister, you're cutting in line." The pimply faced teenage boy behind Irene and Tessa objected to the man's presence.

He nodded to the girls. "I'm with them, if that's agreeable to you."

Tessa didn't give Irene a chance to open her mouth. "Sure, it would be swell to have you join us, love. I don't believe we've had the pleasure. I'm Tessa Wainwright, from England via Hong Kong, and you were correct. This is my friend Irene Reynolds. Have you two met before?"

They had, Irene was sure of it, but she couldn't place him. The look in his blue eyes, though, gave her the willies.

"A friend pointed you out and told me your name. It is a pleasure to formally make your acquaintance."

"Which friend was that?" The second the words came out of her mouth, Irene's stomach took a dive over that waterfall. This was the man with Rand in Father's Garden. The man Rand thought was threatening him.

"Rand Sterling. A business associate of mine. And I'm Frank Covey."

"Rand told me about you."

"Did he now?"

Irene clutched her plate so tightly she was afraid she might bend it. "Yes. He said you have a complicated relationship."

Mr. Covey's mustache twitched underneath his crooked nose. "You might say that. In fact, that is a good way to describe it. But I like Mr. Sterling and admire his business acumen."

Irene wished Mr. Covey would go away.

"Irene is sweet on Rand."

Irene stepped on Tessa's foot. "That is not true. We are friendly acquaintances, nothing more. He was at Hospicio de Santiago at the same time as my aunt. He has been good to me and Anita, and we appreciate his kindness."

"He is a generous man. One of his many fine qualities."

"It is curious to me that, though you were business acquaintances on the outside, Rand didn't mention you to me until a short time ago." She crossed her arms against her chest, her metal plate against her middle.

Mr. Covey rubbed the bald spot at the top of his head. "If you aren't that close to Mr. Sterling, why would he? Has he mentioned to you everyone he knows?"

The man had a point, but Irene's skin itched. "This heat has gotten to me. I'm not feeling all that well. I believe I'll visit my aunt for a while. I'll see you later, Tessa. Good day, Mr. Covey."

Before either of them could stop her, she hustled away.

But Mr. Covey's laugh as she left sent a shiver up and down her spine.

ℊ

Irene kept her head down as she hurried across the campus toward Santa Catalina. She hated to leave Tessa in the lurch with Mr. Covey, but she couldn't stand to be in his presence one minute longer. She would give Tessa her last can of chili as a thank-you gift to make up for her abrupt departure.

She needed to speak with Anita. Perhaps a little perspective would help her sort out the situation and help her decide if she should speak to Rand about Mr. Covey. If they were involved in a shady deal, Irene would be better off staying far away from Mr. Sterling.

Besides, if he ever found out who she was, he would want nothing to do with her.

Having walked this path a hundred times before, she didn't watch where she was going and slammed into something solid.

Not something. Someone. Someone with blue knee-length shorts and hairy legs. Her gaze traveled upward. Someone with a sunken stomach and light-brown hair on his chest.

She gasped when she saw his face. "Rand." Heat rose in her cheeks—and not from the afternoon sun.

"Irene. What a pleasure running into you here." A smile graced his entire face, like he meant what he said.

"I am so sorry. I-you-you usually wear a shirt." Why on earth had she blurted that out?

"I wanted to get a tan."

She raised an eyebrow.

"Actually, I'm saving it for a special occasion. Like escorting you to the camp's dance on Saturday night. A special treat from the Japanese. Magnanimous of them. That is, if you would be comfortable in my arms."

If possible, her face grew warmer. Her hands sweated, but Rand's embrace would be nothing like that of the Japanese soldier's. He would be gentle and careful. She realized she wanted him to hold her and to protect her. "I'd like that. Thank you."

"Good." He stood with one hand on his hip. "Where are you off to in such a hurry?"

"To visit my aunt."

His mouth danced as he tried to hold back a smile. "With your plate?"

"I had a strange encounter in the chow line. Your Mr. Covey cut in and invited himself to dinner with Tessa and me. Isn't that the man I saw you so deep in conversation with that day?"

"Ah yes, Mr. Covey."

"He said you told him about me."

"I never did." Rand's eyes were large. "I never told him your name or who you are."

"What aren't you telling me?"

"Nothing. Just stay away from him."

"I did. I left right away because he made me uncomfortable. You still believe he is the man threatening you?"

"Not believe it. Know it."

"He admitted it to you?" Squeezing milk from a bean was easier than getting information from this man.

Rand grabbed her forearms with a tight grip. Her heart beat faster than an Olympian running a race. He released her. "I'm sorry." He stroked her blazing cheek. "But listen to me. Please drop the subject. Let's never speak of Mr. Covey again. Just tell me if he is anywhere near you or if you see him doing anything unusual or suspicious."

"Rand, you're frightening me." A vise gripped her midsection. "What is he holding over your head?"

"I told you not to ask. I will not answer. Ever. Don't badger me or pester me because I won't tell you."

She wanted to stomp her foot. Never had God made a creature as stubborn as the man in front of her. Instead, she clenched and unclenched her fist and shook her head.

He had the gall to laugh.

"What is so funny?" she asked through gritted teeth.

"You. I think I finally got the best of you."

She decided to let him think that. True, he had said not to ask him what Mr. Covey was holding over his head. But he never said she couldn't ask Mr. Covey himself.

Over the next few days, Irene made a point of being in the dinner chow line at the same time every day. As she waited today, she stood on her tiptoes, searching for a bald head in a sea of bald-headed men.

Tessa tugged on her arm. "What are you doing? Are you looking for someone?"

"Yes, Mr. Covey. If you see him, please let me know."

Tessa felt Irene's forehead. "Are you sick? The other day you couldn't get away from him fast enough, and today you are searching him out. What is going on, love?"

"You wouldn't believe me if I told you. I just want to speak to him."

Tessa squealed, and her green eyes shimmered. "You like him."

"I do not." Irene shook her head so hard she thought it might fly right off of her shoulders. "He's old enough to be my father." She grimaced.

"Admit it. Your face changes when you talk about him."

"Not in a good way, I imagine. I need information from him, information Rand won't give me. I've decided to go directly to the source."

"Getting the goods on Rand. Bangers and mash, it's him you like."

"Stop it, Tessa. Not all of life is about catching a man. Women can make their own way. Look at Anita." Or her own mother. No, she was a bad example.

"And look at all the women in this camp with men to take care of them and to see to their needs. Wouldn't that be swell?"

What would be swell would be having her father here, taking care of her. Like he should be. She couldn't erase the image of that little girl in her daddy's arms. "Look, I think I see him. Over there. Keep my place in line." Irene made her way toward the little man striding in their direction, his chin high. "Mr. Covey."

Confusion suffused his face for a moment before recognition dawned along with a crooked grin. "Miss Reynolds, what a pleasure to see you so soon again. I trust you are well?"

"I am, thank you. Tessa—Miss Wainwright—and I were wondering if you would like to join us today. I want to apologize for leaving the way I did earlier in the week."

"I would love to dine with you, but you don't need to make the overture as an apology. You couldn't help it if you weren't feeling well." He walked with her in Tessa's direction.

"Just a touch of enteritis."

"Well, we all have that, don't we?"

"I mentioned to Rand that I saw you on Monday."

"Ah."

"He doesn't recall telling you about me."

Mr. Covey waved his hand, dismissing her words. "We don't remember everything we say, do we? He must have forgotten that part of the conversation. We were discussing other serious matters."

She decided to play a bit coy and see if that would get him to open up. Tessa did it with great success. "Serious? How serious?"

"Nothing for you to worry about. Business and things you wouldn't understand."

Irene bristled, biting back the hurt at the insult. "Whatever it is, Rand is very concerned and preoccupied."

Mr. Covey nodded. "I should think he would be. The matter is very distressing to him."

"And I would like to be able to help him, but I can't if I don't know what is troubling him. I'm sure he doesn't want to burden me with his affairs, but he has been good to me, and I would like to return the favor."

"You choose your words well, Miss Reynolds." Mr. Covey coughed, and it sounded to Irene like he was covering up a laugh. "I don't want to discuss private matters with you behind Mr. Sterling's back. That wouldn't be ethical."

They returned to the line.

"Miss Wainwright, what a pleasure to see you again." Mr. Covey kissed the back of Tessa's hand, and she giggled. Irene slapped a mosquito and scratched her arm.

"Your mustache tickles. Have you told Miss Reynolds what's bothering Mr. Sterling?"

Again, Irene stepped on Tessa's foot. The girl had no filter on her mouth. Irene would be sure never to share a secret with her.

"As I told her, she needs to speak with Mr. Sterling about it herself. I would never betray a friend's confidence. But I do believe she would be very interested in what he has to say."

One way or another, Irene would discover Rand's secret.

❧

Rand strolled from his shanty in Glamourville toward the Education Building where he had left his razor. These days he only shaved occasionally. What was the point? It took too much energy. He decided that though the dance was still five days away, he should start shaving regularly to be rid of any razor burn before the big day.

He whistled a little tune as he wound his way through the huts and out to the road that ran in front of the Main and Education Buildings. The commandant had his headquarters between the two.

He hoped Irene would drop her questioning about Mr. Covey. If she went snooping, Rand would lose her for sure. He had to protect his secret. She couldn't find out. The world couldn't find out. His social standing, his position in the community, his clubs—they were all at stake.

And he wasn't willing to let any of those slip through his fingers.

As he approached his dorm, he noticed a commotion near the commandant's headquarters. There was shouting and screaming. Little children screaming.

He turned left and hustled to see what was going on. Children were gathered in a cluster, a soldier shouting at them. Other guards made their way to the trouble spot.

What did the Japanese intend to do to these kids?

Blood pounded in his ears by the time he reached the gathering crowd. "What is going on?"

"Who are the parents of these children?" The soldier spoke perfect English.

Rand sucked in his breath when he recognized the pockmarked face. A flick of his eye confirmed the soldier's missing fingertip.

His insides froze despite the sweat pouring from his face.

And they turned even colder when he spotted Sheila King's black head in the group of half a dozen or so children herded together by two other guards.

"What have they been doing? Why are you holding them?"

"They have stolen food from the commandant's garbage bin. You have been warned that this was to stop, yet we find these young ones here. Who are the parents? You do not want to see your children hurt." The man spoke in detached tones, void of any emotion save anger.

A couple of the adults who had gathered stepped forward. A few other of the adults jogged off, either in an attempt to escape possible punishment or to find the offenders' fathers and mothers.

Then Sheila began to cry, huge tears running down her peaked little face. "But I don't have a mommy or a daddy." Even from the distance of several feet, Rand witnessed her tiny body trembling.

Fear radiated from her. He couldn't leave her alone.

The word *punishment* zipped through his mind as fast as an electric current. And just that fast, it disappeared. "I'm responsible for her."

The crowd gasped.

# Chapter Twenty-Three

"Mr. Sterling." Sheila broke from the guard and raced to hug Rand's leg. Her tears soaked his shorts. "Thank you for rescuing me. I was so scared when that soldier started to yell at us. And then I don't have a mommy or daddy to take care of me."

He bent down and stroked her dark, silky hair, aware of the gaze of the crowd—and the guard—on him. "I couldn't leave you all alone. Were you stealing food?"

Her trembling resumed. "I'm so hungry." The words came out in the barest of whispers.

He dropped to his knees. Those rotten Japanese, starving little kids. Kids who just wanted to survive and who had been reduced to foraging for scraps from the garbage to do so. "Don't you worry. From now on, I'll make sure you have plenty. If you're hungry, you come to me."

She nodded and placed a kiss on his cheek. The many kisses he had received from fawning admirers paled in comparison. Never had one been so sweet.

He stood and grasped her hand, planning to return her to the Annex where she lived before heading to his quarters.

"Stop."

He obeyed the guard's order. The soldier stepped in front of him, his face mere inches from his. The smell of sake was strong on the man's breath. "The child may go. You, however, as the responsible party, will be punished, as promised by the commandant."

He released his grip on Sheila. "Go home now."

She nodded, and after he gave her a small push, she raced away.

Rand felt the gazes of those gathered.

The soldier sneered. "You have been warned."

Rand did vaguely remember the announcement made over the loudspeaker. Not having children, he didn't pay any attention to it.

He grabbed Rand by the upper arm with no effort at gentleness. "The commandant will have the final say as to your sentence."

Now even his sweat turned cold. He rubbed the knuckles of his right hand. He tried to block out the memory of anguished screams.

Was he to return to Fort Santiago?

The guard led him the short distance to the commandant's office. The soldier bowed before the stocky Japanese man in control of the camp. His dark eyes were narrow and his mouth drawn into a hard line. He spoke in Japanese, the tone of his words harsh.

Rand's captor answered him in the same tongue.

What could they be discussing? His execution?

The exchange went on for a minute or so. To Rand, it was a lifetime. He locked his knees to keep them from shaking. What trouble had his impetuous words brought him?

Then he thought of Sheila's tears and how she had clung to him.

No matter what happened to him, he would do it again. Just to protect her.

The commandant stood and leaned over the desk, his nubby fingers splayed on top of it. "Three days in camp jail. Next time, not so nice." With a wave of his hand, he dismissed Rand.

It was all he could do to stay erect, his relief was so great.

The soldier led him away to the building that housed prisoners on-site. The internee committee used it to hold their fellow detainees accused of such crimes as theft. Compared to Fort Santiago, it was a palace. No putrid odors. No bloodcurdling screams. No torture chambers.

For Sheila, it was all worth it.

Then his world went black.

# Chapter Twenty-Four

Irene stared out of the hospital window as the nurse recorded Anita's vital signs. Below the window, the internees went about their jobs. The children continued their schooling, though adult classes had ceased as people were too tired after work to try to think. Instead, basic survival held more importance as women tended the gardens and men hauled water to the shanties.

Thank the Lord, her aunt was stable. She hadn't lost any more weight. But neither had she gained any. She remained weak and frail. For the time being, the doctor allowed her to remain here, and Irene was grateful. This way she didn't have to worry about Anita not bowing to the guards.

But if there was an epidemic, Anita's bed would be required, and they would be back to the same problem as before.

*Take therefore no thought for the morrow: for the morrow shall take thought for the things of itself.* Irene remembered the verse Anita quoted to her often. The words of Matthew were true enough.

The nurse finished her work with Anita and moved on to another patient. Her aunt sat up in bed and rearranged her covers to hide her bony legs. "Tell me about this dance tonight. What will you wear?"

"Tessa is lending me the prettiest green dress you ever saw. It's the color of the leaves in the canopy after a rain, sleeveless, with a sheer lace overlay and belted at the waist. She made it herself.

"I know you don't approve, but I'm looking forward to the dancing. Tessa has been helping me because Rand is an expert dancer. I promise to leave plenty of daylight between us."

"I hear the excitement in your voice and the tenderness when you speak of him. I'm concerned."

"Concerned? Why?"

"You're growing attached to this young man."

"He's a good man, Anita. Look at what he did for Sheila." Irene couldn't believe Rand stood up for Sheila knowing the Japanese guards had threatened punishment. "He's not the same person who zipped around Manila in that red convertible."

Anita nodded. "That was an amazing act of self-sacrifice. But does he know about your father?"

Irene wiped her damp hands on her skirt. "No. And I don't want him to find out. I'm not attached to him. When the war is over, we will go back to our old lives. He moves in a different sphere than me. This is a friendship. Nothing more."

Even as she said the words, Irene knew she lied.

By the look Anita flashed her, brows furrowed, she knew it too. "Let me ask you the most important thing. Is he a believer? Does he know and love the Lord and seek to follow Him?"

Irene twirled a curl around her finger and let it spring back. "I don't know. I don't think so, but I'm not sure."

"Then, as far as I am concerned, he isn't a Christian. When a man follows Christ, he doesn't hide his faith under a bushel."

"Don't worry. Like I said before, this is nothing more than a friendship. He has a good heart."

"A good heart does not a believer make."

"After the war, he will find a wife, and Lord willing, I will find a husband."

"But the war hasn't ended yet. Be careful, before you discover yourself entangled with him too much to get free. You know I was married for a brief time."

"Yes." Irene learned never to ask Anita questions about that time in her life before she lost her sight.

"I had been brought up in a Christian home and had given my heart to God at an early age. My parents never had a moment's trouble with me. Walter, your father, was a different story. Oh my, he was a handful from the time he could crawl.

"And then Nigel walked through the doors of the office where I was working at the time and into my life. He was the most dashing, handsome man I had ever seen." Anita's voice took on a dreamy quality. "He was sophisticated and taught me more about the world than I ever cared to know."

Irene had a difficult time picturing her straitlaced aunt doing anything even close to bad.

"All appeared to be well on the outside during our courtship. He said the right words and did the right things. He was polite to my parents and kind to my brother. He didn't attend church with me but did pray before meals. My parents warned me, but I refused to be dissuaded. We eloped."

Irene sucked in her breath. "Eloped?"

With a twinkle in her eyes, Anita laughed. "It was quite the scandal. Walter applauded me when he found out. We were happy for the first few months. Then Nigel insisted that I stop attending church and go to brunch with him on Sunday mornings instead. I was insulting his mother by refusing her repeated invitations."

Those eyes, so merry a moment ago, now shone with tears. "I was miserable. I tried to read my Bible in my room by myself, but it wasn't the same. Nigel and I didn't agree on important issues, and it tore a rift in my marriage and in my walk with the Lord."

Anita wiped her eyes. "When he died three years later, it was a relief. But it took me a long time to repair my relationship with God. Please don't make the same mistake I did."

"I won't, Anita. I promise."

But her heart told her she might already be caught in Rand's web.

Tessa and Irene vied for the one handheld mirror they owned between them. Tessa pinned one piece of rolled hair on top of her head next to another. "My sister who made it to the United States wrote to me that this is all the fashion. They even call it a victory roll to be patriotic."

Irene struggled to pin back her curls.

Tessa handed Irene the mirror. "Let me help you, love. I can't believe you never rolled your hair before."

"Not in the jungle." Irene fingered the lacy green fabric of the dress Tessa had lent her and taken in. She had never worn anything so beautiful.

Tessa spent the next fifteen minutes removing the large curlers from Irene's hair and pinning the sausage rolls to the top of her head. She left soft curls at the bottom. "I wish I had your platinum-blond hair. I've spent my life dreaming of being a blonde or a brunette—anything but a redhead. Well, now for a little lipstick. I've been saving it for just such an occasion."

Irene cringed at the bright-red color. "Rand gave me lipstick for Christmas, and it's a softer color that I prefer."

Tessa laughed, pink highlighting her thin cheeks. "Don't be silly. With your fair hair, this is the color you want. Trust me. You will look fabulous. Bangers and mash, if only we hadn't left all of our jewelry in that safety-deposit box in Hong Kong." She sighed. "Oh well, we look as good as we can."

Irene pulled out the tube Rand had given her. "I'm fashionable enough. I'm going to wear this color." And she applied the coral lipstick. She stood and peeked at herself in the mirror, then sucked in her breath, not recognizing the woman staring back. "If marrying a rich man doesn't work out for you, Tessa, you could always fall back on being a hairstylist or a Hollywood makeup artist."

"You are a beautiful woman, Irene. I'm glad you're realizing it at last."

"What will Rand say when he sees me?"

"He will marvel at the gorgeous creature you have become. And don't tell me you don't like him even just a little bit."

Irene turned and admired Tessa in her stunning robin's-egg blue dress that hugged her body as the silk fabric flowed to the floor. "Bruce's eyes are going to pop right out of his head when he gets his first glimpse of you. You're gorgeous. I just can't believe you agreed to go to the dance with Rand's friend."

"And why not? It's a truth universally acknowledged that a single man in possession of a fortune must be in want of a wife."

Irene laughed. "He's so much older than you."

"But he has what you Americans call rugged good looks. Besides, Rand is almost ten years older than you."

A rap on the door interrupted them. Rand and Bruce Tarpin

stood waiting for them. Rand had a white lily in his hand. "Irene, Irene, prettiest girl I ever have seen."

Tessa hadn't needed to fret over not having rouge. Irene was sure her cheeks were plenty pink. "You haven't rhymed in a while."

"There hasn't been much to rhyme about. But it's true. I have never seen a lovelier woman in my life."

He looked handsome enough himself in his long pants and starched shirt, a dark-red necktie around his throat. The way the clothing hung on his frame told the truth of his weight loss. Even his stocky friend had thinned considerably.

Rand had slicked back his light-brown hair and had managed to tame most of the waves. He rubbed his square chin. A chill of delight rushed over her.

Irene pulled on the elbow-length gloves Tessa had lent her. "That is not the truth. I've heard tales of you with a gorgeous woman on each arm."

"They pale in comparison to you." He tucked the flower behind her right ear, an electric-like jolt racing to her toes at his touch.

Bruce guffawed. "Keep in mind that he's a notorious flirt. And all of the stories you've heard about him are true."

Didn't Bruce like her very much, or was he teasing?

He kissed Tessa's hand, sending her into a spasm of giggles. "Miss Wainwright, thank you for doing me the honor. Wainwright as in Wainwright Jewelers, serving all of the finest families of the Far East, correct?"

Irene tuned out Rand's friend and turned her attention back to him. A bluish-greenish spot on his temple was the only mark of the ordeal he'd suffered earlier in the week. She touched it, careful not to hurt him. "Do you feel well enough to dance tonight?"

"A thousand Japanese soldiers wouldn't keep me from this. I would have been here even if I had to escape." He winked.

She shivered.

Tessa laughed and patted Irene's hair. "Enough of that lovey-dovey talk. Are we ready?"

Rand offered Irene his elbow, and she slipped her hand around his arm. "I've never been to a dance before, so I'm not sure I'll be very good. I hope I don't embarrass you too much."

He turned and looked at her. "You have never danced?"

"My aunt frowned on it. Tessa has been helping me learn."

"Never danced before?" Bruce shook his head. "I don't know of anyone who has never danced."

"Don't pay any attention to my supposed friend. He's jealous of me. Just follow my lead, and you'll be swell."

Couples milled around the yard in front of the Main Building. Lights had been strung around the dance floor, and on the stage, a group of musicians with violins, trumpets, trombones, and clarinets tuned their instruments.

Irene tried to take it all in. Yes, the internees were weary both physically and emotionally, and Santo Tomas was not as pretty as it had been two and a half years ago when they arrived. Shanties dotted the landscape. The beautiful lawns had been turned into vegetable gardens, now weed-infested because the internees lacked the energy to properly care for them.

But tonight, just for tonight, the square was beautiful and the hunger pains forgotten. "This is wonderful. I thought it would be records over the loudspeaker and people dancing in mud."

"Let this camp fade into the distance. Imagine yourself in my club. The tinkling of glasses. The laughter of couples. The whisper of skirts."

"Imagine myself with all of the pretty girls?"

"Only you."

The orchestra struck up a waltz. That's what Rand told her, anyway. She had no idea what was going on. He bowed in front of her and offered his hand. "Shall we?"

She nodded, trembling at the thought of stepping on his toes. He slipped his left hand into her right and his right hand around her waist. "Are you fine with this?"

"Yes." She could hardly breathe. Though he was six feet tall, they fit together like puzzle pieces.

"Count to three, and come along with me."

He began to move. Irene felt as if she were floating. The music lifted her, and Rand carried her across the floor. Her skirt swished around her knees. One song after another played, and she and Rand danced until they could dance no more. The music changed, more of a Lindy Hop according to him, and Irene bowed out. He escorted her to the side.

"You don't have to stand here with me. There are plenty of women who would love to dance with you." She noticed quite a number of young ladies smiling and batting their eyes in his direction. Irene fanned herself with her hand.

"They don't hold my interest. Not like you."

Her heart fluttered. He was a smooth talker. "I see Sheila King. She'd like to have you for a partner."

"Are you trying to get rid of me?"

"You know how to show the young ladies a good time."

"That I do." With a glint in his eyes, he walked over to Sheila, bowed to her, and swung her around the dance floor. Several other of the little girls took their turns with him, and he was red faced and panting when he returned to her.

"Let's take a walk, shall we?" Rand held her hand.

"Can't handle all of the attention?"

"Well, Sheila's very special. She's had it tough. I like to make her smile, if only for a few minutes. However, there's only one lady's attention I'm vying for tonight."

If she were a fainting woman, she'd swoon. "Shouldn't we tell Tessa and your friend Bruce where we're going?"

Rand tipped his head toward the dancers. "I saw them making eyes at each other. I don't think they'll miss us."

"That sounds like Tessa."

Together they walked around the Main Building and toward Father's Garden. The music and laughter faded into the distance. Rand drew her close, and she felt his heart beating furiously against hers. "I'm not frightening you, am I?"

Not in the way he thought. "No. I, well, I like this." She smiled though she trembled from head to toe.

He whispered into her ear, "I meant it when I said you were the most beautiful woman I have ever seen. No one compares to you, Irene. No one. Don't doubt it."

He turned his head, and his lips met her cheek. A soft kiss.

His lips met her cheek again and then her lips, brushing them, setting them on fire. He slipped his arms from around her and held her face in his hands. "I'm falling for you, Miss Reynolds."

She had already fallen.

He kissed her again, harder this time. She wrapped her hands around the back of his neck and kissed him. Too soon, far too soon, he broke away and stepped back. "How are you?"

She nodded, unable to answer, not wanting the moment to end.

She jumped at the thud and the curse that followed.

They weren't alone.

# Chapter Twenty-Five

Rand spun from Irene's embrace upon hearing the sound behind them. "Who's there?" It could be a Japanese soldier, ready to punish them for a public display of affection.

A figure sprinted across the garden and toward Shantytown. Rand started after him, but Irene caught him. "Stop. Don't chase him. It was Mr. Covey."

"You're sure about that? How could you tell in the dark?"

"The man was the right size and shape, and I saw his mustache. I only know one man with facial hair like that."

The warmth that had filled Rand moments earlier as he held Irene in his arms escaped and left a chill in its wake. "Covey. Of course."

"I spoke to him yesterday. He refused to tell me what is going on between the two of you."

Rand stepped back and pursed his lips, but the words exploded nonetheless. "I told you to stay away from him and to let this matter die. It's of no consequence to you. Please, Irene, don't meddle in my business. All you're going to do is make matters worse."

He hated the pain in her eyes at his harsh words, but he hated more what she had done. He could feel Covey's noose tightening around his neck. She didn't want to know his secret. He had to keep her from finding out. He didn't want to face the hurt in her beautiful blue eyes when he told her what kind of man he was.

Because if she did know, so would his entire social circle. Irene would tell Tessa who would tell—well, everyone.

And then he would lose everything.

He walked around her, his arms taut, his jaw clenched.

"Maybe I can help you."

If he gave her a little information, perhaps that would be enough. Then she would drop the matter and never speak of it again. "Yes, Covey is threatening me. He wants to take away my business. If he makes me look bad, the elite of Manila will no longer want to associate with me, and then he will be king of the nightclubs."

"He'll take everything important to you."

"Yes."

"So he was happy when you were sent to Fort Santiago and angry when you came back. Thus, the first note. The first one from him, anyway."

"Correct again. Though it appeared to come from the outside, he had it planted on your desk. I'm sure of it. He will spread rumors about me until I am an outcast. As for right now, he's my business partner." He touched her warm cheek. "But don't you see? If you pester him about this, he will increase his attacks against me unless I give him a larger percentage of the clubs. It will never end."

Irene gasped. "I'm sorry I went against your wishes. I should have trusted you when you told me to stay away."

"Apology accepted. Now will you avoid Covey?"

"I will. I promise." She brushed a kiss against his cheek.

His stomach tightened.

What if Covey saw their other kiss? What kind of ammunition would that give him?

❧

Irene returned to her shanty, floating on a cloud. Whether she experienced a thousand kisses in her life or just this one, she would never forget the one she got tonight. Her first. Rand's lips on hers, so soft and gentle, yet full of passion. She had never known such feelings existed.

Her aunt's warning rang in her head, but she pushed it aside. This was innocent. The war would end, and they would return to their normal lives—Rand to his glittering high society and she to humble charitable work. Two different people. Two different worlds. Two different lives.

Tessa hadn't returned yet. She and Bruce had hit it off and appeared to be having the time of their lives. Before returning to the Main Building to sleep, Irene slipped off the beautiful borrowed dress and hung it where it wouldn't get damaged. She may never wear a gown so lovely again. She fingered the material one last time before gathering a change of clothes. Then she began the trip to her classroom.

Darkness had descended, though stars littered the sky.

She hadn't gone more than twenty steps when a Japanese soldier approached from the opposite direction. Her heart froze.

He strode her way, relaxed, his gun slung over his shoulder. Almost casual. Very different from the guards' patrols. Mercedes's friend?

She dropped her gaze.

*Dear God, don't let it be. Help me to stop seeing him in every Japanese face.*

Willing her legs to move, she stepped to the side to allow him to pass, bowing at the prescribed angle, hoping she would not attract attention.

He stopped in front of her, his once-shiny black boots now dusty and worn.

She trembled as he turned in her direction. What had she done?

"You."

*No. No. No.*

She dared to peer at him.

His laugh morphed into a sneer.

She studied his right hand. Cold rushed from her heart throughout her body.

That hand. Missing a fingertip. Her legs melted. She fell to the ground.

He stepped closer.

Screams tore from her throat. "Get away. Stay away from me." She flailed her arms and legs, stirring the dirt.

He was at her side in a flash, his hand over her mouth, pulling her to her feet. She fought for air, tried to bite him, to kick him in the groin. All to no avail. He held fast.

Where was he taking her? What was he going to do with her?

---

"And God bless Mama, and God bless Papa in heaven, and God bless Mr. Tanaka. In the name of the Father, and the Son, and the Holy Ghost. Amen."

Mercedes tucked the threadbare sheet around her son's small body and kissed him on the forehead. "Good night, my love. Sleep well and may the angels keep watch over you."

He hugged her neck with a fierceness that surprised her.

"What is it?"

"You're sad."

"I miss your father and our home."

"We'll leave soon. I saw my teacher yesterday, and he said the Japanese are going to lose the war, and it won't be long now. Our boys have them on the run."

"From your lips to God's ears." She kissed him again and adjusted his covers before walking out of the room to sit on the sofa in the living area. The stores Charles had laid up for them wouldn't hold out much longer. Right now she needed her husband's strength. The women in the camp shunned her because of Mr. Tanaka, and Irene avoided her. The soldier hadn't brought her food in over a month. Mercedes didn't know how much longer she and Paulo would survive.

Leaning back, she sighed and closed her eyes. Her prayers refused to come. She was as adrift in the sea as a warship without power.

She wished for a deep, dreamless sleep—the only time she wasn't hungry or afraid. For the past few weeks it had eluded her.

Screams reached her ears, jolting her from her stupor. Yelling wasn't unheard of in the camp. Couples squabbled. Children threw temper tantrums. Babies demanded attention. Living in such close quarters, it was surprising there wasn't more of it.

Something about these screams disturbed Mercedes. Like she had heard the voice before. She pulled herself from the depths of the old couch and went to the no-privacy window. The night was dark, and with blackout conditions enforced to the letter of the law, seeing anything was difficult to impossible on this moonless night.

She peered out farther. The screams had stopped. No, they were muffled now. She heard scuffling. Like a struggle was going on.

"Hello." Her voice was tentative. She trembled, wanting the fight to end but not caring to get in the middle of an argument. "Is everything okay?"

For a moment, the muffled cries grew louder. Then they stopped. Rapid footsteps approached, and a sound like someone was dragging something.

The tumult came closer. A figure—no, two—drew near. One shape was tall, regal almost. A soldier. The other? Mercedes squinted. The shape of a woman.

Why would a guard be dragging a woman with him?

Mercedes's midsection turned to ice. She no sooner thought the question than she had the answer. "No." The word was a whisper. With a churning stomach, she ran to the door and opened it a crack.

Not any soldier. The height, the bearing, the way he walked. It was Mr. Tanaka. Despite the darkness, she was sure.

Her heart began pumping at a furious pace, and she clutched her hand to her chest. Irene. *Oh, God, no. Not her. Please, God, not her.*

She shut the door, careful to keep it from banging. What should she do? Should she yell at him? Go and pull Irene away? Get help?

Yes, help. That's what she needed to do. Who? *Charles, why aren't you here?*

Rand. Good idea. She would get Rand.

But there wasn't time. Why was she hesitating? She hadn't given a second thought to getting involved with the man with the fish. So why?

Because this had everything to do with how wrong she'd been.

With shaking hands, she threw open the door. "What is going on?"

In an instant, the soldier removed his hand from Irene's mouth.

"It's him. I told you it's him."

"She is mistaken."

Mercedes lunged in his direction. "I am the one who was mistaken. Get out of here. We don't need your help. Leave us alone. Don't ever come back." Every muscle in her body tensed.

"You will miss me. When your son is starving, you will miss me."

Either way, Mercedes was doomed.

~

Rand held open the door to his shanty, the early-morning sun streaming through. "Come in, Mr. Covey. I've been expecting you."

"That sounds like a very warm welcome. And you were right to expect me."

"I wish you would stop following me."

"Ah, but then I wouldn't glean important information about you, would I? And several interesting tidbits have come to my attention in the past few days. Namely, in regard to Miss Irene Reynolds."

Rand sat on the chair in the living room without inviting Covey to do the same. "Leave her out of this. She has nothing to do with it."

"I beg to differ. She now has everything to do with it. A missionary girl, I believe. Devout. Pure. How would she feel if she discovered your indiscretions? That you have a child you have never met and do not support despite your large bank account?"

"You are twisting the story around so it no longer resembles the truth."

"The truth is you don't want me to tell Miss Reynolds about your daughter, do you?"

Rand sighed and ran his hand over the arm of the chair. Maybe the time had come to see if Mr. Covey was bluffing. Would he really tell Irene about Melanie?

Yes.

But he had no idea how Irene would react. Maybe she would forgive him for his sins. Wasn't that what Christians were supposed to do? She would understand that this happened years ago and that he only found out about his daughter at a time when he could do nothing about the situation.

"The price for my silence will be high. I want to be a seventy percent partner."

"Seventy percent?" Rand's mouth hung open. "We had agreed to controlling interest: fifty-one percent."

"My price has risen." He gave a crooked grin to match his crooked nose. "Of course, you would continue your fine job of managing them and will collect a tidy portion of the profits."

"I would never—"

"Mr. Sterling, I would be careful of using the word *never*."

Rand wanted to break the chair in half. Instead, he pounded his fist on the seat. "Again, I will need time to think about this. I won't hand over large portions of my business without considering all of my options."

Mr. Covey nodded. "I'll be back this time tomorrow for your answer. I saw that kiss last night. You care for Miss Reynolds, and she has strong feelings for you. She is beautiful and kind and everything you could ask for in a wife. Do you want to risk losing her? Will you ever find another as sweet as her?"

Mr. Covey left, the door banging shut behind him.

Rand held his pounding head. Armando had taught him right from wrong, and he had ignored the man's admonition.

His sins had come back to haunt him.

Either way, he would lose one of his loves—Irene or the clubs.

Yes, he loved Irene. She was the most incredible woman he had ever met. She filled a hole inside of him. He imagined her by his side forever. He dreamed of kissing her and holding her far into the night.

He sighed and rubbed his temples.

He couldn't have both.

But which one should he choose?

⁂

It took Rand the better part of the afternoon, but he finally located Irene pulling weeds from between her *talinum* plants. Her arms and legs had tanned, but she wore a large straw hat to protect her ivory face.

"Hello there."

She looked up and smiled, then straightened and rubbed the small of her back. "Rand." She shuffled her feet.

He understood how she felt. It was the first time they had seen each other since the kiss. For whatever reason, he was shy, wondering if she remembered what happened between them and if she cherished it as much as he did.

No other kiss had affected him so.

"What brings you here? Are you going to help weed?"

"Brown thumb. Sorry. You don't want me anywhere near your plants. In fact, why don't we take a walk, away from them, so they don't see me and die."

"Is that the effect you have on them?"

He wanted to ask her what effect he had on her. "You don't want to find out."

She wiped her hands on her dirty pink apron and ran the back of her hand across her forehead. "You will have to put up with the way I look unless you're going to give me time to wash up and change."

"You look as beautiful right now as you did last night."

"No wonder the women like you, with the way you flatter them."

They meandered side by side into Glamourville and down the street. His mouth was as dry as the Mojave Desert and his hands as damp as the Philippine jungle.

He loved her.

And he was about to break her heart.

"On the way back to the Main Building last night, that soldier tried to attack me again."

Rand froze. "What? Are you hurt?"

She shook her head. "Mercedes came from her shanty and ran him off. Told him never to come back."

He clenched his fist. "You sure he didn't harm you?"

"No. I'm so thankful she came out when she did. Otherwise . . ."

"That's good. She'll see now what kind of man he is. That she shouldn't have anything to do with him. And maybe he'll leave you alone." Rand would make sure of that.

"But the harm has been done. I don't know if I'll ever be able to forgive her for choosing that Japanese guard over me."

He squeezed her hand. "I'm just glad you aren't injured. That beast . . ." He tamped down the fury building in his chest. Because the guard may not have hurt her, but he was about to.

If he could just put it off. But no, he had to take away Covey's ammunition. Or part of it, at least.

They came to his hut, and he wished they could go inside and have some privacy. He didn't want the world to see her tears. Maybe she would slap him. "Is it okay with you if we stop here and talk awhile?"

She bit her lip and held up her hand. "You don't have to say anything. There is no need for regrets about last night. It is a memory I will carry with me for the rest of my life. I understand that I'm not the type of girl for you and—"

He placed his finger on her lips and hushed her. "Stop it. Nothing could be further from the truth. That kiss was amazing. And so are you. Irene, I love you and you . . ."

He should have let her go, thinking he didn't want anything to do with her.

"There is something else. I want to tell you what information Covey has about me." He wrung his hands and took a deep breath to steady himself. *Just say it. Just spit out the words.* "He is blackmailing me."

She touched his bare arm, and he couldn't bear the thought of losing her. "You don't have to tell me. Whatever it is, you work it out with him. I should never have gone to him behind your back. That was wrong."

"I have a daughter."

Her eyes widened. "You never told me you were married before."

He had to force the words past his lips. "I wasn't."

"Oh." She stood there, her mouth round, not saying a word.

His heart pounded. "Somehow Covey found out about her. She's six years old. Her mother and I were college sweethearts."

"No wonder you're so good with Sheila."

"I've never met her. I didn't know Catherine was expecting when I graduated and returned to Manila. She moved to Virginia. I only found out a couple of weeks ago myself."

"Oh." Much of the color fled her face, and he was afraid she would faint. He led her to the step to sit.

"I know what I did was wrong. I am sorry for it. Can you ever forgive me?" He held his breath.

"This is . . . this is so much to take in at one time."

He knelt beside her, grateful that no one else walked along the wall this time of day. It was too hot to be out. "Let Covey have my clubs. I can start again." His heart wrenched as if it were being plucked from his chest. "There will be nothing left of them by the end of the war, so I would have had to rebuild either way. What I care about is you."

Could he rebuild his clubs with his tarnished reputation and without financial backing?

Irene smoothed her skirt over her knees. "I understand. It's right that you should see your daughter and marry her mother. You need to make a family with them."

"I don't want to marry Catherine. I want to marry you."

Now Irene stood, tears coursing down her face, making tracks through the dirt. "I can't marry you, Rand. It would never work between us. I had hoped to have a wonderful friendship with you here, but I let myself feel too much for you. I should never have let it go that far. I'm sorry, Rand, I truly am."

And she ran off down the drainage ditch until she reached the end of the road.

He watched as she disappeared from sight.

"Thirty percent is all you will get." Rand stood face-to-face with Covey across his kitchen table and had to restrain himself from spitting in the man's eye.

"So she left you."

"I chose the truth over lies. If I wanted to have a relationship with Irene, it needed to be built on honesty. She had to know about Melanie. And now she does. She has chosen to end our relationship, but that doesn't affect our business. I refuse to hand over controlling interest in my clubs to you."

Covey ground his teeth. Rand had the satisfaction of knowing that he had bested his rival, at least for now.

Bright colors exploded in front of Rand's eye as Covey's fist met his temple. The room spun. He grabbed for the kitchen chair, which toppled over. He stumbled against the wall.

Covey came at him again. He blocked Covey's blows and pushed the man against the counter. Rand socked him in the stomach and chopped him on the neck. Covey slumped to the floor and Rand stood over him.

"Don't *ever* come near me again. Next time I might not be able to control myself. The threats are over. Over. Tell whomever you want about my daughter. I'll shout it from the rooftops. You will get none of my business. I would rather close the doors to the Monarch and the Azure and never own another club than have your dirty hands in the till. Get out of my sight."

Rand stepped back so Covey could get up. He followed the man out the door and down the street.

For the longest time after he returned to the hut, Rand sat on the porch, the picture of Melanie in his hand, watching couples walking and talking together.

He had lost everything.

His clubs. His position. His standing.

Absolutely everything.

# Chapter Twenty-Six

*August 21, 1944*

Irene opened her eyes as soon as light began slanting through the mats that made up her hut. She had slept here last night after seeing Mercedes and Paulo heading for the Annex, perhaps because of the driving rainstorm.

A splitting headache greeted her as it had every morning for a few weeks. As she sat up, she noticed that her hands and feet and abdomen were swollen and her lips were thick. Signs of beriberi. Almost everyone in the camp had early symptoms of it. Subsisting on rice and gravy with a fourth of a can of meat once a week would do that to a body. Gas had been cut and, as a result, there was no more noonday cooking at the shanties unless you could find wood to burn for fuel.

For her, once she moved around for an hour or so, the swelling and headache went away. For the elderly, they suffered day and night. The death rate in camp climbed steadily each month.

She swung her legs over the side of the bed, her stomach

cramping so much that she doubled over in pain. The wave passed, but Irene hurried as fast as she could to what the internees called "The Little House on the Hill." Even at this early hour, a queue of women waited for the restroom. Not in all the time they had been in camp had there been adequate sanitary facilities.

But for Irene today, it took on more urgency. She had contracted bacillary dysentery. She clung to her little can of water and her rag, her only means of cleaning herself once she finished. The new commandant announced that there was not a square of toilet paper left in the entire Philippine Islands. The camp had been making do with four squares per person per week for some time. This, though, was a bitter pill for the internees to swallow.

Tessa met her in line, her usually fair face unusually pale.

"You too?"

Tessa nodded. "Who in the camp doesn't have it? We'll all be laid out by the time the Americans arrive. What is taking your boys so long, love?"

"They dropped a few bombs on Davao at the beginning of the month, or so the rumor goes."

"A few bombs. *Pfff.* What good will that do? We need steak and kidney pie."

"Oh, Tessa, that image is not helping my stomach."

They inched forward. Irene's cramps intensified. A dark-haired woman in front of them in a faded pink dress swayed. Irene reached out to steady her. She almost dropped the woman when she saw her face. "Mercedes. What's wrong? Are you ill?" A ridiculous question, really. They all were sick.

The woman fainted, slumping in Irene's arms. She lowered Mercedes to the ground. Tessa leaned over and fanned the Filipina with her hand.

"Come on. Paulo needs you. Don't leave him alone." The dampness of her hands had nothing to do with illness. Mercedes's face was as pale as Irene had ever seen it. Her own legs began to quiver.

Not getting a response, Irene did the only thing she could think to do. She reached for her can of water and doused Mercedes with it. She spluttered and revived, then sat back when she realized who had aided her. "Irene."

"Do you feel better?"

Mercedes nodded, biting the inside of her cheek.

"You have to make sure you're eating enough. I know times are tight because you've severed ties with that Japanese guard, but giving all of your food to Paulo won't help him if you leave him an orphan."

Mercedes nodded. "It's not that." She lifted the now-empty can of water.

"Like all of us."

Tessa helped Mercedes to stand. "You have to get to hospital."

"No. I have to keep working in the kitchen to get the extra rations for Paulo. I would do anything for him."

It appeared she would. Like Anita did for her. It's what a mother did for her child, she supposed. In a way, she admired Mercedes and the love she had for Paulo. Irene had never known that kind of love from the woman who gave birth to her. "You can go get treatment. Tessa and I will make sure Paulo is looked after until you're stronger. Likely, they'll give you sulfa and send you on your way. There isn't enough room in the hospital to keep you there."

"But—"

"Don't let him suffer because you and I don't see eye to eye. That's not what you want."

"Thank you, my friend."

Irene bristled at the word.

Mercedes studied her broken, dirty fingernails. "I'm sorry about everything."

"I'm helping Paulo. That's all." Irene didn't mean to be short or want to be ill-tempered, but she couldn't forgive Mercedes now. Maybe not ever.

"Do you think you can stand now, love?" Tessa cupped Mercedes under the elbow.

Mercedes rose to her feet. "Thank you both."

"I'll take her to hospital and see you later, Irene. Perhaps they can give me some medication while I'm there." Tessa led Mercedes out of the building.

Irene gasped at the next round of cramps and tightened the muscles of her buttocks so she would make it to the toilet. There was no use asking to move ahead in the line. All of the women were in the same condition.

She made it, just barely, and just in time to line up for roll call in her shanty area. The Japanese had now forbidden all chairs during roll call. Only the weakest could sit on the ground. The rest had to stand in double rows, hands behind backs, eyes straight ahead, facing the Rising Sun in the east. The guards now required everyone to bow every time they passed. The bow had to meet regulations, be a certain angle, otherwise the internee would be slapped, much like she and Anita had been.

Irene no longer gave it a second thought. She bowed, never looking any of her captors in the eye. It was easier that way.

After that twice-daily torture, she stood in line for a very long time for a bit of gruel called *lugao*. It was a tasteless mixture of rice and ground corn and did nothing to ease the constant hunger pains.

The food did give her enough energy to take the short walk to

Santa Catalina to see Anita. Perhaps she and Tessa could walk to the kitchen together afterward.

Anita's beriberi symptoms were much more severe than Irene's. She was often confused and ate very little. Nothing, it seemed, stayed in her stomach.

Irene sat on a chair beside her aunt and held her hand. "Good morning. How are you doing today?"

"Who are you? Why are you here? I want my mother." Anita's voice was thin and hollow.

"I'm Irene, your niece. Anita, do you know me?"

"Why can't I see you?" Anita thrashed. "Turn on the lights. I'm scared of the dark."

Irene rubbed her aunt's arm in an attempt to calm her. "Don't be afraid. I'm right here with you. There is nothing in the dark that will hurt you." Her own heart, however, raced. Anita had never been this confused before. Her memory lapses had lasted only a few minutes and had never resulted in such agitation.

When she was little and frightened, after Father had run off, Anita had sung one particular hymn. Though she didn't have an opera-worthy voice, Irene began to sing in hopes of stilling her aunt.

*"Our God, our help in ages past,*
*Our hope for years to come,*
*Our shelter from the stormy blast,*
*And our eternal home."*

Anita lay more still, her mouth open.

*"Under the shadow of Thy throne*
*Thy saints have dwelt secure;*

*Sufficient is Thine arm alone,*
*And our defense is sure.*

*"Time, like an ever-rolling stream,*
*Bears all its sons away;*
*They fly, forgotten, as a dream*
*Dies at the opening day."*

Irene's voice broke. Was that what God was doing with Anita? Was He bearing her away to her eternal home? *No, Lord, no. Not now. I need her.*

"Keep singing."

Irene finished the hymn.

*"Our God, our help in ages past,*
*Our hope for years to come,*
*Be Thou our guard while troubles last,*
*And our eternal home."*

"I like that song. Where did you learn it?"

"You taught it to me, Anita, when I first came to live with you. The trees in the jungle made scary shadows on the wall in my room at night, and you would sing it so I would go to sleep."

"That's nice. You'll have to teach it to me."

"Don't you remember lying in bed with me, singing that hymn?"

"That's a good idea." Anita scooted over and patted the mattress beside her. "Snuggle next to me and sing the song again."

This was not how it went. Anita came into bed with her and sang to her, not the other way around. Even though her throat threatened to swell shut, Irene climbed in bed beside her aunt and sang the hymn once more.

Anita joined in on the last verse. "'*Our eternal home.*' My eternal home. Do you know what heaven will be like?"

"What?" Irene smoothed back what little hair Anita had left.

"The streets are made of pure gold and the gates of the city from precious pearls. There will be a river as clear as crystal. There will be no more tears, no more pain, no more dying. And the best part? The best part is that we will be with the Lord forever."

Anita made it sound so real, like she could see it and touch it.

"Won't it be wonderful to go there? I can hardly wait." Anita's face shone.

"Yes, it will be beyond our imagining."

"Will you go with me?"

"I can't. But Jesus will be there waiting for you."

"I see heaven opened." Anita closed her eyes and her face relaxed.

Irene sat up. "Anita. Anita." She shook her aunt. No response. "Nurse, nurse, come quickly."

The nurse rushed over.

Irene couldn't breathe.

After feeling Anita's pulse and listening to her heart, the nurse shook her head. "She's in a coma. It won't be long now."

Irene jumped from the bed. "No. No. No." *God, don't do this to me.* She had to get out of this place, away from this. Then maybe it wouldn't happen. Maybe it was a bad dream.

She sprinted through the hall, her *bakyas* clicking on the tile, down the stairs, and out the door. All around her, people went about their business as if this were just another day. Not the day her aunt would die and leave her alone.

*Ack-ack-ack-ack.* The racket startled her, and she jumped higher than she ever had in her life. The internees milling around her stopped. "What was that?"

From somewhere in the crowd a voice answered, "The Japanese are practicing their antiaircraft fire. Our planes will soon be here!"

A roar of approval rose up.

*Ack-ack-ack-ack.*

Irene hated the noise. She covered her ears but could still hear it. It grated on every nerve she had left.

*Ack-ack-ack-ack.*

She fled to her shanty where she began tearing out the white lilies growing in front of it, yanking them from the ground. One after another after another, she ripped them out by the roots and flung them to the side. Sweat poured down her face, hair tangled in her eyes. Her bare arms were wet.

"Stop. Irene, no." A man called to her, but she ignored him. Kept on pulling. Another plant out.

Then arms stronger than hers lifted her and pulled her away from the next stalk. "What are you doing?"

She recognized the voice. "Let go of me. Leave me alone." She tried to kick Rand's shins but didn't have the strength.

He lifted her from the garden and sat her on the ground, then dropped to his knees beside her. "Why are you pulling out your flowers?"

*Ack-ack-ack-ack.*

Irene screamed, "Make it stop. Make it stop."

*Ack-ack-ack-ack.*

"*Shh, shh.*" Rand wrapped her in his arms and held her while she trembled. "That's a good sound. Our planes are coming. We'll be going home soon."

"Make it stop."

"I can't. I don't want to."

"I want you to."

He released her, wiping her hair from her face. "Sweetheart, what is going on?"

"I'm not your sweetheart. I can't be, and I never will be."

"What has you so upset?"

She didn't want to say the words. If she didn't say them, they wouldn't be true. Once they passed her lips, there would be no taking them back. They would be reality.

"I can't tell you."

"You can tell me anything. You know that. I won't hurt you. I promise."

"If I say it, it will happen."

"Irene, I don't understand. Please tell me."

"Anita is confused."

"About what?"

"Everything. She didn't recognize me this morning."

"Was this the first time?"

Irene shook her head. If only . . . if only it had been the first time. "It's been getting worse for a while."

"You're telling me she has advanced beriberi."

This time Irene nodded.

*Ack-ack-ack-ack.*

She stiffened.

Rand held her again until she relaxed.

"She's in a coma."

"This is what we're going to do. You go to the washing station and clean up. I'll replant these flowers."

"You don't have to."

"Let me do this. If they don't live, at least we know we tried."

Irene walked the short distance to the troughs, which had been set up as washing stations and laundry facilities. A few women were there washing their clothes, careful not to rub too hard and put holes in the thin fabric. She splashed lukewarm water on her face and up and down her arms and neck. The hot sun dried her in short order.

By the time she returned to the garden, Rand had replanted most of what she had torn out. She didn't care. It was sweet of him, but it didn't matter. There was no beauty left in the world.

Rand wiped his hands on his khaki shorts and smiled. "Do you feel better?"

"A little."

"Good. Let's go visit Anita. I'll stay with you."

He shouldn't. He was going to marry another woman. He had a family with her.

But right now she needed him. She needed his presence, his strength.

Because she was going to watch her aunt die.

*No, God, no. You can't take her from me too.*

# Chapter Twenty-Seven

Hours upon hours passed as Irene and Rand kept vigil at Anita's bedside. She hadn't awakened from her coma. Midafternoon came and along with it Dr. Young.

"I hear that Mrs. Markham has taken a turn for the worse."

Irene nodded. "This morning."

He examined Irene's aunt, then stood back, his stethoscope around his neck. "Beriberi and malnutrition have taken their toll on her body. Even if I had proper medicine to administer, there would be little we could do for her. I can't tell you how long it will be. It could be a few hours or a few days. I am sorry for your loss. I'm sorry the Japanese did this to her."

Dr. Young left, and Irene watched him make his way to the hall. She had held out hope that the nurse had been wrong, that Anita was merely sleeping so she could regain her strength.

But the doctor only confirmed Irene's worst fear. And what she had known to be the truth all along.

Irene couldn't move, could barely make herself blink. She wanted to collapse but fought to hold herself upright.

Rand rubbed her back. She didn't want to feel comforted by him, but she did. She was thankful he had found her, thankful he stayed with her.

She couldn't do this on her own.

"I'll be right back." Rand left and returned a short time later with a bowl of *lugao* for her.

Her stomach lurched. She pushed the bowl away. "I can't eat. Thank you, but please take it away. I'll be sick." Several times over the course of the day she had to run to the restroom. Her stomach rebelled at the thought of even a taste of the revolting gruel.

He held out a spoon. "Just a little. You need to keep up your strength."

"What does it matter? Don't you see, we will all end up like Anita sooner or later. So if I don't want to eat, don't make me."

He set the bowl on the floor and sat in silence with her for a while again. Irene watched her aunt's chest rise and fall, dreading the moment it would stop.

Rand slid his chair closer to hers so they were touching. "I don't know what to say to you. I've never been good with religious words. That was Armando's department. Tell me what your aunt would say if she was sitting beside you."

What would Anita say? Words that were soothing, comforting, biblical. Like she had taught the village women. "She would say that death is not something to be afraid of. We will all face it one day, but for those who know the Lord and are prepared for it, it is a day they will anticipate and welcome."

"Why would that be?"

"To be at home in the body is to be apart from Christ. This

earth isn't our true home. We look for a city with foundations whose builder is God. She told me right before she slipped into the coma how beautiful heaven would be and how she couldn't wait to get there."

"It sounds like she was at peace."

"She was. She is."

"She was a good woman."

"It's true. She is. But do you know what she would say to that?"

Rand shook his head. "Tell me."

"She would say she was the worst of sinners. Apart from God, she could do nothing righteous. All of her good works, she would say, were as filthy rags."

"And what kind of bad things did she do? Surely not have a child out of wedlock."

"There were times when she got angry with me when I didn't obey her. There were times when she was frustrated. And we don't know what kind of thoughts ran through her mind. We think wrong things all the time."

"But doesn't God count what good she did to her credit?"

"No. He only sees our faith and Christ's blood covering our sins. Christ's good works and His death on the cross are the only things that will save us, no matter what good we do in this life."

"Then why do any good at all? You can be as evil as Hitler and Hirohito and still get into heaven."

"No. When we are truly saved, we put our old selves to death with our sinful desires. We aren't perfect in this life, but we strive to honor God by doing what would please Him."

"It sounds simple. But there are some sins that God can't forgive."

"If you are truly repentant, there are no sins He can't forgive."

"Even what I've done?"

"Even what you've done."

"You preach a good sermon, Miss Reynolds."

"It's only what Anita would say. What God would say to you."

Rand sat forward in his chair. "I remember Armando speaking to me about God. He said many of the same things you did. I would find him in the garden at the end of the day, his Bible open on his lap. When I asked him what he was reading, he would tell me the most wonderful book on earth.

"He told me stories from it, and I learned. To me, they were just that. Stories. Tales. When I got older, I grew bored with them and stopped asking Armando to read to me. But to you and Anita, the Bible is alive. It's real."

"It's a history book. The history of our redemption from sin, of our forgiveness in Christ."

"It will be hard for you to let go of her."

"Other than my father, I have no other living relatives. For all intents and purposes, I will be an orphan. I won't have anyone to talk to, anyone to help me."

"You could have me."

"This isn't the time, Rand. Not now."

They fell into silence once more, and the shadows stretched across the floor. They had to leave for roll call but came back right afterward. Rand again brought her *lugao*, and this time she made an effort and ate several bites, her stomach having calmed a little.

Darkness fell, but both of them stayed at the hospital. She leaned her head on Rand's shoulder, fighting sleep. She wanted to be alert when Anita passed from this life to the next.

Somewhere deep in the night, Anita stirred. Her eyes fluttered open.

"She's awake, Rand. She's awake." Irene fell to her knees beside her aunt. "I'm here, Anita. It's me, Irene."

"Irene, my sweet girl. And Rand is here too."

"Yes, yes, he is." Irene's breath came in short gasps. The doctor had been wrong. Anita would recover.

"Rand?"

"Yes, ma'am?"

"You take good care of Irene, you hear? You promised me once. Promise me again."

"I promise."

Why was Anita saying these things?

"And, Irene?"

"Yes, I'm here." She clung to her aunt's hand.

"You be a good girl. Be good to Rand. Love God, and tell others about Him. Forgive. Forgive each other."

"I will."

"The Lord has been good to me all these years. He's calling me home now."

"No, Anita, you can't leave me. There is no one else here for me."

"You have Jesus. He is your help and your shield. He will watch over you far better than I ever could. It is time for me to go home. And what a beautiful home it is."

Irene had never seen such radiant joy as she saw in Anita's face at that moment. The sun was not brighter. And peace. The lines that marred Anita's forehead and mouth softened. She took a deep breath and then no more.

Irene's throat burned. She swallowed hard. Her vision blurred. She blinked, and the tears began to fall, one after the other, in a cascade she couldn't control. As she held her aunt's cooling hand, she sobbed. Sobbed for the infant robbed of a mother. Sobbed for the little girl robbed of a father. Sobbed for a young woman robbed of the aunt who was a better parent to her than those who gave her life.

She could think no more. Wave upon wave of sorrow crashed over her. She was vaguely aware of Rand at her side, his arm across her shoulders, tucking her hair behind her ear. At one point, he handed her a handkerchief, and she wiped her eyes. But it wasn't large enough to absorb all of her tears.

Exhausted, her crying slowed. Morning broke, and Rand pulled her to her feet. Her legs were stiff and unusually swollen this morning. A round of dizziness sent her crashing into him.

A nurse came by, and he called out to her, "Mrs. Markham has passed away. Irene is in no shape to go to roll call right now. Can we find a bed for her and get her excused?"

The nurse made the arrangements, and Rand carried her to the clean bed they had prepared for her. She didn't fight him but gave in to his ministrations. For right now, for this moment, she didn't have to be alone.

After he pulled the sheet to her chin, he kissed her on the forehead. "I know it's difficult, but try to get some sleep. I'll be back in a little while."

She nodded and drifted off in a haze of pain.

Rand wandered from Santa Catalina, so many thoughts whirring through his mind. He went to roll call in a daze. While most of the internees continued from there to the mess hall, he knew his stomach couldn't handle breakfast this morning.

He thought of the story of redemption that Irene had told him. Was it true? She believed it. Anita believed it. Armando believed it. But did he?

Too much muddled his brain this morning for him to think much on it. Later, he would. Yes, later.

But he couldn't forget the look of sheer joy on Anita's face as she slipped from this life. Not pain. Not fear. Joy.

If he lived a million years, he would never forget that moment.

What did it all mean? If only he could know. If she would come back and tell him if what Irene said was true. Never had his clubs given him such radiant joy. In all his life, he had never known such peace as Anita had. Anita Markham. A woman who was blind, suffered from ill health, lived in the jungle.

In the end, she had it all.

In that moment, he wished he did too.

She had never complained. Never grumbled. In fact, she praised God every day.

What would make someone live like that?

The grounds were quiet, most people busy consuming their meager meal. They lived for the two times during the day they got to put nourishment, such as it was, into their bodies. Soon the children would fill the yard, internees would shuffle by on their way to their duties, and old people would sit on the patio to chat.

He strolled in front of the Education Building. A movement caught the corner of his eye, a young man walking, then running across the yard. Rand paused, curious. What was he doing?

The boy, likely no more than nineteen, sprinted now. A Kempeitai ran after him, his rifle in his hands. Rand shielded his eyes from the morning sun.

The boy stumbled and fell. The Kempeitai caught up to him, pulled him from the ground by his hair.

Without saying a word, the soldier dragged the teenager outside of the gate.

Then Rand heard a single gunshot.

# Chapter Twenty-Eight

*Early September 1944*

Even if we get the food smuggled in, I don't see how we are going to store or distribute it." John Mitchell pounded so hard on Rand's table he thought it might collapse. "We don't have a warehouse, and we can't let the Japanese find out." The diminutive man pushed his wire-rimmed glasses up on his nose.

Rand stood and ran his hands through his hair, cigar smoke billowing around him. He, John, and Bruce Tarpin—they had been the Three Musketeers before the war—had been at this for over two hours now and were no further than when they began. Rand was almost sorry he brought John into the plan with them. With rampant inflation, their contact could no longer sneak in the large pile of bills as he had been. He didn't have a case big enough. Food was more useful to them. Since their contact's office shared a wall with the gymnasium—now a dormitory for the older men—they might be able to get the precious supplies into the camp.

Desperate to save their families, the men had banded together to figure out a solution to the problem of getting food. "No, we don't have much storage, but we don't need it. We can only smuggle in so much every day. We'll take it to the kitchen and use the furniture closet in the gymnasium if we need more room."

"And how long before some Lucy Loose-Lips blabs to the guards? Does the thought of returning to Fort Santiago appeal to you, Sterling?" John pushed up his glasses again.

"That's not fair." Bruce splayed his large hands on the cherry table. "Isn't the risk worth it to at least save the women and children? For now I'm fine, but that's not the case with so many others who didn't start with as much as us."

Rand thought of Irene. She must be down a good twenty pounds from the time he first met her almost a year ago. She never complained, but he knew she was hungry. "To me, yes, it's worth the risk. I, more than any of you, know what awaits me if we are caught. But our contact is offering to do this for us at great risk to himself."

Bruce murmured in agreement.

Rand grasped the back of one of the kitchen chairs. "Listen, Mitchell, if you don't want to be a part of this scheme, say so. Just promise us you will turn a blind eye to the hole in the wall and to the activity taking place over there."

John scratched his cheek. "I never said I wouldn't do it. All I meant was that we need to have a plan, a good, solid approach to this so we don't jeopardize the operation. If we get caught, no one will benefit. We might even do more harm than good to the camp in that instance."

Bruce swished the last of his brandy around in his glass. The last bottle of the cache Rand had brought into Santo Tomas with him. The last of his old way of life. This was the best plan he could figure to get the men to see his way of thinking. "Then I say let's tell our friend we'll be ready to do this in a week's time."

"Wait. I thought I heard a sound outside." John pushed back his chair.

Bruce snickered. "You're paranoid. I didn't hear anything."

John tipped his head. "I'm sure there was a noise."

"We have to get back to the issue at hand." Rand scoped out the men at his table. "Can we be ready in a week?"

John shook his head, his glasses sliding down their perch. "No. We need to figure out rationing and distribution—that is, once we have the storage problem solved."

Bruce gulped the last of his drink and set the glass on the table with a *thunk*. "How did you ever get ahead in business, Mitchell, if you weren't willing to take a risk, if you didn't know how to think on the fly?"

"Risking money is very different from risking your life."

"You mean risking your father's money." Rand slapped the table and laughed, Bruce joining him.

John's face turned as red as a sunset over Manila Bay. "Hush. Do you want one of the guards to hear us and turn us in before we even get started?"

Rand wished he had a little more brandy to pour for John to calm him down.

"There is nothing wrong with a group of friends getting together for an evening of fun and a cigar or two." Bruce puffed on his favorite local brand, making Rand's point.

"There's that thump again."

This time Rand heard it. "I'll check it out." He motioned for John to stay seated before making his way to the porch and peering through the screen into the darkness. People laughed, a phonograph blared music, and a couple down the way argued. Nothing out of the ordinary for Glamourville this time of the evening.

Rand took a deep breath of the heavy, humid air, a sight better than the smoky atmosphere inside his hut. He never used to mind the drinks and the cigars. Now he found he didn't care for them.

He didn't hear any more sounds. John Mitchell always did have a vivid imagination. In the past, he liked to envision that every young lady in Manila had her eye set on him. None of them ever did.

He spun around to return to the conversation, hating to be left out of any of it. A movement to his right caught the corner of his eye. A shadowy figure moved across the path along the wall.

Rand stepped out of the porch and down to the yard. Was it Ramon again? "Who's there?"

The interloper picked up speed, and Rand kept pace, then overtook the panting man. He grabbed the man's arms and pinned the flabby body against the flimsy wall. "I thought I told you never to come back here."

"Mr. Sterling, really, you don't need to speak in such a harsh tone."

Frank Covey. Rand would have preferred the eavesdropper to be Ramon. He didn't believe Ramon would betray them. Covey might. "What are you doing sneaking around my shanty?"

"Who said I was sneaking? I was out for a walk in the cool of the evening."

"You don't even live in Glamourville."

"That"—Covey spit in Rand's face—"is the arrogance I despise about you."

Rand wiped his cheek on Covey's T-shirt. "Not arrogance. A fact." Rand grew tired of Covey's verbal dance moves. "Why are you here?"

"What are you and your little band plotting?"

"We are enjoying a friendly round of poker. Would you care to join us?"

"Would you be willing to put more of your business at stake?"

Rand's fists itched to lay into Covey's cheek, to break his nose further. "Would you be willing to wager your share?"

Covey's mustache twitched, his scar glowed in the dark. "I don't play poker."

Rand grinned. "I didn't think so." He leaned closer to Covey. "The next time I catch you anywhere in the vicinity of my hut, I will not exercise such restraint." He stood straight. "Now get out of here."

"I'd be careful about making threats if I was you, Mr. Sterling. What would your business associates think about your little escapade?"

Frank Covey slithered into the night. After taking a moment to still his shaking hands, Rand made his way back to his hut. "What did I miss?"

John shook a finger at him. "I told you someone was out there. We heard your voice."

"Just a couple out for a stroll. We chatted about the weather for a few minutes before they continued on their way." Rand turned his attention to taking his seat so he didn't have to meet any of his friends' eyes. "Are we decided on next week, then?"

Bruce nodded. "Let's not blow this. It may be the only way to save the camp."

John traced the rim of his highball glass. "I wish there was another way."

Rand tented his fingers. "The Japanese have hamstrung our leadership. Our friend cannot continue doing what he was. Things will get worse before our boys arrive, mark my words. We must act."

"But it might be at the cost of our own lives."

Rand remembered the teenager shot by the Japanese.

He shuddered.

❧

Though the deep of the night had fallen and the camp was still and quiet, Rand never felt more alive. He, Bruce, and John had gathered at a hole in the gymnasium wall. On the other side was their Filipino friend's office. A clever disguise of furniture and curtains hid the hole where he fed through rice and mongo beans and tinned meat.

They would take turns running the precious sacks to the kitchen.

No moon shone tonight, and the guards, sure that no internees would escape to conditions that were just as bad on the outside, had become more lax with their patrols. Still, each one of Rand's senses was heightened. He strained to hear approaching footsteps, adjusted his eyes to the lack of light due to the blackout, sniffed the air for the odor of hibachi.

A whistle sounded on the other side of the wall and John answered with a whistle of his own. The exchange reminded Rand of Armando. He wondered how they were faring.

He shook his head. He couldn't be distracted tonight. One wrong move could jeopardize the operation. Not only would they suffer, but so would the entire camp.

Their contact shoved the first bag of rice through the hole, and John ran off with it. About five minutes later, another bag came through, and Bruce took this one. John returned just as the next bag made its way through. Rand hefted it on his shoulder and started in the direction of the kitchen.

He hadn't gone very far when he had to stop and rest, setting the bag on the ground and sitting on it. They were living on very few calories. Meat, eggs, and milk disappeared from the camp long ago. He estimated that he had lost sixty or so pounds of the almost two hundred he started with. He picked up the bag and continued his journey. Jobs that had been effortless for him before now left him winded. Beriberi was rampant.

The children, though thin, remained the healthiest. That wasn't the Japanese's doing. They would starve the little ones too. The internees' executive committee made sure the children received the most calories. The one thing they had gotten right. But even they were hungry.

After dropping off his precious cargo, he stood with his hands on his knees for a moment, trying to catch his breath and clear his dizziness.

Once his vision returned—the vision he had in his left eye—he made his way back to the hole in the wall as fast as possible. Another bag of rice was waiting for him. He had to keep up a strong pace. Bags of rice piling up against the wall would only arouse Japanese suspicions.

After a half-dozen trips, Rand was exhausted. Sweat poured down his forehead and into his eyes. His shirt was soaked and his muscles screamed in pain. One last bag. Their contact had given the signal that he had delivered all he could for the night.

As soon as they were liberated, this man would be the first person Rand would go see. Even if they never got another grain of rice into the camp, this would be helpful. Lifesaving.

Rand hefted this last bag of rice over his shoulder and slipped into the dark night. The air hung still and heavy. No crickets chirped. No cats screeched. No cars honked outside of the walls.

Then a sudden noise broke the quiet.

What was that?

Who was that?

He played statue, not daring to breathe.

Footsteps.

Rand squeezed his eyes shut.

# Chapter Twenty-Nine

Every muscle in Rand's body tensed as he listened to the sound of footsteps growing closer. The weight of the rice sack on his shoulder threatened to collapse his weak knees. He held his breath, sure whoever would pop out of the shadows could hear him inhale and exhale. Terror iced his veins.

The footsteps stopped.

"I know you are here." The unmistakable nasal accent of a Japanese soldier.

Had Covey betrayed them?

Rand had never been more thankful for a moonless night.

He heard the guard slide his rifle from his shoulder.

Sweat poured down Rand's face and dripped into his eyes, stinging them. The world buzzed around him.

A heavy footfall sounded on his left, then on his right. The crazy guard was lunging in the dark. Rand imagined the bayonet slicing into his stomach.

He couldn't stand here and wait for the soldier to find him at sword point.

He had to run.

But what about the rice? He couldn't let it go. It meant life to too many people.

Still clutching the precious bag of grain, Rand set off at a sprint. He heard nothing but the whooshing of blood in his ears, the pounding of his feet on the hard-packed road.

The soldier shouted something in Japanese.

Rand remembered the feel of the hammer on his fingers and pumped his legs harder. He recalled the bone-chilling wet of the Fort Santiago cell and drew in deeper breaths.

The well-fed soldier gained on him. He grabbed Rand by one shoulder and pulled him to the ground. He landed on the bag of rice.

Before the soldier could stab him, Rand grabbed the burlap sack, rolled from under his assailant, and swung with all his might.

The thud of the bag against the man's head was more satisfying than any brandy had ever been.

❧

*September 21, 1944*

The Japanese guards roamed the columns of internees like hyenas searching for the next carcass. Irene squirmed under their gazes, the merciless sun increasing her discomfort. The roll call had lasted almost two hours already. Several of her fellow prisoners fainted. The world around her buzzed. She would be next, she knew.

One of them barked out a speech, much like she imagined a drill sergeant would. "A Japanese guard. Pummeled with a sack of rice. Illegal grain someone had been hoarding. Left for dead on the street."

Irene shifted her weight from one aching foot to the other.

The soldiers' boots beat out a tempo echoed in her pounding head. "We will find the culprit."

The entire camp fell into silence. Only the bees hummed.

"And bring him to justice."

Irene's knees quivered. Fear? Malnutrition? She didn't know.

The soldiers walked the length of the columns and back again, hands gripping their rifles. Which one of them would receive a bullet to the head? Or a bayonet through the stomach?

She saw spots in front of her eyes.

"Dismissed."

To her great relief, the torture ended. They had endured these unending roll calls twice a day for three days now.

"You look terrible, love. Let's get you into the shade." Tessa took Irene by the elbow and led her in the direction of the hut they now shared.

"We need to eat. They can't keep cutting back our rations this way."

"Tell your boys to hurry up, then. And the man who clobbered that soldier over the head to give himself up."

Irene stopped short. "No. No. We can't hope for that. No one should be subjected to what the Japanese have in mind for him." She thought of Rand's hand and took a deep breath. "We'll endure what we have to until the commandant feels we've all been punished enough."

"Whenever that may be."

They arrived at the shanty. Irene sat in a chair, a glass of water in her hand, feeling better already. "Go on. I know you have plans to meet Bruce on the patio. I don't need a nanny."

The sparkle in Tessa's green eyes lit the dim interior. "If you're sure . . ."

"I am. Thank you."

Her friend just about skipped from the hut. Irene heard her singing "Cheek to Cheek." *"Heaven, I'm in heaven, and my heart beats so that I can hardly speak."*

You'd think a two-hour ordeal in the sun would have dampened Tessa's enthusiasm. Then again, Irene reasoned, that was impossible.

Bruce may not care for her very much, but he had taken a liking to Tessa. And she to him.

A visitor announced his arrival, and she went to answer the door. Rand checked on her every day, and she anticipated his visits. They were the only good left in her life. He never stayed long, but just long enough to lift her loneliness.

She opened the door and found not Rand but Mr. Covey. She started to shake. According to Rand, he should no longer be a problem.

"Good morning, Miss Reynolds." He pushed his way inside without an invitation.

"I'm sorry, but you aren't welcome here. Please leave." She didn't have the strength to deal with him right now.

"I wish to express my deepest sympathies for your loss. I was sorry to hear that your aunt passed away."

"How do you know so much about me?"

"I know more than you think I do."

A slithery shiver worked its way up and down Irene's spine. "I'm going to have to ask you once more to leave. Rand will be here soon, and he won't be happy to see you. He told me about your last meeting."

"Rand is occupied with a business meeting in his shanty. He won't be here for a while."

"Are you following us? Why go through all of this just to get Rand's clubs?"

He tented his fingers over his bent nose. "Can we please sit down? You'll be interested in what I have to say."

"I have no interest in anything you say. No, I will not sit." She crossed her arms.

"I'm sure Mr. Sterling wouldn't want the Japanese to know what business he is discussing with his associates just now."

"What are they talking about?"

"That will be for Mr. Sterling to tell you. If he cares to."

He was baiting her. "What do you want?"

"As you know, your father embezzled money from Mr. Sterling, then disappeared."

She straightened. "Where did you get that information?"

"I have my sources, Miss Reynolds. And I have my ways of getting the information I want."

"No one would have told you that. No one but Anita knew." She sucked in her breath and stood on her tiptoes to look him in his scar-marred face. "You took advantage of a dying woman. You are the rottenest man I've ever known."

"That is quite a compliment. But as you know, I don't go fishing for information unless I intend to use it."

"You have nothing on Rand anymore. He would rather the news about his daughter get out than give you any portion of his clubs."

"And that is where you come in. I need you to convince him that word of his daughter would be detrimental to him. Unless you want me to tell him about your father and his relationship to Mr. Sterling's business."

"And if I decide to tell Rand myself?"

"The Japanese would also be interested in his recent activities."

Rand had been brave enough to tell her the truth. Yes, and look at what she did—she walked away from him. Right now she needed him. She knew they had no future together beyond these walls, but for the here and now, he was all she had. She couldn't lose him too. If he walked out of her life—or was taken from her by the Japanese—she would be alone.

She paced the tiny room for a minute, twirling her hair around her finger, then turned to Mr. Covey. "What is it you want me to do?"

❧

When Rand arrived at her shanty later that morning, Irene tried her best to act as if nothing out of the ordinary had happened. "Come in." She pasted on a smile she didn't feel.

He gave her a chaste peck on the cheek. "You sound better today."

"Do I?" Her voice was too high. She cleared her throat. "Do I?"

"I would say you're almost chipper."

"One day closer to liberation."

"Mm-hmm." He didn't believe her.

Nor should he. "When our boys arrive, the first thing I'm going to do is find the biggest roast I can and make you a proper dinner. You come every day, and I never have anything to offer you, not even a cup of tea or coffee."

"You don't need to do anything for me, Irene, and you know that. You're more nervous than a squirrel whose nut stash has been discovered."

"I'm not." She stilled her hands. "You had a meeting this morning?"

He grinned, his face thinner than ever. "Irene, Irene, prettiest little spy I've ever seen."

"What was it about?"

His smile faded. "It's better that you not know."

"And the Japanese?"

Now his face blanched. "What about them?" He grabbed her upper arms with a viselike grip.

"What aren't you telling me?"

"Nothing." Now his voice sounded too bright. He frightened her.

"Are you in collusion with the enemy?"

He released her. "If I was, would they have sent me to Fort Santiago?"

"Is that why you came back?"

"No. Quite the opposite. That's all you need to know."

She couldn't decide if she should be relieved or worried. She wrung her hands. "I'm sorry. I'm out of sorts."

"This confinement has gotten to all of us." He embraced her. She drew comfort from his strength, his closeness. He kissed the top of her head. "To help myself, I think more and more about what I'm going to do to rebuild my life when we walk out of here."

"Aren't you afraid of what Mr. Covey will do when he is released? You need to put Melanie's welfare ahead of your own."

He creased his forehead. "What do you mean?" He drew out each word.

She made a circuit around the room. "We both know Mr. Covey to be an underhanded, sneaky type of man who will do whatever he has to in order to get what he wants. Once we are free, what's to stop him from going to Virginia and threatening either Catherine or Melanie?"

"Threatening them how?"

She clutched her hands so her knuckles whitened. "Their lives. He might go after them physically if you don't give in to his demands."

Rand rubbed his square chin. "I hadn't thought about that."

"You should."

"He might go after you too."

Irene stood with her back to Rand. "He might."

"You're right here in camp."

"Like I said before, I think their lives are in danger. Both of them. If you want to protect them, you have to give Mr. Covey what he wants." This lie was getting harder and harder to keep up. All of the lies—the one about her father, the ones Mr. Covey forced her to tell. She longed to reveal the truth. Every bit of it.

Anita would tell her she should. Her aunt would urge her to accept whatever consequences would come from it.

But she couldn't lose him. Since Anita's death, he had been by her side whenever she needed him. She hated that she relied on him this much, but she did. He was the best friend she had in camp. In the world. Without him, she would be emptier than ever.

Rand cracked his knuckles. "I don't want to see Melanie or Catherine get hurt because of me."

The thundering roar of aircraft filled the air. It shook the ground and reverberated in her bones. They both ran to the window. "Rand, look! Planes coming from the south. Look at them all. Are they ours?"

He shrugged. "Let's hope so."

*Ack-ack-ack-ack.* Intense Japanese antiaircraft fire split the day.

Then the air-raid sirens shrieked. A command boomed over the loudspeaker. "This is an air raid. Seek shelter immediately."

No more practice. This was the real thing.

Those horrible days of the beginning of the war flooded back. The bombs falling around them. The Japanese marching into the open city of Manila. Moisture gathered on her hands. "Rand, these are our planes."

He whooped and picked up Irene, swinging her in a circle. "*The Yanks are coming, the Yanks are coming,*" he sang.

"This isn't a time for dancing. We have to take cover."

They scurried under Irene's bed, beneath the bamboo slats holding her mattress. Rand had to fold his long legs as much as possible in order to fit. Together they listened to the music of the American planes in the sky. Rand squirmed and wriggled. "I can't sit in here and listen to it. I want to see our planes. Wave to our boys."

"I'm coming with you."

"A little scared?"

"More like scared of you getting into trouble with the guards again." They were under strict orders from the commandant not to watch the fight over the city. Yet she noticed many eyes peeping from the shanties.

"The guards just like to get under my skin. They're as harmless as a cobra's bite."

"Very reassuring."

Planes peeled off from their formation and dove toward the earth, releasing their cargo over the city and zooming high into the sky again. It was a dance so amazing to watch. Black clouds from the antiaircraft fire puffed upward.

"Can you believe it, Irene? There is our hope. There is our liberation."

A short while later, the explosions came closer, and shells and shrapnel showered the camp. Rand and Irene dove back under the bed. The ground rocked. She jumped and scooted closer to him. "What were those? Are the Americans bombing the camp?"

Rand rubbed her back. "No, those must be Japanese pom-poms. From what I've heard, they only explode on impact."

With his words, another detonation rocked the ground. "What if we take a direct hit?"

"Pray. That's all I can say. If one of those pom-poms did hit this hut, we have no real protection."

Irene's body went limp.

# Chapter Thirty

With pom-poms detonating around them, Irene sat quivering on the bamboo floor, Rand beside her, and pleaded with God. "Dear Father, please keep us safe from this shelling. We thank You that You have sent the Americans to free us. We pray that You would watch over the pilots and all of those on the ground. Protect us, Lord, and keep us in the palm of Your hand. Be our shelter from the stormy blast. We ask this all in Your Son's precious name. Amen."

Rand shifted positions, holding Irene's tiny, trembling hand in his. "Do you believe what you pray?"

"Of course."

"I wish I could." He did too. He'd been watching Anita and Irene. They didn't have the aching emptiness he did. They were full. Like he wanted to be. "But what if a pom-pom falls on us and we die? God will have failed you."

"He may choose to answer my prayer in a different way than I intend. I want to be kept safe on this earth to live another day. He might choose to keep me safe by taking me to be home with Him where no harm will ever come to me again."

He shivered. "But you're afraid."

"Not afraid of death, but yes, dying scares me. Does that make sense?"

"I suppose it does. I wish I had the assurance you do, that when I die I will go to heaven. When that guard caught me—"

"The Lord watched over you, even in Fort Santiago."

Why had he opened his mouth? He hadn't wanted her to know this. "No, when he caught me last week, smuggling rice."

"He what?" She tried to sit up and smacked her head on the bed frame.

*Ack-ack-ack-ack.*

The shelling continued unabated.

"On the day Anita died, I watched a guard chase a teenage boy. Who knows what the kid had done. When the soldier caught the boy, he hauled him out of camp and killed him. When the guard caught me with that sack of rice, I thought for sure my time had come. You can only be lucky so many times. I was terrified. Petrified."

"You're the one who injured that guard."

"I never meant to get anyone else into trouble. I'm sorry the camp is suffering because of me. So you see, God won't forgive me. I'll never have what you have." He had failed to earn God's favor. In fact, he had brought His wrath on himself.

"All you have to do is believe. It is that simple. Nothing is too much for God to forgive. Don't make it more complicated or intellectual than it has to be. Just have faith."

Just have faith. So easy to say. But wanting faith and having it were two different things.

The day wore on, planes droned overhead, and bombs whistled to the ground. As they sat huddled in the shelter, Rand wondered what would be left of the city he loved by the time the Americans arrived. He thought of the millions of people who called Manila home. Many of them were very poor, and they had no shelters to run to when the shelling began.

A pom-pom hit nearby. Dirt sprayed the side of the shanty. Irene grabbed his hand. "Is this hut going to hold?"

He didn't know what to tell her. Though the bombs weren't falling here, the shrapnel and Japanese pom-poms were. Would the little bit of bamboo and *sawali* protect them? He fingered the picture of Melanie in his pocket.

Another ground-shaking hit.

What about Armando and Ramon? Were they safe? Where were they hiding?

"You're worried about Armando."

"How did you know?"

"You get this crease across your forehead when you're concerned. There is just enough light for me to see it. I took a guess as to why."

"I remember when I was about five, there was a terrible thunderstorm. My parents were out and my *amah* was asleep, which was fine with me. I would rather spend my time with Armando.

"As the lightning brightened the nursery, I scurried downstairs to the servants' quarters and found Armando sitting in bed. He lifted the sheet and I crawled beneath it."

Rand drifted to that day. He could almost smell the rain.

"I don't like the storm." The little hairs on his arms stood at attention.

Armando pulled him close, like a father would. Like a father should. "I don't like them much myself."

"So what do we do?"

"We trust God to take care of us and we pray to Him." Armando bowed his dark head.

"How?" Another great crash shook the house. Rand's heart beat fast as he snuggled against Armando's solid frame. He just wished Armando would make the thunder go away.

"We pray like this. Dear heavenly Father, please take care of us. Protect us from the storm. Help us not to be afraid. Amen."

Maybe praying would stop the storm. It was worth a try. Another low rumble came, and it felt like an earthquake. Rand closed his eyes and folded his trembling hands the way Armando did. He bowed his head and prayed, "Dear heavenly Father, take care of me and Armando. Keep the storm away and help us not to be afraid. Amen."

A great peace washed over him. For the first time in his life, he wasn't afraid of the thunder or the lightning or the pouring rain. He fell asleep next to Armando.

The thunder of an exploding pom-pom jarred him back to the present day. Irene quaked beside him. "That was close."

He pulled her to himself, relishing the way she fit in the crook of his arm. "Let's hope they don't get any closer."

They listened to the battle as it raged outside. He held Irene's hand and squeezed it. "And what if one of those pom-poms explodes over our heads?"

"What about it?"

"I want the assurance you have."

"I told you how you can get it. Armando told you how to get it."

Could he surrender control like that? Give everything over to the Lord—all of his fears, his worries, his sins? The fighting in the skies above him frightened him much the same way the thunderstorm had all those years ago. He remembered the peace that flooded him at that time. He wanted that peace again. That feeling of fullness. Completeness.

"I can't kneel in here."

"You don't have to. You can pray anytime, anywhere, in any position." She slid her arm around his shoulders and pushed a strand of hair away from his face.

He took a deep breath, knowing that his life was about to change forever. He was about to change. God was about to change him. "Dear heavenly Father, I pray that You would take away all of my sins. Help me put my faith and trust in You. Protect us here, Lord, and keep those shells away. And if they come, take us to heaven with You. Amen."

He knew it wouldn't go down in the annals of history as the greatest prayer of all time, but that peace that he had so longed for since he was a child once again filled his soul. It seeped in and covered him completely.

He was full to overflowing.

He knew every sin he had ever committed, even his sin with Catherine, was covered by Jesus' blood. He knew he was clean, a new creature in Christ.

And he knew what awaited him after this life.

And then the loudest explosion he had ever heard rocked the shelter.

# Chapter Thirty-One

The pom-pom struck mere feet from where Rand and Irene huddled under the bed. The rocks and twigs it pummeled against the shanty tore a hole in the *sawali* wall right beside Irene. Sand filled the air, stinging Irene's eyes, making them water. Dirt choked her and she coughed. The acetone-like odor of cordite hung in the air.

Rand rubbed her back. "Are you hurt? Let me look at you."

He helped her crawl from under the bed and sit, stroking her cheek with his misshapen fingers. "Your face has been gashed. You're bleeding."

It wasn't until that moment that she felt the pain across her forehead and the stickiness of blood running down her temple.

"Let's get you cleaned up."

Shrapnel continued to rain around the shanty. Another pom-pom exploded about twenty or thirty feet away, sending a shower of dirt into the air.

She shuddered.

Rand sat her on the chair and went for a bowl of water and a washcloth. As gentle as any nurse, he washed her wound and wiped her face. He dabbed and dabbed at the area. "I can't get the bleeding to stop. You need stitches."

The *rat-a-tat-tat* of antiaircraft fire continued around them. "We can't go out now. Just bandage it the best you can, and I'll go once this is over. Maybe by then the bleeding will stop on its own." She couldn't bear the thought of needle and thread being pulled through her skin.

"Let me see what I can do." He left the room, and she heard him ripping cloth. When he came back, he no longer wore a T-shirt but carried strips of material.

She sat back in horror. Horror at his bony frame, his ribs and collar bones protruding, his stomach shrunken, more so than when she'd seen him bare-chested a few weeks ago. And horror at the thought that he had torn up his last T-shirt for her.

He turned sideways and flexed his muscles. But skin hung from his bony arm. "One hundred twenty-nine pounds this morning. What do you think?"

"You have no more shirts."

He came and wrapped the soft cotton material around her head. "I have more. This is my last T-shirt, true, but I have two dress shirts. Don't ask me why I brought them with me, but I did. One I'm saving for when our boys get here. The other I can wear in the meantime."

He tugged and tied a knot in the back. "There you are. You look like a warrior."

"Just call me Alexander the Great."

The shelling raged on. His voice softened as did his golden eyes. "You are a warrior."

They rode out the remainder of the air raid huddled under Irene's bed. At about five o'clock, the all-clear was sounded at last.

As they left the shanty to walk to the hospital, Rand pointed to the sky in the direction of the harbor. The heavens glowed red and smoke smudged the sky all around the city. "The bombing must have been heavy."

*O Lord, let this be over soon. Bring us peace quickly.*

Rand squeezed her hand. "I know what you're thinking."

"We're all thinking it tonight. But don't say it. Please don't say a word. If we talk about it, it won't happen."

Rand nodded, understanding in his eyes. "The entire camp is holding its breath and won't release it until our boys walk through those gates." He licked his lips. "I hope the hospital won't be too crowded, that not too many were injured."

Or killed. "Let's hope not. We had enough practice leading up to this day. We knew what to do."

With relief, Irene and Rand entered the clinic and found only a handful of people waiting to be seen. Most of them were suffering from dysentery. The rest had minor cuts or bumps.

Dr. Young had a chance to see her at last. He numbed the area around her gash, the pain of the needle worse than the pain of her injury. She closed her eyes while he worked so she wouldn't have to watch him sewing her back together. Rand held her hand the entire time.

What would she have done without him? He could never know about her father. More than ever, she wanted to preserve that secret.

Once the doctor finished, he laid aside his work. "I've been meaning to come and see you, Irene. Wait here. I have a package for you."

He disappeared, and she turned to Rand. "What do you suppose it is?"

He rubbed his square chin and shrugged.

The doctor returned in a few minutes with a small box tied

with brown string. "I saw your aunt every day she was in the hospital. We spent much time talking about many different subjects. At one point, when she spoke to me about the Lord, she gave me a Bible so I could read it. She changed my life. I'm not the same man I was when I first met her. I wanted you to know that. God brought good from her illness, at least for me."

He handed her the box. She bit her lip, not wanting to make a public scene. Tears, however, rolled down Dr. Young's face, and she allowed hers to flow. "Thank you."

Rand held her hand, and a sad smile crossed his angular face.

"Your aunt was an extraordinary woman," the doctor said. "Remember that. I'm sorry I couldn't do more to help her."

"I understand. You did everything possible under the circumstances."

Rand saw her back to her shanty and brushed a good-night kiss across her cheek. "Are you going to be okay?"

She managed to nod. "I have something to remember her by."

For a long time Irene sat in the dark, the package unopened on the table in front of her as she wondered what it contained. The hole left in her heart by Anita's disappearance hadn't shrunk. She missed her as much today as a month ago.

With her stomach tied in knots, Irene pulled the twine loose. She slipped it from the box and opened the flap. She withdrew her aunt's watch, her most expensive and prized possession. Her parents had given it to her when she left for the mission field. Irene didn't have to turn it over to know the inscription on the back. *Look on the fields; for they are white already to harvest.*

She set the watch aside and reached into the box again. The only other thing her fingers brushed was Anita's Bible. The small one she had before she went blind. Irene retrieved it.

The markings in the front indicated that her parents gave Anita this Bible on her wedding day. Anita had underlined scores of passages throughout the book and had written a plethora of notes in the margins before scarlet fever robbed her of her sight.

She turned to Jeremiah 46:27, the verse Anita had read to her the day after she had been attacked. "But fear not thou, O my servant Jacob, and be not dismayed, O Israel: for, behold, I will save thee from afar off, and thy seed from the land of their captivity; and Jacob shall return, and be in rest and at ease, and none shall make him afraid."

Off to the side, Irene saw a note written in a hand other than her aunt's. *This is for you, Irene. Cling to it and don't lose hope. Your salvation is near.*

Irene picked up the book and pressed it to her chest. She wondered who Anita had recruited to write the words for her and when. Had it been some time ago or just before she passed away? The Americans were making their presence known, and Irene's salvation was near.

Either their boys would come riding into camp in the next couple of weeks or months, or Irene would starve to death.

The sun was barely over the horizon when Frank Covey stood on Rand's step. Rand's mouth went dry as he opened the door.

It was as if his conversation with Irene yesterday morning had made Covey appear. Strange coincidence?

Excitement shone in Covey's bright-blue eyes. His mustache twitched, and he practically danced as Rand ushered him in. "Mr. Sterling, good morning."

In that moment, Rand was convinced this wasn't a coincidence. Had Irene been up to something? Her concern for Catherine's and Melanie's lives came out of nowhere. And suddenly Covey was here.

"I need to talk to you." The man was downright gleeful.

Rand pulled out a kitchen chair and motioned for Covey to sit.

Rand himself remained standing, his instincts screaming caution. "I have something to say to you first. I think you're blackmailing Irene Reynolds."

Covey's eyebrows rose. "Why on earth would you say that?"

"Because suddenly she wants me to make a deal with you."

"That doesn't mean I'm blackmailing her. She's a shrewd woman who has your best interests at heart. Now let's sit down and draw up paperwork to seal the deal. I believe we were at seventy percent before you had your little tantrum?" He smiled, the scar across his cheek bunching as he did so.

"You hold no sway over me, Covey." Rand's mind raced. The man denied having anything on Irene, but Rand would bet his nightclubs on it. And he was about to. "Nothing. Nothing at all."

"Are you out of your mind?"

Rand leaned on the rickety table. "I have no reason to give you any part of my business."

"Do you want the world to find out about your daughter? Do you want your daughter to find out about you? Do you want her to have an accident?"

The new threat made Rand stand up. Covey now had his attention. Irene had been right.

"That's correct. I know where the little angel lives. I know where she goes to school and to church."

"You wouldn't involve a child in this."

"Do you want to take the chance? And what about Irene?"

Rand went numb. This wasn't money or his clubs on the line. This was his daughter's life. And the life of the woman he loved. Did he want to gamble with them? Did he dare?

He didn't want to do this. It would be easier for him to stab a knife into his heart than to let this man into his business. But Irene was right. It had to be done.

The only way to protect his child was to keep Covey on a very short leash. Right in front of him.

He swallowed hard, praying Covey didn't notice the quiver in his voice. "Thirty percent. I'm prepared to walk away from the table and take my chances if you don't accept my terms."

"Seventy percent. Take it or leave it. How much are two lives worth?"

All the man wanted was controlling interest. He wanted to be in charge.

And if Rand lost the clubs? Could he live with that?

Was there more to life than success? Than being someone people stood in awe of, who waved to you when you drove past, who fawned over you?

Maybe. He didn't know. But he did know he could never live with being the one to bring harm to his daughter. Or with losing Irene.

He drew in a deep breath and held it.

Then he nodded.

The gleeful glint returned to Covey's eyes. "I'll draw up the papers and send them over to you for your signature. This time we'll have it all in writing. Nice and legal. And the contract will include the stipulation that you'll reopen the clubs within one year of the end of the war."

Rand didn't argue.

Covey was about to get everything Rand ever wanted.

❧

*October 19, 1944*

Irene bent over her flowers, her legs and hands swollen and painful from the beriberi. She ached all over and was so tired.

With all of the air raids in the past month, she hadn't had much time to tend to her garden. She wanted at least to pluck off the spent blooms. Soon the weeds would choke out all of her flowers.

After the first few days of heavy raids, several days without bombings had passed, and so it continued. Planes would come one after the other, then stop for a while. Hopes would soar. Hopes would fall.

She wanted to look up and stretch her neck, but the commandant's new decree kept her eyes fixed on her flowers. Whoever looked to the skies was to be punished. And who knew what form that punishment would take?

Irene sat back in the dirt. Rand came from her shanty with a glass of water in his hand. "Drink up. You look thirsty."

"No wonder the ladies all swoon over you, with the way you flatter them." She gave him her best smile.

"You've discovered my secret. I hope it doesn't mean you'll be immune to my charms."

"You won't win me with your sweet-talking ways."

He brushed her cheek. "Rest for a while."

The word *rest* brought to mind the Bible passage her aunt had recited to her. *Jacob shall return, and be in rest and at ease.* She studied Rand—shirtless, skinny, sunken-chested. *How long, O Lord, how long? How long until You deliver us?*

No answer came.

After a while of sitting in silence, he pulled her up. "Come on, let's go get some *lugao* and pretend it's chocolate cake."

She nodded. "Oh, that would be so good. I could eat an entire one by myself."

"I've done just that."

"And borne your *amah*'s wrath, I assume."

"No, Armando covered for me."

She gave him a gentle elbow to the side. "No wonder you're so spoiled."

"A genuine brat." He grinned, full and wide.

They were still crossing the yard when they heard the rumble of approaching planes. Rand looked up, and Irene followed his gaze. Were they American planes or the Japanese? Their boys hadn't bombed in a few days.

From the corner of her eye, she spied a guard with a fixed bayonet. She nudged Rand in the ribs. "Look down. The soldier is watching you."

They picked up their pace, but the guard caught them, moving in front of them. He spat at Rand. "You were looking up."

"I was stretching my neck."

"Not true." The soldier struck Rand, and he stumbled backward. "If you wanted to see upward so much, now you will."

Rand clenched his fists.

The soldier led Rand, a bayonet in his back, to the front gate and tied him to it.

"Now look up."

~

Fire raged inside of Rand. The rule was the most ridiculous he had ever heard in his life. The Japanese wanted so much control over them, they now told them where they could and could not look.

Crazy.

He dug his fingernails into his palm.

He tilted his head upward, the glare of the sun robbing him of the sight in his good eye for a moment. He closed his lids.

The guard struck him. "No closing eyes."

All of this because of the natural instinct to watch a plane.

He would bake to a crisp.

# Chapter Thirty-Two

Irene sat on the ground near Rand as he stared into the perfectly blue sky. He felt her presence, unable to see her below him. A group of internees gathered, most of the spectators sympathetic to his plight.

"Hey, Mr. Sterling, you have to play ball with us again." A young boy held up his basketball.

"Kind of hard to dribble now. It will have to wait till later. Then I'm going to get more baskets than you because all I'll be able to see is the net."

"Bet you won't."

"Bet I will."

Others in the crowd shouted encouragement to him.

He had never been one to shy away from entertaining an audience. "Rand, Rand, leader of the band, here he must stand, feet stuck in the sand."

The crowd laughed and applauded.

"All because he looked to the sky, watching for our boys to come by, looking as they fly, in the blue so very high."

Cheers this time. The guard crossed his arms and frowned.

"Please don't be like me, hoping you will see, the boys that make us free, how happy we will be."

The people roared their approval.

The guard uncrossed his arms, spread his legs wide, and screamed, "Get away. Leave now. No one here by this man." He moved forward, and the crowd dispersed.

A few of the men called to Rand as they left. "Stand tall."

"Hang in there."

"Don't give in to them."

He stood alone, the minutes ticking away with maddening slowness. His face grew hot, his lips parched. He longed for a drink. He could see nothing but searing bright white.

Then Irene's quiet voice from several feet away broke the silence. "I'm here, Rand."

He had never heard a more beautiful sound in all of his life. "You didn't leave?"

"I'll stay as long as that guard allows me."

"I'm glad you're here."

"You've been there for me when I needed you. Now it's my turn to be here for you."

The words washed over him like a cool shower. "You should be back at your hut resting."

"I'll be able to do that later. I remember those long Nebraska winters. Have you ever seen snow?"

Rand nodded. "When I was in school in California, yes. We went to the mountains to ski at Christmas. The first time I saw it I was amazed. It was cold and white and there was so much. Snow was more beautiful than I had imagined."

"It can be quite pretty. Think of the prairie covered in white,

white as far as the eye can see. And then the sun shines on it, and it sparkles like tens of thousands of diamonds. One time the boys at school teased some of the girls by shoving snow down our backs. I don't think I've ever been so cold in my entire life. For the rest of the day, I sat in my wet clothes and shivered, even though Miss Peters allowed me to sit next to the stove."

He shivered along with her. "I see what you're doing, Miss Reynolds, trying to keep my mind off of the heat."

"Is it working?"

"Yes. Keep talking to me. I know you never knew your mother. Tell me about your father. What did he do for a living?"

Irene took a long moment to answer. "He held a variety of jobs over the years. After my mother left, he was sad and never found fulfillment in work. That's why Anita suggested we move to Manila."

"You never told me you lived in Manila with your father."

"We weren't here long before Father disappeared."

"Why?"

Again, an extended silence stretched out before Irene continued. "It's not important. One day I woke up and he was gone, a Filipina in his place. The woman took me to the mission. What really matters is that's when Anita took me in. From that point on, I lived with her, and she was both mother and father to me."

"That's hard on a child." He heard the pain in her voice and something else. A bit of fear? "I caught a man embezzling from me once, a manager of mine, and I had to turn him in despite the fact that he had a family. He disappeared before he was prosecuted. Walter Reynolds was his name. Do you know him?"

"No, no. It's a common last name. You know, Reynoldses all over the world, and I don't know a tenth of them. It's a strange coincidence, nothing more. It's not the same man. That wasn't my father who embezzled from you."

He hadn't accused him of being her father. But she protested too much. Could it be?

No, she would have told him.

❧

Two mornings later, Irene sat on the doorstep of her shanty, the one she now shared with Tessa. Her lilies were making a valiant effort at reviving after she pulled them up the day Anita died. They refused to bloom, however.

She clutched Anita's Bible in her lap, unopened. Even without reading the words, Irene knew them. She didn't miss her aunt as much when she touched the book Anita had touched.

How she longed for her aunt's words of wisdom. Rand had probed close to the truth about her father the previous day. She had slipped when she mentioned that her father had disappeared. Words she wished she could take back.

If he kept asking questions, he would get suspicious and would try to find out about her father, no doubt. If only their boys would arrive soon so that she didn't have to keep up this charade any longer.

She dreaded not spending time with Rand, not hearing his voice at her door, not seeing his smiling face each day. He kept her going when she wanted to roll over and give up.

She couldn't tell him until they were free. He was her survival.

As if she'd conjured him up, he appeared, whistling down the street, settling on the step beside her. She couldn't tell that he had been tied to the gate and forced to look at the sun until dusk.

"How are your eyes?" With sight in only one, his vision was precious.

He squinted, hiding his liquid-gold orbs. "I can see a fair amount, but there are still lots of spots. Or do you have chicken pox?"

"It's the pox, and I'm contagious."

"Then I should run away." He made no attempt to move.

But run away he would when he discovered her secret. Or rather, her father's secret. "Why aren't you going anywhere?" She flashed him what she hoped was an impish grin.

He responded in kind, the lines around his mouth deepening, the skin sagging. "You can't get rid of me that easily."

He didn't understand.

They sat for a while, enjoying the birds' morning songs. Just his presence cheered her. What would she do if she lost it?

"Did you hear the rumors?" Rand's voice held near giddiness.

"About the overdue rice shipment arriving?"

"That, too, but about Leyte?"

"Who hasn't? The camp has been buzzing with it. They say some heard it on the secret radio. Do you believe that our forces have actually landed in the Philippines? This isn't some trick?"

"It has to be true. I can feel it in my bones. General MacArthur has his feet on Filipino soil again. The end can't be far off. It just can't be. Maybe weeks. Some are saying that we will celebrate Thanksgiving in our own homes this year."

Yes, Rand would celebrate it in his grand home on Dewey Boulevard. They would go their separate ways. Irene would begin her new life alone.

Yet, not quite.

She rubbed the cracked leather cover of the Bible. "I'm so

grateful that Dr. Young gave this to me. I hear Anita in the words she wrote in the margins. At times it's like she never left."

"I'm glad you have it."

"She was everything to me. I'd like to go thank Dr. Young. Are you up to a walk?"

He helped her up and held her hand as they wove their way through the huts of Shantytown. Their path to Glamourville took them across the main lawn. A surprising number of people filled the square, even for so early in the day. It no longer held the jovial atmosphere of the early days when there were concerts and activities, but couples strolled along and friends laughed together. Gone were the strings of lights that provided a festive feeling. Gone were the merchants selling treats. Still, the soft hum of voices filled the air.

The loudspeaker that brought them news, however censored it might be, crackled to life. The announcer cleared his voice and noted the delay of the daily announcements. "This has come a little late, but better Leyte than never."

A stunned silence fell over the crowd. Leyte was pronounced *late-ay.* The Japanese might not understand the connection, but the internees did. Smiles broke out on all of those assembled.

Rand stopped and squeezed Irene's hand. She squeezed his back. It was true. The Americans had arrived. Just having them in country brought a measure of hope and comfort. They were here. It was now just a matter of time.

No celebrations broke out among the crowd, though. How could they? The Japanese would punish them for sure if they shouted and danced and sang. No, except for the brightness of the faces, all went on as it had before.

"I told you." Rand laughed.

Irene stroked his thin cheek, the cleft in his chin more prominent than ever with his weight loss. "That almost makes up for this." She tipped her head toward the gate.

"The dump." A host of military supplies littered the front lawn of Santo Tomas, including caches of ammunition. "And rumor is that the Japanese have buried huge drums of fuel outside of the gate."

"So that if one bomb hits us, we'll be blown to kingdom come." Irene shivered.

Rand wrapped his arm around her and rubbed her shoulder. "Some say that the Japanese are using us as a shield. The Americans won't bomb us, so they can concentrate their soldiers and supplies here where they're safe. Others say they mean to . . ."

"Mean to what?" Her pulse throbbed in her ears. Irene wasn't sure she wanted to hear the rest.

"Mean to make this place a target so the Americans will blow it up. And us with it."

"I pray you're wrong."

"Me too. I've grown rather attached to all my body parts."

Seeing the military dump robbed the joy of the news of the American landfall.

Rand held her a bit tighter. "Our boys will get here in time. God will bring them."

"Like the verse Anita read to me after my escapade in Manila. God will return Israel, and they will be at rest. Or something like that. I can't remember now." She opened the Bible she was taking to Dr. Young and thumbed through the pages to the passage in Isaiah she wanted.

A paper fluttered out. Rand picked it up before the wind had a chance to blow it away.

"What is that?"

"I don't know. It fell out of the Bible. I thought you had put it there."

"No, I don't have any papers tucked inside. Read what it says."

He unfolded the sheet.

Dearest Irene,

As I have the nurse pen these words, I know my days on this earth are nearing an end. I will be happy to see my Savior. I worry about leaving you, but I know you will be in God's hands. Rand is a fine young man, and I believe he is coming to see the truth. If he does, you will have my blessing.

A smile curled Rand's mouth. "She always liked me."

Irene tipped her head. "Keep reading."

First, though, you must tell him the truth. It is time he knew. The hour for secrets is over. Whether there is a future for you with him or not, tell him the truth.

I love you with all of my heart. I could not have loved you more had you been born from my own body. Remember to walk humbly with our Lord in all your ways.

Much love to you,

Anita

Irene's breathing grew erratic. She ripped the paper from Rand's hand.

He stared at her. "What is it you need to tell me?"

"I can't tell you. Not right now." Not when their liberation might only be weeks away.

He ran his hands through his wavy light-brown hair. "You can tell me anything. You know that. I confided in you about my daughter. I promise, whatever it is, I won't walk away. I want to commit myself to you. Nothing you say will drive me away."

Her entire body tingled. "I can't. Don't you see, even if I wanted to, I can't."

"It's Covey, isn't it?" His eyes searched her face, and she squirmed under the scrutiny. Why couldn't Anita's words simply have been ones of encouragement? And why did she allow Rand to read the letter?

She dragged her *bakyas* through the dirt. "No."

"He'll win if you don't tell me."

"Rand, you didn't want me to badger you. Please don't hound me. I promise I will tell you when the right time comes. But this isn't it. Not now."

"Now is the perfect time."

# Chapter Thirty-Three

Irene stood on the front lawn of Santo Tomas, a munitions dump in front of her, the iron gates covered with *sawali* mats so the Filipinos couldn't see in and the internees couldn't see out. The crowd diminished, off to celebrate the landing at Leyte privately. Her entire body ached, and she wished Rand would go away. But that's what she feared—that he would leave and never come back to her. He promised he wouldn't, but he didn't know who she was.

And once he found out, that would change everything.

She was afraid of Mr. Covey as well. The man gave her the heebie-jeebies. She rubbed her sweaty hands together.

In her mind, she heard Anita begging her to tell Rand the truth. Anita hated secrets and said that no good ever came from keeping them. She never threw Irene a surprise birthday party because of it.

But so much havoc could be wreaked with the telling of one. "You will hate me when I tell you."

"I could never hate you."

There was no way around it. She had to tell him the truth. Now.

She swallowed hard and drew in a deep breath to steady her shaking limbs. "My father is Walter Reynolds. The man who embezzled from you."

His jaw dropped wide enough to land an American bomber. "Walter Reynolds." He paced in front of her. "Of course. I don't know why I didn't figure it out the moment I heard your name. You even have the same turned-up nose and blue eyes as your father. You're Walter Reynolds's daughter. The little girl he had."

She couldn't see the expression in his eyes. Her airway constricted so all she could do was squeak, "Do you hate me?"

"Oh, Irene." Rand stopped, studied her, and ran his fingers through her hair that hung loose around her shoulders. His voice softened. "I could never hate you. You and your father are two separate people. You shouldn't pay for his crimes. Don't you see? I love you. No matter what."

"Please don't say that. You can't love me." When this had time to sink in, he would hate her for all her father had done to him. And then his rejection would be even more unbearable. She had to walk away now and let him live his life.

"If this is about Catherine and Melanie . . ."

"It is and it isn't. When you look at me, you will see the man who almost ruined your young business. Then you will realize that Catherine and Melanie need to be the most important people in your life."

Rand sighed and rubbed his square jaw the way Irene loved.

Yes, she loved him. When he almost ran her over with his red convertible, he was the last person on earth she thought she would ever love.

But she did.

"I'm not walking away from you."

She touched his whisker-roughened cheek. "When the war is over, you will. You need to figure out where your life goes from here and so do I."

"We could do that together."

"You signed the paper with Covey that states you must reopen your clubs. You will return to that lavish, glittering lifestyle. Don't you see? We live in different circles."

"And you belong with me."

"Nightclubs aren't what I'm interested in. They are the furthest thing from the orphanage I want to open. Please don't try to make this work when it won't. Let's agree to be friends. Nothing more. Nothing less." Her heart ached more than her body.

"Is that what you truly want?"

"It is what I truly want." Oh, how she truly wanted him.

*December 23, 1944*

Bruce sat with Rand in the shade of his little screened porch. Someone in the area played "Jingle Bells" on the phonograph. In his hand, Rand held a piece of the kitchen table's leg and a whittling knife.

"What on earth are you carving?"

"Irene's Christmas gift." Part of it, anyway. "It's supposed to be a lily."

"*Supposed to be* are the right words."

"It would be nicer if I could use my right hand better."

"Excuses, excuses, Sterling. I hope she's worth it."

"She is."

"At least Tessa's family has money and connections."

"Is that all that matters?"

Bruce rubbed his mouth. "Honestly, not as much as before this war."

"Would you feel the same way about Tessa if she didn't have a penny to her name?" Rand hadn't failed to notice the way Bruce's hard face softened when he was around the woman. He bore all of the signs of a man in love. Rand ought to know.

"You have me there. I'll admit, it's what first attracted me to her, but now that I know her, it doesn't matter. But she isn't a missionary girl."

"That's what makes Irene better than all the rest. Someone I'd give my last bag of rice for."

"And that's about all I have left."

"Me too. And then what will we do?"

"What can we do?" Bruce rubbed his ruddy face. "There's no rice remaining in the entire city."

Rand stared into space. Their friend had stopped delivering food. There just wasn't any to be found. "How long can we hold out?" He knew the answer but had to ask the question.

"Weeks. Not much more. Some of the elderly men won't last but a few more days. We're going to start having deaths from starvation."

In his former life, Rand would have cursed then. "Those Japanese. Do they intend to kill us all?"

"If the kitchen staff doesn't kill us first."

Rand grabbed his stomach. "Don't remind me. I don't know who decided to cook the cassava root that way for Thanksgiving, but my stomach still hurts thinking about it."

"Well, one way or another, this will be our last Christmas here. Our boys are so close and yet so far away."

"Let's pray they're here sooner rather than later." Not only for the sake of the internees, but for the civilians of Manila. He wondered how Armando and Ramon were faring. *Please, Lord, keep them safe too.*

The loudspeaker hummed and screeched, and then a voice sounded. "Everyone must report to their rooms immediately. You are not to stay in your shanties. Report to your assigned rooms at this time."

Rand looked up from his work. "What might this be about? I didn't hear an air-raid siren, did you?"

Bruce shook his head. "I have no idea. The commandant is so fickle, who knows what the reason is. I wouldn't doubt that they're going to take this opportunity to search all of our quarters. Off to the Education Building, I suppose." He rose from his chair with a bit of effort.

If they were going to go through his belongings, he didn't want to be caught with a knife. That he slipped into his pocket. Not wanting them to take or damage his crude carving, he wrapped the wood in a piece of cloth.

He tucked the little flower through a rip in the material on the underside of the couch, along with his picture of Melanie. They were his most prized possessions. No way was he going to let the enemy get his hands on those.

They followed the stream of men making their way to the Education Building. Bruce pointed to the sky at the low-flying planes. "Those are land based, I'd bet my last can of Spam on it."

"Land based?" Rand didn't dare look to the skies.

"I'm positive."

"That means our boys have taken and now hold an airfield."

A wide grin brightened Bruce's craggy face. "It sure does. Maybe they'll be here by the new year." He slapped Rand on the back. "No more worries about our lack of food. We'll be free before we run out."

"I don't know."

They wound their way around a group of slower-moving, older men as the stream of internees headed to the classrooms increased. "What's the problem?"

Rand shook his head to clear his thoughts and chase away his unease. "Nothing. I pray you're right."

They came within sight of the iron gates that robbed them of their freedom. Bruce harrumphed. "At least they got rid of that military equipment they had piled on the front lawn, thanks to those old priests."

"But what about the drums of fuel rumored to be buried just outside?" Rand's heart seized. "With all of the bombs falling around the city, we're in as much danger as ever."

"Now that's the Christmas spirit."

"It's contagious."

"Old Mr. Scrooge has nothing on you."

"Just don't let the Ghost of Christmas Past visit me."

"We have to stop them."

"How? Dig up barrels of gasoline outside of the gates with our bare hands? If there are even any there. You're out of your mind, Bruce."

"We can't let them murder more than three thousand people. Women and children."

Sweat dripped down Rand's forehead. "We're powerless. Sick. Starving. Our boys need to come. And soon. There's nothing we can do but pray that God will bring them. That's the only way."

"What happened to your fighting spirit?"

"Fort Santiago. A soldier with a bayonet. I know this command to report to our rooms is a practice for our death. They want to collect us together to make it easier."

"You've tried to escape, and you've smuggled rice. Why stop there?"

Rand turned to his friend. "You tell me what we can do."

His friend didn't answer.

"Just pray like you've never prayed before."

They dragged their feet until they came to the steps of the Education Building where they lived when not in their shanties. "You've become all religious on me."

"Because when you come down to it, God is our only hope." Everything had been stripped from him. All he had left was God. He needed that to be sufficient.

The men separated after they climbed the steps to the third floor, each into the classroom allotted to him in the first days of their captivity. Rand found his cot and settled in, staring at the sheet hanging over him with a change of clothes.

Not five minutes passed before Covey moseyed over. "I haven't seen you in a while, business partner."

Rand's hackles went up at the sound of those words. "A good thing."

"Come, come. We want this to be a profitable venture for both of us."

"What is it you want?" Rand didn't have the energy to deal with this problem right now.

"I think it's about time we sit down and discuss the reopening of the Monarch and the Azure as soon as we can after the war. I have some ideas sure to attract many customers." He scratched his cockeyed nose.

Rand bit back a retort. If he had all of these grand schemes, then why didn't he use them and make money himself? "We'll see. Not until January, for sure. The holidays aren't a time for conducting business."

"On the contrary. It's only a matter of time before we're free. We need to be ready, up and running, as soon as possible. If we want to make Manila the Pearl of the Orient again—"

"If?" Rand jumped from the bed. "There is no if. Of course I want to see this city I love restored to its former glory. But are nightclubs the answer? What about these children who are losing parents in the fighting? What will happen to them?"

A brief shadow crossed Covey's face, a sort of sadness. Then the hardness returned. "They are of no consequence to me."

But they occupied Rand's thoughts. He had been blessed. He had been somebody. And now he knew what it felt like to be nobody. What about all of the other nobodies out there? The children, the most innocent of them all. "Go away, Covey, and leave me alone. We may not even live to see the new year. We'll talk when we know we're going to survive and not a moment before. You're going to get what you want, so don't pester me anymore about it."

Covey humphed. "Have it your way. But mark my words. When—and I mean when—we survive, I will hold you to our agreement. I will bring the Monarch and the Azure out of the ashes." Then he stomped away, much to Rand's relief.

He couldn't stop thinking about what he'd told Covey. Were nightclubs really going to help restore Manila to her former glory? It could never be what it once was while children roamed the streets, hungry and sick. Irene had told him about the children she'd seen when she was out in the city.

He thought of Paulo and Sheila and the other tens of thousands of children in Manila, alone on the streets. He could imagine what it was like to be hungry or lonely or scared.

And Irene wanted to care for them.

If he could help in some way . . . maybe work beside her?

Crazy. It was an insane thought.

But one that took root in his heart. He'd be somebody to those children.

Not more than five minutes passed before soldiers with fixed bayonets stormed into the classroom. Not their usual guards. The Kempeitai. Like the ones from Fort Santiago. "We will search everyone. We must see all of your possessions."

They were looking for weapons. A way for the internees to fight back against what they planned to do to them. A way to stop an uprising as the Americans approached. Rand fingered the knife in his pocket.

The secret police came to Rand's area. He rubbed his goose-pimple covered arm with his bent right hand. The Japanese had no hearts.

They searched through the hammock hanging above his bed where he placed his personal items. Here he kept a razor and a change of clothes in case he decided to take refuge inside in the face of a typhoon. He stored all the rest of his earthly goods in his shanty.

Who could read the mind of the Japanese? Especially the fickle commandant.

One pointed his sword at Rand's heart. "Empty your pockets."

With an icy cold finger, Rand touched the knife.

# Chapter Thirty-Four

Empty your pockets." The Japanese guard took another step forward, his bayonet aimed at Rand's stomach.

What could he do? If they found the knife, he would be headed back to Fort Santiago. Or worse. They could shoot him in the head right here and now like they did with that boy he saw running from them. He was sure the soldier could see his heart beating in his chest.

Then his fingers brushed his handkerchief, worn and stained as it was.

But useful.

Carefully and with as much deftness as he could muster, he wrapped the knife in the cloth, along with a metal band he also had in that pocket. Grasping the items tightly, he pulled the handkerchief from his pocket. The knife thunked as it hit the table.

Rand held his breath, waiting for the stab through his midsection that would end his life.

It never came. Didn't the soldier hear?

He let his breath out, careful not to let it whoosh.

He glanced at the handkerchief beside him, hoping it appeared just to be in a pile, not hiding a weapon. And hoping that no bit of the knife peeked through.

"Turn them inside out."

Rand did so. A coin that he didn't realize was in his pockets fell out, clinking on the tile floor. The soldier picked it up with a smile. "Thank you."

He turned his attention to the handkerchief. Rand's mouth went dry. The soldier wouldn't be as sloppy as not to lift it. He'd gone through everything else.

Rand could feel the pain as the hammer hit the fingers of his left hand this time. No, the Japanese would do much worse to him.

He stood tall and lifted his chin but felt no confidence whatsoever.

The soldier grunted, then jabbed Rand in the stomach with the rifle butt. He landed on his cot as the soldier walked away.

*Oh, Lord, You had mercy on me. Thank You for blinding his eyes.*

Before the guard changed his mind and returned to search him again, Rand returned the items to his pocket. He was relieved that he maintained possession of his knife. He was even more relieved that the soldier hadn't found or confiscated the little metal ring.

*Christmas Day, 1944*

Irene couldn't help it. She just couldn't help it.

Couldn't help comparing this Christmas with the last. Last Christmas Anita had been with her, and they had a wonderful time at Rand's shanty eating ham and mashed potatoes and cassava cake.

And now? She sat alone in the empty shanty. Anita was dead.

She had lost Mercedes's longtime, precious friendship. Rand had a daughter and would build a life with the child's mother. As he should. As she had wanted him to.

The commandant, beneficent as he was, gave them an extra hour before curfew that Tessa and Bruce were out enjoying. They had been inseparable since the dance. Irene paced from one side of the tiny hut to the other. Some who had rice left burned their furniture in order to cook it. She and Tessa didn't have that problem.

*How long, O Lord? How long? Will we ever be free?*

More than anything, she ached to be out of here, to get to work with the children of Manila.

But she had ears. She heard the rumors about what the Japanese were planning.

Like she had told Rand the day the bombing began, she wasn't afraid of being dead. She was afraid of dying.

Outside, a group of children sang "O Come, O Come, Emmanuel." How appropriate. Yet she had no desire to sing along with them.

One of the little ones knocked on the door. Carolers. Just what she didn't want in her melancholy mood. She opened the door, not to children, but to Rand. She sucked in her breath. It had been a few weeks since she had seen him. He looked thinner than ever. "What are you doing here?"

"Merry Christmas to you too." He bowed. He had tamed the waves of his hair and put on a shirt, hiding his ribs. Straightening, he handed her a bunch of Philippine lilies.

"Merry Christmas. And thank you for the flowers. From your hut, I assume?" Their sweet perfume lifted a bit of her gloom.

He nodded.

"I thought you had a brown thumb."

"I happen to have the best gardener in Santo Tomas." He winked.

Heat filled her face. "The promise of new beginnings. Of all things yet to come."

"I haven't gotten mine to bloom yet."

"They will. May I come in?"

"Bruce and Tessa are out enjoying our extra hour before curfew tonight."

"Then let's do the same. Shall we?" He offered her his elbow.

She shouldn't. She knew she shouldn't. But then again, they might all be dead in a matter of hours or days. Why not enjoy this time they had left? If they survived the war, then she could worry about mending her broken heart. She slipped her hand through the crook of his elbow.

"I've missed you." His voice was low and husky.

She smiled. "Me too." As soon as the words slipped out, she regretted them, not wanting to give him false hope. But then, perhaps each of them was living with false hope for tomorrow.

They came upon the carolers. Sheila skipped to them. "We'll sing a song for you. What would you like to hear?"

Rand pulled at her pigtail. "Are you good singers?"

"Oh, the best, Mr. Sterling. We've been practicing real hard since Thanksgiving and we're real good now. You could sing with us, if you like."

Rand laughed. "Not me. You don't want me to ruin your beautiful singing. But Miss Reynolds has a nice voice."

"That's not really true."

"Adequate, then. Good enough."

Sheila looked up at her with those clear, innocent sea-green eyes. "You will sing with us, won't you, Miss Reynolds? Then we'll sound even better."

The ice in her soul began to melt. "Only if you sing 'It Came Upon the Midnight Clear.' That's my favorite."

*"It came upon the midnight clear,*
*That glorious song of old,*
*From angels bending near the earth,*
*To touch their harps of gold;*

*"'Peace on the earth, goodwill to men,*
*From Heaven's all gracious King!'*
*The world in solemn stillness lay,*
*To hear the angels sing.*

*"Still through the cloven skies they come,*
*With peaceful wings unfurled;*
*And still their heavenly music floats*
*O'er all the weary world;*

*"Above its sad and lowly plains,*
*They bend on hovering wing,*
*And ever o'er its Babel sounds*
*The blessed angels sing.*

*"And ye, beneath life's crushing load,*
*Whose forms are bending low,*
*Who toil along the climbing way*
*With painful steps and slow;*

*"Look now! for glad and golden hours*
*Come swiftly on the wing.*
*O rest beside the weary road,*
*And hear the angels sing."*

Irene had tears in her eyes by this time and had difficulty getting out the words. The internees were bending low, and all of their steps were painful and slow these days. Rand squeezed her hand when they sang of glad and golden hours coming swiftly on the wing. For today, the skies remained void of American planes.

Rand applauded wildly as Irene bent to kiss the girl's tanned cheek. "Thank you, Sheila. You have made my Christmas."

"And mine." Rand kissed the child's other cheek and patted the other carolers on their heads. A wide grin caressed his narrow face as they walked away. "Now that is what Christmas is all about."

"I agree."

"And your voice is very nice."

"You must be tone deaf." They walked in silence for a while, their feet quiet on the hard-packed road. "So what made you come to me today?"

"I wanted to give you time, Irene, to come to the realization that it's you I want in my life, not Catherine. And Catherine doesn't want me."

"That sounds like you're settling for me."

He stopped short and looked her square in the face, his golden-brown eyes searching hers. "Not at all. I haven't loved Catherine in more than seven years, if I ever loved her. I've never felt about a woman the way I feel about you. Never. You have to believe that. And who your father is has no bearing on my feelings for you. He is he and you are you. You bear no responsibility for him."

Irene couldn't stand to see the feelings written on his countenance or continue this discussion, so she directed her attention to the groups of people gathered on the front lawn.

*"Glad and golden hours come swiftly on the wing."*

Irene blinked away the tears. "I hope—I pray—that this song is a foretelling of what's ahead. But it's been so long since Leyte, and nothing."

They stopped and sat in the grass.

"Our release will happen. In time. God's time. For today, I'm happy you agreed to see me. It's been too long."

She shushed him with a finger on his lips. "Don't read anything into this. It's Christmas. That's all."

Rand reached into his pocket, then handed her a small package wrapped in old copies of the *Tribune*, the camp paper that had been discontinued due to the lack of supplies. "I hope you like it."

She untied the string and pulled back the paper. Inside was a perfect Philippine lily carved out of golden wood. Her stomach fluttered. It was so delicate she was afraid she would crush it. "Oh, Rand, I don't know what to say. It's the most beautiful thing I've ever owned." She turned and gave him a peck on the cheek. Fire shone in his eyes. He wanted more. The one thing she could not give him.

"I almost didn't get to finish this. The day we had to report to our buildings, I hid it in the couch but took the knife with me. The guard searched me, demanding I empty my pockets."

Irene dug her fingernails into her palms.

"I put my hands inside them, meeting nothing there but the knife and my handkerchief. I slid the knife into the folds of the handkerchief and set it on the table, holding my breath. He never looked under it."

She shook her head. "You are bound and determined to get sent back to Fort Santiago, aren't you?"

"No way. I'm not leaving you." He kissed her on the forehead, lightly but enough to send her heart racing.

She slid back a bit. She had to protect herself. "But I don't have anything for you."

"Just you spending time with me is present enough. There will be other Christmases."

But Irene knew that to be untrue.

"I hope you saved some room for my surprise." Rand dipped his hand into his pocket again and came out with something round, also wrapped in paper. "A Christmas cake."

Irene sat forward. "How did you? Where did you? Who made it?"

"I did. Cook always ruled the kitchen, but my culinary skills have improved over the years."

"With what?"

"Don't be so skeptical. I charmed one of the kitchen girls into selling me a bit of brown sugar and cassava flour. I had a little coconut oil left in the bottom of the jar. Violà. Christmas cake."

Irene didn't want to be unkind, especially since he was so excited about the cake, but she had to pull up her nose. "Wasn't your oil rancid?"

"Let's hope the sugar hides the flavor." Rand broke the dense little cake in two and handed half to Irene.

She popped it into her mouth, then spit it out. "Don't touch it." She pulled Rand's hand away from his lips. "It's terrible."

Poor Rand's shoulders slumped. "It can't be worse than weevils."

They had long ago stopped picking the disgusting bugs from their rice, figuring the extra calories were beneficial. "It is. Your oil was rancid. You'll end up as sick as you must have been at Thanksgiving if you touch it."

"I'm sorry."

"Why?" She stroked his smooth cheek, his mouth downturned. "It was a lovely thought. Truly it was."

"Next year I'll make a real Christmas cake."

"You will use a recipe?"

"Who needs a recipe?"

Irene laughed.

ண

Irene's laughter was one of the most beautiful sounds in the entire world. Rand would never tire of listening to its music. He wanted to wake up to it every morning and go to bed with it every night. He ached to be with her.

He fingered the loop of metal in his pocket. His heartbeat was off the charts, and the twists and turns his stomach was doing would give circus tumblers a run for their money. He knew the perfect way for this wretched Christmas to end.

Irene looked stunning tonight in the filmy green dress she had worn to the dance, though it hung on her frame more than it had before. She had once again molded her white-blond hair into curls pinned to the side of her head. She wore no lipstick, but her lips were as red as the earlier sunset.

Only the edict against public displays of affection kept him from kissing her right then and there.

Last night, during the long hours when he couldn't sleep, he memorized a speech for this moment. The trouble was, he couldn't remember a single word of it.

What if he botched it? What if she said no? He swallowed.

And that was a very real possibility. He knew what her objections would be, and he knew how he would rebuff them. If he could recall his arguments.

She was talking to him, saying words he couldn't comprehend. The air around him buzzed.

"Don't you agree? Rand?"

"I'm sorry. I lost the train of thought."

"What were you thinking about?"

"About how beautiful you are. That green is a swell color on you. I love the dress."

Even in the near darkness, he saw her cheeks turn pink and a smile spread from one side of her face to the other. "You look rather dapper yourself."

"Yes, I went all out for you. I put on pants and a shirt."

There was that laugh again, as intoxicating as any brandy.

He cleared his throat, having decided to speak the words that came to his mind. "You know how much I love you, Irene."

She opened her mouth, but he shushed her. "Please let me say what I have to say. I love you from the bottom of my feet to the top of my head." He took a deep breath. "I can't bear the thought of not having you with me when we leave here. You are the most generous, thoughtful, loving, caring woman I have ever known. You think of others before you think of yourself. And you love the Lord and have taught me to love Him too.

"I've prayed about this, and I know it is right. Catherine made her choice when she chose not to tell me about my daughter. She and Melanie have made a life for themselves. It's what she wants.

"I'll support my daughter every way I can, but I gave up my right to raise her when I walked away from her mother seven years ago. It's in you that I see my future. It's with you that I want to build a family, whether here in Manila or in the United States."

He pulled the metal ring from his pocket and got down on one knee. "Irene Reynolds, would you please marry me and make me the happiest man on earth?" Surely she heard his heart pounding.

She sat and stared at him. He didn't venture a guess as to

whether her speechlessness was a good thing or not. She blinked her eyes and clasped her hands.

Then she got up and ran away.

He stared at the ring in his hand.

# Chapter Thirty-Five

Rand searched the grounds for Irene. She wasn't in her shanty, nor was she in her room. He hoped to find her in Father's Garden, but the place was empty. Each moment she slipped further through his fingers.

Curfew approached. He didn't have time to look anymore. He would have to wait until tomorrow to speak to her.

He had prayed she would accept his proposal. Had braced himself for the very real possibility that she would say no. He never expected that she would run off and leave him kneeling in the grass by himself.

He had said something wrong. That had to be it. His prepared speech had been perfect. He should have written it down and read it. Then he wouldn't have bungled it the way he did. Had he lost his chance with her?

The familiar empty ache filled his chest.

He returned to his shanty and lay down on his mattress in frustration. *Lord, will any good thing come from this camp?* He managed a smile as he knew the answer. Yes, he had found his strength and his help in the Lord. If God meant for him to be married to Irene, God Himself would have to make a way.

But that didn't mean that Rand couldn't play his part. When he went to Irene's shanty the following day, hoping to convince her to spend her life with him, Tessa told him she refused to see him. A crushing pain raced through his abdomen.

Then he lifted his chin. All his life he'd gotten what he wanted. His parents bought him the toys he wanted. Cook prepared the meals he wanted. Father gave him the money for the club he wanted. He wasn't about to stop now. He would win Irene, one way or another.

He was determined to make a pest of himself until she broke down and spoke to him. Each day he would sit on his *sawali* mat outside of her bedroom. He would spend the hours talking to her about anything and everything—camp rumors, his hopes, her dreams.

He woke up this morning with dysentery. He suspected that almost everyone in camp suffered a bout of the affliction. The illness left him weak and exhausted, and walking across the campus to see Irene or get meals was difficult. But he wasn't about to be deterred. If he had to crawl on his hands and knees, he would continue his quest to win her.

On his way to her hut, he spied a group of four internees being led by a horde of Japanese soldiers toward the camp's prison. Through the guards, he managed to make out who the men were. He knew three of them. E. E. Johnson, Carroll Grinnell, Alfred Duggleby. Members of their executive committee. The fourth was an internee by the look of him, but not one Rand recognized.

He stood rooted to the spot, his knees weak. The Japanese were arresting them. And their end couldn't be good. Neither could the other internees'.

He shared the grim news with Irene as he sat outside of her shanty. "Our boys must be closing in, otherwise why would they arrest the committee now?"

Silence.

Most of the day he spoke to her the thoughts that came to his head. There were no air raids. Their boys must be taking the holiday week off, giving him the most time possible to speak to her. He tried to catch Irene on the way to roll call and meals, but she ignored him. Her walk, however, concerned him. She moved like a seventy-year-old woman, her legs paining her.

The week passed, Rand spending his days outside of Irene's hut, making a general nuisance of himself.

On New Year's Eve, the last day of the wretched year of 1944, Rand again sat on his mat speaking to Irene. "Sweetheart, I am sorry if I hurt you in any way. But please don't push me to marry Catherine. She told me in her letter that she wants to be left alone. I know I've read it to you a thousand times."

Silence. Utter silence. He didn't have much strength left. He couldn't go on much more. How long could she hold out?

"When I convince you to marry me—and I will convince you—I've thought about what we will do. I have to reopen the nightclubs, but they won't consume me. I want to do meaningful work. I want to help you with your orphanage."

Irene's silence remained icy.

How long could he continue to beat his head against a wall?

An orphanage? That's what Rand wanted to do with the rest of his life?

Yes, he was good with the children of the camp, playing games with them, making up rhymes for them, asking them about school. He bore up well under these living conditions and didn't complain about his lack of a butler or cook or chauffeur. He worked hard.

But could he be happy with that kind of life forever?

She had been considering his proposal, praying about it whenever he would go away and leave her in peace and quiet. At any rate, he was making sure she didn't forget about him.

She imagined spending every night for the rest of her life in his arms. She wondered what it would be like to be loved by him. Oh, the joy that would be.

And then Catherine's face would pop to mind. Or what she imagined Catherine looked like. She had never seen a photograph of her, but she must have some of Melanie's features. Rand said she didn't want him to disturb the life they had built for themselves. But would he want to stay away? How could he not desire to meet his daughter?

He would make a wonderful father. And now he wanted to work with orphans. He wouldn't be able to turn his back on Melanie.

When he saw Catherine again, the spark that had existed between them would flame, and they would fall in love. Who could help but love him? Irene would be left at the side of the road.

*Oh, God, help me know what to do. Tell me what is right. How can I be sure that he will love me and only me for the rest of our lives?*

Tessa came to her and sat on the edge of Irene's mattress. "You'll have to talk to him at some point, so why not make it now? We all have to listen to his chatter and would prefer if you would just accept his proposal."

"There are hindrances you don't understand."

Tessa tucked a strand of red hair behind her ear. "That's where you're wrong, love. We understand—very well. We've been listening to him all week, remember? Yes, he has a daughter in Virginia he's never met. So what? Catherine should have told him right away that she was expecting. She shut him out of Melanie's life. It wasn't his choice."

Irene smoothed the sheet over her swollen legs. Tessa was right.

"Don't you think if he had known about her from the beginning, he would have chosen to make a family with them?"

"I know he would have. I complicate matters. If I'm not in the way, he can still do that."

"But it's not what Catherine wants. Bangers and mash, don't you see? Rand is doing what is right for his daughter. He doesn't want to disturb her life. She's happy, and his appearance would only upset her. That part of his life has been decided for him. He does want a family—with you."

"And what if, in the future, Catherine tells Melanie the truth? Then what?"

"Then Rand will get to know his daughter, and she will have a wonderful stepmother." Tessa got up but stopped and turned around. "Think about what I said."

And Irene did think. Whether it was right or wrong, Catherine had made her choice. It would be great if Rand could know his daughter, but he knew she was happy. To him, she was but a face in a picture.

"I don't know what to do."

Tessa laughed. "Marry him."

From outside, Rand cheered.

Irene lay back on the bed. They were ganging up on her. But she had to be sure.

❧

*January 1, 1945*

The new year started with a bang. The vacation was over for the Americans, and they once again began bombing the city. The raids went on all day, with only short breaks. The shrapnel and pom-poms falling all around made Mercedes nervous. Any moment a shell might crash right through the roof and explode in front of their feet. They needed to go to the Annex where the ceiling was thicker and stronger.

Paulo jumped with each and every sound. Her little boy was thin and nervous and withdrawn, not the happy child of even a few months ago. She longed to provide him with peace and stability.

She met Irene and Tessa leaving their shanty. Mercedes nodded at Irene's suitcase. "We have the same idea. It's not safe to stay in the huts anymore."

"No." Irene took a couple of feeble steps forward.

A heart attack couldn't hurt more than the pain in Mercedes's chest at Irene's coldness. After she had been kind to her at The Little House on the Hill, she had thought Irene was coming around. Tessa had even watched Paulo for a few hours. Mercedes had to make this right. "I haven't seen him since the night he hurt you. Please talk to me."

Irene stopped, leaning on Tessa. "You're fortunate he didn't hurt me worse."

"I don't know who to believe or what to believe anymore. I miss Charles. I need him here to tell me what to do. But I'm not willing to lose our friendship over a Japanese soldier. You will never know how sorry I am for the things I said to you. For what I did to you."

"Could you have lived with yourself if he had taken advantage of me? Or worse?"

Mercedes clutched her throat and shook her head.

"Then why didn't you listen to me the first time? Why did you get involved with him at all?"

"I told you. You know what it's like to be alone."

The truth dawned on Irene's face. "But I didn't turn to one of our captors."

"We all make mistakes. I'm asking for a second chance." She longed for the companionship of another woman.

The air-raid siren called out its shrill warning. Tessa motioned to the Main Building. "We have to go and so do you."

Mercedes didn't want to let this chance to speak to Irene be for nothing. "What would Anita say?"

"That I am to forgive you. Anita was a better person than I am. But I'll think about it."

Mercedes deflated and dragged her feet toward the Annex for mothers with small children, pulling Paulo behind her. What would the rest of the war be like, cooped up in a room with women who despised her?

If only Irene could find it in her heart to forgive her.

# Chapter Thirty-Six

*February 3, 1945*

Rand missed seeing Irene, but she had been wise to move to the Main Building. It was better to be closer to all they needed. He preferred his shanty only because it kept him away from Frank Covey. One of the first things Rand planned to do when he was freed was contact his lawyer and have the document ripped to shreds.

He didn't plan to resurrect the clubs, and he didn't want Covey to force him to do so. He would pay for protection for Catherine and Melanie if necessary.

Roll call this morning was a miserable affair. His joints ached so much it reminded him of his grandmother when she was seventy. That's about how old he felt. Word from the secret radio was that their boys had landed at Lingayen on January 9. Excitement had been high then, but no Americans showed up. Now they all wondered if their boys would make it in time.

After eating his single scoop of watery mush at one of the long tables outside, Rand wandered over to the patio, hoping to spend time with Irene today. Smoke drifted from the Japanese area of the camp where they had their offices and barracks. They were getting nervous. They knew their time was running out. Their captors were burning large numbers of papers.

He rubbed the goose bumps from his arms.

Bruce ambled over and sat beside Rand. "You're looking rather forlorn."

Rand tried to crack a smile. "Nice way to compliment someone."

"I wasn't complimenting you."

Rand noticed how this once-burly man had been reduced to a pile of skin and bones. All of the men resembled walking skeletons these days.

"Where is your lovely lady?"

"Now you think she's lovely?"

"For a missionary girl, she's pretty swell. Sweet isn't so bad. I give you my blessing."

"Thanks. It's good to know I have it. I wouldn't feel good about pursuing a relationship with her without it."

"That's why I gave it."

"Tessa is softening you."

"You know, she's not here. I hope neither of them are sick."

"The women can't keep on like this. None of us can."

Bruce flapped his bony hand. "Our boys have to be near. The Japanese are jumpy. I just hope they don't blow us clear to China. Or slaughter us the way they did those American POWs in Palawan."

He couldn't even think about it. Their own executions here at Santo Tomas became more and more of a reality with each passing day. *Lord, watch over us. Protect us and send our boys here soon.*

His hopes of seeing Irene this morning weren't disappointed. She and Tessa arrived and joined them.

Irene gave him a wan smile. Her face was pale and drawn, her knuckles and wrists swollen. Her beautiful blond hair had lost its luster. He rubbed her knee. "How are you?"

"Alive. That's the best we can ask for today. And you?"

"Alive." Even now, in her condition, she didn't complain.

She worried the hem of her mustard-yellow dress. "I'm scared, Rand. They're going to starve us all."

"What would Anita tell you?"

"That dawn will break. And we should pray in the meantime."

"Then let's do that." He joined hands with Irene and Tessa. Even tough old Bruce joined them. "Dear heavenly Father, we pray that You would be near us right now and that You would send our boys here very soon. Sustain us until that time. Deliver us, Lord. Give us Your peace and take away our fear. We ask this in Your Son's name. Amen."

The roar of jets drowned out all else as they dove low, silver bodies glinting in the sun. "Look at those planes." Irene pointed to the sky.

"I'd rather not." Rand grinned. Then leaflets dropped from the bellies of the planes, floating down to earth like a thousand birds.

Along with many other internees, Rand hurried to the yard to pick up the fliers. What did their boys want them to know? Any word from an American on the outside would be so welcome.

"Away, away." Bayoneted guards rushed toward the crowd. "Do not touch those." Rand took a step back, as did those around him. A few words from home weren't worth risking his life.

All day planes swooped low. They didn't bomb or strafe.

"What are they doing?" Irene dared to shade her eyes and gaze heavenward.

Rand kept his eyes low. "Reconnaissance, possibly."

Bruce hazarded a guess. "Troop transport, I think."

Irene's mouth formed a perfect O. "Are they bringing our boys in that close to Manila?" She was almost breathless.

*God, if that could but be true.* "Let's bring our boys in, we'll give them a grin, because then we'll win."

Irene tipped her head in the direction of the yard. "Don't let the Japanese hear you. They aren't wasting time with Fort Santiago these days."

Rand nodded. The committee members he'd seen being arrested had disappeared, along with all hope for them. "Let's pray whoever is up there is careful in their shooting."

"And hope they see that." Bruce pointed at the machine gun nest the Japanese were constructing at one end of the compound.

"All the better to kill us with."

Irene grabbed his arm. "You're scaring me, Rand. Please tell me our boys will get here soon."

"I wish I could."

From somewhere outside, in a home across the street from Santo Tomas, a radio crackled to life. "General MacArthur's forces are converging on Manila from three sides and now control all the major roads and railways in the Central Plain. The Americans coming in on the city from the north are about twenty miles away. A second force . . ."

*Ping, ping, ping.* The shots from a Japanese gun silenced the radio.

Rand was afraid the radio man was injured—or worse—but he couldn't stop the smile that broke out across his face. "Twenty miles." He wanted to kiss Irene right then and there, but really didn't want the wrath of the Japanese to fall on him at this point. "Days, just days before they are here."

Bruce asked the question all of them were thinking. "But will we be here?"

*8:40 p.m.*

Rand lay back on his bed in his room in the Education Building, staring at the hammock-sheet above him. Worry, peace, anger, love all warred for dominance in his mind. What was going to happen to them in the next couple of days?

*Lord, if it is Your intention to take me home, please prepare me. Forgive me of my sins, cleanse me, and fit me to be with You forever. Above all, give me peace. And if it be Your will, protect Irene from all harm. Keep her safe, please.*

From outside of the gates came the sound of shooting. In the past few days, the internees had become accustomed to the noise. A guard signaling to his late-arriving reliever. A Japanese shooting a poor Filipino caught in the wrong place at the wrong time.

As long as they didn't aim at the internees.

Anything but that.

The entire camp held its breath.

Then he heard the low, deep rumble of tanks. What would Japanese tanks be doing here? What was going on?

Had they come to begin the slaughter?

His heart beat out an uneven, jazzlike rhythm.

He wasn't the only one wondering. Many of the men from his room made their way to the window and peered at the scene below, down on the front gate of Santo Tomas. Their home for more than three years.

He grabbed his shirt, stuffed his trembling arms into it, and went to the window. As he stood on shaky legs, he knew he would never forget the sight that met his eyes. A huge, gray metallic vehicle stood at the iron bars, then rumbled forward, smashing the gate, the driver rolling over it with his tracks until he stopped not far from the building where Rand was.

The markings on the side were not Japanese.

The words read *Battlin' Basic.*

English.

Their boys had arrived.

He couldn't stop the tears that poured down his face. Who cared that he was crying? They all were. He turned and hugged the men in his room. Cheering filtered upward and men, women, and children poured from their shanties and dorms.

Japanese soldiers filed out of the gates. Their captors but moments ago, now the captured.

He had to get down there. He wanted to shake an American soldier's hand. He wanted to touch the *Battlin' Basic.* He wanted to be in the midst of the action.

He moved through the hall with the other men and down the stairs.

And he could go no farther.

Japanese soldiers blocked his way. These guards stood their ground, their weapons sighted on the American troops.

"Get back. Get back," someone shouted. Rand fell back.

One of the soldiers turned around. "Get upstairs. No one is going anywhere."

Rand's shoulders slumped as he climbed the steps. So close. Liberation was so close he could see it, feel it, taste it.

And he couldn't grasp it.

He was now a hostage.

Gunshots rang out. A body hit the ground with a thud. "Crazy fool," someone shouted. One of their fellow building denizens had attempted to escape out of the third-floor window, a rope tied around his waist. The Japanese guards riddled him with bullets.

That might have been him a year and a half ago.

Rand continued to wait out what he knew would be a battle. Many avoided the window, but he couldn't. To lose sight of their boys might be to lose sight of freedom forever. To not lose hope, he had to watch their every move.

What was happening to Irene? People spilled out of the Main Building. Surely that meant Irene was safe. She was not still holed up in her room, held hostage by the Japanese guards.

Relief filled him. If nothing else, she was safe. Nothing else mattered. If she came through this alive, that would be enough for him.

"How are we going to get out of here?" Covey's voice at his elbow surprised him, but it shouldn't have. Panic laced the man's words.

"We'll get free."

"But how? We're going to be stuck in here forever."

"God will deliver us. Wait and see." Rand wiped his clammy hands on his pants, trying to believe his own words.

Bruce joined their conversation. "If we could get our boys to start a commotion up front, a distraction, the Japanese would be too busy to notice us slip out the back."

Rand shook his head. "There have to be at least two hundred of us in here. That will never work. In no time the guards will figure out what we're up to and turn their guns on us."

Covey jiggled his bony leg. "There has to be a way. We could attack the soldiers."

"A bunch of weak, unarmed men? It will never work." The talk made Rand anxious. Though, if they could find a way out, a way for this to be over, a way for him to get to Irene, they had to try. He paced, running his hands through his hair. "If we armed ourselves . . ."

Bruce grunted. "With what? Like you said, we're weak."

"We will have to wait on the Lord, then."

"That's not good enough for me." Covey made his way to the end of the hall. "I'm getting out of here, one way or the other."

"What do you mean? Where are you going?" Rand hurried to catch up with him.

"Out."

"You can't walk out the front door. You'd never even get past the guards."

"What can they do? Shoot me?"

"You'll get yourself killed."

"I'll be out of here."

Rand turned and stood in Covey's way. "You're insane."

"I refuse to spend one more night as a prisoner in this place. One way or another, I'll be free."

Rand spread his legs and pushed his palms against Covey's chest. "There's no love lost between us, but I can't let you do this."

"Why not? Then you'll be out of your contract. Your daughter will be safe. I'm a rotten man. No one will miss me. Not even my own daughter."

Rand's breath stuck in his throat. "Your daughter? You have a daughter?"

"Think about it for a moment, Sterling."

He couldn't. "Who is it?"

"Look at my eyes."

Rand did. He had seen those eyes before.

"Picture me without this scar. Imagine what my nose would look like if it hadn't been broken."

In the semidarkness, he studied Covey. "You have the same eyes as her. And if your nose wasn't broken, it would turn up . . ." Praying he'd remain on his feet, Rand gripped Covey's arm. Why had he never made the connection?

"It's all we have in common."

"Does Irene know?"

Covey—Reynolds—shook his head.

"Why haven't you made yourself known?" Rand's head pounded.

"Before I could tell her who I was, I had to have a way to provide for her. I failed her when she was young, too much and too often. Without the means to take care of my little girl, I couldn't reveal myself to her.

"It was risky, coming back to you, someone who might recognize me. And then when I saw you with my daughter, it grew even more dangerous. But I had discovered your secrets even before the war. And being confined in here gave me the chance to come up with a plan to use that information to my greatest advantage. I banked on the fact that I've changed so much, neither of you would know who I was."

And it was true. Covey—Reynolds—had changed. He'd been a rotund man, now as skinny as the rest of them. He'd aged in the eight or nine years since he disappeared.

"She'll want to know you're alive. She'll be happy to see you."

The man turned away, his shoulders heaving. A few minutes passed before he spoke. "No, she won't. Look at what I've done. I was blinded by my greed. She'll want nothing to do with me. The jig is up. It's time I face the music. Please don't let her know it was me. Do that for me."

The man ducked under Rand's arms and skittered down the hall toward the stairs.

"Covey, stop. Stop!" Rand sprinted after him, then tackled him on the top step.

"Get off of me. Leave me alone. Let me die."

They wrestled, as much as two almost-starved men could. Rand landed a punch on his cheek or eye while Covey kicked him in the stomach.

Men poured out of the classrooms and separated the two. Bruce hung on to Rand's collar. "What is going on here?"

Rand stood and wiped the sweat from his forehead. "I'm trying to save this man from sacrificing himself to the guards." What would he tell Irene if he watched as her father threw himself into the line of fire? He could never live with himself.

With a glowering glance, Covey walked away to nurse his black eye.

All the better. "We have the Japanese to fight. Let's not go after each other. The worst thing you can do for your daughter is to get yourself loaded up with Japanese lead."

The squeal of wheels drew Rand's attention away from his aching middle. One of the tanks that had forced its way through the main gate now rolled toward the Education Building, then stopped in line with the front door.

"To the back of the building." Rand didn't know where the orders came from—perhaps from outside—but in this instance, it appeared wise to obey. Without electricity and no lights other than those on the tank, it was difficult for Rand to pick his way through the building. He stumbled over beds and chairs and men's belongings and down the hall until he arrived in a back room.

Then the big guns on the hulking monster blazed to life.

Machine gun fire spit from the long barrels. The building shook as the rounds hit the concrete. Windows on the first floor shattered.

Rand covered his ears. Never before had he heard such a loud noise. It shook his bones and rattled his teeth. The building trembled with each shell that struck it.

A shriek threatened to rupture Rand's eardrums. White heat seared his face as the shell exploded not far from him.

"I'm hit. I'm hit!"

In the light of the tank's headlamps, Rand turned to see Covey on the floor, blood pouring from his side.

Rand ripped off his last decent shirt, the one he'd been saving for this day, and threw it to the men nearest Covey. Keeping Irene's father alive was proving difficult. "Wrap this around him to stop the bleeding. Our boys are going to kill us. I have to see what I can do."

Crouching low, Rand made his way to the front of the building. Bullets and shells whistled all around him. Another shriek had him flat on the floor, his face pressed to the cool tile. He had to work to steady his breath.

A momentary lull allowed him to reach the window. He flung it open and hung out. "Stop. Stop. We have a casualty." A shell whistled passed his ear, and he ducked. His heart stopped, then began pounding at an alarming rate. He rose and waved his arms to get the Americans' attention. "Cease fire. Cease fire."

Those in the *Battlin' Basic* heard his message. The firing stopped. The guns fell silent.

Sounds of jubilation wafted on the evening air. People sang and danced and cried.

How he wanted to be in the midst of them. Not cooped up in here.

For well over three thousand of the internees, the war had

ended. But not for the couple of hundred in here. Why hadn't he gone to the shanty? He would have been safe there. He could be out dancing on the lawn with Irene in his arms, convincing her to become his wife.

The Manila sky glowed red with fires that burned in every part of the city.

Would this nightmare ever end?

# Chapter Thirty-Seven

Irene watched from her window in the Main Building with tears in her eyes as the American tank crashed through Santo Tomas's iron gate, the gate that had held them in for the past thirty-seven months.

Their captivity was over.

It was finally over.

"Tessa, do you see that?"

Her friend whooped like an Indian. "We're free. Let's go. We have to find the men. I want to kiss Bruce. Come on, love." She tugged on Irene's arm and pulled her from the room.

On weak, swollen, shaky legs, she made her way through the third-floor hall, down the stairs, and out to the lawn. The lawn where Rand had proposed a few weeks ago.

Now a great, hulking tank stood on the pathway, and it was the most beautiful sight she had seen in her entire life. She ran her hands over the warm metal.

She had heard about hearts bursting for joy. She felt the sensation now. Her chest couldn't contain her happiness.

If only Anita had held on for a few more months, she could have been here too. She could have witnessed God's deliverance, as she had predicted. As He had promised.

Rand. She had to find him. She turned around and around, searching for his light-brown head above the others. By now he should have located her. Where could he be?

"I don't see Bruce." Tessa's voice was laced with concern. She bit her pale-pink lip.

"I can't find Rand either. We must have passed each other. They're probably at the Main Building looking for us." Though Irene stood on her tiptoes and surveyed the crowd, the bright lights on the tank illuminating the scene, she didn't see him. And Tessa couldn't find Bruce.

"Let's look at the Education Building. Rand said he was going to spend the night there." Holding hands so they didn't get separated, the girls swam upstream against the surge toward the Education Building.

"Stop right there, ladies." A lanky, redheaded kid not much more than twenty stood in her way.

"I have to get to my . . . to Rand. I can't find him."

"The Japanese are holed up in there. You have to stay back in case of any shooting. If he's in there, he's not coming out for a while."

Her stomach fell clean out of her body.

"Shooting? Not coming out?" Tessa just about screeched.

"That's what I said. It's best if you go back to where you've been. We'll get him free as soon as we can, and then he'll find you."

"But—"

"I don't want you to get hurt. Not now."

Irene stared up at the third-floor window, the one Rand had pointed out as his. She thought she made out shapes by the glass, men moving around. Was Rand one of them?

Tessa squeezed her hand. "Bangers and mash, they have to be at their shanties. They must have changed their minds about sleeping here tonight."

With her heart racing faster than Rand's little convertible, Irene nodded and pulled her friend in the direction of Glamourville.

*God, let him be at their shanties. Either one.*

Rapid gunfire cut through the joyous celebrations. Irene came to a sudden standstill. Her green eyes round in her face, Tessa pulled to a halt beside Irene. "The Education Building."

Irene spun on her heel and headed in the opposite direction. "Those are gunshots."

With each heavy step, she prayed, "God, keep him safe. Watch over him. Don't let anything happen to him. Protect him. Deliver him."

"Keep praying, love. I'm so afraid for Bruce."

As she approached the building, Irene saw a figure hanging out of a third-floor window. Not any window, but the one in Rand's room.

"Cease fire."

She would know the sound of that voice in a sea of a thousand voices. "Rand!"

"Cease fire."

One more shell. Then the guns fell silent.

She shrieked, "Rand, Rand."

Silence. Eerie silence.

"Rand! I need you." What happened to him? Why wasn't he in the window anymore?

"Get out of here, ladies." A soldier pulled her away.

She fell to her knees in the dirt, sobs tearing at her chest. "Rand, Rand."

Had they come this far, this close, for God to rip him away from her now? "God, I need him. I need him so."

Tessa knelt on the ground beside her, tears also pouring down her cheeks. "Bruce must be in there too."

"Ladies, you have to move." The American soldier was insistent. They staggered to their feet.

"What are we going to do?" Tessa swiped at the wetness on her face.

Irene did the same. "Pray for them." It didn't seem like enough, but what else could they do?

Around them, the celebration continued. People wept, opened any canned goods they had left, and lit fires with chairs.

"Bangers and mash, I can't watch this. All of the joy has gone out of the evening. I'm going back to our room."

Irene went with her, but instead of going inside, she sat on the front step of the building.

*Why, God, why?* She was free, but the man she loved wasn't. Even in this happy time, they couldn't rejoice together. "Will it ever end?"

Then she remembered words she had seen underlined in Anita's Bible, ones she had memorized. From Psalm 37. *The salvation of the righteous is of the* Lord*: he is their strength in the time of trouble. And the* Lord *shall help them, and deliver them: he shall deliver them from the wicked, and save them, because they trust in him.*

*The Lord shall help them.*

Rand had been so good to her, had been there when she needed him the most.

*The* Lord *shall help them . . . deliver them from the wicked, and save them, because they trust him.*

She brushed the dirt from her knees, even as tears coursed down her face.

Hordes of former prisoners milled around, talking to the American soldiers, sitting on the tanks, accepting any food offered to them, especially chocolate bars.

Her merriment had fled. "God, You have to keep Rand safe. Don't let him die. Bring him out of there. I've told You I need him."

*He shall deliver them and save them.* Tears ran on either side of her nose. "Is that what I've been doing, Lord? Relying too much on Anita and Rand and myself and not enough on You?"

Her heart knew the answer. Yes, she had been. She had lived the past three years as if she could take care of herself. And when she couldn't, she turned to fallible, weak human beings to take care of her. Ever since her father had deserted her, she had been looking for someone to be there for her. To watch over her. To provide for her. She looked to everyone but God.

In the end, when it came right down to it, only God could help her. He used Rand and Anita and the US Army 1st Cavalry Division, but He came to her aid. All the while, when she had been longing for a Father the most, she already had one.

How foolish for her to have spent her life thinking otherwise.

She gazed at the Education Building, at Rand's window.

The mighty tank stood silent in the yard, its guns pointed toward the Japanese inside. How long until the Lord delivered those prisoners?

She had to believe Rand would come out alive. Her mind refused to allow her to think the worst. She wanted him out here, to experience freedom with her. It was amazing and frightening and strange all at the same time.

"Good night, Rand. God be with you. God deliver you."

A vise tightened around her heart. How long would it be before the Lord came to his aid?

*February 5, 1945*

Rand sat on the end of his bed. The Japanese had kept the men confined here for two days. The rest of the internees enjoyed their second day of freedom. Not yet him, nor the couple of hundred held hostage here.

He heard the shouts of the crowd as the American flag was draped from a window in the Main Building. The Rising Sun had set. The Stars and Stripes again flew high.

And he could do nothing.

The hours passed with maddening slowness. From time to time he peered through the window. He imagined the woman with the hair the color of foam on the waves was Irene. She stood out in the crowd.

And then she turned her head, and by the angle of her cheek and the curve of her neck, he knew it was her.

Even from this distance, she took his breath away.

Every bit of him wanted to jump from the window and run to her. But he didn't relish a barrage of Japanese bullets.

He wanted to shout to her, tell her how much he loved her. Again, he thought better of it. She knew he was here. She knew how he felt about her.

"Have a piece of chocolate." One of the guards held out a piece of candy that must have come from the Red Cross boxes the internees had never received.

Rand struggled. This young man spoke perfect English, much as the soldier at Fort Santiago. But the Japanese were their enemies, those who had kept them locked in here all of this time, those who were starving them to death.

A Japanese soldier had attacked Irene. Had hurt her and would have raped her if given the chance. He clenched his fists.

The chocolate looked delicious. He imagined the creamy sweetness on his tongue. His mouth watered and his stomach grumbled.

Why would this soldier be kind to him now? A week ago this man would have slapped him if he hadn't bowed properly or shot him if he'd found out about the rice smuggling. Rand narrowed his eyes and gazed long and hard at the man's round face, dark eyes, flat nose.

"No. Leave me alone." Acid ate at his stomach.

The soldier continued to hold out the sweet treat. "My peace offering."

"You think you can buy me with candy? That one square of chocolate will make me forget what your people did to me?" He held up his right hand. "To us?" Ludicrous. Rand's body shook.

"No, it can't. But it's a start. I'm asking for your forgiveness."

Rand exploded like a pom-pom. "Forgiveness? You want forgiveness? After the deplorable living conditions, the starvation, the disease? We have lived little better than animals. For thirty-seven months, you have kept us caged. And you expect me to walk away and forget about it? To become your friend?"

The hopeful light in the man's eyes darkened. "It is a hard thing, yes. I know this. I have no right to ask so much of you. But we have to make a start. I have seen you and watched you. You are a good man. And I have seen you read that book about your God. In America, I went to church with a friend. They talked about forgiveness."

"It is one thing for God to forgive you. Quite another for me."

"Why?" Furrows marred the man's brow.

"Well . . ." Rand had no answer for that. He knew of God's forgiveness firsthand. He stood before the holy Lord with his slate wiped clean. But he hadn't detained innocent civilians and starved them to death.

And conviction hit him between the eyes. He was just as guilty in God's eyes as that soldier. His hands were as much bloodstained. His heart equally corrupt.

Yet when he'd come to God, begging for forgiveness, his heavenly Father had granted his request.

*Forgive us our debts, as we forgive our debtors.*

God had forgiven him. And now He expected Rand to forgive this man before him.

But it was so hard. He had carried this anger and hatred with him for thirty-seven months. For that long, it had harbored and festered inside of him.

He forced himself to relax his fists. Could he let it go? He took a deep breath. *Let me mean it, Lord.* "I forgive you."

Angel choirs didn't exactly begin singing at those words, but relief flooded Rand in that moment. A smile, at first tentative, then growing stronger, spread across the soldier's face.

And what Rand saw in his face was a man, just like him. Perhaps with a wife and children at home. He fought because his country required that he do so. If Rand hadn't been caught in Manila, he would have been on the front lines doing much the same for his country.

In the end, wasn't that what they all were? Just men and women? The war had blurred class distinctions. The Japanese had stripped them of their funds, reduced them all to the same pitiful state. And when rich and poor went away, you were left with people.

Extraordinary people. People who lived their lives with grace and dignity despite their circumstances. Or maybe because of them. People who had been poor, who had more dignity than any of those who had been his friends and acquaintances before the war.

And this Japanese man before him, just a man with hopes and dreams and aspirations. Longing to get home to his family. To love. To live.

Like any other man on the planet.

Rand took the square the guard held out to him. "Thank you." He had never tasted anything so wonderful in all of his life. He ate just a little bit and very slowly. His shrunken stomach would allow him no more. The last thing he needed now was worse dysentery.

"You're welcome. We are waiting until the Americans will let us out without killing us. You saw what they did to our commander?"

Rand shook his head. He had heard nothing about the captain of the guards.

"They shot him, and then your countrymen gloated over his body. They refused to let him rest in honor."

"I'm sorry about that." And Rand truly was. "I understand your desire to survive. You have to understand that we have that same desire. We want to be free. How long do you plan to keep us here?"

"As I said, until we are allowed to leave peaceably. I don't know how long. Would you like a cigarette too?" The soldier now held out a good-quality American cigarette. Rand could only guess it also came from a Red Cross box.

He shook his head. "I don't smoke. But thank you."

The day wore on. The soldier offered him a few more squares of chocolate. They didn't provide the nourishment he needed, but they helped with the gnawing hunger pains. More than that, the burning in his chest, with him for far more thirty-seven months, subsided.

Rand noticed Covey in his bed, fever-induced sweat dotting his brow. The wound he received the night of their boys' arrival had become infected.

He should talk to Covey before it was too late.

It was time to let go.

# Chapter Thirty-Eight

With surprising peace, Rand wound his way through the mass of men toward Covey. He was about to give up what he had wanted and fought for and dreamed about the entire internment.

And he was happy.

Happier than he remembered being for a long time. Maybe ever.

"How's the pain?"

"Getting on my good side won't earn you points with my daughter." His voice was weak and raspy.

"That's not why I asked. I want to know how you're feeling."

"Why?"

"I don't wish you ill."

"I already am. What do you want?"

"As soon as we're released and life returns to normal—"

"You're going to turn me in." Covey ran a shaky hand over his partially bald head. "I won't be here."

"No, I'm not."

"Your generosity won't make a difference with Irene."

"I want to change the terms of our deal."

Covey tried to move but winced with the effort. Instead, he narrowed his eyes. "Because you see that I'm dying."

Rand licked his lips, his mouth dry. "If you want the clubs, they are yours. I will hand them over to you."

The man's shrunken cheeks blazed. "This is a trick."

"No trick. The Monarch and the Azure are yours. You control them. Do with them what you wish. I'm getting out of the nightclub business."

"You can tell Irene after I'm gone that you did this."

"No. I plan to work with orphans and street children here in Manila."

"Why?"

"The life of glittery high society holds no appeal for me anymore. Not since I've become a follower of Christ. I thought I was somebody. He reduced me to a nobody, then made me a somebody in Him. He saved me. Now I want to save the most forgotten victims—the nobodies—of this war. They're humans, just like us, who want joy and happiness and peace."

"You are . . . Out of your . . . Mind." He struggled for breath.

Rand shrugged. "Maybe. But I've forgiven you for stealing from me. That is the only way I could do this."

The man's breathing became more labored. "Do. Me. A favor?"

"Is this a trick of yours?"

"No." Covey swallowed. "Irene. I loved her. I did it. All. For her." Then he closed his eyes.

"Covey? Covey. Reynolds?" Rand shook the man but didn't get a response. He checked Covey's pulse in his neck.

None.

Irene's father had died.

*

Irene was dozing on her bed when a buzz ran through her room in the Main Building. "They're leaving. Look at them go."

"Who? What?"

Tessa called to Irene and the others. "Bangers and mash, the Japanese are walking out of the Education Building. Just surrendering. Bruce and Rand are free."

A cheer rose among the women.

Could it be? Could it really be? Irene held her breath, not daring to hope.

She got up and crowded around the window with the other women. Like ants following one another, the Japanese guards marched from the Education Building.

"Rand. He's free." She turned to Tessa. "He's free."

Tessa gave her a little nudge. "What are we waiting for? Let's go to them."

Though it had been just two days with a better diet, the pain in Irene's legs was subsiding. She hurried outside and hustled to the Education Building. The internees had begun to leave as well. Where was he? She bounced up and down, hoping to catch a glimpse of him.

And then, the most beautiful sight. A shock of wavy, light-brown hair all askew. A familiar, tall figure made his way down the steps. His stride was sure and confident. Some might call it cocky. He had sticks for legs and arms, but his smile lit his face.

She sped toward him, and he took her in his arms, lifting her from the ground, swinging her around and around in circles.

She laughed. "You're making me dizzy."

"Dizzy with love, I hope."

"Dizzy with being near you."

He kissed her, right out in public. Sweet, delicious, delirious. The world buzzed until he put her down on shaky legs and released her. "Look at this. We're free. Irene, do you know what this means? It's over. It's all over."

"Wait until you taste the food. The soldiers are sick of these rations they've been getting, but to me they are delicious. Tinned meat and fruit, powdered eggs and milk. The finest restaurants don't have better fare."

"Are we still talking about eating? There are a million other things I'd rather talk about. Like . . ."

She sent him a warning glance. Her heart was wary, afraid. Not now, not yet.

"Like when we get to leave this place." His impish grin almost did her in.

"Manila is still in the hands of the Japanese. We can't go anywhere right now without being shot. Our boys have told us to be patient while they clear the city. And they are clearing it. See?" She pointed at the blazing sky.

"The poor citizens. They didn't ask for any of this. They are losing their homes, their livelihoods, everything. I meant it when I said I wanted to help the orphans and the street children. There will be so much work to do when we get the Japanese out of here at last."

Irene squeezed his hand. "You are a wonderful man, Rand."

"What took you so long to figure that out?"

She laughed, but she didn't know if she would be able to commit her heart to him.

ꟹ

*February 8, 1945*

Rand scurried from Glamourville and headed to the chow line, not knowing how temporary the lull in the constant shelling would be. Santo Tomas may be in American hands, but much of the rest of the city was not. The Japanese and Americans continued their fierce fighting for the Pearl of the Orient. Santo Tomas sat as an island in the midst of all of it.

The sun beat down on Rand as he crossed the campus to the kitchen, yawning all the way. The constant whining and whistles of the shells kept sleep at bay. The sky above the city continued to glow with fire. The Japanese intended to burn Manila to the ground.

Rand hadn't seen Irene yet today and was anxious to look at her, to touch her, to be with her. When they were apart, he missed her more than he thought possible. And if it was this bad when he saw her almost every day, what would it be like if she walked out of his life forever?

The ache in his chest grew.

He hadn't told her about her father yet. He didn't even know if he should. What difference did it make now? Then again, if they were able to start a life together, he didn't want to keep information from her. Yes, he needed to tell her.

But the right moment never came.

He passed shanties with holes in the roofs and *sawali* mats. Between the embers from blazes across the city to the shells the Japanese continued to lob over the wall, it was amazing that none of the huts had burned to the ground yet. The fire brigade the internees had organized was doing its job well.

He walked into the open space between Glamourville and the chow line. No one stood still but all hustled, scurrying to get back under cover before the firing began again.

Across the yard, Rand spotted a woman with hair the color of Irene's. She had the same swing to her hips as Irene did.

She hurried beside a woman with blazing-red hair.

It had to be her and Tessa. Their heads were bent together as if they shared a secret.

Irene lifted her head and laughed. Even from this bit of a distance, the music of it charmed him. She turned in his direction, smiled, and waved. His face warmed and he waved back.

*Pop, pop, pop.* Without warning, the gunfire resumed. The internees screamed and rushed to the nearest, safest place.

Irene took three strides in the direction of the kitchen.

A whistle.

A bright light.

Dirt and grass spewed up.

Then she fell.

Hit.

By a Japanese shell.

A rush of adrenaline surged through his body. Heedless of the firing around him, Rand shot forward to Irene's side. "Are you hurt?"

She stared at him, her blue eyes unblinking. Her lips moved, but her throat produced no sound.

He examined her, patting her head, her arms, her stomach. The shrapnel had torn her blue dress, her prettiest. Blood poured from a wound on her leg. She looked at it and screamed.

He tamped down the panic in his chest and forced himself to breathe.

He pressed his hand to her thigh to stop the blood. It did little good in ebbing the warm, sticky flow. She needed more help than he could give. "You need a doctor. This is going to hurt, but I'm going to carry you to the hospital. Tessa, hold your hand over the wound."

*Shee-boom, shee-boom.*

With the greatest of care and the utmost of speed, he scooped Irene into his arms. She weighed next to nothing, but he had little arm muscle left. He didn't know how he'd make it to the nearby building. Shells sent up sprays of dirt and rocks.

He and Tessa dodged the shells as they trotted toward the hospital.

"It hurts. Oh, it hurts." Tears coursed down Irene's pallid cheeks.

"Remember the lilies, Irene, like in the Bible. God is watching over you, taking care of you." He held her close. "We're almost there. You'll be fine. Don't worry now. The doctors will take good care of you. Tessa, press harder."

"I'm doing my best, love."

"Hurry, Rand, hurry."

"Just hold on, Irene. Stay with me. Don't leave me." *God, don't let her leave me.*

He hustled as fast as his weakened body allowed.

Then she slumped in his arms.

"No!" Rand's heart threatened to jump ship. His lungs and legs burned as he raced across the yard. Santa Catalina had never seemed so far away.

By the time he reached the door, he was panting, his chest heaving. Irene hadn't regained consciousness. Tessa pushed the door open with her shoulder. The two of them sped to the Army doctor they spied down the hall, Irene still in Rand's arms.

"She's been shot. She's losing blood. Please help her. She's fainted or something."

The man in the olive-drab uniform with eyes to match took Irene from Rand. "Where?"

Tessa pushed back a strand of hair with bloody fingers. "Her thigh. I tried to hold my hand over the wound to stop the bleeding, but it didn't work."

Rand's heartbeat hadn't slowed. "Is she going to survive?"

The doctor nodded in the direction of a group of chairs. "Have a seat while I take her back and examine her. We'll go from there." And with that, he disappeared into another room, Irene in his arms.

Rand sat in the rickety wooden chair beside Tessa, crossed his legs, uncrossed his legs, then rested his own bloody hands on his knees. *God, help her. Preserve her life. Don't take her from me.*

"She'll be fine. Bangers and mash, she didn't survive this long to die from a bullet now."

"I pray you're right, Tessa. I pray you're right."

The clock on the wall ticked away with maddening slowness. The time had to be wrong. Surely they had been here more than a few minutes. He stood and paced the waiting area, quiet now. Irene had been the only casualty of this round of firing.

"I can't live without her, Tessa."

"And you won't have to. She's plucky, so I know she'll be fine."

He rubbed the back of his neck. "I have to convince her to marry me. As soon as possible."

"She wants to be sure you love her and only her. Not Catherine. And she wants to be sure there will never be the chance you might come to love Catherine again."

"Jeepers creepers, how can I be with a woman who doesn't want me?" He lowered his voice. "I don't love Catherine now, if I ever did. And she's made her choice. She and Melanie have a life they don't want disturbed."

"I understand that. Irene's just a little more hardheaded than I am."

"She is awake and asking for you." The doctor's voice startled Rand. He hadn't heard the man come down the hall.

He turned to the doctor. "She is?"

"Yes. She's going to be fine. You can go see her."

"Yes, sir." Rand followed the doctor. They had settled Irene into a sunny room, and she had an IV in her arm. In just a few days, with only a few supplies, the hospital had taken on a much different look.

The doctor ushered him in. "It's a good thing the Army brought provisions with them. I was able to give her some blood, and she should make a full recovery very soon."

"Thank you, thank you so much." Rand went to her and knelt beside her bed. "How are you? Is the pain bad?"

Irene shook her head. "They gave me a painkiller so I don't have much discomfort. The doctor sewed me up and told me I'll be as good as new. He thinks I'll be able to leave the hospital in a few days."

Rand wilted. "Thank the Lord. That's the best news."

She clutched his hand, her fingers cold. "Just before I passed out, Covey's face flashed in front of my eyes. Isn't that strange? Why would that happen?"

He didn't answer. Couldn't.

"Rand, what aren't you telling me?"

He shivered.

Now he needed to find the words to share with her the most shocking news of her life.

# Chapter Thirty-Nine

Rand refused to look Irene in the eye. He studied the floor in the hospital room and the wall and the window above her head, but not her. Was the news he had to tell her so bad? Covey had been weasely, and she had to know. "Please, whatever it is, I can handle it."

"I'm not sure. You're weak. You've lost so much blood. Perhaps when you're stronger, in a few days."

Had he decided to go back to Catherine after all? The thought robbed the breath from her. She squeezed his hand tighter. That would be the worst possible scenario. She braced herself for whatever he had to say. "I'm fine."

"You fainted once today already."

"I'll faint from anxiety if you don't tell me. Secrets aren't good. We've learned that we can trust each other and walk through anything that comes our way. That proves our strength."

"This has nothing to do with me. Not much, anyway. It may not have anything to do with us."

In addition to being confused, now she was frightened. She

turned to face him better, her leg throbbing as she did so. She settled in and caught his gaze, his soft brown eyes unblinking. “Please.”

“Give me a minute.”

He didn’t hesitate this much when he told her about his daughter. What was going on?

She lay back against the pillows. A few minutes passed, then Rand touched her cheek. “Covey isn’t his real name.”

“Is that all?” She sat up. “You frightened me, and it turns out to be nothing more than Covey has an alias? Is it all that surprising?”

Rand’s lips curled upward the slightest bit. “Let me finish.”

She nodded and clamped her mouth shut.

“I don’t know why I didn’t put it together earlier. The nose, the eyes, his story. Your story.”

“You’re talking in circles again.”

“He’s your father.”

Her head swam. She must have heard him wrong. That had to be it. “My . . . my . . . father?”

“Yes. He lost a great amount of weight, he’s partially bald, and that scar and broken nose changed his appearance. But he’s your father.”

Irene brought Mr. Covey’s face to her mind. She examined it. Rand was right. He had her nose and their eyes were identical in color. She grasped the edge of the sheet. “The man who stole from you.”

He nodded. “He told me when we were holed up with the Japanese. He asked me not to say anything.”

“Thank you for telling me now.”

“But there’s more.”

She didn’t like the paleness of his face. “What?”

“He’s gone.”

She pulled her eyebrows together. "Gone? As in to-the-hills gone or . . . ?"

"He was hit when our boys shelled the building the night they arrived. Without medical care, the wound became infected."

She wiped away the single tear that fell. "He didn't have the courage to tell me who he was." She tugged the sheet so hard she was afraid she would rip it. "He must not . . . must not . . ." She couldn't bring herself to say the words. Pain exploded in her chest at the thought that her father hadn't loved her.

"In his own way, he loved you. He broke down when he told me who he was. He was sorry for using you the way he did. He understood that greed blinded him. But he wanted it all for you, to be able to provide for you."

"I would have rather had a father in my life, no matter how poor we were. He should have taken me with him when he left."

"What kind of life would that have been for a child? Hiding out, moving from town to town when my investigators got close. He would have had to take you out of school and away from friends over and over. He did what was best for you under the circumstances by leaving you with Anita."

"Is it wrong to be angry with him?"

Rand rubbed her hand. "No. But don't stay angry with him. While I sat in that Education Building, I discovered the freedom of forgiveness. Freedom that transcends these walls. A Japanese soldier wanted to befriend me. I refused, until he asked for forgiveness. God forgave me, Irene, of sins as heinous as those the guard committed. If God could forgive such a sinner as me, shouldn't I forgive the soldier? It took courage to say the words, determination—with God's help—to mean them. But the release was amazing."

"So you've forgiven my father too?"

"I don't condone what he did, but I've forgiven him."

"He doesn't deserve it. He left his thirteen-year-old daughter alone."

"None of us deserve God's forgiveness. The Bible says to forgive because God forgave us. It doesn't say anything about deserving it or even asking for it."

For years the thought of her father made her sick to her stomach. She hated him for leaving her. Alone. With no mother. Just an aunt who lived in the jungle.

Forgive him? Not for a very, very long time.

# Chapter Forty

Mercedes sat on the front step of the Main Building, enjoying the warm early morning. The sun rose over the still-smoking city. Sporadic gunfire broke the stillness, though it was farther away. The soldiers had begun to allow some Santo Tomas residents to leave the shelter of the compound.

Paulo ran around on a small patch of grass, playing tag with an invisible friend. Already he was healthier and stronger, and he grew in confidence each day. He ran to her and slapped her arm. "You're it, Mama. Now you have to catch me."

She chased after him, pretending she couldn't reach to tag him. After a few minutes, she stopped, her hand on her knees. "I give up. You are too fast for me. You win. Now I must sit down and rest." Laughing, she returned to the step.

Paulo came and wrapped her in a bear hug. "When I go to Grandpa and Grandma's house in America, will you play tag with me there? And Grandma and Grandpa too?"

She slicked back his curly, dark-brown hair from his sweaty

face. "Of course we will. Papa told me they have a big lawn with plenty of room for a little boy."

A voice behind Mercedes startled her. "You're going to Charles's parents?"

Mercedes held her hand over her heart. "Irene, I didn't see you coming."

"We're going to see Grandpa and Grandma in America. They have a big house, and I will have a room of my own. I never had one before."

Mercedes crinkled her forehead at her son's words. "Of course you did. Don't you remember our house before the war?"

"Mama, I was only four years old." He stood with one hip jutted out. "I just remember packing to come here." The boy kissed Mercedes on the cheek and scampered off in an attempt to catch a butterfly.

Irene sat beside Mercedes, covering her knees with the hem of a red dress Mercedes had never seen. The Red Cross had sent them clothing.

Mercedes clasped her hands. "It's for the best."

The two women sat in awkward silence for several moments.

"Paulo seems excited to go."

"He is. And so am I. No one there will know my past or what I did during the war. It will be a fresh start for us. If I stayed here, I would be shunned by my old friends." Like Irene shunned her. She took a deep breath, the smell of smoke still heavy in the air. "And what will be left of my home, if anything? I don't have the means to start over here. There, Charles's parents will help me. They will get us settled and help me find a job."

More awkward silence. Mercedes swallowed hard, her words barley a whisper. "You know, I did it all for him." She tipped her head in Paulo's direction. "You don't understand a mother's love until you have a child. He's all I have left of Charles. I couldn't bear to lose him too. I had to protect him. Maybe I didn't go about it the best way—"

"Including fraternizing with the enemy?"

Irene's words struck Mercedes in the heart like a knife. "It wasn't like that. Not at all. We talked. He brought me food when he could. He was kind to my son. Nothing more."

"You're right. I don't understand a mother's love. But I've watched you with Paulo these past three years. A mother's love is powerful. I don't blame you for wanting to do what you could to help you and your son survive this awful place. You have tenacity."

Mercedes rubbed her palms together. "Do you think we could ever be friends again?"

"Rand talked to me about forgiveness. How God expects us to forgive and forget. It doesn't come easily to me." Irene shifted her feet back and forth.

"I'm sorry. For whatever it's worth, I wish I would have believed you over him."

Irene gave a tentative smile.

Mercedes reciprocated, her shoulders lighter than they had been in a long time. "Thank you. We can see each other sometimes in America?"

Irene shook her head, a shadow falling across her fair face. "I plan on staying in Manila and opening Byaya Children's Center like I always wanted."

"And what about Rand?"

"He'll be here too. I don't know what will happen to us. This freedom is all so new. He's mentioned that he wants to work with me."

"What about your heart?"

"I love him. And I'm beginning to believe that it's me he loves, not Catherine. We'll wait and see what God plans for us."

Irene swept Mercedes into her arms, and they hugged for a good long time. Mercedes relished the feeling. Peace.

Gunfire once again interrupted the morning. Peace on the inside, at least.

"I'm going to miss you." Irene stood and brushed off her skirt.

"But we part as friends. I could ask for nothing more." Mercedes couldn't wipe the smile from her face.

Rand bounded from his shanty. The sun beat down even at this early hour, but it only brightened his mood. He had a surprise for Irene and couldn't wait to share it with her. He had told her to be ready first thing.

And there she was, sitting on the step in front of the Main Building, the sun coloring her hair red and yellow. She had on a new red dress this morning and looked beautiful.

She greeted him with a peck on his cheek, as light as a breeze. "I couldn't sleep all night, wondering what this surprise might be."

He motioned to an Army jeep idling on the drive, a private at the wheel. "Your chariot, mademoiselle."

Her sparkling blue eyes widened. "We're leaving this place? You're taking me out?"

"It frustrated me that it took me this long to locate Armando and arrange for transportation, but we're going to see him. I'm desperate to find out how he's doing. I pray the food I was able to get to him was enough. And that he survived the bombing."

"I can't wait to meet him. Thank you for sharing this with me."

"Armando is important to me. You're important to me. It's time you two get to know each other."

He held the jeep's door for her and jumped in the back with her. They moved out of the gates for the first time in over three years without fear, breathing free air. A smile dawned on Irene's face. "We're out."

"And we don't have to worry about getting caught. We can go anywhere we want."

"That's safely in American hands, you mean."

He directed the driver through Manila's streets. Wherever they looked, they found destruction. The great churches had been heavily damaged, the steeples torn off, the beautiful carvings and reliefs pocked with bullet holes. The shops, once bustling with patrons, now were filled with rubble. Even the humble homes of the average citizen, small, much like their huts at Santo Tomas, were now piles of smoldering *sawali* mats.

The driver swerved often to avoid pieces of concrete and gaping holes in the road. With the lack of landmarks, Rand had a difficult time finding his way. They turned from the commercial part of the city into a residential area.

Beside him, Irene gasped. Craters yawned where homes had stood. Rand gripped the edge of the seat. What would they find when they got to Armando's house?

Irene rubbed her eyes. "All of these people? What has happened to them?"

"If they survived, many have likely been reduced to begging. They've lost what little they had."

They passed a group of children dressed in rags, sifting through rubble, searching for something. Their faces were thin and peaked, their arms and legs nothing more than sticks.

Rand's heart clenched. The children spied the jeep and ran alongside. "Mister, you have money?"

"Stop the jeep." Rand got out, Irene behind him. "Where are your parents?"

The oldest of the group shrugged. "A few days ago they went to get food. They don't come back."

Irene touched Rand's arm. "We have to do something for them."

"I don't have any money." He had been reduced to much the same state as these kids, at least until he got access to his funds in Taiwan. "Private, what do you have?"

The young man rummaged through his pockets and pulled out a wrinkled dollar bill. "It's my last until payday."

"Good. You don't need to spend it at the bars." Rand took the money and handed it to the oldest boy. "I wish it was more. When I have some money, I'll come back to help you."

"You promise, mister?"

"I promise."

The boy grinned, dirt in the creases around his cheeks.

"Go get food for you and your brothers and sisters."

The kids scurried away toward the main road.

"What am I supposed to live on until payday?" The soldier stood with legs apart and arms crossed.

"What are those kids supposed to live on for the foreseeable future?"

Irene hugged him. "Thank you."

Rand shook his head. "It wasn't enough. Not nearly enough. And there are hundreds, maybe even thousands, like them."

"We'll be back. We'll help them."

He gazed at her, her cheeks red. Did she realize she spoke in the plural? As in, the two of them? Oh, the joy to have her by his side as he worked to restore his city. To have her in his life forever. He couldn't imagine what it would be like, but he sure wanted to find out.

Soon afterward, they came to Armando's neighborhood. Rand breathed a sigh when he saw the houses all standing. He instructed the driver to stop the jeep, then helped Irene out.

"This is it."

"It's nice, Rand."

And it was. A small stucco home, two stories, with glass in the two windows on each level. A row of lilies bloomed for all it was worth.

She grabbed his hand and squeezed it. "Look at the flowers."

Rand smiled and squeezed her hand back. He understood.

"I've been praying for Armando."

"As have I. I just hope . . ."

"No reason to stand out here and hope. Let's knock and find out."

He loved this no-nonsense woman. "Come on." They approached the door and announced their presence.

A stooped, gray-haired man answered the door. He looked them over. "May I help you?"

Rand would recognize that face anywhere, despite the deepness of the wrinkles and hollowness of the cheeks. "Don't you know me?"

Armando studied him more, then clasped his hands. "If it isn't my boy Rand. Praise the Lord, look at you, so thin. Come out of the sun. And you have a beautiful woman here too."

Rand glanced between the two people he loved most in the world. "Armando, this is Irene. I met her at Santo Tomas and she has, well, I can't begin to describe to you all she's done for me. Most importantly, she helped me see my need for the Lord."

Tears streamed down the weathered old face. “Like Simeon when he saw the Christ child, I can now die in peace.”

Fear prickled Rand’s skin. “Don’t say that. I’ve been praying for many more years for you.”

Armando led the way to a small, tiled living area, the furniture worn, the place spotless. “None of us knows when He will call us home. I’m an old man, and this war has been hard on me.”

“Didn’t Ramon bring you the rice and beans?”

“He did. But it’s more than the physical hardships. It breaks my heart to see what has become of my city and the evil that men inflict on each other. I am ready to be gone from this place. But no more talk of that. Let’s enjoy whatever time the Lord gives us.”

Rand couldn’t think of anything he’d rather do.

Irene stepped from Armando’s home, back into the sunshine, her arm linked with Rand’s. “I now understand why you were so desperate to see after him. He’s a wonderful, godly man. You are blessed to have him in your life. Thank you for including me today.”

Rand looked up, shielding his eyes with his right hand, the fingers stiff. “I didn’t always realize how lucky I was to have him in my life, caring for me when my parents weren’t there. As I’ve gotten older, I’ve appreciated him more. His job didn’t include taking care of me. I had an *amah* for that. But he took me under his wing when I was giving my *amah* a difficult time and gave me direction.”

“It’s been one of the best days of my life.” She couldn’t remember a time when she was happier, when she was more at peace.

Rand stopped before they reached the jeep. He wiped his hands on his pair of hand-me-down trousers. The driver had gone off somewhere or another. He couldn't be far. Lines appeared in Rand's forehead. "I know you have questions about Catherine and Melanie. I've made my decision to respect her wishes. If Melanie wants to know me at some point in the future, I'll cross that bridge when I come to it. But I don't love Catherine. I love you."

Irene held her breath. He loved her. And her heart answered in kind. The Lord had torn down every roadblock in their path. He had prepared the way for her to Rand and a life with him.

And when Rand stopped earlier to help those children, they had torn at her soul. They were little, the oldest not more than twelve, fending for themselves in a war-torn city. How would they survive? They needed someone to take care of them, to provide for them.

And she wanted to be that person. She hated the thought of them on the streets. That was no life for a child. She'd had Anita. Now she could turn and help other parentless children. And that's what Rand wanted too.

Most of all, they could do it together. They could work side by side all day and spend the nights with each other, too, for the rest of their lives. If she had Rand and God, she would be the richest woman in the world. Nothing could compare to that.

She released her breath little by little. "I love you too."

His brown eyes shone like the Philippine Sea. "You love me?"

"I do."

"You won't be marrying the most successful nightclub owner in the Orient."

"I don't need to. I need you. That's all."

He pulled her close, and his heart throbbed in his chest. Hers answered his beat for beat.

"I want you to work with me. Together we can make a difference."

She nodded but wanted so much more than working beside him. "We can."

He brushed his lips across her cheek. She warmed through.

"I want to have you by my side always. Not just working with me but as my wife. I can't imagine my future without you." He knelt there on the scarred street, her hand in his. She bit back the bubble of joy that rose inside her.

"Irene Reynolds, be mine, until the end of time, now wouldn't that be fine?"

She knelt beside him and nodded. "That is why I love you. Yes, yes, yes. I would be honored to be your wife."

They laughed together and hugged, falling to the ground.

The driver picked that moment to return. "What's going on here?"

Irene stood, brushing the dirt from her knees. "I said yes."

"I'm the luckiest man on the planet." Rand bent and picked a singular white flower from the stalk by Armando's front door. He held it out to her. "I don't have a ring, but until I can get one, will this do?" He stuck the flower behind her ear.

"It most certainly will."

And he wrapped his arms around her and kissed her hard, his kiss full of hope and promise for the future.

A future Irene couldn't wait to start.

# A NOTE FROM THE AUTHOR

According to records, there were only two escape attempts made from Santo Tomas during the more than three years of captivity, both in the early months. During the first attempt, three men were captured and executed. The following day, one made it to freedom. Rand's attempt is purely fictitious.

According to the camp doctors, not a single woman died of starvation at Santo Tomas, though some died of other diseases. Anita's death, then, would have been an anomaly.

There was a Filipino man, Luis de Alcuaz, who worked at the university and had a relationship with the Japanese. They would drive him into the compound to work. The briefcase on his lap would often be loaded with currency for the internee committee to purchase rice and other staples. Once inflation became so high that he could no longer bring in enough cash without arousing suspicion, he began smuggling in rice, beans, and tinned meat through a hole in the wall between his office and the gymnasium.

The Japanese often brought in food and spoiled it in front of the internees for fun. While it did happen, there is no evidence that it happened on the day mentioned in the story.

Mother Superior at Hospicio de Santiago was a real person, a

Frenchwoman by birth. She was just as described—calm, unflappable, and would do anything to protect the Americans under her care. She suffered from a painful leg condition that partially disabled her. During her tenure, the Japanese discovered no Americans during their occasional raids, though Mother Superior did hide American soldiers at Santiago Hospital. The incident with Mr. Jennings is pure fiction.

# READING GROUP GUIDE

1. Which character resonates with you the most? Why?
2. What do the lilies represent?
3. How does Rand change from the beginning of the book to the end? What precipitates the change?
4. Was Mercedes justified in trusting the Japanese guard? Why or why not?
5. What effect did Rand's and Irene's secrets have on their relationship?
6. Would you have bowed to the Japanese soldiers? Why or why not?
7. What was Frank Covey's motivation for blackmailing both Rand and Irene?
8. What do Rand and Irene discover is the hardest part of forgiveness?
9. Who was more headstrong and foolish—Rand or Irene? Why?
10. What gave Anita her courage and strength? What has given you courage and strength in a difficult situation?

# ACKNOWLEDGMENTS

While an author often feels that she leads a very isolated life, always chained to her computer, that is not the case. A novel cannot be born without the help of many talented people. A very special thank-you to Sascha Jansen. Your unique insight on Santo Tomas Internment Camp, actually living these events, was beyond helpful. I'm so glad we share the same vision of recording this period of history as accurately as possible. Thank you for taking the time to speak with me. It's an experience I will never forget. I would like to thank my critique partner, Diana Brandmeyer. You always push me to be the best I can be. I appreciate your encouragement and support. Thank you to my fabulous agent, Tamela Hancock Murray. It's good to know you're always on the other end of the line or the computer when I have a question. Thank you for cheering me on for all of these years. Thank you to the amazing team at HarperCollins Christian/Thomas Nelson. Becky Philpott, I have so enjoyed working with you and getting to know you. Your faith in me is a great encouragement. Julee Schwarzburg, I could not ask for a better editor. I've taken to channeling you when I write! Your gentle but forthright manner is spot-on. Elizabeth Hudson, you are a joy to work with. Thank you for catching my vision and translating it into an amazing marketing plan. Daisy Hutton, I owe you so much for taking a chance on these books and making them a reality. Thank you also to Jodi Hughes and Katie Bond. You ladies are an invaluable part of my team. To the outstanding group at Litfuse Publicity, thank you for all of your hard work. Amy and Elizabeth, my hat's off to you. You are social media geniuses! To my husband, Doug, God gave me the most incredible gift when He gave me you. You must get sick of frozen pizza for dinner and overflowing laundry baskets, but you don't complain. Thank you for your love and support. It means the world to me. And thank you to my wonderful children. Brian, you are great at promoting my books. Are you sure you don't want to join my marketing team? Alyssa, your domestic skills amaze me. Thank you for being willing to step in and make dinner, watch your sister, and do a hundred other things when I'm on deadline. This family wouldn't function nearly as well without you. And, Jonalyn, thank you for being your sweet and loving self and reminding me that there are things more important in this world than others. Thank you, Mom, for being such a great beta reader. I appreciate your good eye and your kind words. Dad, thank you for inspiring me to work as hard as possible. Thank you to my influencers, endorsers, and street team. I owe you all a debt of gratitude. And above all, *Soli Deo Gloria*.

# A STRANGER'S LIFE HANGS IN THE BALANCE. BUT TO SAVE HIM IS TO RISK EVERYTHING.

"In an adventurous tale that reads like a movie script, Liz Tolsma weaves faith in seamlessly, moving the reader with her characters' convictions to create a captivating debut novel."

—*Bookpage*

Available in print and e-book

9781401689148-A

9781401689148-B

**Looking for more riveting historical fiction?**
**Check out *The Butterfly and the Violin* by Kristy Cambron.**

*A mysterious painting breathes hope and beauty into the darkest corners of Auschwitz— and the loneliest hearts of Manhattan.*

"In her historical series debut, Cambron expertly weaves together multiple plotlines, time lines, and perspectives to produce a poignant tale of the power of love and faith in difficult circumstances. Those interested in stories of survival and the Holocaust, such as Eli Wiesel's *Night*, will want to read."

—*Library Journal*, starred review

Available in print and e-book

9781401689148-C

# AN EXCERPT FROM
# *THE BUTTERFLY AND THE VIOLIN*

*by Kristy Cambron*

## *Chapter One*

PRESENT DAY, NEW YORK CITY

"Is this it?"

Sera James bounded through the front doors of the Manhattan gallery, so excited that she nearly slipped for running across the hardwood floor in her heels. She came to a flustered stop in front of the large canvas hanging on the back wall. Breathless, she asked, "You've confirmed—this is her?"

"Did you run all the way here, Sera?"

"Yes. Wouldn't you?" She wasn't ashamed to admit it. From the second she'd received the phone call, Sera had pushed and shoved her way off the subway in a frenzy and had run the eight blocks back to the gallery, dodging taxis and cracks in the sidewalks all the way.

Penny nodded. "The guys in the back just opened the crate. Can you believe it's been there for a week and we didn't even know it?"

She shook her head in disbelief. "Unfathomable."

Sera unwound the chiffon scarf from her neck and shrugged off her trench coat as she stepped away for a moment, draping them both over the antique wooden counter stretching across the back of the room. She twisted her long ebony hair and tucked it into a loose bun, then secured it atop her head with a pencil she found nearby. It wasn't until she turned back to her assistant that she noticed the girl hadn't moved an inch. Penny stood like a statue, her only movement an index finger that twirled a lock of strawberry blond hair at her nape.

Sera laughed. When her assistant took to whirling a strand of hair around her finger, something had to have completely captured her attention.

"You're doing it again, Penny."

The action was telltale. But Sera didn't blame Penny in the least. This moment was special. If the painting was what they both thought it was, standing in awe was warranted. The rest of the city could have flown by outside the front windows and neither one of them would have noticed. Or cared.

"I'm just sorry it's not the original." Penny offered Sera an envelope without looking away from the canvas. "But it is another step closer and that's what matters."

"You've inspected the borders?"

"My hands were shaking like crazy the whole time," Penny admitted, tilting her head to one side. "But yeah. Even though I knew this was paint on canvas, I still checked to be sure. The negatives are inside."

Sera opened the envelope and held the negatives up to the light. Penny was right—the painting before them was eerily similar to the one they sought. Checking the borders was the only way to distinguish the original from a copy. And if the borders didn't match, then this couldn't be the one they'd been searching for. Her heart almost sank a little before she realized that while it may not have been *the* portrait, it was still a portrait of *her.* The borders didn't matter much when those piercing eyes continued to stare out, haunting the viewer.

Sera swallowed hard, thinking how long they'd waited for the moment to arrive. She replaced the negatives in the envelope. "It may be a copy, but I still have to know. How did you find it?"

"An estate sale," Penny answered, her voice sounding almost dreamy. "Just north of San Francisco."

"And do we know for whom?"

Penny nodded again, and this time cocked an eyebrow in a curious fashion. "That's the mystery—it's some businessman. A financier in real estate. William Hanover is his name. I called his office with a basic inquiry and he contacted us back immediately. Said he was liquidating his late grandfather's estate. The name doesn't ring a bell for me at all and I've been chasing this painting for more than two years, same as you. Nobody in the art world has ever heard of him."

The name was foreign to her too. Who was this William Hanover, and how did he manage to get his hands on a painting that was a virtual copy of the one she was looking for?

"And did we make an offer?"

"Mmm-hmm. I figured you'd want to, so I made a generous one."

Penny's answer didn't inspire a lot of confidence. Sera shook her head. "Then why do you sound as if you've got some bad news for me?"

"Because he said he's not going to sell. Money isn't enough, apparently."

"But you just said it was an estate sale."

"Right," Penny cut in. "But it was a chance encounter that I found the painting on an Internet auction site. It was the image and not a bill of sale that caught my attention. I was sifting through old photographs of estate sales from last fall, jewelry and such. You know, the usual. I'd been through an exhausting file of artwork when I came across a photo of this—faded and barely noticeable in the background, behind a vase that had been highlighted for sale. But there's no doubt—it's her."

Her assistant stood back and eyed the painting, then pulled a clipboard up to her chin as if entranced by the vision of the ethereal beauty.

"It was her eyes, Sera. They pierced right through the computer screen and pulled me in, if that's possible."

"It's possible." The same thing had happened to her the first time she'd seen the painting. Only hers was a patchy memory, of an image she'd once seen as a young girl. Thinking back on it now made the moment all the more surreal.

"I spilled a whole mug of coffee down my front when I saw it on the computer screen." Penny smiled, one of those youthful, dimple-cheeked grins so characteristic of the young art student.

"Remember that ivory sweater I borrowed? Hope you didn't want it back anytime soon."

"No," Sera answered honestly and, lost in thought, took a step closer to the canvas. "Forget about it. This is better."

"It is, isn't it?" They stood for a moment, speechless, transfixed by the beauty of the portrait. Penny shook her head and on a hushed breath whispered, "After all this time. She's finally here."

It had been far too long, that was for sure.

From the moment Sera had laid eyes on the work of art when she was eight years old, she'd been haunted by the otherworldly beauty. A simple three-quarter silhouette of a young woman of perhaps twenty years of age, with flawless, iridescent skin and those ever-piercing, almost animalistic blue eyes. The softness in the mouth, the sadness in the features . . . the stark coldness of the shaved head, showing a young beauty who had been shorn of her crown and glory . . . the tattooed numbers, shouting out from the left forearm that cradled a violin.

"So, let me get this straight." Sera stood tall in her pencil skirt and classic white oxford, with arms folded and foot tapping while she tried to work things out in her mind. "We found a painting by chance, but it's not the original. And though it happens to be an image of our long-lost girl, it's not for sale. The owner won't take money for it."

"That sums it up. I wish I could say it didn't."

Sera stood back for a moment, puzzled as to how the painting could be in her gallery under the circumstances. "So . . . how did it end up here again?"

"It's been sent here on loan."

"Why on loan?" Sera leaned in, nodding at the exquisite brushstrokes.

"That's just it." Penny paused with a hitch in her voice.

With her attention piqued, Sera half turned to find Penny chewing the edge of her thumbnail. Penny furrowed her brow as if she were staring into the bright summer sunshine. Sera stood up straight then, as her hands found their way to her hips. She almost smiled at her friend's behavior.

"Penn—what on earth is the matter with you? Is there something you're not telling me?"

"He wants to talk in person." Penny looked close to cringing. "About his terms."

Sera did smile then. The man had terms? "His terms for what?"

"For hiring you," Penny admitted with an almost too reluctant smile herself. "Or us, rather. He's willing to pay close to an obscene amount of money for the services of the gallery that's looking for the very same thing he is—the original painting of our girl."

"Did you explain why we're looking for the painting?"

"Yes, of course I did. I told him we had interest in acquiring Holocaust era art for the gallery, but I had to soften it a little. After all, something to the tune of 'She's been dreaming of finding this painting since she was a girl' didn't seem appropriate to confess to a complete stranger we might have to negotiate with. I mean, if he has a copy of the painting, then he may be our ticket to finding the original. I told him the truth." Penny pulled a paper free from the clipboard and handed it to her. "Enough of it, anyway, to get you an invitation and a plane ticket to the West Coast. Your flight leaves tomorrow—on his dime."

Hesitating, Sera toyed with the idea that the man could have his own agenda.

"Okay. We both know why I'm looking for the painting. But why does this William Hanover want it? Did he say?"

Penny shook her head. "I guess that's what this ticket will help us find out."

Sera reached for the ticket with trembling fingertips.

Two years.

It'd been two years since her world had fallen apart, since she'd thrown herself into work and once again found herself consumed by the intrigue of the painting's mystery. She may have first learned of the painting as a girl, but her real dedication to unraveling its mystery hadn't come until she had nothing left. If finding the last piece of the puzzle meant that Sera had to work with this William Hanover, then she was game.

*Thank You, Lord.* The unspoken prayer somehow made her heart feel light. *We're this close to finding her.*

"Penny." Sera smiled. "We're finally bringing her home."

The story continues in
*The Butterfly and the Violin*
by Kristy Cambron.